MORNING GLORY CIRCLE

MORNING GLORY CIRCLE

Pamela Grandstaff

Books by Pamela Grandstaff:

Rose Hill Mystery Series:

Rose Hill

Morning Glory Circle

Iris Avenue

Peony Street

Daisy Lane

Lilac Avenue

Hollyhock Ridge

Sunflower Street

Viola Avenue

Pumpkin Ridge

Copyright © 2009 Pamela Grandstaff
All rights reserved.
ISBN-10: 1439258422
EAN-13: 978-1439258422

For Betsy

Chapter One – Monday

Margie Estep sealed the entrance to the hiding place where she kept all her secrets, or rather, the stolen evidence of other people's secrets. A frisson of fear and excitement ran up her spine at the prospect of setting into motion one of the most clever schemes she had ever concocted. One day, after she disappeared and was living her new life somewhere far away, she hoped someone would figure out what she'd done and how she'd done it. Her only regret about leaving the town she had lived in all her life was not being able to witness the havoc she would leave in her wake.

The home health nurse was with her mother in the front room. The young blonde woman glanced at Margie with barely concealed dislike as she entered the room. This one was called Cindy and had a chirpy voice that grated on Margie's nerves.

"We need to eat our dinner now, Mrs. Estep," Cindy said. "We can't let good food go to waste, now can we?"

Cindy had draped a dish towel across the cardigan and housedress that encased the older woman's sagging bosom and was trying to coax her into eating a spoonful of tapioca pudding. Enid Estep's hands, crippled with arthritis, lay curled into gnarled fists on each arm of the recliner in which she sat all day.

"Where are you going, Mary Margaret?" Enid asked her daughter in a sharp tone, as Margie took her coat off the peg by the door.

There was tapioca on her mother's chin, glistening in amongst the few long whiskers growing there. It seemed to Margie that everything about her mother was worn out and failing, from the sagging, spotted lids of her pale blue eyes to her swollen ankles and misshapen feet. She was helpless,

1

and something about this great vulnerability enraged Margie, made her snap out answers instead of being patient and kind.

"Out for a walk," Margie said, averting her eyes. "I won't be gone long."

"She does this every night," Enid said to Cindy. "I keep telling her she shouldn't go out alone after dark, but she won't listen."

"I'll be fine," Margie said through clenched teeth.

"I'm going to Mountain View tomorrow," Enid said to Cindy. "She can't wait to get rid of me."

"I'm sure that's not true," Cindy said.

Margie waited until the door shut behind her before saying quietly, "It is true."

Margie and her mother lived in a small house on Lotus Avenue, in the shadow of the defunct Rodefeffer Glassworks building, which sat next to the railroad tracks by the Little Bear River. Most everyone on Lotus Avenue heated with coal, so the smell of coal smoke permeated the air. It had also permanently stained the peeling white paint on the houses built by the coal companies to house workers in the early part of the 20th century. It was, as Margie knew all too well, considered the wrong side of town, and only the poorest people lived there.

Down at the end of the block Margie spied Sue Fischer unloading groceries from her car and carrying them into the house she shared with her husband, Calvert. Cal and Sue had purchased one of the neighborhood's small houses and fixed it up. Margie resented their optimism. As she approached Sue, the woman nodded at her in as bare an acknowledgment a civilized person could make without being rude, and Margie took that as an invitation to speak. Sue stopped, with six heavy bags of groceries dangling from her arms and hands, lips pursed and countenance straining to conclude as quickly as possible whatever conversation it was Margie wished to have.

When Cal Fischer came out the front door a few minutes later to see what was keeping Sue, he found his wife threatening to dip Margie in tar and roll her in feathers before forcibly running her out of town. As he hurried down the steps to the front walk, Sue dropped her groceries in the snow and advanced on the small dumpy woman with what looked like every intention of following through on her threat.

"What's going on?" Cal asked as he rushed forward to restrain his wife.

"Margie's up to her old tricks," Sue said bitterly. "She's just picked the wrong person to try it on this time."

Margie just smirked and said, "You think about what I said and get back to me."

"I'll see you in hell first," Sue said, and Cal took his wife more firmly by the arm.

"Sue!" he said, and she seemed to come to her senses.

As Margie walked away, Cal helped Sue gather up the grocery bags and retrieve the items that had rolled out when she dropped them.

"What in the world did she say to you?" he asked her.

"We'll talk about it inside," Sue said, looking around to see if anyone could have overheard her argument with Margie.

"I thought you were going to hurt her," Cal said. "That's not like you."

"Somebody needs to do something about that woman," Sue said. "And if she doesn't watch herself someday I will."

Margie walked up Pine Mountain Road past the newspaper office and bakery, which were closed for the evening. Davis's Diner was open, and she could see some college students and a few regular customers seated inside, but no one with whom she had business dealings. She turned right, crossed the street, and walked down toward the college. She stopped in front of the post office, which up until a few weeks previously she had been postmistress of for over twenty years. It was closed as well, of course, so she could only stare into the dark interior and feel her resentment build. With a vengeful smirk on her face, she drew out a thick handful of stamped, addressed envelopes from her coat pocket and dropped them into the mailbox outside the building. To anyone watching it would have looked like a perfectly ordinary, innocent activity when actually it was as wicked of an act as a madman poisoning a well.

Maggie Fitzpatrick came out of Delvecchio's IGA grocery store just as Margie was dropping her letters and although Maggie greeted her, it was no friendlier than Sue's greeting had been. Margie felt stung by the snub. There was not a person in town she didn't have something on, some little nugget of unpleasantness she could take out and polish when her feelings were hurt. Maggie Fitzpatrick's family provided a treasure trove of such gems.

'That stupid policeman must have told her lies about me,' Margie surmised. Her resentment at losing her job was still fresh in her breast, and her frustration at not being able to get back at the person she blamed was driving her mad with desire for revenge. Taking it out on Maggie was the next best thing to getting back at Police Chief Scott Gordon, so Margie lashed out with the only weapon she had left: over twenty years' worth of vicious Rose Hill gossip.

"Heard from Gabe?" she asked Maggie in a syrupy sweet voice.

Maggie was so visibly taken aback that Margie knew her poison dart had found its mark.

"Why would you even ask me that?' Maggie said, and her face could be seen under the streetlight to become suffused by a deep red flush.

"I bet you'd give a lot to know what happened to Gabe," Margie said.

"You know, Margie," Maggie said. "Scott told me about all the awful things you've done, and I would think you'd need to be on your best behavior right about now."

"I bet Scott would give a lot for you not to find out what happened to Gabe," Margie said with a cackle.

"You don't know what you're talking about," Maggie said. "Stay away from me and mind your own business."

Margie felt all her anger and bitterness rise up and burst out, and it felt good to let it fly on someone instead of bottling it up and storing it somewhere deep, dark, and dank.

"Everyone knows your father's a drunk and Theo Eldridge was screwing your sister-in-law," Margie said. "You've got no right to look down your nose at me."

Maggie advanced on Margie much the same way Sue Fischer had a few minutes earlier.

"Don't you hit me," Margie yelled. "I'll have you arrested."

"You listen to me, Margie Estep," Maggie said. "I wouldn't pollute myself by touching you. Besides, there's not a thing I could do to you that's worse than what you've done to yourself. You're hated in this town, truly hated, and there's not a person here who'd miss you if you went to jail, which is where you belong."

"Maggie, what's going on?" Matt Delvecchio said as he came out of his grocery store to see what the yelling was about. "Margie, are you making trouble again?"

"You'll be sorry you said that," Margie said to Maggie, and then looked at Matt. "You'll all be sorry."

But Maggie Fitzpatrick had already turned her back and walked away, crossing the street to her bookstore.

"You better keep your nose clean, Margie," Matt said. "You've just about worn out your welcome in this town."

"You better keep a closer eye on that wife of yours," Margie snarled. "I hear she's been spending a lot of time in the hardware store, but she never buys anything."

"You'll never learn, will you?" Matt said, shaking his head. "You better go on home now, and try to stay out of trouble."

Matt went back inside the grocery store, and Margie stomped back the way she came. She wished she had time to exact revenge on everyone who dared to underestimate her. She retraced her steps to the center of town where Pine Mountain Road and Rose Hill Avenue met. The heavy snow that was forecast began to fall, and the last vestiges of daylight disappeared behind the mountains to the west, on the other side of the Little Bear River.

She crossed Rose Hill Avenue and trudged uphill, toward the higher streets in town where the homes were bigger and sat on wide, manicured lawns. From Lilac Avenue Margie crossed through Rose Hill City Park and lingered in amongst the trees at the far edge, where she could stand unobserved but with a very good view into some of the finer houses on Morning Glory Avenue. She was particularly interested in Morning Glory Circle, the cul de sac at the end of the street where the wealthiest Rose Hill residents currently resided.

There, in a Gothic monstrosity of a mansion, lived Mamie Rodefeffer, the great-granddaughter of the glassworks founder. The cranky old woman spent her days bullying her staff and walking around town acting as if she owned it. She blamed Margie for any rise in the cost of stamps, and flung her mail on the counter in an imperious manner rather than put it through the slot like everyone else. Margie took her revenge on Mamie by making sure some of her mail never reached the intended recipients, and by occasionally stealing the old woman's National Geographic magazines. She also knew something about Mamie she was pretty sure the old lady would not want to have revealed.

In a Federal style home next to Mamie's lived Knox Rodefeffer. He was Mamie's nephew, president of the local bank, and his wife had recently been seriously injured in a car accident that Margie suspected Knox had engineered. She didn't have any actual proof, but sometimes, Margie had found, an accusation was worth as much as real evidence. Knox never lowered himself to come to the post office, preferring to send that whore of a secretary instead. Anyone who looked at her could tell she had the morals of an alley cat. Margie had heard from the cleaning woman at the bank the kinds of things found in Knox's garbage can after he had closed-door meetings with his secretary. Her imagination could easily fill in the blanks. Everyone knew Knox was poised to run for political office and couldn't afford a scandal.

At the very top of Morning Glory Circle sat a large Edwardian home in which lived Gwyneth Eldridge, one of the two Eldridge heiresses who inherited a fortune when their brother Theo was murdered back in January. Margie didn't have anything on Gwyneth, but she knew plenty about Theo and thought his sister might be willing to pay plenty to keep those secrets hidden. Gwyneth was positioning herself as a powerful influence in town and would be anxious to keep any unsavory information out of her spotlight.

The Eldridge Inn was next door to Gwyneth's house, and the walled grounds of Eldridge College could be seen behind. Margie could see movement where she hoped to see it. She took a small pair of binoculars out of her pocket and focused them on the object of her interest. It all looked very promising.

A few hours later Margie pulled her dead father's coat close around her as she turned down the alley behind the fire station. The snow, flying sideways, stung her cheeks and ears. She made her way down the narrow lane by walking in the deep ruts that the city snowplow's tires had made the night before. The tire tracks, already filled in with a couple of inches of fine, white powder, ended behind a building that used to house a tire store, closed now for several years. Stacks of used tires still lined one side of the narrow lane, with many weeks' worth of snow plowed and drifted up against them, creating a white wall of whitewalls.

She had stayed away the night before, when the drop off was supposed to have taken place, not wanting to take the chance that anyone would be waiting for her. Better to come like this, before sunrise the next day, when most folks were still in bed or just waking up. Margie was certain her victim was just as anxious as she was to maintain confidentiality, and hardly likely to send the police to arrest her. With way more to lose than most people in this town, regarding reputation, wealth, and power, she was certain this target would pay just about any price to eliminate the merest breath of scandal. The wealthy, socially prominent citizens of Rose Hill may have enjoyed a certain amount of power, but their status carried with it a vulnerability to scandal that Margie found irresistible.

Margie's focus was on a rusted metal barrel that stood next to a set of stairs leading up to Rose Hill Avenue. Down in the bottom of the barrel, she found the grocery bag, placed just as she had instructed it be done. The weight of it seemed to indicate the money was in there, but she used a small flashlight to make sure. It was during this brief lack of attention to her surroundings that someone moved out of the shadows behind the wall of discarded tires, grabbed Margie around her waist, and clamped a gloved hand over her mouth and nose. That handheld a cloth soaked in a strong smelling chemical that choked her as it filled her lungs. As Margie struggled she also gasped in the fumes, and passed out within seconds.

Over the years, many people in Rose Hill had discovered that Margie Estep tended to stick her nose in where she ought not, to seek out and spread vicious gossip, and to create malicious mischief wherever and whenever she could. These people often complained to each other that something should be done about Margie Estep. A few people in town also knew that Margie was dangerously malicious and vindictive, and incapable of feeling either empathy or remorse.

One person, in particular, knew very well what awful acts Margie was capable of committing. This someone had finally had enough, was not going to put up with it anymore, and was willing to wait for a long time in the cold and dark for the opportunity to finally do something about Margie Estep. Once the deed was done and Margie's body was disposed of, all that was left to do was retrieve the money, eliminate the evidence, and let Mother Nature do the rest. Snow had a way of making everything in Rose Hill look clean and innocent, even the scene of a murder.

Morning Glory Circle by Pamela Grandstaff

Chapter Two – Tuesday

Police Chief Scott Gordon swallowed some aspirin along with the last of his hot coffee as he drove down Peony Street toward the river. When Scott felt that familiar headache twinge nowadays, he didn't take any chances lest it turn into another debilitating migraine. A brutal migraine incapacitated him during a crucial moment in a recent murder investigation, and he was determined that must never happen again.

It may have seemed to outsiders that policing a town with one traffic light and just over 500 permanent residents would be a piece of cake, but lately, the troubles in Rose Hill seemed to be multiplying as fast as the feral felines that threatened to overrun the town. Scott had a nagging feeling that the dark vein of corruption exposed by Theo Eldridge's murder had not been eliminated by his death. He now believed it had always been there, flowing under the town of Rose Hill like an underground spring; now that he knew about it he seemed to see evidence of it everywhere.

This morning Scott was providing security for 78-year-old Enid Estep, who was leaving her home of over fifty years to go live in the best retirement home in the county. Nurse Ruthie Postlethwaite, the intake registrar of the Mountain View Retirement Home and a former schoolmate of Scott's, was providing transportation. Enid's good friend Lily Crawford was providing moral support. Scott was just making sure Enid's daughter Margie didn't interfere with the transition.

Scott turned left on Lotus Avenue, the street closest to the railroad tracks and the Little Bear River. As Scott approached Enid's house, he saw there was a "for sale" sign in her front yard, put there no doubt by realtor Trick Rodefeffer, a descendant of the glassworks founder. Scott knew Enid had deeded her home over to the owners of the retirement home to pay for her care.

Ruthie had parked the van from Mountain View at the curb and was standing on the sidewalk next to it talking to Lily Crawford. Ruthie was a tall, athletic woman with dark hair and eyes, and had worked with Enid for a few years as her home health nurse. Lily, who was short with a round figure, white hair, and wire-rimmed glasses, was a kind woman Enid loved and trusted. Ruthie and Lily both looked worried as Scott drove up, and then relieved to see him arrive.

"Margie won't let us in," Ruthie told Scott. "I didn't want to make too big a ruckus and upset Enid, but..."

Scott sighed deeply, shook his head, and produced a key from his pocket. He gestured for the two women to follow him to the door.

He knocked on the door and called out, "Enid, it's Scott Gordon. I have Ruthie and Lily with me, and we've come to help you move."

There was no answer, and the curtains were closed so he couldn't see inside.

"Enid, I'm coming in," he said and held his breath as he inserted the key and turned it.

There was no one in the little sitting room, which was cold and quiet. Scott led the women in and gestured for them to stay behind him.

"Margie," he called out. "I've come to take Enid to Mountain View. We discussed this."

There was a faint cry from the next room. Scott crossed the hall and opened the door to Enid's bedroom, where he found her lying in her disheveled bed, her hair falling from its usual tight knot at the back of her head. She looked frail, confused, and ill.

"Mary Margaret isn't here," she said in a weak voice and started to cry. "I called and called, but she never came."

Lily and Ruthie rushed to her side.

"I'm sorry," she said to them. "I've made a mess."

The two women gently helped the older woman out of her bed and into the bathroom. Meanwhile, Scott searched the house, but Margie wasn't in it. Her little attic room, accessed by pull-down stairs in the hallway between her mother's bedroom and the bathroom, was plain and bare, with only the most essential toiletries and very little decoration. The twin-size bed looked like a child's bed, and the quilt on top was faded and worn.

Scott went back downstairs to the living room, perplexed. Margie's handbag and coat were hanging on pegs by the front door. Why would Margie skip out on her mother like this at the last moment? Moreover, where was the home health nurse who was supposed to have stayed the night? Scott stood in the middle of the living room and looked around for clues, but the house seemed the same as it always was, slightly shabby but neat and clean.

On the mantle in the living room were two photos. One was a black and white photo of Enid and Eric on their wedding day; Eric was wearing his army uniform, and Enid was wearing a dark calf-length dress suit, with white gloves and a hat, clutching a white Bible. The other was a studio portrait of Margie in her first Holy Communion dress and veil, holding what looked like the same white Bible. There was a white Bible on a TV tray next to Enid's recliner this morning, amid the pill bottles, cough drops, and discarded tissues. The book's white leather cover was peeling, and it curled up at the edges. Scott took the prescriptions, the framed photos, and the white Bible and placed them on the kitchen table so they would be sure to include them in the personal effects Enid took with her to Mountain View.

At loose ends and feeling twitchy, Scott left the house, took a shovel out of the back of his Explorer, and cleared the sidewalk. This winter had been generous with snow, and the latest forecast predicted even more. Rose Hill's Winter Festival was scheduled to begin later that week, so more snow was welcome. After he shoveled the walk, he scattered salt on some icy patches and returned the shovel to the SUV. Lily Crawford came out and joined him there.

"Enid hasn't seen Margie since yesterday evening," Lily said. "She's beside herself with worry."

"Why didn't she call somebody?"

"There's only one phone in that house, and it's in the kitchen. She couldn't get to it."

"Where's her home health nurse?"

"I don't know," Lily said. "She's so fragile right now that I hated to keep questioning her."

"Damn that Margie," Scott said. "We almost got through this with no trouble."

"I know Margie resigned from her job at the post office," Lily said. "I've heard gossip that I know you shouldn't comment on, but is it true you saved Margie from going to jail?"

"I should have arrested her for mail tampering and embezzling her mother's money," Scott said, "but I made her a deal. If she helped her mother get moved into Mountain View and resigned from her job, I wouldn't arrest her. I was trying to protect Enid."

"I also heard she fabricated the evidence that sent Willy Neff to prison."

"She did. She confessed as much to me when I confronted her about it after he died. I don't have any proof, though, so I can't prosecute her for it, and I doubt she'd repeat her confession in court."

"I knew she was nosy, but I had no idea she was doing such vicious things," Lily said.

"I thought she was a harmless gossip. After you tipped me off about the mail, I looked in the station files and found a thick file of complaints made about her before I started working there. The chief was her father's best friend. He dismissed it as gossip and refused to do anything about it, so I guess people quit complaining. There's no telling what else she was doing."

"I appreciate you telling me. You know it won't go any further."

14

"You're one of the few people in this town who can keep a confidence."

"Was it you who ordered the home health care she's been getting?"

"I did," Scott said. "I thought Margie might harm her mother."

"Surely not," Lily said.

"I had her cornered. I thought she might do something desperate."

"You don't think she's killed herself."

"I doubt it. Margie thinks far too highly of herself."

When they went back inside, they found Ruthie had got Enid dressed and seated at the kitchen table. Lily made her something to eat while Ruthie cleaned her room and packed her belongings.

"I can't think where she's got to," Enid told Scott. "She knew I was going this morning."

"When did you last see her?" Scott asked, trying to make it sound more friendly than official.

"Last night after dinner she went out for a while, but I heard her come back in later. She often takes walks late at night, although I told her this is not the same town she grew up in. Bad things can happen to young girls out on their own at night. She can be stubborn, that girl, when she wants to be."

Scott knew Margie was older than he was by about ten years, and he was in his mid-thirties, so she would hardly be considered a "young girl" by anyone except her mother.

"Where is your nurse?"

"That was Cynthia. When she came last night, she gave me dinner and helped me to bed, and then I sent her home. Her child is sick, and she appreciated it. I didn't worry, knowing Mary Margaret would be here. Oh, Scott, you don't suppose anything has happened to my girl."

"I'm sure she's fine," Scott told her and gave her his clean handkerchief. "She's probably just upset about you leaving and didn't want to see you go."

"She was the one who arranged it," Enid protested. "She was the one who quit her job and said we had to sell the house."

"You don't mind going to Mountain View, though, do you?" Scott said.

"It's a nice enough place," she conceded. "Ruthie took me to see it. I guess there's some would say it's a palace compared to this place. It's just that I've lived here most of my life, and it's all happening so fast. I don't know whether I'm coming or going."

Scott felt a bit guilty, as he was the one who pushed Margie to act so hastily.

"I heard you met some old friends over at Mountain View," Lily said.

"Oh yes, some girls I went to school with. My people are from Pendleton, you know. Imogene and Ivy are their names, the Dale sisters. They had the most beautiful blonde curls back then, and their mother dressed them up just like Shirley Temple. I couldn't believe those girls remembered me, but they sure did."

"They'll keep you busy in that place, I bet," Scott said.

"Don't I know it. They have a snack bar, a game room, and a craft room. Do you know they have a television in the parlor there that's the biggest one I've ever seen? Every day it'll be like going to the Bijou for a matinee."

Ruthie returned from loading Enid's meager belongings into the van, and after getting her to eat a little breakfast, they cleaned the kitchen. Lily assured Enid she would take the soiled bedding and towels home and wash them for her. Ruthie told Enid what was going to happen next, and all the fun activities she had to look forward to, trying to divert her from worrying.

"Hannah's going to bring a kitten to visit you," Ruthie said, knowing how much Enid would love that.

16

"Mind she doesn't leave one with you," Lily said, "or seven or eight."

Hannah was the local animal control officer and was very good at facilitating "temporary foster placements" that turned into permanent adoptions.

Ruthie and Lily got Enid on her feet and helped her shuffle toward the door, chatting the whole way to try to keep her distracted. Still, when they got outside, she turned for a last look at her home, tears heavy in her eyes.

"You'll check on my girl?" she asked Scott.

"Don't you worry," he told her. "You just tell Imogene and Ivy they'll have to share you with all of us. You'll have lots of visitors this week, including me."

"You'll bring Lily?" she asked. "She's like me; she doesn't have a car."

"I'll bring her, I promise. She knows all she has to do is call me. You call me too if you need anything."

Enid was weeping as Ruthie and Lily helped her into the van. After Ruthie got Enid secured in her seatbelt, she hugged Scott and said, "thank you" before going around and getting in on the driver's side. Lily and Scott watched the van pull away from the curb, taking Enid to what they all hoped would be a better place.

"Where do you think Margie's gone?" Lily asked Scott.

"I haven't got a clue," he replied. "And as much as I don't care where she is, I don't want to lose track of her either. That woman's a danger to herself and others."

Lily Crawford lived at the end of Morning Glory Avenue Extension, a narrow lane known locally as Possum Holler. It was little more than a dirt and gravel driveway that began where the prestigious avenue ended, at the top of Peony Street by the library. It wound around the hill past a few old farmhouses and the Rose Hill Cemetery before it ended at Lily's farm, a narrow, rolling valley with a big pond in the middle.

Crawford's farm was where the majority of the town's children (and many adults) went sled riding every winter, on a steep incline that began in front of the house and ended in a wide flat meadow below. When Simon Crawford was alive, there were cows grazing in the meadow and hay and corn growing in the fields beyond. The Crawfords did not have children of their own, but they were generous to the town's children with their time and attention. The same tractor tire inner tubes that carried shrieking kids down the snow-covered hill in the winter floated them atop Frog Pond in the heat of summer. Scott had been one of those kids.

As Scott pulled into Lily's driveway, Betty Lou the basset hound came charging out through the dog door from the back porch, baying at the top of her lungs. Behind Betty Lou, who was furiously waddling toward the truck, was a scrawny little white, gold and brown striped kitten, mewing in a hoarse voice, trying to keep up.

"Who's that with Betty Lou?" Scott asked Lily.

"That's her new kitten," Lily said as she got out of the SUV, lugging Enid's linens in a plastic laundry basket.

Scott kept a box of animal crackers in the glove compartment just for Betty Lou, and when he offered her one, she quickly snuffled it up, tail wagging. The little kitten rubbed itself against the dog's haunches and purred loudly between hoarse mews. When Scott reached down to pick up the kitten, it arched its little back, hissed at him, and hopped sideways, the purr turning into a deep growl. Scott quickly pulled his hand back as Lily laughed.

"I should have warned you," Lily said. "It's a feral kitten. I can't touch it either."

"Is it one of Hannah's?" Scott asked, taking the heavy laundry basket from Lily.

"No, Hannah may be sneaky, but she wouldn't just drop one off. There are lots of feral cats out here. They keep the rabbits out of my garden and the mice out of the barn, so I don't mind them. Hannah leaves humane traps and fixes the ones she catches, but they breed faster than she can keep up. This one just appeared one day, curled up in Betty Lou's bed with her on the back porch. It must have got separated from its mama somehow and imprinted on my girl here. I feed it, but it won't come near me."

"I can't believe Betty puts up with it. I thought she hated cats."

"She loves this one," Lily shrugged. "It follows her everywhere."

Lily led Scott in through the back door to her kitchen, which was cozy and warm, and smelled like vanilla, cinnamon, and coffee. Betty Lou turned in a circle a couple of times before laying down in her basket by the stove. The kitten hopped in and curled up against her, kneading the dog's fur and purring loudly, eyes closed in ecstasy.

Scott sat the laundry basket on the floor and shrugged off his coat.

"Let me fix you some breakfast," Lily said, "and we'll get caught up."

Lily had been peripherally involved in a recent murder investigation in Rose Hill. After Theo Eldridge, the great-grandson of the founder of nearby Eldridge College was found bludgeoned to death in the back room of the local veterinary clinic, Scott found a threatening message in his undelivered mail. It turned out to be a card Lily had given Theo, along with a photo of his deceased brother, a kind gesture that postmistress Margie Estep had altered to make it look like a death threat. An offhand comment of Lily's had alerted Scott to the issue of Margie tampering with the mail, and his subsequent search through the police station's file archive uncovered a history of complaints that stretched back over two decades. It was through investigating those complaints that Scott had uncovered the false accusation Margie made against Willy Neff that sent him to prison.

Willy was with Theo the night he was murdered, and his death was also connected with that crime. Even though no one in Rose Hill was surprised someone hated Theo enough to kill him, the murder shook up the whole town. A greedy, wealthy bully, Theo had been known to pressure local people into selling their homes to him just so he could turn around and sell the properties to big city folks for a huge profit, or act as slumlord over the students he duped into renting them. If threats and coercion didn't always get Theo what he wanted, blackmail and arson often did. He also ran a dog breeding scam, and some believed he trafficked in drugs.

"How are you and Maggie doing?" Lily asked Scott.

"Slow progress," Scott said. "It's been almost seven years since Gabe left her, but she still isn't over it."

"You know, it's been five years since Simon passed away and I don't think I'll ever get over it," Lily said. "Maggie's still young enough to start over, though. I hope she won't let her grief keep her from living her life."

"I'm not giving up," Scott said. "She's worth the wait."

"I hope you two work it out," Lily said. "I'd love to see you settled with a family."

"Me too," Scott said. He neglected to confide in Lily about the tests he had undergone during his first marriage, the ones that determined he would not be likely to father anyone's children.

Full of biscuits and gravy, Scott left Lily's house an hour later. As he fastened his seatbelt, a large black luxury car pulled into the driveway next to his SUV. Scott couldn't see anyone through the darkly tinted windows, so he waited until Lily greeted whoever it was and then waved to Scott to let him know she was fine. He glanced in his rearview mirror as he rolled down the lane, and saw a gray-haired woman dressed in a dark business suit get out of the car and walk with Lily to her back door. Scott decided it must be a friend of Lily's from the city. He was glad she wasn't lonely.

It seemed to Scott as if Lily Crawford didn't want for anything, but he knew that very few farmers' wives had retirement accounts on which to live after their husbands died. Scott didn't know anything about the financial status of Lily and her husband, Simon. They were good people and hard workers, and they used to be rock concert and motorcycle enthusiasts when they were younger. Maybe they saved a lot of money, or maybe one or the other came from a wealthy family. Scott guessed that if Lily ever needed money, she could sell some of the farm property, but as far as he knew, she hadn't.

Scott passed Rose Hill Cemetery, where they had buried Willy Neff a few weeks ago. He drowned after his truck rolled down Pine Mountain Road into the river with him passed out inside. After finding out Margie framed Willy for a crime he did not commit, and feeling deep remorse over the way the whole town had mistreated him after he returned from prison, Scott and a few friends got together and paid for a proper burial and a stone.

Just beyond the cemetery was all that remained of Maggie Fitzpatrick's house after it burned down almost seven years' previously, just a stone foundation and part of a brick fireplace? Most everyone believed Theo Eldridge had set fire to the house, with Maggie in it, because she wouldn't sell it to him. It was the only property left on that side of the road that he didn't own at the time, and he had been determined to have it. Theo had warned her, ominously, that it was a firetrap, and as much as bragged about doing the deed later, while drinking in the Rose and Thorn. The fire chief at that time, Eric Estep, had determined it was faulty wiring so Theo could not be blamed. Scott had recently discovered, however, that Theo was blackmailing the fire chief, which may have led to him taking his own life.

Farther down the lane, Scott saw Ava Fitzpatrick and her two children walking up the snowy, rutted road toward the farm, dragging a large tractor tire inner tube by a rope. Scott slowed down and rolled down his window.

"Why aren't you in school?" he asked Charlotte, who was twelve.

21

A police officer, especially one that came to dinner at her house a couple of times a month, did not intimidate the poised Charlotte. A mirror image of her beautiful mother at that age, she flipped her long dark hair over her shoulders and said, "It's an administrative day for teachers. You know we would never skip school."

Ava laughed at her daughter and winked at Scott, which made him feel a little dizzy. He loved Maggie, but her sister-in-law Ava was the most beautiful woman in Rose Hill, maybe in the world, as far as Scott was concerned. She owned the local bed and breakfast, was a good neighbor, a good mother, and seemed amazingly normal despite the dramatic effect she had on every man she met. Her husband, Maggie's oldest brother Brian, had abandoned the family just after young Timothy was born, not long after Maggie's house burned down. Scott had recently discovered Brian was living in Bimini, reportedly with no intention of ever returning.

Six-year-old Timmy pulled on his mother's arm until she bent down, and then whispered something in her ear. He was a blue-eyed, freckled redhead just like his father and Aunt Maggie.

"Timmy wants to know if you've ever arrested any pirates," Ava asked Scott with a straight face.

Timmy half hid behind his mother but peered up at Scott with keen interest.

"I've never seen any pirates around here," Scott told Timmy, "but as long as they were nice, well-behaved pirates, I guess they could visit for a spell. But let me tell you I won't tolerate any shenanigans on the river, like firing off cannons or making people walk the plank."

That answer seemed to satisfy Timmy. Ava thanked Scott, and he went on his way.

When Theo Eldridge was murdered, most of his estate went to his two sisters, the snobby Gwyneth from Manhattan, and the humanitarian hobbyist Caroline, who was currently in South America. He also left a large amount of money in a trust for Ava Fitzpatrick, and that surprise bequest had set the town buzzing with speculation as to why.

There had never been any love lost between the Fitzpatrick family and Theo Eldridge. As a teenager, Maggie's brother Patrick had once beaten Theo within an inch of his life for trying to drown their brother Sean. After Theo's brother drowned in similar circumstances, Theo blackmailed Sean so that he would not implicate him in the crime. Theo also loaned Maggie's brother Brian a huge amount of money right around the time he disappeared, using Brian's home and life insurance on his wife Ava and their children as collateral. Add to all that the belief that Theo burned down Maggie's house and it was not surprising when a Fitzpatrick brother was a suspect in Theo's murder.

Back in town, Scott stopped in the Rose Hill Sentinel newspaper office to see if his buddy Ed, the owner, and editor-in-chief, had any insight into Margie Estep's disappearance. Hank, Ed's big black Labrador retriever, was snoring on a red cushion in front of the gas stove. Ed was staring dolefully at a dozen cinnamon- and sugar-covered doughnuts that were sitting on a plate in front of him.

"What's up?" Scott asked him.

Ed shook his head sorrowfully.

"She keeps bringing me pastries. I can hardly button my pants as it is, but she just brings me more."

"We're talking about Mandy, I guess."

"She won't listen to me. I keep telling her I'm too old for her, but she just smiles at me like I said the cutest thing."

Mandy's son was Tommy, Rose Hill's only paper-carrier, whom Ed had rescued a few weeks earlier when a car almost ran over him. During the emotional 24 hours that followed the accident, Tommy's mother had fallen hard for Ed. Mandy worked at the Fitzpatrick's bakery during the day and the Rose and Thorn bar at night, and if her constant tokens of appreciation were any indication, she seemed intent on making Ed her fat, drunk boyfriend. Scott found it hard to feel sorry for Ed, who hadn't had a date that Scott knew of since his wife left him several years ago.

Scott helped himself to a doughnut and took a seat at the table. He refused the coffee Ed offered, knowing from experience it would look like tar and have a similar taste. Ed got more coffee for himself but resisted the sweet siren call of the deep-fried dough.

"Men have often dated women who were much too young for them," Scott told him. "Why don't you just enjoy it?"

"It's not just that she's so young," Ed said. "I hate to say it, but she's not very bright. We have nothing in common and nothing to talk about except Tommy. Don't get me wrong, she's sweet as molasses and very pretty, but I can't get over the feeling that she should be riding around in some young guy's sports car, listening to America's top forty."

"You could always buy a sports car, you know. Then all you'd need is an earring, a tattoo, and some baggy pants."

"Very funny. I won't lie to you; I'm tempted. I'd have to be dead not to be. But you know as well as I do that this is a very small town, and if I end up the bad guy in all of this, there will be a price on my head that any Fitzpatrick would be glad to collect. Plus, I like her kid, and I don't want to get him mixed up in a situation that could hurt him as well."

"Sounds like you've talked yourself out of it."

"Now if I could just convince her."

"Ah, the life of a Rose Hill playboy," Scott said, and Ed threw a doughnut at him, which he caught and bit into.

Between chewing bites of doughnut, Scott told Ed what was going on with Enid and Margie.

"I've meant to tell you this," Ed said. "Tony Delvecchio mentioned to me that Margie asked about getting a life insurance policy on her mother."

"When was this?"

"Last week. Tony told her it would be nearly impossible, given Enid's age and health, and Margie didn't follow up on it."

"That woman," Scott said. "I think she's got an important screw loose."

"The one that keeps the conscience securely fastened."

"The thing that continues to astonish me is how immune to any consequences she believes she is. Instead of being grateful I didn't arrest her, she's now convinced she can do anything she wants and get away with it."

"Is that an indication of a sociopath or a psychopath? I've forgotten my college psychology."

"It's an indication of a dangerous loon, and that's my official diagnosis."

"At least Enid is safe now."

"Yeah, that's a relief. Ruthie is going to make sure Margie doesn't get in to see her mother without someone else present."

"I'll ask around about her today and let you know what I find out."

"Thanks."

"Speaking of victims and their potentially murderous relatives, have Anne Marie and Knox returned from their cruise?" Ed asked.

"His brother says they're having such a great time that they're extending their vacation by two weeks."

"Do you think he's spending all this time persuading her not to press charges?"

"I don't know if she even remembers the accident; I haven't been able to talk to her. As soon as she was released from the hospital, he whisked her off on this vacation."

"I wouldn't stand too close to the railing on that cruise ship if I were her."

Scott snagged another doughnut and left the office. He turned right and crossed the alley where Theo's murderer had followed him the night he died, and passed the new antique store that was slated to open later in the spring. The new owners had poured tons of money into renovating the place but had been strangely absent so far. There was a narrow walkway between that building and the next, where newspaper carrier Tommy had hidden the night of Theo's murder and had seen almost everything that happened. He had been too afraid to tell anyone for fear of the killer harming him and his mother. He kept that horrible secret until the day he was almost run over in the alley as the murderer fled town.

Tony Delvecchio was on the phone when Scott entered the agency, which was on the ground floor. The floors above the office held apartments most often rented to Eldridge College students. Tony was a few years older than Scott and had been a basketball star at Rose Hill High School. He was one of Sal Delvecchio's sons, all of whom owned businesses in the town. His oldest brother Sonny owned the hardware store, his older brother Matt owned the IGA grocery, and his younger brother Paul and wife Julie owned PJ's Pizza. Their father Sal was a very small, unattractive man married to a very tall, Sophia Loren-like beauty named Antonia. All the sons had inherited their mother's height, but only Tony had been lucky enough to inherit her beautiful features as well. He was the only unmarried brother and still lived at home with his parents.

"Hey Scott," Tony said, as soon as he got off the phone. "How are you?"

"I'm doing well, Tony, how about yourself?"

"I can't complain," Tony said, and then gestured to a chair. "Have a seat."

Scott sat down and told Tony what was going on with Enid and Margie, and what he had heard from Ed.

"So, is that pretty much what happened, or is there more?" Scott asked when he was finished.

"That's about it," Tony said. "It's pretty late in the game for her to be looking for life insurance, and no one would underwrite the policy, considering her mother's age and medical condition."

"Margie is known to do some strange things. I didn't know until a few weeks ago that she was tampering with the mail."

"I had mail go missing, so much so that I got a post office box in Pendleton several years ago. A lot of Rose Hill folks have Pendleton P.O. boxes on account of Margie."

"I feel awful about that," Scott said. "Sarah Albright, from the sheriff's office, is always telling me I need to listen to gossip if I want to find out what's going on in this town. I hate that Margie proved her right."

"I think it would be hard to sift the truth from the lies around here," Tony said. "Margie likes to embellish quite a bit, from what I understand."

"How did she seem the day she was in here?"

"This may sound weird, but I want to say she seemed smug. Like she had a secret and was enjoying it."

"Other than the policy business, did she say anything else?"

Tony hesitated before he spoke.

"She did make some odd remarks. At the time I didn't think it meant anything, but since then I've heard some of the gossip going 'round about her, and it makes what she said seem more sinister."

Scott listened patiently, which was something he did better than most. He had a high tolerance for the long silences that allowed people to decide to disclose information.

"She was angry that I wouldn't write the policy. Even though I told her I just brokered policies, I didn't personally underwrite them; she seemed to think I would personally put up the money for her mother. She argued with me about it. I thought she just didn't understand how my business worked, but before she left, she said something that, upon reflection, sounded almost like a threat of some sort."

Scott just nodded and waited.

"It was probably nothing," Tony said. "I feel stupid even repeating it. I may have misunderstood."

Scott listened patiently but said nothing.

"She said I should think about my decision and get back to her. I said there was nothing to think about, it was a business decision. She said I should give it some more thought. Then she said she hoped my mother's heart wasn't broken by the kind of life I was leading."

Scott's curiosity was piqued, but he let the silence do its work.

"At the time I thought she meant my mother would be ashamed of me for not helping her out. I told her there was no way I would personally underwrite a policy on her mother and she left in a huff. When I look back on it now, though, I wonder if she wasn't trying to blackmail me into underwriting a policy and that if I refused, she would tell my mother something about me that I wouldn't want her to know."

"And is there something?"

Tony's face flushed, and he seemed agitated, but even after a long, uncomfortable silence, he wouldn't say more. Scott realized he was going to have to help him over the next hurdle.

"I'm a police officer, Tony, but you and I have known each other our whole lives. If it's just something embarrassing and not criminal, I can be counted on to be discreet. If it's criminal, you need to tell a lawyer, a priest, or both."

"It's not criminal, and I'm not embarrassed about it, it's just nobody's business but my own," Tony said.

"Whatever it is, how could Margie know about it? You said you switched mail deliveries, so she didn't have access to your mail."

"She walks around late at night. You know that, right?"

"I've heard that, but I've never run into her."

"She probably hides from you. I think she must do a lot of hiding and watching."

"So you think she saw you doing something?"

"I think she saw me with someone and speculated about what was going on."

"You're right, that's nobody else's business," Scott said. "Consenting adults and so forth."

"Exactly."

"Well, I appreciate your confidence in me, and it will go no further. I'm not a bit surprised, by the way, that she would threaten to blackmail you to get what she wanted. She's a real piece of work."

"This town," Tony said. "If it isn't busybodies using police scanners to listen in on your phone calls, it's nosy parkers roaming the streets after dark looking for ways to blackmail you."

"And people think I have an easy job," Scott said.

"Not me," Tony said. "I don't know how you do it. Between the good old boy politics and the freelance critics we've got in this town..."

"I appreciate your sympathy," Scott said and rose to leave.

"Anytime," Tony said and shook Scott's hand.

"When did this happen?" Scott asked him, as they walked toward the door. "When was Margie here?"

"Last week. I'm pretty sure it was Wednesday."

"Have you seen her since?"

"No," Tony said. "I haven't been out late at night, though, since I realized she might be following me."

"If you do see her give me a call," Scott said. "I'd like to catch her in the act and give her a good scare."

"Will do," Tony promised, and Scott left with a wave.

Scott walked back up Pine Mountain Road past the newspaper office to Fitzpatrick's Bakery, where owner Bonnie Fitzpatrick was waiting on a long line of customers crowding the counter. Ed's number one fan, Mandy, was ringing up their orders. In the back, Scott could see Alice Fitzpatrick, Bonnie's sister-in-law, taking multiple trays of flaky golden brown turnovers out of one of the commercial ovens.

Maggie's mother Bonnie was a sturdy woman with a no-nonsense demeanor, steely blue eyes, white curly hair, and an accusatory look. She raised an eyebrow at Scott in a greeting that felt more like a warning, as if to say, "don't you start with me." Scott stood to the side out of the way and waited.

"What'll it be?" she asked him, once the line had dissipated.

"Have you seen Margie Estep today?" he asked both Bonnie and Mandy. "Enid moved to Mountain View this morning, and she says Margie went out early this morning and didn't come back."

"Maybe she's done away with herself," Bonnie said. "You better start dragging the river."

"I don't think we need to jump to any dire conclusions yet," Scott said.

"Maybe she had a breakfast date," Mandy suggested, but Bonnie scoffed at that notion.

"If she did, it will be the first date she's ever had."

Bonnie poured Scott a cup of coffee to go and motioned for him to follow her out the front door.

"I'd like to know what's going on between you and my daughter," she said once they were outside.

"I'm crazy about her, Bonnie, you know that."

"You know how I felt about that last one," she said. "The first time he came in here sniffing around our girl, I knew it would end in tears. I saw right through him, but Mary Margaret thought he could do no wrong. With those big dark eyes, he looked just like a gypsy, and he stole her away from us, just like a gypsy would."

"He was a good friend of mine," Scott said. "He fooled me too."

"I thought after he left she'd eventually get married, maybe give me some more grandchildren, but it looks like she's never going to."

"I think she'll come around, given time. I'm willing to wait."

"I hope you aren't going to tempt her to live in sin as well."

"I'll take her any way she'll have me. I'm sorry if that offends you."

"Well, that's honest, at least," she said, crossing her arms. "Stupid, stubborn girl. I don't know why you bother."

"Same reason Fitz bothered when he was chasing you around this town," Scott teased her. "We both have a weakness for bossy redheads with bad tempers. I bet you're a good kisser too."

"Watch your mouth, sonny Jim," she warned, but then she winked at him. "I only let Fitz think he was the one doing the chasing. That's the trick."

Scott kissed her on the cheek before she went back inside.

The whole town was gearing up for the Winter Festival, and Mayor Stuart Machalvie was supervising the raising of two banners above the crossroads of Rose Hill Avenue and Pine Mountain Road. Route 1 brought tourists south from the four-lane highway and then turned into Rose Hill Avenue, and Pine Mountain Road took them east from the Little Bear River up over Pine Mountain on a winding two-lane road past the state park to the Glencora Ski Resort. The Winter Festival drew a big crowd, and that crowd brought a lot of money into town. The main goal of the festival was to extract as much of that money as possible before they left.

The mayor flagged Scott down.

"I've had a brilliant idea," Stuart said.

"I can't wait to hear it," Scott said, but his sarcasm seemed to be lost on the mayor.

"As you know," Stuart said, "the town council picks a Snow Queen to reign over all the festivities. She's crowned on Friday night at the bonfire, leads the parade Saturday morning, and judges the baking competition on Sunday."

"I've only been to about three dozen of these festivals, Stuart, but I do remember what happens."

"So what lucky gal do you think I have lined up to be our Princess of Precipitation this year?"

"Isn't it usually one of your relatives?"

"That's not fair, Scott. It isn't always a relative, just frequently. The women in my family just tend to be naturally vivacious. I can't help that."

"Well, which one is it this year?"

"It's not a relative of mine, I swear to you. I'll give you some clues and see if you can't guess. Who is a new resident of Rose Hill?"

"The young couple opening the antique store?"

"No, no, no. Who is a new, influential person, a fine lady who I am anxious should feel welcome and at home here in Rose Hill?"

"You wouldn't."

"I would! I have! It's all fixed up. I'm going to make the announcement later today. Hold a press conference and everything."

"I see many flaws in your scheme."

"Such as?"

"Well, for one thing, Gwyneth Eldridge won't do it. She hates anything small town or quaint, and she wouldn't be caught dead wearing a sash and riding a fire truck down Rose Hill Avenue."

"She might, given the right persuasion. Say, if she knew the town council vote was unanimous, or that her picture would be on the front page of the local newspaper."

32

"She probably hasn't successfully digested a carbohydrate in thirty years, Stuart. She's not going to taste twenty pies."

"She can preside over the contest, and let the city council taste and judge."

"She's over forty."

"There's no age requirement; I looked it up."

"Well, good luck," Scott said. "I hope you have a backup plan."

"We won't need it, you'll see," Stuart said as Scott walked away. "Your problem, Scott, is that you're not a team player, and your attitude stinks. You need to start thinking positive."

"I'm positive your idea stinks," Scott said under his breath. Behind him, he could hear the sound of the fire truck ladder being raised to assist in the banner application process, and Stuart yelling encouraging words to the intrepid volunteer who was climbing above the traffic below.

When Scott got back to the police station, Hannah was there, trying to talk his deputy Frank into taking a trembling, growling little dog she was holding. Frank was backing up and shaking his head.

"I have a small child at home, Hannah, no way."

Hannah turned as Scott came in, and he got a better look at the dog.

"What is that?" he asked.

"She's a Chihuahua mixed with some other things. Isn't she cute?"

Scott shook his head sadly as the little dog pulled its lips back to show two full rows of small, pointed teeth, and growled at him like a rabid chipmunk.

"Mixed with piranha, maybe," he said.

"Ah, come on now," Hannah said. "You aren't afraid of an itty bitty wittle thing like this."

The words were no sooner out of her mouth when the small dog threw a wild, writhing, screaming fit, and Hannah quickly stuffed it back into its crate.

"Where'd you get the little precious?" Scott asked.

"I know. She's awful, isn't she? I traded four pit bulls for her to a no-kill shelter in Maryland."

"Four pit bulls."

"They were raised to fight and weren't nearly as vicious. I thought I was getting the better deal."

"It seems like she might need some extra work," Scott said.

"Or an exorcism," Hannah said. "Maybe I'll try Father Stephen."

"Father Stephen's a cat person. I don't know who would want to take that on," Scott said.

"It would have to be someone hard as nails and mean as a snake," Frank said.

"Too bad Theo's dead," Scott commented.

Hannah suddenly looked as though a light bulb had come on over her head.

"See ya!" she trilled as she went out the door with the dog in the crate.

Scott spent some time cleaning off his desk, considered addressing the station's current budget deficit, and then decided that was too depressing. He couldn't quit thinking about Margie and wondering where she was. He knew he was more likely to get a lead on her by walking around town asking for the latest gossip, and even though that was against his nature, he decided to try it.

He left the office and walked down to the service station to see if his friend Patrick wanted to shoot hoops later, but got a chilly reception and a 'no, too busy' brush off.

'This is the price I have to pay,' Scott thought to himself. 'Now that I'm the chief of police I have to get used to the fallout from making unpopular decisions.'

Scott had cleared out the Rose and Thorn the previous night when they went way beyond fire code capacity due to a busload of rowdy tourists from one of the ski resorts. Fire Chief Malcolm Behr, who should have been the one to make the call, was, unfortunately, one of the more drunken revelers in the bar at the time, so he had a conflict of interest. Patrick, the bartender on duty (and primary tip recipient), was not too happy about losing the extra business. It looked like he wasn't over it yet.

Scott went over to the veterinary clinic to see Dr. Drew Rosen, but the office was still closed. The yellow crime scene tape was no longer up, but he still wasn't open for business. There was a "Help Wanted" poster in the front window with Drew's telephone number on it. Since Theo's murder took place in the back room of the clinic, the doctor was having trouble finding a receptionist. It didn't help that the pay was low and the patients often pooped on or bit the help (and sometimes did both).

Scott walked down to Little Bear Books. Maggie was behind the front desk, talking on the telephone and holding what looked like a tame version of the little dog Hannah had just been trying to pawn off on Frank. The dog seemed calm and content now curled up in the crook of Maggie's arm with one of her long red curls draped over its little head. As soon as she got off the phone, Maggie gave Scott a look that reminded him of her mother Bonnie, complete with a "don't you start with me" eyebrow raise.

"What's that you've got there, Mary Margaret?" he asked.

Maggie rubbed the little dog under the chin with the crook of her finger, and it looked up at her adoringly.

"I'm dog sitting for Hannah while she goes on a house call with Drew. She was pretty desperate."

"Just dog sitting, huh?"

"I'm well aware of Hannah's tactics, but she wouldn't dare try them on me."

Scott reached out to pet the dog, which now looked so docile, and it bared its teeth at him.

"Here now," Maggie hissed at the dog, in a perfect imitation of her mother. "I'll not be having that."

The little dog closed its eyes and snuggled against her generous bosom, but Scott thought he detected a brief warning glance in his direction, and the tip of one long, sharp tooth was still sticking out over its bottom lip.

"Have you seen Margie this morning?" Scott asked.

"No, what's she done now?"

"Disappeared," he said. "Went out early and wasn't there this morning when Ruthie showed up to get Enid."

"You think she's run off?"

"It's a possibility," Scott said.

"Good riddance," Maggie said. "I saw her yesterday, and it was all I could do not to punch her lights out."

"When was this?"

"It was early in the evening, out in front of the IGA. She asked me..." Maggie hesitated before continuing. "Well, she said something very rude and I told her off. Now that I know all the rotten things she's done, I can hardly stand to look at her. She's lucky not to be in jail."

Scott wanted to stay longer, but the store was busy, and he could tell he was in the way.

"I'm going to run across the street to ask about Margie at the grocery store," Scott said, "but I'll be back."

As soon as he moved out of the way, senior citizen Mamie Rodefeffer slapped a book down on the front counter with such force that she startled Maggie and caused the small dog to growl deep in its little throat.

"I don't know why they make up such silly names instead of using normal names like Tom or Nancy," Mamie complained.

The quarrelsome old woman fixed Maggie with a fierce glare, magnified through the thick lenses of her dirty cat-eye glasses. The over-excited, under-dressed couple featured on the cover of the offending article seemed to indicate a "pirate and convent girl" romance theme.

"'Mamie Rodefeffer' is a pretty unusual name," observed Maggie quietly, as she rang up the paperback bodice-ripper.

Mamie, who had excellent hearing, waved her off in dismissal.

"I was christened Mary Margaret, which is a perfectly normal name, the same as yours and half the women in this town. Mamie's what my father called me."

Maggie liked to tell her staff members that "Mamie" was short for "cockamamie." She smiled as she thought it but didn't say it.

"I hope it's not too boring," Mamie said, gesturing to the book. "I like lots of action."

Maggie turned the book over and read aloud from the description on the back cover.

"'Although determined not to be ensnared by Trinity's smoldering green eyes, riotous golden curls, and long, silken limbs, nevertheless Captain Dominic Cordoba longed to probe the full depths of her wanton womanhood. In many ways still an innocent child, Trinity found this reckless pirate's rough embrace awakened ravenous carnal desires hidden deep within her. The ecstatic joining of their savage passions threatened to drown them both in a whirlpool of liquid fire.' Sounds pretty steamy to me, Mamie."

"We'll see," Mamie said. "That last one I bought kept skipping over the juicy parts."

Mamie finally seemed to notice the dog Maggie was holding.

"What have you got there, Mary Margaret, a baby possum?"

"It's a dog. I'm watching him for Hannah while she runs an errand."

The little dog gave Mamie a dirty look, one long fang still visible.

"Hannah Fitzpatrick!" Mamie snorted. "If she tries to pawn one of those mangy mutts off on me I'll tie a rock to it and throw it in the river."

"Her name's been Hannah Campbell for ten years now, and I doubt she'll ask you," Maggie said.

She handed the paperback and a receipt to Mamie, who thrust them down into one of the many ancient tote bags she carried everywhere she went.

"You fell for that one!" Mamie declared, pointing a knobby, blue-veined finger at the dog. "That little possum is yours for life!"

Maggie regarded the little dog and thought that maybe "Possum" would be a good name for it, if she kept it, which she probably wouldn't.

Mamie patted her coat pockets to make sure she had her coin purse, house keys, and a canister of pepper spray before taking up the ornately carved cane that was leaning against the counter and making her weaving, lurching way out of the bookstore. She knocked over a cardboard display of paperbacks with one of her swinging tote bags, and almost knocked over a customer who was entering the store.

"Your stock is getting old!" Mamie yelled back as she went out. "I've probably already read this one!"

The bookstore staff kept a list of what Mamie had read just so she wouldn't duplicate purchases, and Maggie had consulted it before she rang up the sale. She added the most recent title to the long list and then went back to the romance section to straighten out the mess the older woman always made of it. The bells attached to the front door jangled and Maggie turned to find Scott walking back in with Trick Rodefeffer close behind.

"Out!" yelled Maggie, and Scott stopped in his tracks, thinking she meant him.

"Ah Maggie, aren't you over that yet?" whined Trick, as he stopped just inside the door and looked to the left, where the list of people Maggie had banned from the bookstore was written on the dry erase board of shame.

"Not yet. Out!"

Maggie pointed to the door, and Trick sighed before he slouched back out.

"What did he do?" Scott asked Mitchell, the pierced, tattooed, and dreadlocked young man who was working behind the coffee bar.

"Oh man, you should have seen it," Mitchell said in a quiet voice, as he prepared Scott's usual order of cappuccino and a blueberry muffin. "Trick brought a lady friend in here who was not Mrs. Trick, if you know what I mean. Maggie caught Trick slipping his hand up Not Mrs. Trick's skirt, and she went ballistic. It was awesome."

"She doesn't even like Mrs. Trick, I mean, Sandy."

"She told Trick this was not a whorehouse, and he was not to bring his whores in here."

"Wow. What did Trick say to that?"

"He told Maggie she needed to get laid and lighten up. I thought she was going to have a stroke."

"He's lucky to be alive," Scott said.

"Oh yeah, for sure," Mitchell said admiringly. "She threw a teapot at him. It hit the wall over there and broke into about a million pieces."

Scott took his cappuccino and over-sized blueberry muffin to his usual table at the end of the coffee bar, by the window. From this vantage point, he could see a large section of Rose Hill Avenue, from the college entrance to his left to just beyond the diner at the crossroads to his right. He saw Trick outside, giving a young woman some money and then pointing at the bookstore. The young woman came in and ordered an extra-large iced latte to go.

Hannah came in and plopped down next to Scott, then reached over to steal his muffin. He grabbed his plate out from under her hand and held it beyond her reach.

"You are not seriously thinking of leaving that dog with Maggie," he said.

"Hey Mitchell," she called out. "Scott's buying me an extra-large caramel latte with whipped cream and two cheese Danish."

"Is that a bribe?" Scott asked her.

"Let's just call it an alternative foster placement fee."

"Alright, then. Where did you go with Drew?"

"To the Eldridge Inn. You know Connie's old cat, the one who attacks all her guests? We had to put it down. Kidney failure. It seemed kinder to do it there, and Drew wanted someone to hold hands with Connie."

"How'd she do?"

"She's a mess, of course. You'd think someone that germ phobic wouldn't have a pet in the house, but she adored that wicked old cat. It was eighteen years old."

"Are the college president and his wife still staying there?"

"You mean since Gwyneth inherited the house they were living in and kicked them out in the snow? He is, but the wife's gone to Florida to stay with their daughter. You know, I don't think Connie and the president are getting along very well."

"I hear she drives everyone crazy who stays there, following them around with sanitizing wipes and air freshener."

"Yeah, she's a nut, but no, what I mean is when we got there, Connie and the man were having a huge fight in the kitchen."

"What about?"

"I think he wants to move out, and she was telling him he couldn't go."

"Seems like it would be up to the paying guest whether he stayed or went."

"Sounded to me like he'd reserved the room for a long time and she'd turned away other customers. This is a really busy time right now with the festival coming up."

Scott shrugged, saying, "None of our business."

"You're no fun at all," Hannah said, and then thanked Mitchell for bringing her order to the table.

"Is that going to be your breakfast?" Scott asked her.

"Are you kidding? I had breakfast hours ago. This will just about tide me over until lunch."

"How can you eat like that all the time and stay so skinny?" Scott asked her.

"Thin genes, I guess," she said. "My brothers are all the same way."

"Are we square about the dog?"

"I know I often forget to pick up animals when I leave them with people, but I am going to take that dog with me. I've got a gal up at the library who loves Chihuahuas, and I'm going to take it up there to her."

"What did she ever do to you?"

"Now, don't be hateful. We can't all be pretty and precious. Speaking of which ..."

At that moment, Ava Fitzpatrick came in the bookstore with her children, and Hannah snorted in derision.

"What have you got against Ava?" Scott asked her.

"She may have all you men wrapped around her little finger, but she doesn't fool me. She's no saint."

"I never said she was. She doesn't look like any saint I ever saw. An angel, maybe."

Hannah rolled her eyes.

"Well, if you'd been hearing what I've been hearing..."

"That's just gossip, Hannah; you know that."

"It may be, but you're missing out on some pretty interesting theories about why Theo left her all that money."

"Speaking of vicious gossip, have you seen Margie today?"

"Speaking of crazy criminals, I can't say that I have. Why?"

"Even though she knew Enid was scheduled to move to Mountain View this morning, Margie went out early and didn't come back."

"That's weird, even for her."

"I thought so too."

"I can ask the scanner grannies if you like."

The scanner grannies were a group of senior citizens in town who used their older model police scanners to listen in on cordless and cellular telephone calls. It was illegal and immoral, of course, but it was also very useful in gathering information.

"That would be great, thanks."

"You know, Scott, for someone who doesn't listen to gossip you sure don't mind asking me to, except of course, when it comes to Saint Ava."

Maggie came over to their table and handed the small dog to Hannah.

"It's scaring the customers," Maggie said.

"Well, off with its little head then," Hannah said. "Let's not let a poor little homeless dog get in the way of your profit margin."

Maggie put her hands on her hips and glared at her cousin, who also happened to be her best friend.

"Are you saying I care more about making money than anything else?"

"I am."

"Well, you're right," Maggie said, and then turned on her heel and walked away.

Scott spent the afternoon asking people if they'd seen Margie that day, but no one had. Many people took the opportunity to share stories of their past unpleasant run-ins with the former post-mistress, and Scott felt renewed regret over how long Margie had been allowed to make malicious mischief in Rose Hill, especially on his watch.

He checked back at her house again before he went off duty. Her handbag and heavy winter coat were still hanging by the door, with her gloves and hat sticking out of one pocket. Up in her room, despite feeling squeamish about it, Scott checked her dresser and closet, which were both full of clothes. There was an old cardboard suitcase under her bed, but it was empty. Where could she have gone without a coat, purse, or a suitcase full of clothes?

Scott hated to think the worst, but he was beginning to.

Morning Glory Circle by Pamela Grandstaff

Chapter Three – Wednesday

aggie called Hannah at 2:30 in the morning. Hannah's husband Sam answered on the first ring, as he was still up working in his home office. Sam owned a network security-consulting firm and had contracts with several large corporations and government agencies. He worked odd hours from a room that looked more like the command center of a futuristic spaceship than a home office in a hundred-year-old farmhouse.

"I know she's sleeping," Maggie told him, "but Caroline just called from the Pittsburgh airport, and Hannah and I said we'd pick her up."

"Wasn't she supposed to come home next Sunday?" Sam asked.

"That was the original plan, but you know Caroline, she said she had a premonition she needed to be home sooner."

"Are these her 'guides' talking to her again?" Sam asked in a sarcastic tone.

"She didn't say that," Maggie said, "but it wouldn't surprise me."

Caroline Eldridge was a free spirit, and a generous trust fund had allowed her to dabble in many different religious and charitable organizations. As a result of this decade-long spiritual and cultural exploration, Caroline espoused a mélange of ancient mystical and new age beliefs that transcended any single philosophy or religion, with rules and rhetoric that often contradicted one another.

"That woman needs a shrink more than a guru," Sam said, not for the first time.

"Give her a break," Maggie said. "She has more money than she knows what to do with and good intentions."

Maggie could imagine Sam shaking his head, but he just said, "I'll get Hannah."

They were on the road by 4:00 a.m., driving Scott's Explorer. Hannah wasn't allowed to take the animal control vehicle out of the county, Sam's wheelchair adapted van employed hand controls that Hannah just could not get the hang of using, and Maggie didn't think her vintage VW Beetle would survive the trip. Luckily, Scott was always glad to give Maggie anything she wanted, including the use of his SUV. He offered to drive, but she quickly declined as graciously as possible. Maggie wanted Caroline to feel free to talk, and Scott's casual conversation technique often tended to come across, albeit unintentionally, as a police interrogation.

Two and a half hours later Maggie and Hannah were in the baggage claim area of the Pittsburgh airport, looking for the friend they hadn't seen since they dropped her off at the same airport over six years previously. Back then she was volunteering on a humanitarian aid trip to Haiti and had been her usual exuberant, sunny blonde self, eager to be off on a new adventure. The woman who approached them this morning and flung her arms around them, on the other hand, they at first mistook for a much older homeless person.

Maggie and Hannah tried to hide their shock, but it was difficult. Caroline stank to high heaven, for one thing, an overpowering mixture of body odor, patchouli, and mildew. Dressed in a stained t-shirt, torn jeans, and sandals, she had only a huge, filthy backpack for luggage. The previously attractive young woman now had lank, dirty hair, leathery skin, a deeply lined face, bloodshot eyes, and some seriously chapped lips. Hannah and Maggie exchanged horrified glances behind her head as she hugged them.

Maggie didn't know what to say other than, "Where is your coat? It's February."

Caroline held her friends out at arms' length and beamed at them.

"I'm so glad to see you guys!" she said. "You haven't changed a bit!"

Caroline excused herself to go to the restroom, and Maggie and Hannah just stared at one another, speechless for a few seconds.

"I pity the people who just flew several thousand miles with that stench," Maggie finally said.

"I pity the two of us for the next few hours," Hannah said, and the realization of what she meant sank in for Maggie.

"Oh no," she said. "We probably need to stop and get her something to eat."

"We'll drive through somewhere," Hannah said. "We can't inflict that malodorous pong on any of our favorite places, or we'll be banned for life."

"How do you tell someone they stink?" Maggie asked.

"I don't," Hannah said. "But you let me know how that works out for you."

"Thanks a lot."

"Is that a pot smell or perfume?" Hannah asked.

"I think it's the patchouli. I associate that smell so strongly with pot that I get them mixed up as well."

"I never liked that stuff," Hannah said. "It just made me sleepy."

"You know, it just occurred to me that you haven't had a cigarette yet today," Maggie said. "Have you finally quit?"

"It's the weirdest thing," Hannah said. "This past weekend they started to make me feel queasy. I stopped on Sunday, got a huge headache on Monday, bit Sam's head off all day, and now I don't want one. It can't be that easy."

"Maybe you're pregnant," Maggie said.

"I seriously doubt that. If it hasn't happened in ten years of using no birth control, I think the odds are against it happening at all."

"You could get tested."

"Yeah, but if nothing's wrong with my equipment, then Sam would have to get tested. I can't see him bouncing back quickly from bad news on that front. I'd rather just leave it a mystery we don't talk about."

"I'd say I'm glad to see you quit smoking but I think you'd start back up just to spite me."

"I've been thinking about quitting ever since your Grandpa Tim had his throat zapped, and of course Sam nags me about it all the time. I think I'm just ready."

When Caroline came back, they ascertained that she did not, in fact, have a coat, and didn't seem a bit concerned about the sub-freezing temperatures outside.

"I'll just think warm thoughts," she said, and Maggie could hear Hannah groan, although it was a quiet one.

Caroline pulled a ratty looking wool sweater out of her backpack and pulled it on over her ensemble, and this helped Maggie and Hannah identify the main source of the mildew smell. She happily accepted Maggie's gloves for her hands and Hannah's mittens for her feet.

"You can keep those, by the way," Hannah assured her.

Maggie was ashamed of how embarrassed she was to be seen with and smelled with her old friend. The odor was so bad that it made her eyes water and her nose run. When she licked her lips, a big mistake it turned out, she felt as though she could even taste it.

Caroline declined a drive-through meal, saying, "I'm vegan, and I don't eat anything fried."

"What does that leave?" asked Hannah, who considered French fries with ketchup two healthy servings of vegetables.

They stopped at a giant grocery store where Caroline was equally bowled over by and critical of the abundance of choices. She explained she didn't have any U.S. currency yet, so Maggie bought the hummus, pita bread, and the glass bottle of organic apple juice her friend picked out. She was appalled at how much they cost. Caroline's smell had killed both their appetites, so Maggie and Hannah each just purchased something to drink.

"You know, Hannah, the carbonation and high fructose corn syrup in that soda will ruin your liver and kidneys," Caroline told her as they got back in the SUV. "You should also know, Maggie, that if people quit buying bottled water, the cities would have to clean up the public water supply, and everyone would have access to clean water."

Back in the SUV, neither Maggie nor Hannah could think of anything to say, so they just listened to Caroline smack her lips as she chewed with her mouth open while telling them all the ways in which gas-guzzling SUV's, like the one currently being used to retrieve her from the airport, were ruining the environment. After Maggie stopped at a gas station to fill up the tank for the return trip, Caroline lectured them on the evil deeds of all the oil companies, and how they manufactured the oil crisis to drive up prices and justify drilling on protected lands.

Maggie, who recycled, conserved water, turned off the lights when she left a room and contributed both time and money to local charities, agreed with most of what Caroline said. Still, she dreaded spending the next two hours listening to how woefully inadequate she and Hannah were in preventing the suffering of third world populations and in how many ways they were constantly contributing to the ultimate destruction of the planet. Maggie wondered why it didn't bother her to read about it online or listen to it on television, but having someone she knew preach it to her in person was incredibly irritating.

Hannah must have been thinking along the same lines, because she suddenly changed the subject by saying, "We are so sorry about Theo."

"Gwyneth said someone hit him over the head and he bled to death," Caroline said as if they were discussing the weather and not her older brother's murder.

"Yes," Maggie said. "The person who did it died in a car accident soon after."

49

"That karma was pretty instant," Caroline said. "Why'd he do it?"

Maggie was amazed at Caroline's seeming detachment but still chose her words carefully, trying to be sensitive.

"As well as Scott can determine, he thought he might inherit some of Theo's money if he died. He got the idea he was Brad's son."

"Not possible," Caroline said immediately, about her brother Brad, who had drowned when he was 15. "Brad was gay."

Maggie almost turned around in her seat at that but remembered she was driving. Hannah, however, spun around instantly.

"Brad was gay?" Hannah asked, incredulous. "How do you know?"

Caroline caught Maggie's glance in the rearview mirror, smiled, and said, "I saw him with someone once."

Maggie knew 'that someone' was most likely her brother Sean. Hannah, however, did not know about any of that, and Maggie hadn't planned to tell her, so she was grateful when Caroline didn't. Maggie considered her brother's sexual orientation private family information, and she wasn't about to gossip about any of her brothers, even with Hannah.

Maggie thought about Margie's recent remarks about her father and sister-in-law, and was just relieved she didn't also know about Sean. Margie's hostile accusations about Maggie's family had been uncomfortably right on target. Her father was disabled due to a back injury, and he did supplement his pain medication with alcohol. During the investigation into Theo's murder, Hannah and Maggie found a wall in Theo's house covered with photos of her sister-in-law Ava, and as a result, Maggie wondered if there was anything to the rumors about her beautiful sister-in-law and the deceased. Maggie was used to speculation about her family and had learned to deflect it by pointing out that it was no one's business but their own. It was bad enough to have to live in the soap opera, let alone to have to explain the plot to curious onlookers.

Caroline told them all about the mission she had been on, taking much-needed medical supplies to rural communities outside Concepcion in Paraguay, and the trip to California that preceded that.

"I stayed with some great Buddhist monks in Santa Cruz," she said. "A few weeks ago their monastery burned down in the wildfires out there, and I've invited them all here to stay with me until they find a new place."

"I can't wait," Hannah said quietly, and Maggie gave her a warning look.

"How will they get here?" Maggie asked.

"I haven't thought that through," Caroline said. "I'm sure the universe will take care of it."

Hannah sent Maggie a stern look that she understood immediately. Hannah didn't want her to do it, but Maggie's first inclination was to help Caroline, so she ignored her cousin.

"You should call Midge at Sacred Heart," Maggie said. "She's the church secretary, and her dad Elbie drives the church van; I think it holds twenty people. If you make a donation to the food bank and pay for the gas, they will probably help you out."

Hannah rolled her eyes in disgust as Carolyn thanked Maggie.

"Why don't you come home with me instead of going straight out to the lodge," Maggie suggested, "I hate to think of you being up there alone with no supplies. At my place, you can get a shower, wash your clothes, and we can shop for provisions."

Caroline agreed, and then delighted her two companions by laying down in the back seat to have a nap. Through an ingenious method Hannah improvised of sliding down every window in the Explorer less than an inch and cranking the heater, the cross ventilation took most of

Caroline's body odor out the back window, and everyone still stayed warm. When they got to the other side of Pittsburgh, Maggie offered to take Hannah home first, but Hannah quickly refused, saying it would probably be better not to spring a visitor on Sam without warning, and that Caroline would probably want to "freshen up" before she visited anyone.

"I think she's asleep," Maggie whispered.

"Maybe she's just having an out of body experience," Hannah said.

"Do you think she can hear us from the astral plane?" Maggie asked.

"Maybe she's checking the ozone layer to see how big the hole is we're making," Hannah said.

"I do care about the environment," Maggie said. "I buy recycled paper products for the store."

"I do too, you know," Hannah said. "I'm the one who made you go see that movie about it."

"She's just very passionate about it," Maggie said.

"She just thinks we're idiots," Hannah said.

"Let's talk about something else," Maggie said.

They discussed the upcoming festival, and all that still needed to be done in preparation. Because the Fitzpatrick families owned so many businesses in town, and because they benefited so much from the influx of tourists that the festival attracted, Maggie, Hannah, and every family member and friend they could recruit would be working morning 'til night during the festival. Maggie felt like she had enough coverage at the bookstore to allow her to focus solely on the family bakery, and Hannah planned to split her time between the bakery and the bar. Patrick would be stretched the most between the bar and service station. Maggie had hinted in an e-mail to her brother Sean that he was not only welcome but also needed in Rose Hill this weekend, but he had only sent back a weak "we'll see." He hadn't been home for so many years that she wondered if he could still find the place.

Hannah's four brothers were all too busy with their own lives elsewhere to come home, and Hannah's and Maggie's cousin Claire (Delia and Ian's only living child) was overseas doing hair and makeup on a movie set. This sounded glamorous, but Claire assured them it often meant months of grueling work dealing with childish egomaniacs in substandard accommodations with little or no edible food. They were sometimes called upon to send care packages of coffee, toilet paper, and junk food, so there must have been some truth to that claim.

Back in Rose Hill, Maggie dropped Hannah off at her parents' house on Iris Avenue, a couple of blocks from Maggie's parents' house. Luckily Alice and Curtis were both working and couldn't come out to see (and smell) Caroline. She was still sleeping when Maggie pulled in next to her VW Beetle in the alley behind the bookstore. She hoped to get Caroline upstairs and into a shower before anyone could experience her funk and form an indelibly bad first impression.

She had been friends with Caroline since kindergarten, and Maggie wanted her friend to be accepted back into Rose Hill in a positive way, unlike Caroline's sister Gwyneth, whom Maggie had tossed out of her bookstore the first day Gwyneth was back in town. As far as Maggie was concerned, Gwyneth was pretentious, condescending, and insufferable. Most people who met her agreed.

Maggie gently woke her friend, who looked momentarily confused about where she was but still sat up with a big smile on her face. Caroline wanted to go to Maggie's bookstore and look around, but Maggie steered her up the back stairs to her apartment instead. As soon as Caroline sat her backpack down, Maggie fetched her a big fluffy towel and a bathrobe and pointed her to the bathroom.

As soon as she heard the shower running, Maggie opened the soiled backpack and dumped out the contents in the middle of the kitchen floor. Maggie's mother Bonnie wouldn't have thought the contents were fit for dust rags, but Maggie dumped the clothes in the washer and used hot water with lots of soap powder. A few other things fell out of the backpack, and after she started the washer, she went back to the pile. There was a passport, a journal, a wooden flute, and a prescription bottle. She resisted the temptation to look at the passport or journal and put them back into the filthy bag. She foresaw a hate/hate relationship with the flute, but carefully placed it in the bag instead of hurling it from her back balcony into the trash dumpster in the alley below. She did, however, glance at the label on the prescription bottle before she returned it to the bag, and was surprised to see it was for an antidepressant. Combining that information with Caroline's appearance made Maggie doubly glad she had brought her home instead of abandoning her in the isolated lodge house up on Pine Mountain.

Caroline took a quick shower, to conserve water no doubt, and then appeared in the kitchen before Maggie had the opportunity to find some clothes for her to wear. Maggie found a new toothbrush still in its package in the kitchen's junk drawer and gave that to her, so Caroline obediently returned to the bathroom to use it. Maggie went into her bedroom and opened some drawers, wondering what she had that wouldn't hang on her friend's gaunt frame.

After she'd finished brushing her teeth, Caroline came into Maggie's bedroom and flopped down on the bed, saying, "I had forgotten what a luxury hot water is."

Maggie pulled out several pairs of pants and set them to the side, saying, "I have three sizes of clothes in here. I have eights I haven't worn since high school, tens I haven't worn in this century, and twelves I am just about to burst out of, but I refuse to buy fourteens."

Maggie feared her friend was about to lecture her on the negative effects of obesity on the earth's resources, but Caroline just said, "It doesn't matter to me what I wear, anything is fine."

54

Caroline graciously accepted and obediently put on every article of clothing that Maggie handed her. Her emaciated frame alarmed Maggie, who could see every rib and vertebrae protruding underneath her friend's skin. The eights were still way too big, but with a belt, the jeans stayed up.

"This must be like dressing a tall skinny doll," Caroline laughed.

'Homeless Barbie,' Maggie thought, and then felt ashamed for even thinking it.

Dressed in jeans, a turtleneck, a fleece pullover, and some warm wool socks, Caroline looked just like a ski resort tourist. She admired each piece of clothing as if it was the nicest thing she'd ever had, and indeed, Maggie thought, although Caroline could afford anything she wanted, she seemed to prefer dressing like the people she helped.

Maggie was dying to use some moisturizer, deodorant, and chapstick on her friend, but didn't want to risk offending her. Maggie made her a care package of several size eight outfits, which although they were out of fashion, were still in good shape. She put it all in a laundry basket, which was the closest thing to luggage that Maggie owned. Caroline tried on all Maggie's snow boots until she found some that were close to her size. Maggie chose a down coat for her next, a ski parka that was too small, not her style, and a gift from her Aunt Alice. It fitted Caroline perfectly.

Caroline submitted to Maggie's insistence that she dry her hair with a blow dryer, even though it probably increased her carbon footprint by one micron, and she plaited her long hair into one skinny french braid.

Caroline looked in the mirror afterward and said, "I look like an American."

Maggie laughed until she realized Caroline wasn't making a joke.

"Do you hate it?" she asked her, worried she had gone too far.

"No," Caroline said, hugging Maggie with one arm. "It just took less time for me to reassimilate than I thought it would. Next thing you know, I'll be buying a gas guzzling SUV to take my spoiled kids to a theme park."

Maggie's feelings were a little hurt by that, but she let it pass. She took Caroline down to the bookstore, introduced her to the staff, and set her loose among the books, telling Jeanette that anything Caroline wanted went on Maggie's tab. Then she went back upstairs, took Caroline's clothes out of the washer and threw them in the dryer, where she willed them to shrink into doll size rags. She knew she shouldn't want to change Caroline, to make her comply with whatever expectations she or anyone else had for how one should look, dress, or behave, but she argued with herself that she had good intentions.

'If I went to one of her countries and she tried to change my appearance,' Maggie reasoned, 'it would be so that I fit in better with the indigenous people.' The indigenous people of Rose Hill responded more favorably to people dressed as they did, who didn't smell bad, so Maggie further rationalized that she was only trying to help Caroline assimilate with the natives.

Maggie was perversely unwilling to let Caroline go out on her own, but she knew that was ridiculous, so she gave her friend the extra keys to the back door and apartment before she took Scott's Explorer back to him. She gassed it up at her uncle's service station, and then drove it to Scott's house with the windows down, hoping to air out the vehicle by the time she arrived, shivering in the frigid winter air.

Scott invited her in, made her some hot tea, and told her Margie was still missing. He also told her about Margie trying to get an insurance policy from Tony but did not share what Tony had confided to him about the blackmail.

"I'll ask around about her," Maggie said. "One thing I forgot to tell you yesterday was that when I ran into her the other night, she was dropping letters in the box outside the post office. It looked like a big handful."

"Thanks," Scott said and wrote that down in his notebook. "What was it she said to you that made you so mad?"

"Just mean stuff about my family," Maggie said, "about Dad and Ava."

Maggie quickly changed the subject by telling him all about Caroline, including the prescription she found in the backpack.

"Do you think she's had a nervous breakdown or something?" he asked her when she was through.

Maggie sipped the English Breakfast tea, which was her favorite, and shrugged in response.

"I don't know how you could tell," she said. "She's so relentlessly cheerful and positive that she seems fine, but that may be because of the antidepressant. Her appearance is awful. She looks at least ten years older than her real age."

"Are you going to talk to her about it?" he asked.

"I feel like I should," Maggie said. "She doesn't look healthy."

"She probably hasn't been to a doctor or a dentist in a long time," Scott said. "Maybe you could suggest that as a start she should get a check-up from Doc Machalvie."

"I'll try," Maggie said, "but I don't want to come over too bossy and alienate her completely."

"You boss me around all the time, and I don't feel alienated," Scott said and gave her a sly grin. "In fact, I think you're pretty wonderful."

"If you're going to talk to me like that I'll have no choice but to leave," Maggie said sternly.

"See what I mean," Scott said. "I think you're pretty sexy when you're irritated."

"That explains a lot," Maggie said, then got up and went to the front room to put on her coat.

Scott just laughed and saw her out, saying he'd call her later. Maggie remembered to thank him for letting her use the Explorer and then walked down the hill toward downtown and home.

Back in the bookstore, Maggie found Caroline sitting at a cafe table in deep conversation with Dr. Drew Rosen, the new veterinarian in town. This surprised Maggie at first, and then she realized how much the two had in common. Drew was very interested in political causes and animal rights, and lived a very healthy, vegetarian lifestyle.

Drew and Maggie had been on a few tentative dates, but Maggie quickly realized that although she liked him quite a bit, and he was a great guy, they were destined just to be good friends. Maggie believed in getting those kinds of conversations over with as soon as possible, and while Drew was gratifyingly disappointed, he was sincere in his intention that they not let a few dates make things weird between them. This was something people often say before they find out how hard it is to do, but Drew had so far been true to his word. Maggie believed any residual awkwardness between them would soon resolve itself. Now that she thought about it, Caroline and Drew would make a really good match. She would have to put Hannah on that project; she was the amateur matchmaker in town.

Neither noticed Maggie, so intent were they on what they were discussing, so she retraced her steps and went to the grocery store across the street to look for something she could feed her vegan friend. Delvecchio's IGA yielded very few organic choices, plenty of vegetables, but no hummus or pita. Owner Matt Delvecchio was helpful, but although he was used to stocking Italian, Polish, Kosher, and German specialty foods, and every kind of junk food a college student could crave, he did not cater to organic vegans.

"Some of those Amish farms in Garrett County might be organic," Matt said, "and I'll ask the folks out at Pumpkin Ridge Farm if they know where we can get the stuff. They raise free-range chickens and feed their dairy cows organic grain. They probably have a source."

"She'll probably be a good customer for you," Maggie urged him, "so it would be worth it to try."

He said if Caroline would stop by he'd see what he could order for her.

Maggie went down to the bakery to get some whole grain bran muffins. Her mother was busy working the counter, so she asked her Aunt Alice if she knew how to make pita. Alice said she didn't, but said she thought Mrs. Haddad made her own pita bread, and that she would give her a call.

Next Maggie went to Machalvie's Pharmacy and found some organic, natural toiletries for Caroline. She was shocked by the high prices. Meg Kelly rang up her purchases and told her the tourists and college students bought the majority of the expensive natural products.

"But I like the beeswax lip balm, myself," she said.

Maggie decided to get one to try out.

"Hey," Maggie said, remembering she had promised to ask around. "You haven't seen Margie lately, have you?"

Meg frowned.

"I've been trying hard not to speak ill of others," Meg said. "Father Stephen says we should not judge lest we be judged."

"Come on," Maggie encouraged her. "I won't tell Father Stephen."

"He says God sees everything we do," Meg said. "He says you can't hide anything from God."

"Maybe God would want you to help keep Margie from hurting other people," Maggie said. "Maybe telling me what you know will help someone else."

"That Margie is just awful," Meg said, now that she believed she had God's permission to gossip.

"What'd she do?"

"You know her mother has rheumatoid arthritis," Meg said. "Doc Machalvie prescribed her a new anti-inflammatory pain medication that is supposed to be great for that. Well, Margie came in to pick it up, and when she saw how much the co-pay was, she refused to pay it. Delores was the pharmacist on duty that day, and she told Margie she was going to report her for elder abuse. Margie bought the medicine, but when Delores left that night, her tires had been slashed."

"Did she tell Scott about that?"

"No," Meg said. "She didn't have any proof it was Margie who did it."

"I have just recently begun to find out how vindictive that woman can be."

"Ask around," Meg said. "Almost everyone I know has a Margie story. She got mad at me because she wasn't invited to my wedding shower, so my wedding invitations somehow went missing for a few weeks after I mailed them. Some people never received theirs."

"Did you report her?"

"If you can't prove it what's the point? She's wicked, but she's clever."

As she was leaving Machalvie's, Maggie ran into her brother Patrick, who was crossing the street from the service station, where he worked all morning, to the Rose and Thorn, where he worked all evening.

"Aren't you going home for lunch?" she asked him.

"Can't," he said. "Ian got held up, and I have to open the bar by myself."

Their Uncle Ian used to be the police chief before he retired at the beginning of the year, and now he drove a school bus and managed the family bar. Maggie headed to her parents' house to get lunch for her dad, known as Fitz, and her Grandpa Tim.

"I was beginning to think you'd forgotten about us," her father said gruffly, but Grandpa Tim smiled and blew her a kiss as she passed his recliner. The Irish setter known as Lazy Ass Laddie only stirred from his cozy spot next to the heater long enough to thump his tail at Maggie, then curled it back up and closed his eyes.

Back when Maggie was still in grade school, her father had fallen off a ladder while painting the trim on the house and broke some vertebrae in his back. Her mother often said the only thing that cushioned his fall was the six-pack he consumed before he got on the ladder. After a couple of surgeries failed to help relieve his pain, Fitz declared he was done with hospitals and had since relied more heavily on medication mixed with alcohol to control his pain.

Maggie heated up some leftovers, made Lazy Ass Laddie go out in the backyard to pee, and then served the two men on TV trays in the front room. Maggie washed up their dishes when they'd finished, and her grandfather winked at her as she left. Grandpa Tim was Bonnie's father and reportedly started smoking back in Scotland at the tender age of six. He suffered from emphysema and had recently undergone surgery and radiation treatments for throat cancer. He couldn't talk above a whisper.

Maggie stopped back in at the bakery to tell her mother she'd taken care of lunch, and found her mother resting behind the counter during an unusual lull. She told her mother a bit about Caroline.

"All the money she's got and you're buying her toothpaste and groceries," Bonnie said. "That makes no sense to me."

"She just got back in the country and didn't have any American money yet."

"There's a bank, not twenty yards from here full of American money, and her the richest woman in the county. That's how the rich stay rich, daughter. They're always looking the other way when the bill comes."

When Maggie returned to the bookstore, she found out from Jeanette that Caroline had gone upstairs for a nap. Maggie looked at her tab and saw she had picked out a few news magazines, two big city newspapers, and chamomile tea. Maggie went upstairs to her apartment and took her purchases to the kitchen, after closing the door to the bedroom, where she could see a Caroline-shaped lump under her quilt. She fired up her computer and looked up some vegan recipes to see if she could make lunch out of anything she had purchased.

Caroline slept through lunch clear until 3:00 p.m., at which time Maggie warmed up the baked sweet potatoes, green beans with garlic and onion, and whole grain muffins she had prepared for lunch. Caroline ate a couple of little bites of everything, and pronounced it all delicious, but didn't consume more than a half-cup of food, all told.

She told Maggie about meeting Drew and already seemed to know more about him than Maggie did. Maggie knew Drew had been in Belize with the Peace Corps for a year between college and vet school, but she didn't know he'd been back to visit several times.

"He was in the Peace Corps with a person who I know well," Caroline said. "It's such a small world."

Maggie made her friend some hot chamomile tea, and then gently broached the subject she was determined to discuss.

"Are you feeling okay, Caroline?" she asked her, as she reseated herself across from her friend at the table.

"I'm fine," Caroline said, but she was shaking her head as she said it. "I'm just tired."

"Would you say we have the kind of friendship where complete honesty is acceptable?" Maggie asked her.

"Gosh, I hope so," Caroline said, sounding surprised.

"You look like you might be ill," Maggie told her, as gently as she could. "I'm really worried about you."

"I'm fine, really," Caroline said and jumped up to take her plate to the sink. "You made way too much food. Do you think anyone downstairs would want some?"

It would never have occurred to Maggie to offer her staff food from her kitchen. For one thing, she rarely cooked for herself. For another, she kept her private life very separate from her work life. Most of her employees had never even been upstairs in her apartment. Caroline had quickly changed the subject, and Maggie sensed that any more questions about her health would be shut down similarly.

"What are your plans?" Maggie asked her instead.

"Up in the air, really," Caroline said. "I need to go over the bequest issues with the executor, and probably sign a million papers at my bank trustee's office, and then I'm just going to relax. I need to take some time to process Theo's transition, both spiritually and mentally."

"You mentioned some monks were coming?"

"Oh yeah, they might. There are about twelve of them and some staff members. Their abbot recently transitioned planes, and their retreat center was destroyed in a wildfire. The lodge is plenty big enough for all of us."

"What do they do exactly?"

"They're Zen Buddhists," Caroline said. "They spend most of their time meditating or chanting, but they also train candidates who are seeking ordination into the order, or who just want to teach meditation."

"Isn't meditation just praying?"

"Meditation can be different for everyone. For me it's all about putting aside my ego, ignoring the constant chatter inside my head, and finding that stillness where there is peace and the knowledge that we are all one."

"I'd sign up for that," Maggie said. "The voice chattering inside my head is most often my mother's."

"I can teach you," Caroline said. "It helps keep you in the now moment instead of worrying about the future or regretting the past."

"What else is there to do?" Maggie asked her. "I mean, besides working to make money, taking care of the family, and all the church and community stuff that I have to do. Worrying is just watching out for the bad stuff that might happen so that I can be prepared, and regret is what I feel when I fail."

"Regret and worry don't change anything; they're just unnecessary suffering. Try just being," Caroline said. "Just accept what is."

Maggie couldn't imagine accomplishing all she had to do, looking after all the people she cared about and keeping vigilant against the potential troubles that seem always to lurk nearby if all she did was relax and accept "what was" all the time.

"So, besides meditating and teaching meditation, what do the monks do all day?"

"Not much else. Some orders keep bees, garden, or perform community services, but their particular mission is to teach others to meditate."

"There may not be a big call for that in Pine County."

"The universe will bring them what they need, and will draw to them the people who need what they have to offer."

"Just meditating all day would get old after a week or two, I would think," Maggie said. "Don't they ever get bored, lonely, or depressed?"

"The Buddhist way to approach suffering is to serve others to get away from feeling sorry for yourself," Caroline said.

Maggie thought Caroline looked so sad when she said that. She wondered if all her frantic running around trying to save the world was just an attempt to distract her friend from how unhappy she was deep inside. Maggie then had the uncomfortable thought that she might be guilty of the same thing, running around Rose Hill taking care of everyone, and keeping so busy she didn't have time to think about what she was missing in her own life. Maggie decided a change of topic was called for, so she told Caroline about the Winter Festival coming up, and all that had to be done to prepare for it.

"I would love to help," Caroline said.

"Great," Maggie said. "You can help out in the bakery with Hannah and me tomorrow. My mom will appreciate the extra hands."

"Count me in," Caroline said. "Sounds like fun."

"I need to go to a committee meeting tonight, and I might be home late. I'll sleep on the couch when I come in this evening so I won't wake you," Maggie said. "You'll need your rest if you're going to work in the bakery tomorrow."

"Thank you so much for letting me stay," Caroline said. "I'm so glad we'll have a chance to catch up tomorrow. I've spent all our time together today telling you all about me, but I want to know what's going on with you."

Caroline went to the front room, and Maggie cleaned the kitchen. She tried to imagine how she would feel if she, like Caroline, was alone in the world with only that pretentious pill Gwyneth for family, with no home or friends to return to when she was tired and cold. Maggie didn't think any amount of money or any number of worthy causes could fill that kind of deep pit of loneliness in her soul. She decided to do her best to make sure Caroline didn't feel lonely. She would be a good friend to her and help her however she could.

Maggie left Caroline lounging in the sitting room with her newspapers and magazines and walked up to the community center to attend the final Winter Festival prep meeting. Hannah was already there and had saved a seat for Maggie. The mayor's capable secretary Kay was running the meeting in his absence, as usual, and she had everything planned down to the smallest detail. Stuart and his wife Peg may have taken turns being mayor every four years, but Kay was the one who ran the town on a day-to-day basis.

Maggie looked around until she found where Scott was sitting, with his chair tipped back against the wall at the side of the room, looking right at Maggie with that blatant warm regard that made her feel nervous and happy all at the same time. When she crossed her eyes and stuck her tongue out at him, he grinned and shook his head.

When the meeting was over, Maggie told Hannah that Caroline would be there to help in the morning.

Hannah said, "I'll believe it when I see it," in a way that irritated Maggie.

"Don't be like that," Maggie said. "She'll be there."

"We'll just have to wait and see about that, now won't we?" Hannah said with a smirk.

Hannah left, and Maggie found Scott waiting for her outside the community center, which used to be Rose Hill High School.

"May I walk you home, Miss?" he said and offered her his arm.

She smacked his arm away, saying, "I don't need police protection to walk three blocks, thank you very much."

"Then can I buy you a drink somewhere?"

Maggie considered him a moment, then said, "I'm really in the mood for a beer and a bowl of pretzels. I ate a healthy lunch, and I need something bad to balance it out."

"I better come along if you're going to be bad," he said, "just to keep an eye on you."

They walked down to Rose Hill Avenue and crossed the street to the Rose and Thorn, which was full of people. Maggie snagged them a booth and Scott got their drinks: beer for Maggie and a soft drink for himself. Scott smiled at her warmly from across the table, and Maggie was equal parts irritated and pleased.

"Any sign of Margie?" she asked him.

"No one has seen her. I have this feeling she's somewhere laughing at us all worrying about her."

Maggie told him the stories Meg Kelly had told her, about Margie slashing Delores's tires and sabotaging Meg's wedding invitations, and Scott shook his head.

"Why don't people tell me about these things?" he asked. "That's what the police are for."

"No proof," she said.

"I guess," Scott said and rubbed his forehead.

"Aren't you worn out?" Maggie asked him over the loud Irish folk music Patrick was playing.

Scott had worked night shifts for the past three nights and was now switching to three days in a row.

"No," he said, "I had a long nap this afternoon."

"How's the head?" she asked.

"No problems," he said.

Patrick was filling glasses and flirting with some women at the bar, and Mandy, who worked in the evenings, was serving drinks at the tables and booths. Their Uncle Ian was holding down the far end of the bar next to the entrance, greeting new customers, and encouraging the ones who left to come back and visit. As Maggie and Mandy tried to hold a conversation over the loud buzz of the crowd and music, Maggie noticed Scott rub his forehead again, and realized the combination of noise and cigarette smoke was probably getting to him.

"Let's go," she said and drained the last of her beer.

Scott walked her to the back door of the bookstore, and, as they were away from prying eyes, gave her a warm hug and a lingering kiss. Maggie let herself enjoy his warm embrace, the smell of his skin, and the intensity of the attraction between them. She was tempted to invite him up but stopped herself just as the words were about to leave her lips. There was no halfway with Scott Gordon; if she slept with him, they were as good as engaged in his eyes.

"I don't want to stop," he said.

He pushed her up against the back door and kissed her again, with an urgency that thrilled her and scared her to death. She was quickly losing control of her senses and pushed him away.

"Maggie," he said, and the longing and desire in his voice almost persuaded her. "Let me come in."

"Get out of here," she said. "You're as bad as that cat of yours, always following me home and wanting to come inside."

"You're considering it, though," Scott said. "I can feel it."

"I don't know what you're talking about," Maggie said and unlocked the back door.

"You're weakening," he taunted as he went down the steps and walked away.

The cafe was busy even though it was late, and Maggie hoped the noise wasn't keeping Caroline awake. She needn't have worried. When Maggie went upstairs, she found a note from Caroline saying she'd gone to Drew's for dinner.

"That was quick," Hannah said when Maggie called to tell her. "I hadn't even got my matchmaking juices flowing yet."

Drew was now living in a much nicer, warmer place than the sad shack he had been renting from Theo Eldridge the month before. Maggie, Hannah, Scott, Patrick, and Ed had helped him clean, paint, and move into one of the small, one-bedroom apartments that used to be servants' quarters over Mamie Rodefeffer's vast garage. Mamie loved having someone close by to observe and criticize, and if that irritated Drew, he had only to remember the drafty fire hazard he'd left behind to find a good reason to put up with it.

"Let's make a bet about how soon they sleep together," Hannah suggested

"She's not likely to start a new relationship so quickly," Maggie protested.

But she was wrong. Caroline didn't call or come back to Maggie's that night.

After Scott left Maggie's, he walked down to Lotus Avenue to check in again at Margie's. Everything looked just as it had when he left earlier. Scott went back up to Margie's room and looked around, determined to find some clue as to where she went. Frustrated by the lack of personal effects in the room, Scott picked up Margie's pillow to see if anything was hidden under it. There was nothing. He knelt down and felt under the twin mattress, and found a manila envelope. Inside was a first class ticket to Maui, a new passport, a travel agent's packet of brochures, and a detailed itinerary. She had rented a suite at a luxury hotel right on the beach. This was obviously her plan for after her mother moved into the retirement home, but how could she afford it? The plane tickets were for today's date.

'She's missed her flight,' Scott thought. 'Where in the world is she?'

Scott searched the room again, not worrying this time if he displaced anything or made a mess. The only other clue he found was a pamphlet hidden between her neatly folded nightgowns in a dresser drawer. It was from a plastic surgery center in Los Angeles that touted "Extreme Makeovers."

'How could she afford all this?' he wondered.

Scott had arranged for her bank accounts to be frozen when he found out about the embezzling, and if she wanted any money she had to get approval from the bank trustee assigned to her.

'Maybe she has a large amount of cash squirreled away somewhere,' he thought.

Scott was reminded of the secret room in the lodge Theo had used to hide money, drugs, and blackmail fodder. He wondered where Margie's secret room was. Scott ran his hand along the paneling all around the room, below the slanted ceiling. There were no doors into the crawlspace, and the paneling looked and felt continuous. He checked the floorboards and couldn't find any that lifted up.

Scott walked home wondering if he could make a missing person claim on Margie without Enid getting involved. He decided to wait until morning, check the house again, and then call someone at the county sheriff's office to see what he could do. Sarah Albright, the county sheriff's office investigator, would no doubt know, and Scott had her number on speed dial. He didn't want to stir up that wasp's nest, though, if he could help it. Sarah got under his skin, but not in a good way, and certainly not in the way she wanted.

As he passed the mobile home park, Scott saw Ed walking Mandy's son Tommy home, and he met them at the corner of Iris Avenue.

"Any sign of Margie?" Ed asked him.

"No, and I'm starting to think there's cause to worry."

"I'm going up to the Thorn after this, want to join me?"

"Sure."

They walked Tommy home and made sure the doors of the trailer were locked tight before they left him. The trailer next door, which belonged to Phyllis Davis, had a light on inside.

"Phyllis isn't back, is she?" Scott asked.

Phyllis had been Theo's lover and blackmail accomplice and had unwittingly provided his killer with the motive to murder him.

"She's living in one of the rooms behind the Roadhouse, near the highway," Ed said. "We heard she'd rented the trailer to someone, but we haven't seen who it is yet."

Scott told him about the plane tickets, hotel reservation, the plastic surgery pamphlet, and the keys, purse, and coat being in Margie's house.

"That doesn't sound good," Ed said. "I asked everyone I saw today if they'd seen her, and no one had. According to everyone I spoke to since she quit at the post office, Margie's been staying home all day and walking around town late at night."

"If she hadn't missed that plane, I'd say she's taken off. That was an expensive ticket to let go to waste."

"Maybe she set it up to look as if she's disappeared, and she's created a new identity for herself somewhere else."

"She's certainly devious enough," Scott said.

The bar was packed with tourists, loud fiddle music was blaring, and a thick layer of smoke hovered near the ceiling.

"Let's just go back to my house and have a beer," Ed said, knowing Scott couldn't handle the smoke.

"If you don't care," Scott said, "I'm just going to head home. I'm beat."

"No problem," Ed said and waved goodbye as he entered the noisy bar.

Scott crossed Rose Hill Avenue and turned right down the alley. Duke, the huge striped tomcat that used to belong to the vet, had recently moved in with Scott and was coming down the alley from the other direction. He meowed at Scott.

"Hey buddy," Scott said as they met. "Are you coming home?"

Duke twined around Scott's legs briefly in an affectionate greeting before continuing in the direction he'd been headed. Scott shook his head and watched him go.

"Be careful," he told the big cat and then headed toward home.

Chapter Four - Thursday

Maggie was so mad at Caroline for ditching them that she couldn't quit talking about it. She vented all evening to Hannah on the phone and was still complaining about it the next morning while the two of them carried supplies from a delivery truck in the alley through the back door into the bakery kitchen.

"That's why she didn't eat much of the food I fixed," Maggie said. "She had plans for later."

Hannah had the 'I told you so' look on her face.

"I guess she's done with us," Maggie said. "She needed a ride home from the airport, and that was all."

"You're only mistake was in forgetting what a flake she is," Hannah said. "This isn't the first time she's done this to us, you know."

"I know, I know," Maggie said. "I always fall for it. I'm such an idiot."

"You're not at fault for trying to help a friend," Hannah said, as she handed Maggie two big tins of baking powder to shelve. "You just forgot who you were dealing with."

It was coming back to Maggie now, all the times Caroline had canceled at the last minute because of the "cool" people she had just met, or the "awesome" place she had an opportunity to go to, always on the spur of the moment. Often Caroline forgot to call and let her know she was canceling, and Maggie would only find out why Caroline didn't show up at the concert venue in June when she got a postcard from her in December.

Maggie was wondering now why she had even bothered to stay in touch with Caroline over all these years. Caroline, Hannah, Maggie, and their cousin Claire had all been close friends as little girls, but that was a long time ago. If she had let go of her, Caroline probably would have been content to drift away, and never look back. Maggie stewed about this as she and Hannah helped bake the merchandise they would sell at the festival.

Hannah and Maggie worked in the kitchen all morning making many dozens of cookies, brownies and flaky turnovers using recipes they knew so well they hardly had to refer to them. It helped that they had an industrial size mixing machine and two large professional ovens, each of which held several pans on the wire racks inside. It was hot, thirsty work, and they drank what felt like gallons of ice water, stepping outside frequently to enjoy the cold air in the alley behind the bakery. Hannah and Maggie had been doing this work since they were old enough to see over the edge of the counter, and they worked well together, never getting in each other's way.

By mid-morning, there was still no sign of Caroline. When Maggie went back to her apartment during a break, she saw that Caroline had taken her backpack and the clothes she had lent her, as well as the magazines and newspapers she took from Maggie's store.

"She came and got all her things while we were working here this morning," Maggie said to Hannah when she returned to the bakery. "She left this note."

Hannah read the note out loud, "Thanks for the hospitality. We'll get together soon. Love and Light, C."

"I can't believe she did that," Maggie said. "She said she was going to help us today."

"And once again, we've been used and discarded by Caroline Eldridge," Hannah said.

"I feel like such an idiot," Maggie said. "I thought we were friends.

"Are we done now, with her and her bullshit?" Hannah asked Maggie.

"Oh yeah," Maggie said. "We're done."

Ed Harrison, editor-in-chief, and owner of the Rose Hill Sentinel was standing in the front room of the newspaper office, arguing with Ethel Birch. Ethel, who was 79 years of age, was a homemaking enthusiast and the writer of the "Home Matters" column in the weekly newspaper. She was a stickler for tradition, and still typed her columns on an old Royal manual typewriter. She was a stout, dour-looking woman who hadn't changed her hairstyle in half a century, still sewed all her own clothes, knitted her own cardigans, and enjoyed crocheting covers for inanimate objects. Her gardening claim to fame was growing huge Dahlias which were as big as dinner plates.

"It's too long," Ed told her. "You have to cut twenty words."

"It's the same length it always is," she insisted. "I used the same size paper and the same margin settings I have used for almost fifty years. I ought to know how long my own column is."

"I have explained this to you many times, Ethel," Ed said. "What fits on your paper does not necessarily fit in the column."

"Your father always made it fit."

"You need to cut twenty words."

"Your grandfather always made it fit."

"Fine," he said. "I will cut them for you."

"Oh, no you won't," she said, clasping the page to her prodigious bosom. "You butchered it once before, and I'm not going to let that happen again."

Ed calmly handed her a red pencil. Ethel huffily arranged herself at the extra desk by the window and put on her half-moon reading glasses, which hung from a beaded chain around her neck.

Ed went back to his desk, where he was wrestling with a web-site-building program. He had recently decided to bite the bullet and put up a Sentinel website and was determined to do it all by himself. He purchased the domain address and set up an account with a service provider, and was now working on designing the site. When he followed the instructions that came with the software it worked, but he couldn't understand why it worked, and that frustrated him.

The front door opened and Mandy came in smiling, carrying a plate of hot doughnuts.

"Hey good lookin'," she said, but then stopped talking when she saw Ethel, who was giving her a stern look over her reading glasses.

"Good morning," Ed said, as he jumped up and took the plate from her, conscious of Ethel's eagle eye and bloodhound nose for gossip. "You really shouldn't keep bringing me these. I'm getting fat."

Mandy just beamed at Ed, flashing her big green eyes, dimples, and white teeth. A Fitzpatrick Bakery apron was wrapped around her slim, petite frame, and her long blonde hair was twisted up on top of her head.

"Well, I know how much you like 'em," Mandy said in her Tennessee twang.

Ed glanced at Ethel, who wasn't even pretending not to listen.

"Doughnut, Ethel?" he offered.

"No," Ethel said, obviously enjoying Ed's discomfort. "I can't have the sugar, but you two enjoy yourselves."

Ed felt awkward, and Mandy just stood there, smiling up at him like a child waiting for a pat on the head.

"Well, thanks," Ed said.

"You goin' to the bonfire tomorrow night?" Mandy asked.

"Yes," he said. "I have to take photos for the paper."

"Would ya mind if Tommy tagged along with ya? I gotta work, and I don't like him runnin' around alone after dark."

"No, that's fine, I don't mind," Ed said. "Tell him to come over here after dinner, and we'll go together."

"Thanks," Mandy said. "See ya later."

She was still flashing those white teeth and dimples as she went out the door.

Ed braced himself for Ethel's comment.

"She's too young for you," she said.

"I know," Ed said. "We're just friends."

"Hah," Ethel said. "She's got a big crush on you."

"That may be true," Ed said, "but I'm not going to do anything about it."

"Fiddlesticks," Ethel said. "Most men would give an eyetooth to have a pretty young thing like that chasing after them."

"Well, I'm not like most men, I guess."

"You aren't made of stone," Ethel said.

"I'm not an idiot, either."

"We'll see," she said, smirking as she returned to her copy editing.

Ed didn't know what to do about Mandy. As improbable as it seemed to him, she was seriously infatuated, and he just kept hoping it would pass, like the flu or the measles. He was attracted to her, how could he not be? She was young, pretty, and sweet.

'If I was ten years younger,' he told himself.

But that wasn't true. Ten years earlier, Ed was married to and madly in love with the sexy, ambitious Eve, whom he met in their college journalism program. After they graduated, they worked on the same newspaper in Philadelphia. When his father died, Ed came back to Rose Hill to take over the family's newspaper business. He and Eve tried to keep their relationship going long distance for a while before realizing they wanted very different things out of life. Being the wife of a weekly newspaper editor in the sleepy little town of Rose Hill was not what Eve had in mind.

Ed suddenly realized he had eaten half the doughnuts on the plate and done no work on the website since Mandy left. He pushed the plate away.

"She's fattening you up," Ethel said, "so you can't get away."

"Twenty words," Ed warned her. "Or I'll do it myself."

The Rose Hill Winter Festival was held in the field behind the Foxglove Mobile Home Park, between Rose Hill Avenue and the Little Bear River. One of the city's snowplow drivers plowed wide swaths into and around the four to six-foot drifts of snow that covered two acres of roughly flat ground. The fire department set up a temporary fence to mark off the boundaries and keep small children (and drunken adults) off the train tracks and out of the river.

There was a string of food vending caravans lined up on Marigold Avenue, waiting to be towed into place. While Scott directed traffic, Patrick drove the tractor that pulled each caravan. Maggie's sister-in-law Ava was setting up the games area for the littlest children, and some volunteer firefighters were designating the other contest areas with red flags atop six-foot-tall metal rods, which could be seen over the highest drifts.

At noon Hannah and Maggie took a break from the hot bakery kitchen, went to the diner, and ordered late breakfasts. Evidently, Caroline had been making the rounds, because lots of people came up to them and mentioned seeing her, surprised she was back a week early. Maggie was very polite but vague, saying she didn't know what Caroline's plans were.

"Everyone thinks we're still her best friends," Maggie said to Hannah, "so of course, we should know what she's doing."

"You gotta let it go now," Hannah said. "That's just the way Caroline is, and she's never going to change."

But Maggie couldn't let it go. She knew she should, but she felt used and discarded.

"Did she give your keys back?" Hannah asked her.

"Yes," Maggie said.

"Did she leave any money to repay you for all you spent on her yesterday? You know, for the gas for the evil SUV we drove for two and a half hours to pick her up at the crack of dawn, the magazines and newspapers made out of all those defenseless trees, and all the other stuff you bought?"

"No," Maggie said. "But that's my problem, not hers. She didn't ask me to buy her that stuff, I offered."

"You're not going to give yourself a break, are you?" Hannah said while mashing her fried eggs up in a gross looking puddle of soft yolk she planned to scrape up with toast. "Let's melt some candles, make a Caroline doll, and stick it with pins so you'll feel better."

Maggie didn't answer, but she didn't think she was going to get over her hurt feelings quickly just because Hannah was already tired of hearing about it. She knew she was pouting, but she didn't care.

"Okay, let's think up her comic book name," Hannah suggested. "That'll make you feel better."

"I don't feel like it."

"C'mon, you know you want to. How about 'Rich E. McBitchy?'"

"She's not bitchy, her sister is."

"Yeah, but Gwyneth already has her comic book name. She's Twiglet, the British Bumstick. Her superpower is sucking all the fun out of a room just by entering it. She's a member of the League of Fantastic Funsuckers."

Maggie cracked a smile at that.

"That's right," Hannah said. "Now you're back on board. Tell you what, Caroline can be 'Stinky Megabucks.'"

"How about 'Stinky Megabucks, the Vegan Menace?'"

"Perfect," Hannah said. "I will enter that in the official handbook."

Caroline had gone to school with Hannah, Maggie, and their cousin Claire, from kindergarten through seventh grade at Rose Hill Elementary, and the four had been inseparable. Mrs. Eldridge may have looked down her nose at the local girls, with their hand-me-down play clothes and a clumsy way around her fine china, but they were Caroline's only friends, so she tolerated them.

The summer after seventh grade Caroline's brother Brad drowned, and their mother used that as an excuse to send her youngest daughter to boarding school. Caroline came back each summer and palled around with Hannah, Maggie, and Claire, but as much as they loved her, she grew up in a much different culture, with different types of friends and interests than those of her small town counterparts. They saw less and less of her until, after her father passed away and her mother went back to England, she rarely came back to Rose Hill.

Maggie had once driven to Dulles airport in DC to see Caroline during a long flight layover after Caroline called and begged her. Maggie ended up holding her friend's backpack for forty-five minutes while Caroline argued with the boyfriend who had come to the airport expecting to join her on the next leg of her trip, only to get dumped as soon as he arrived. When he got there, he found out Caroline was going with a man she'd met at the Glastonbury Music Festival in England the week before. The new boyfriend drank in the airport lounge while the old boyfriend, who had turned down a prestigious internship and sublet his apartment to go on this trip, cried in front of everyone at the departure gate. Maggie couldn't remember the dumped boyfriend's name, but the new one from London was memorably named "Giles Thripps-Maythorne III." Maggie had later named a goldfish after him.

Caroline's setups sometimes included Hannah as well. One summer Caroline invited Maggie and Hannah for a week-long stay on the outer banks of North Carolina, but once the two got down there, they discovered a house full of Caroline's hard partying, condescending friends from college. Alarmed and repulsed by all the pretentious posing, cocaine snorting, and partner swapping that took place on the first night, they had driven home early the next morning.

"Your trouble is," Hannah said, as she pointed a fork full of hash browns at Maggie, "you keep expecting her to be like you and me when she's nothing like us."

"I know," Maggie said, "and I know that shouldn't matter so much."

After lunch, Maggie checked in at the bookstore, and Jeanette came to her with a concerned look on her face.

"Your friend Caroline came in and got a big stack of books," she said quietly. "I mean hundreds of dollars' worth. She said you wouldn't care."

Maggie's hurt feelings zoomed into anger, and she took a few moments to calm her temper before she spoke.

"The next time Caroline comes in, tell her she needs to see me before she takes anything else. Also, please total up everything she's taken so far, and give her an invoice, due upon receipt."

Maggie could tell Jeanette was pleased with her answer, but she didn't go into it with her.

Caroline Eldridge dropped the books she'd taken from Maggie's store down on the polished table in the formal entry of her sister Gwyneth's house. The stately Edwardian home had served as the Eldridge College president's residence after their father died up until the time Gwyneth claimed it, after their brother Theo's death. The college president and his wife barely had time to put their belongings in storage and move into the Eldridge Inn before Gwyneth's moving van arrived.

"As you can see, there were some hideous attempts at amateur interior decoration which I have yet to address," Gwyneth said, by way of greeting, as she grandly descended the central stairway. "The college president's wife had an unfortunate fondness for pastel floral wallpaper."

"Hello Gwyneth, how are you?" Caroline said, and the two sisters, who hadn't seen each other in many years, shared an air kiss to each side of the face.

"My interior designer, Blaine, is coming down this week to show me some new sketches. Unfortunately, I am at the mercy of a vanishing contractor and the ignorant local tradesmen. There is no sense of urgency or a strong work ethic among them that I can detect. It's all, 'We'll get to it,' and 'I'm waiting on the supplier,' until I just want to scream. You can't even throw money at problems down here; it doesn't do any good."

"How are you, though? Are you well?"

"As well as can be expected, I suppose, considering the conditions. I had to import staff from the city, and they're all suffering from culture shock."

"It's not that bad, surely," Caroline said.

"I warned them," Gwyneth said. "'This is not a lark in the Hamptons,' I said. 'This is a safari into deepest, darkest Appalachia.' They didn't believe me, of course. Now they're frantically calling their families to send them care packages, like Oxfam."

"They'll get used to it," Caroline said.

"Their cell phones and wireless laptops don't work here," Gwyneth sighed, "and they act like someone's pulled their IV's out. I've had to double their salaries just to keep them here. They've taken to referring to it as hillbilly boot camp."

"It's hard to get good staff, that's what Daddy always said," Caroline said. "At least they're being paid fair wages."

"More than fair, I'd say. The locals are unemployable, of course, and so hostile. This town is trapped in the past, and not in the charming, marketable way that Martha's Vineyard is. The mayor and his wife are the only semi-civilized people I've met, and the only ones interested in my suggestions for improvements to the town. I'm glad you're here, darling, although I have to say, you look a mess. What are you wearing?"

"This is an improvement on what I arrived wearing. I wish you and I were the same size, Gwyneth. I need some natural fibers, and I know you have them."

"As it happens, I just bought the most divine cashmere wrap in the palest oyster color. Come up and see."

Gwyneth crossed the foyer and ascended the stairs with Caroline following.

"The cashmere trade is terrible for the goats, you know, Gwyneth. They're often ill-treated."

"Not these goats, I can assure you. My stylist Marissa says they gather just the tiniest bits of chin hair from each one. It probably feels like the barest tickle, and they are all so spoiled and fat. They grow the most heavenly filaments. It's the softest, lightest, warmest thing you've ever felt. You'll want to wash your hands first, of course, before you touch it. Your cuticles are beyond help, I fear. They've run amok."

Caroline dutifully washed her hands before she made her way to Gwyneth's dressing room for the show-and-tell portion of the visit.

"I can't tell you how much I've missed hot water and hand cream," Caroline said. "Although I wish you'd read the labels and make sure there's no animal testing involved."

"You're always so serious, Caroline. Lighten up, please, will you? Let's not worry for ten seconds about lab rabbits, and just enjoy my beautiful clothes together, shall we?"

"Alright, but it is the most frightful waste of resources and a shameful display of excess."

"Oh, I know it, but don't be cross. Tell you what, I'll have Louise fix us a nice lunch and then you can tell me about all the dreary things you've been doing in all those awful places you go."

Caroline sighed but acquiesced. Gwyneth was her only living relative on this side of the Atlantic, after all.

Later, after lunch, Gwyneth broached the delicate subject of money.

"When you talk to Paxton, my love, just tell him you're broke, and he simply must advance you some of your inheritance. That's what I did, and the coffers immediately opened wide. Now there is as much money as I need, right there in my account, whenever I need it. It's all electronic these days."

"Except Theo didn't leave mine to me in the same manner he left yours to you," Caroline said. "Mine's all tied up in trusts, and Paxton will probably put me on some horrible budget and make me submit receipts."

"How dreadful," Gwyneth said but smiled as if it was delicious to hear. "I'm sure I could help you out if you're desperate."

"Well, not exactly desperate. I got Paxton to pay for the plane fare."

"But how did you get here from the airport? Why didn't you call me? I would have sent my car for you."

"It was two in the morning, and I didn't have money for a hotel room or a rental car. I know how you hate to have your sleep disturbed, so I called Maggie, and she came to get me."

"Oh, that odious bookstore woman. I don't know how you could stand her for five minutes, let alone for two hours in a car."

"I slept most of the way. The thing about Maggie is I knew she'd do it. She's like that. You call, and she comes."

"Like a faithful, stupid dog."

"Handy to have around, though, and she's got great taste in books. Her store is well stocked."

"I wouldn't know," Gwyneth said, still smarting from being banned from entering that particular establishment, after literally being thrown out of it.

"She introduced me to a great guy, too; Dr. Drew Rosen, have you met him?"

"A doctor, and on your first day, how lovely," Gwyneth said with a marked lack of enthusiasm.

"He's a veterinarian."

"Oh, I see. Not a real doctor, then."

"Gwyneth, you haven't changed a bit."

"I had a little work done, does it show?"

"That wasn't what I meant."

Ava Fitzpatrick put the finishing touches on the flower arrangement she had created for the library table in the entryway. The snow was falling in downy clusters, making her three-story Victorian home turned bed and breakfast look like a Currier and Ives illustration come to life. Every available room was booked for the festival, and guests were due to begin arriving soon.

Ava stacked firewood in the fireplace of the front parlor and lit the crumpled up newspaper beneath it so a warm blaze would greet the new arrivals. She checked her makeup in the hall mirror, smoothed her hair back from her face, and practiced a friendly smile. It would be nonstop for her over the next several days, with long hours of hard work and not much sleep. And no Patrick, she'd resolved.

When Ava's husband Brian deserted her and their two children, his brother Patrick stepped in to become a rock she could lean on. Patrick and the rest of Brian's extended family helped her transform a falling down money-pit into a showplace that supported her family over the intervening years. She sacrificed much, went without any personal luxuries, and worked her fingers to the bone to make the business a success. In part because of Patrick's presence in their lives, her children were secure and well adjusted, so Ava felt it was all worth it. Unfortunately, and almost without realizing it, she had fallen deeply in love with Patrick along the way.

They managed to keep their affair hidden for a long time, but since Theo Eldridge died and left a large sum of money to her in his will, the town's gossip mill had been grinding at her heels, and people were suddenly noticing things that had gone on under their very noses before. People like Patrick's mother, for instance, the fierce and devoutly Catholic Bonnie Fitzpatrick, who had taken to making surprise visits to bed and breakfast, and making knowing remarks.

When Patrick became a suspect in Theo's murder investigation, in part because of his close relationship with her, Ava had put a stop to his late-night visits, and made every effort never to be alone with him. It was difficult though, to resist the lure of his strong arms around her and his passionate kisses. She longed for him all the way down in her bones and suffered. Patrick had slowly mended Ava's heart after his brother Brian broke it, and now she had to reject him, no matter how difficult it was to do so. It was the best thing for everyone.

Ava heard the back door open, and Patrick came in with her six-year-old son Timmy, both red-cheeked and stamping their snow-covered feet.

"Stay on the rug, please," Ava said automatically, avoiding Patrick's eyes when she joined them in the kitchen.

"Mom, Mom, Mom," Timmy said. "Patrick wants to take me and Charlotte snow-tubing at Mrs. Crawford's farm tonight. There's going to be a fire and everything. Can we go? Please? Please? Please?"

Ava looked at Patrick, who was also giving her the "please, please" look that hurt her heart so.

"We'll see," she said, and both their faces fell. "Let's see how cold it gets."

"That means no," Timmy told Patrick sadly.

"I know," Patrick said, in the same tone.

"Go wash up, please," Ava told Timmy. "Cricket and Tiffany will be here shortly, and I need you to show them where everything is."

"New recruits," Timmy proudly told Patrick. "I have to show 'em the ropes."

The small boy ran off to the bathroom, and Patrick tried to grab Ava around the waist.

"Stop it, Patrick, I mean it," she said sharply, and he backed off with a hurt look on his face.

"You make me feel like a molester or something," Patrick said. "How can I be this close to you and not touch you?"

"I don't want to talk about it," she said. "It's hard for me too, you know."

Timmy came back in, and Patrick swung him up in the air, making him squeal with laughter.

"Cricket and Tiffany?" Patrick asked him. "What kind of silly girl names are those?"

"Her real name's Chrissy," Timmy said, as Patrick sat him back on the floor, "but everyone calls her Cricket."

"Well my real name's Patrick, but no one calls me Caterpillar."

Timmy giggled.

"And no one calls your mom Lady Bug."

"You could call me, um, you could call me, Tickle Bug," Timmy giggled.

The sleigh bells attached to the front door jingled, and Ava said, "That's enough now, Timmy. Say goodbye to Uncle Patrick, please."

Timmy hugged Patrick.

"I love you, Uncle Patrick," he said.

Ava immediately misted up, and Patrick looked at her as if to say, "Why are you doing this to me?"

"I love you too, Tickle Bug," he said and leaned down to kiss the top of the boy's head.

Ava said briskly, "Thanks, Patrick," and went to greet the new recruits.

After checking in at her bookstore, Maggie met Hannah back at the bakery, where both their mothers and Aunt Delia were working hard, getting all the extra baked goods ready for the vending caravan. Hannah and Maggie spent the afternoon wrapping single servings of brownies, cookies, tarts, and turnovers in plastic wrap, and packing them in boxes.

Scott came in at just past five o'clock, and Maggie gave him some fresh coffee and a couple of doughnuts left over from the morning. Scott was adept at reading Maggie's moods and waited until she went to the backroom before asking Hannah what was up.

"Just Caroline Eldridge's usual bull crap," Hannah said. "She does this to Maggie every time. Sets her up as if she's Maggie's friend, and then pulls the rug out from under her. She's a user."

Scott was very familiar with Caroline's lack of dependability and follow through, and it irked him to see her take advantage of Maggie, who had a soft heart beneath a very prickly hide. When Maggie returned to the counter area, he cornered her.

"Let me buy you a pizza for dinner," he said, and then held his hands up, "and no funny business. I promise."

Maggie looked at him, rejection on the tip of her tongue, and then surprised herself and everyone else in the room by saying, "Sure, why not?"

She waved goodbye to her astonished audience and left the bakery with Scott.

"Come and see what all we got done," he said.

They walked down Pine Mountain Road to Marigold Avenue, where they took a right and walked toward the festival grounds. A big banner stretched over the entrance to the festival grounds proclaimed, "Welcome to Rose Hill Winter Festival." All the vending caravans were in place, with the generators and electrical cords behind them, and the bandstand was being set up in a central location. The volunteer firefighters were building the log teepee that would be surrounded by chain link fencing (for safety) and set on fire Friday night. A group of contestants was already working on their entries. "Snow Structure" could be loosely interpreted as any building made of snow, and one contestant seemed to be making a temple or castle of some sort.

"Who's guarding this tonight?" Maggie asked Scott.

Scott pointed to his deputy, Skip, a lanky twenty-something local boy who was currently attending community college part-time in pursuit of a criminal justice degree, just as Scott had done. Deputies Frank and Skip had conveyed a small prefab shed to a point just to the side of the entrance and had equipped it with chairs, a table, and a heater connected to a generator outside.

"Skip is officially in charge, but the Whistle Pig Lodge is providing volunteers," he told her. "It's just an excuse for them to stay up all night drinking and playing cards."

After they fully surveyed the festival site, they walked up Peony Street and crossed Rose Hill Avenue to PJ's Pizza, where they placed their order. They then cut through the alley behind the restaurant and turned up the connecting alley that separated Sunflower Street and Pine Mountain Road, to Scott's back door.

Duke was on the back porch and meowed to be let in.

"I still can't believe you're Duke's new daddy," Maggie told Scott.

Duke originally belonged to Owen, the vet before Drew. Owen had passed away the previous summer, and when his wife sold the practice to Drew, he also got custody of the large cat. Duke refused to stay inside to the point of viciously attacking anyone who tried to make him. Duke also hadn't forgiven Drew for mistaking him for a feline blood donor, which he most decidedly was not. When Drew moved into his new apartment, landlord Mamie forbade him to keep a pet, so Scott offered to take Duke. Duke belonged only to Duke, had several ports in town he called home, and could often be found performing his rodent control service in many of the backyards and alleyways of Rose Hill. When Scott made his rounds late at night, often on foot, Duke kept him company some of the time, trotting along beside him, and looking both ways before he crossed the street.

Scott let Duke and Maggie in the backdoor into the kitchen.

"I'm afraid if I install a door flap he'll bring me a rat for breakfast in bed some morning."

"He used to bring Drew dead animals all the time. I think Duke sees them more as edible gifts."

"You need to talk about this Caroline business," he said to her, taking off his coat as she slid off her own. "It'll make you feel better."

"I'm afraid I'll just sound whiny or jealous if I do."

"Not to me," Scott said and got a couple of bottles of beer out of the fridge.

Maggie sat at the kitchen table and picked at the chipped Formica at the edge.

"I'm mad at myself for expecting too much, and for being such a bossy boots," she said. "But I'm also feeling taken advantage of."

She told Scott about Caroline taking so much merchandise without paying for it, and ditching her for Drew.

"It's the same way when she calls. She never asks how I'm doing," Maggie complained. "It's always all about her and what she's doing, plus whatever favor it is she wants me to do for her."

The doorbell rang. Scott opened the front door to accept the pizza from the delivery person on duty and tipped him three dollars on a nine-dollar pizza.

"My mother would call that throwing away good money," Maggie said, about the amount of the tip.

"I call that guaranteeing my pizza is hot every time it's delivered," Scott said and sat down.

"You know," Maggie said, as she opened the box and selected a slice, "this experience with Caroline has made me really thankful for the good friends I do have. The ones who call when they say they will, follow through on their commitments, and appreciate everything I do for them."

Scott nodded, his mouth full of lava-hot pizza.

"Do I take you for granted?" she asked him, causing him to choke a little.

Scott swallowed the mouthful of pizza he had almost inhaled.

"What did you just say?" he choked.

Maggie sat her slice of pizza down and wiped her hands and mouth with a paper napkin.

"Do you feel like I take our friendship for granted or take advantage of you? You know, like when I show up at 2:00 a.m. to borrow the Explorer, or call and yell at you to come and get Gwyneth Eldridge out of my store just before I fling her out into traffic."

"Well, you did refill my gas tank and air the stink out before you returned the Explorer, and as far as Gwyneth is concerned, I'd help you toss that witch out on her bony butt anytime."

"But what do I ever do for you except tell you 'no,' 'go way,' and 'leave me alone?' You continually offer your hand to me, and I usually bite it. Why do you put up with it?"

Scott got up and took their empty beer bottles to the sink, rinsed them out, and placed them in the recycling bin before he got them each another one. Maggie recognized the evidence of his mother's strict housekeeping training. Scott sat back down and handed her a beer.

"Who rescued me from the Roadhouse when I had my last migraine?" he asked her.

Scott had a whopper of a headache in the middle of investigating Theo Eldridge's murder a few weeks previously. He called Maggie, and although she was on a date with Drew, she came running to get him and nursed him through a long, painful night.

"Who helped me investigate Theo's death when no one else cared who killed him, and were all just thrilled he was gone?"

He didn't bring up the fact that Maggie also interfered in that investigation, and he almost arrested her for tampering with evidence.

"The reason I keep running after you," he said, "even though you're hard-headed and stubborn as all get out, is because I know if you ever commit to being with me, I'll never be bored, I'll never be lonely, and I'll always have my best friend watching my back."

Maggie felt tears well up in her eyes, and she said, "But I don't know if I'll ever be ready for that, and it's not fair to make you wait."

"You let me worry about me, and you work on getting yourself straightened out about what you want. I have faith in you and me, so I'll be here when you're ready. I'm willing to wait as long as it takes."

He smiled at her sweetly and selected another piece of pizza. Maggie smiled back, tenderly, at the man whom she believed really, truly, and finally understood her.

"Thanks," she said. "I'll work on that."

Duke jumped up on the table, grabbed a piece of pizza, and ran down the hall with it before either of them had time to react. He left a greasy trail of toppings and sauce as he went.

"My son needs a mother," Scott said, "so don't take too long."

Ava locked the front door of the inn and allowed herself to exhale. All the guests were tucked in, and the girls had gone home. They were a little silly together but were also sweet and friendly, and they would have to do. She needed them to work the next four days so that she could participate in the festival. Her two housekeeping helpers and Delia Fitzpatrick were also going to work, so she felt she had everything covered.

Back in the kitchen, she kicked off her shoes, put on her fuzzy slippers, and sat down at the kitchen island to go over her lists. There was a tap at the back door, and when she turned around, Patrick was peeking in.

"No," she mouthed to him, and firmly shook her head.

He held up the bakery boxes he was carrying, the delivery from his family bakery she had neglected to pick up.

She unlocked the door and let him in, saying, "I'm sorry, Patrick. I completely forgot about that. Thank you for bringing them."

Patrick sat the boxes down on the counter, said, "Alright then, see you later," and left the way he came in.

Ava was surprised. She had expected him to at least stay and talk to her for a little bit. It was stupid, she knew, to be disappointed when someone does exactly what you've been telling him you want him to do, or in this case, not do. Now that he was complying, how could she complain?

But her feelings were hurt, and she felt rejected in a way she had never been with him. It stung. Something outside caught her eye just then, so she opened the back door, and saw Patrick out in the backyard. She went out onto the porch and could see he was walking around in the knee-deep snow. Once she reached the steps, in the glow from the streetlight in the alley, through the softly falling snow, she could see what he had done. With his feet, shuffling through the deep snow, he had drawn a huge, yard-sized heart, and wrote "AVA" in the middle of it.

After Patrick finished, he stood at the end of the walk, looking back at her, but his face was in shadow. She blew him a kiss, not sure if he could see her in the gloom of the porch. He turned and walked on down the alley, and Ava stood on the porch, watching the falling snow fill the indentations until she could no longer make out her name. The heart shape remained, though, past the point when she got so cold she had to go back in.

Unbeknownst to Ava, someone else had witnessed Patrick's adolescent declaration of affection. Someone who had been spending a lot of time in the cold, dark shadows of Rose Hill lately, waiting for opportunities to present themselves. This person waited until every light in the back of the bed and breakfast went out, signifying everyone had retired to their beds, before creeping up to the back porch and using the sharp blade of a pocket knife to flip up the flimsy hook and eye latch of the screen door. The locked door on the other side was no obstacle to someone with a key, and that key had just been inserted into the lock when a voice in the alley startled and distracted the intruder. As the town's police chief walked down the alley behind the bed and breakfast, talking to someone he could not see, the lurker slipped off the porch into the shadows of the giant evergreens, away from the house. An opportunity missed, perhaps, but one that would come again soon enough.

Scott parted ways with Duke at the end of the alley, telling him, "Be careful."

It had become his habit to talk to the cat as if it understood everything that was said, but Scott rationalized that as long as he didn't imagine the cat responded in an intelligent way, there was no harm in it. Scott knew he should catch up on his sleep while he could, but he was so bothered by Margie's disappearance and the stories that were coming to light as he asked around town about her, that he decided to take a walk around town just to see if he couldn't catch her on one of her moonlit forays.

There was no doubt in Scott's mind that Margie had been threatening to blackmail Tony, and he wondered who else she had threatened. Having her access cut off to the money she'd embezzled, she must have been getting desperate for cash. All those years of prying into people's mail and sneaking around town at night spying may have provided her with a lot of fodder for blackmail schemes. Scott wondered if she realized just how dangerous a game it was she was playing.

Scott walked down Peony Street past the mobile home park to the entrance to the festival grounds and checked in with the Whistle Pig Lodge members who were "guarding" the site. Inside the small prefab shed, they were deep into their poker game, with money on the table and beers at every elbow. They didn't even try to hide what they were doing when Scott entered the shack, just greeted him warmly and offered to deal him in. The cloud of cigar and cigarette smoke hung in a haze down to the tops of their heads, and Scott politely declined as he backed out into the fresh air outside.

Scott continued down Peony Street to Lotus Avenue and stood for a long time looking at Margie's house before continuing down to the end of the block and making a left on Pine Mountain Road. Cal Fischer lived on the corner there, just across the street from the old train depot, and he was standing out on his front porch while his English setter peed in the deep snow of his front yard.

"Hey Scott," Cal called out, and Scott walked up to his front porch. The dog danced around his feet until Scott patted him on the head.

Cal Fischer was a volunteer firefighter and a rescue diver and had also been peripherally involved in Theo's murder investigation. Pine Mountain Road started on the other side of the mountain, in Maryland, and wound along the Mason Dixon line through three states before it ended in Rose Hill, on the shore of the Little Bear River. Cal had, on a few occasions, taken down the barriers that were installed there (to protect people from accidentally driving into the water) to back his boat into the water, cross the river, and hunt for out of season deer. On one such occasion, on a very foggy night, someone had rolled a truck down the last block of Pine Mountain Road into the river, drowning the unconscious Willy Neff inside. On a subsequent outing, Cal found the submerged truck and discovered the victim. He hadn't had the barriers down, his boat out, or done any illegal hunting since.

Scott asked Cal if he'd seen Margie, and he asked Scott to please come inside. Cal brewed some coffee, and they sat at the kitchen table together with the dog on the floor at their feet.

"I just heard from Sue this evening that Margie's missing," Cal told Scott. "I planned to call you tomorrow to tell you about this weird thing that happened."

Scott sipped his coffee and listened attentively.

"Living just down the street from her, we see Margie a lot, because she doesn't have a car and walks everywhere. Sue doesn't like her on account of something that happened with the mail, but I've never had any trouble with her. I know her well enough to wave on the street and say hello, but that's it. Anyway, a few days ago Margie stopped Sue outside the house and told her she knew what happened the night Willy Neff drowned. She said she saw me back my boat into the river with my dog and gun, and she knew I was hunting out of season. Well, you know I confessed to my boss about taking the barriers down, but only you, me, and Sue know about the deer hunting, so Sue figures Margie must have been spying on us that night. Margie says to Sue, 'What do you think the game warden would have to say about that?' This made Sue so mad that she told Margie off."

"Did Margie ask Sue for anything, to keep quiet about it?" Scott asked.

"You mean, like to blackmail us or something?"

Scott nodded.

"Sue said she thought Margie was threatening to tell the game warden just to make trouble for me, and she went ballistic. You know Sue, she's sweet as pie, but if you threaten her family, she'll blister you like hot paint."

Scott was very familiar with Sue Fischer's devotion to her husband and wished he could have seen her go after Margie.

"I don't want you to wake her," Scott said, and about that time Sue walked into the kitchen. She didn't look happy to see Scott.

"What's happened?" she asked worriedly, with a grim look on her face.

"Nothing, honey," Cal reassured her and looped an arm around her waist. "I was just bragging on you to Scott, about how you tore Margie a new one for threatening to tell the game warden I was hunting out of season."

"Did you find her?" Sue asked Scott.

"Not yet," Scott said.

"Well, I hope wherever she is, she stays there."

"What did she say, exactly?" Scott asked her.

"Said she'd seen Cal take the barriers down, saw him take the dog and gun out on the boat. Asked me what I thought the game warden would do if he found out. I told her if she called the game warden on my husband I would take her to court and tell the judge all about the dirty tricks she's been playing on the people of this town for the last twenty years. I said I knew fifty people who would line up to testify against her. I told her when I got through with her she'd be tarred, feathered, and driven out of this town like the low down lying criminal she is," Sue said. "Or something like that."

"It must have been effective," Scott said. "I think she's skipped town."

"Good riddance to bad rubbish," Sue said.

"If you see or hear from her, will you let me know?"

"Sue could deliver her covered in tar and chicken feathers," Cal said.

Sue smacked her husband on the arm but smiled at him affectionately. Scott thanked them and left. As he walked up Pine Mountain Road, Scott reflected that there was a whole lot that went on in this town that he didn't know about, and wondered how much more he would find out on account of Margie going missing. There didn't seem to be one person, save her mother, who cared about her or was sorry she was gone.

Ed Harrison lay in bed and stared at the ceiling. He had purposefully not gone to the Rose and Thorn that night because he was avoiding Mandy. His regular evening ritual of two beers and a ballgame on the bar's big screen TV was ruined now because Mandy wanted to sit on the stool next to him and talk, at least until Patrick fussed at her to get back to work.

Mandy never ran out of things to talk to Ed about, although he couldn't think of a thing to say to her. She'd ask him, "Do you believe in horoscopes?" and then she'd read both of theirs. She'd tell him a dream she had and ask him what he thought it meant. She'd tell him every single thing she'd done from the time she got up until the time she was sitting there, and ask him a hundred questions, like a child. When Ed told her he wanted to watch the game, she asked him all sorts of questions about basketball, and then asked him, related to the cheerleaders, "Which one do you think is the prettiest?" Even worse, all this took place under the amused gaze of the locals seated nearby, and his friend Patrick, who kept rolling his eyes and laughing from behind the bar.

The phone rang.

"I'm just checkin' to be sure you ain't sick or somethin'," Mandy said when he answered.

"No, I'm fine," Ed said. "I just felt like making it an early night."

"Can I bring ya somethin'?' she asked.

"No, but thanks," he said. "I'm going to get an early start on some sleep."

"You still takin' Tommy to the bonfire tomorrow night?"

"Yeah, glad to do it."

"Well, I sure do appreciate that. I hate to think of him all alone at night with all these strangers in town."

"It's no problem."

Ed could hear Patrick yelling in the background and Mandy told him, "Shut up, I'll be there in a minute."

"You better get back to work," Ed said.

"Yeah, I guess I better," Mandy said. "I'm sure missin' you tonight."

"You've got to stop this," Ed said. "I'm too old for you. I don't want to hurt your feelings, but this is not going to work out the way you want. I'm sorry, but it's just not."

"I ain't givin' up," she said. "I ain't no quitter."

"Mandy, you are a sweet girl and any man would be lucky to have you, but it's just not going to be me."

"I had a dream 'bout ya last night," she said. "You and me and Tommy were a family, and we lived in the newspaper office."

"Mandy."

"My dreams always come true," she said. "I believe in my dreams."

"I'm sorry," Ed said. "I don't know what else to say."

"Just don't count me out," Mandy said. "Ya gotta at least give me a chance."

"Mandy."

"I know. I better go. Patrick's having a hissy fit over here. I'll see ya tomorrow."

"No more doughnuts, please."

"Turnovers then," she said with a giggle and hung up.

Ed hung the phone up and covered his face with a pillow. He'd been having dreams about Mandy, too, but what they'd been doing in the newspaper office in his dreams wasn't rated G for family viewing.

Hannah was staring at the kitchen calendar in disbelief, flipping back and forth between the last few months.

"Maybe I just forget to mark the day," she said.

"Mark what day?" Sam asked her, as he rolled his wheelchair into the kitchen from outside, letting a huge gust of cold wind and some blowing snow in with him.

"Oh, nothing," Hannah said. "Maggie and I have the next few days so tightly scheduled I didn't put in enough time to go to the bathroom, let alone shop for groceries. You're on your own for the next few days."

"I don't mind," Sam said, rolling up behind her and bumping her so that she fell back in his lap. "As long as I don't have to go to the festival, I would gladly eat dog chow with these two."

Jax and Wally collapsed on the kitchen floor, panting from the outdoor romp Sam had just taken them on.

"How were the inmates?" she asked him.

"They're fine. I miss the pit bull boys, though. I was kinda getting used to them."

"Don't worry; there will always be more where they came from. As long as there are idiots who breed them to fight and people who are afraid of them, we'll have plenty on hand."

"What time do you have to be at the bakery in the morning?" he asked her while nuzzling her neck.

"Eight a.m."

"You better get to bed then."

"Why don't I think you mean so I can get some sleep?"

"Maybe it's just a feeling you're getting," Sam said mischievously.

"I think I can maybe muster up enough strength to have my way with you," Hannah said. "But it's probably the last time for a few days. It will all be a blur from tomorrow until Monday."

"I'll take what I can get," Sam said.

"You're one of the last of the great romantics, you are."

"Oh my darling," Sam said, in a fake foreign accent, "Come with me to the Casbah, so that we may make the sweet, how do you say, love."

"You sound just like that cartoon skunk."

"I'll try to stay downwind."

Later, after Sam had gone back to work in his home office, and before Hannah turned off the lights in the rest of the house and locked up, she flipped through the calendar again while she rubbed her flat tummy.

"I can't think about it," she said out loud. "I don't have time to even think about it."

She did, though, way past the time when she should have been asleep.

Morning Glory Circle by Pamela Grandstaff

Chapter Five – Friday

Maggie, Patrick, and Hannah met at the bakery at 8:00 a.m. Friday morning, where their mothers had been working since 4:00 a.m., and loaded up Patrick's truck with the baked goods they planned to sell that day at the festival. The sky was still black with a thousand bright stars. It was the kind of frigid cold temperature that tightens your chest and freezes your nose hairs when you breathe in.

Once the boxes were secured in the bed of the pickup, Maggie and Hannah climbed in the back and sat on the wheel wells for the two-block journey to the festival grounds. Deputy Skip had taken down the chain that blocked the entrance, and other vendors were preparing their caravans for the crowds that would soon gather. They would include tourists from the nearby ski resorts, students from the Eldridge College campus, and residents from the surrounding towns.

Because her brother Patrick had placed each caravan himself, Fitzpatrick Bakery and the Rose and Thorn bar were side by side in a prime location near the entrance to the grounds. The other locally-run food caravans included PJ's Pizza selling Italian fare; the Interdenominational Women's Society selling homemade fudge, peanut brittle, and chocolate candy; the Catholic Women's Guild selling homemade apple butter, apple jelly, and apple dumplings; the Whistle Pig Lodge selling funnel cakes, cotton candy, and caramel corn; and the Pine County Boosters selling hot dogs, pepperoni rolls, and assorted hot and cold drinks. A hoagie shop and a Greek restaurant from nearby Pendleton had also been licensed to sell food.

Once the caravan was set up and ready for the noon opening, Maggie went back to the bookstore to see if all was ready there. Jeanette, whom she relied upon so heavily, had everything well in hand. Jeanette was a retired schoolteacher who was supplementing her pension and social security with part-time hours at the bookstore. A no-nonsense, sensible, stalwart right hand, she could deal with any crisis that came up during the morning shifts during the week. Maggie knew that in any situation Jeanette would do what Maggie would have done herself, but in a kinder way, and as a result she gave the older woman a free hand.

This morning she was marshaling the extra troops Maggie had hired for the weekend, teaching them how to do the basic tasks they would be called upon to do. Although it wasn't the ideal time for Benjamin, who ran the espresso bar every morning like a well-oiled machine, to be out of town, Maggie could not refuse him the reasonable request of a week cross country skiing with friends in Maine. Her second best barista, Mitchell, an articulate and outgoing college senior who looked more like a Rastafarian, was subbing for Benjamin during his week off.

Mitchell was showing his temporary help where the supplies were kept, and how best to assist him without getting in the way in the close confines of the area behind the counter. For this year's festival, Maggie had splurged on more temporary staff than usual, anchored by well-trained regulars so that she could spend all the time at the festival helping her mother. She hoped the additional sales from the influx of tourists would more than make up the added expense. If it did, after the weekend was over she planned to reward her staff with some small bonuses, something she rarely did. It's not that Maggie was cheap or begrudged her staff little extras; it was just that she learned at her mother's knee to be frugal, and it was hard to go against that conditioning.

After Maggie felt assured her bookstore was in good hands, she walked down to the Rose and Thorn to see if Patrick needed any help. She waved to her Uncle Curtis as she passed Fitzpatrick's Service Station, where he was holding court with his morning buddies, drinking coffee and eating doughnuts. Her Uncle Ian was driving the school bus like he did every morning and afternoon, so Patrick was left on his own getting the Rose and Thorn caravan ready for business.

At the side door of the bar, which opened onto Peony Street, Scott was helping Patrick roll kegs into the bed of his pickup truck. They were using a piece of plywood as a ramp between the side door and the pickup bed, and Maggie watched as the wood sagged but did not break when they rolled the kegs across it. Patrick was rolling, and Scott was catching. Both men acknowledged her presence with a brief nod and returned to concentrating on their task.

Maggie stood next to the truck and watched, enjoying a chance to admire Scott while he worked. He had on his police uniform of khaki pants, hiking boots, and a navy blue ski jacket with ROSE HILL POLICE appliquéd on the front left side and across the back. On his head, he wore a navy blue wool ball cap with the same city logo on it. Maggie was admiring his rear end when he caught her and grinned.

She felt herself blush and asked her brother, "Anything I can do?"

Patrick stood still a minute as he thought.

"Yes," he finally said, "Go upstairs and get me some plastic cups and paper napkins. They're in the crawl space in the attic."

Maggie went around to the front door and let herself in with her key, then walked all the way to the back of the bar to the office, where the door to the stairs was. Maggie hated the upstairs room, which was dark and spidery, but she didn't dare tell Patrick "no" after offering to help. She found the boxes of cups and napkins right where he said they'd be, and drug several out to save him time later. The boxes were not that heavy, but she slid them down the stairs on their sides, so she didn't have to carry them.

She heard her Aunt Delia yelp "hey!" from downstairs, and Maggie hurried down. Delia wasn't hurt, just surprised when boxes came flying down the stairs at her as she entered the office. Patrick, standing in the doorway behind Delia, laughed at Maggie, saying, "lazy ass," before effortlessly picking up each box and tossing it to Scott, who was still standing in the pickup.

"Sorry," Maggie told her aunt sheepishly when she got downstairs and closed the door behind her.

Delia just hugged Maggie, telling her, "It's awful nice of you to come and help us out, with your store and all you have to do for your mother."

Maggie, who was not a hugger by nature, did not mind when her Aunt Delia, who had always been so sweet and kind to her, insisted on doing so.

"I hear our Caroline's back," Aunt Delia said.

"She's not ours anymore," Maggie said sadly. "I don't know whose she is, but she's not ours."

Delia smoothed Maggie's bright red curls with her hand, cupped her chin, and looked at her with real sympathy.

"It's hard when people grow up and change into someone you don't recognize," she said.

One of the things Maggie loved most about Aunt Delia was that she didn't say, "Life's unfair, get used to it," as Maggie's mother would have. Instead, she listened and empathized. Delia was always available with a shoulder to cry on or a cup of tea if Maggie needed to unburden herself. While she didn't often avail herself of the privilege, it was nice knowing it was there when she needed it.

"How are you doing?" Maggie asked her. Delia suffered from a variety of health problems, but she didn't list them and fret over them like some people.

"Oh, I'm fine," she said, patting herself down as if checking. "There are still lots of years left in this old carcass."

She turned and pointed at Scott, who was helping Patrick shift the kegs, so the weight was evenly distributed in the back of the truck.

"When are you going to make an honest man out of that one?"

"Probably not until his mother dies."

Delia tut-tutted but smiled.

"I know Marcia Gordon well," Delia said. "I can see why you'd want to wait, but please don't defer your happiness. You never know what life has in store, and I'd hate for you to miss out."

"I'm just not sure," Maggie said. "I don't want to make a mistake."

"I blame Gabriel," Delia said. "He left you while the bloom was still on the rose, and now you think no one can take his place. No man is perfect, Maggie, and you need to take Gabe down off the pedestal before you miss your chance with Scott."

They were interrupted by Patrick, who grabbed the keys to the truck off the desk where Delia worked on the bookkeeping for the bar.

"Are you done then?" Delia asked Patrick. "Because we're freezing to death in here and heating the whole town on our gas bill."

Patrick answered by leaving and kicking the door shut behind him. Maggie hurriedly told her aunt goodbye so she wouldn't have to talk any more about Gabe, saying it was so Delia could get on with her bookkeeping. Delia let her go with a sad smile, and Maggie went out the front door of the bar, locking it behind her. She went around to the side of the building where Scott and Patrick had just removed the plywood from the doorway and slid it in the truck bed for use in transferring everything into the caravan at the festival grounds.

Scott hopped out of the back of the truck and came toward Maggie.

"Are you ready for this weekend?" he asked her, smiling that ornery smile of his, the one that knew her so well and still loved her.

Maggie had a sudden urge to hug him and moved toward him to do so. Just then, however, they were startled by a scream from down at the festival grounds.

"That sounds like Hannah," Maggie said and started running down Peony Street toward the entrance to the site, with Scott and Patrick right behind her.

She could hear Hannah yelling, "Scott!" at the top of her lungs, and the slender figure came running toward them as they rounded the entrance to the site.

Hannah was white as a ghost and frantic, could hardly talk she was so shaken up. She fell into Maggie's arms.

"A body!" she said, breathless and gasping, "Blood!"

A crowd of people working on various caravans quickly gathered and Deputy Skip came running out of the security shack, where he had fallen asleep.

"Skip, you keep everyone back," Scott directed him. "Radio Frank to get down here. Hannah, can you show me where it is?"

Hannah, with Maggie and Patrick supporting her on each side, led Scott to where she had been working. Hannah had been preparing one section of the festival site for the snowball throwing competition by using a snow blower to create a low flat area where the competitors would stand and throw snowballs at a row of soft drink cans perched on top of a wall of packed snow at the far end. At the end of the flat area she had created, after six or seven passes with the snow blower, she had uncovered, encased in a solid wall of compacted snow, an arm clothed in a dark nylon coat sleeve. The snow beneath the arm was soaked red with blood. Hannah had suddenly noticed bright pink snow flying out of the snow blower, and that had alerted her to what she'd uncovered. Luckily the snow blower blades had not touched the arm, just the blood-soaked snow next to it. The hand and wrist looked like that of a small adult. The jacket sleeve was made of insulated nylon, like a hundred others they saw every day during the winter months.

Hannah was making a funny sound, and when Maggie turned to look at her friend, she realized Hannah was saying, "Oh my God, oh my God, oh my God," over and over, with her hand held over her mouth.

Scott squatted down to look at the arm, the unclothed part of which was a bluish white color and decided there was no point in checking for a pulse.

Patrick said, "Who is it?"

"I don't know," Scott said, but he gave Maggie a pointed look.

Then they both knew.

"You okay?" Scott asked her.

"Yeah," Maggie said. "It doesn't even look real."

"Take Hannah somewhere and get her something warm to drink," he said, "and let me know where you are later."

"You'll have to call Sarah," Maggie said.

Scott nodded, but said, "Go on now, take Hannah someplace warm."

Maggie and Patrick led Hannah back to the entrance of the festival grounds, where Frank was just arriving.

"C'mon girls," Patrick said. "Let's go back to the Thorn, where it's nice and quiet."

Once he had delivered Hannah to Delia inside the bar, Patrick wanted to go back to the festival grounds to set up the caravan, but Maggie made him wait. Her Aunt Delia made Hannah some coffee, and Maggie called Sam, Hannah's husband.

"She's okay," Maggie assured him, but he just said, "I'll be there in fifteen minutes."

When Patrick heard Sam was coming, he went outside to make sure the accessible parking space next to the bar on the Peony Street side was shoveled and cleared a path from it to the side door, which had a ramp. After he finished, he went back to the festival grounds.

Delia was sitting on a bar stool next to Hannah, with a hand on her arm, talking to her in a soft voice.

"Sam's coming," Maggie told her.

Hannah had started crying now that the shock was wearing off.

Maggie asked, "Do you want your Dad?"

In response Hannah started crying harder, but nodded, so Maggie quickly crossed the street to the service station and brought her Uncle Curtis back with her.

"Here now, little bird," the older man tenderly said when he got to his daughter. "What's this I hear about you murdering people at the festival?"

As Hannah let herself be gathered into her father's arms, Maggie teared up and had to blink several times to get control of her own emotions. She felt a sudden urge to see her dad, who was probably snoring in his recliner at home. It had been a long time since Fitz had been able to be strong for her, and she missed that just now. When Sam arrived, Curtis handed Hannah off to him, and went back to the service station, shaking his head.

"There's been far too much murder going on in this town lately," he told Maggie and Delia as he left.

Now that Hannah's husband Sam was there, Maggie felt like it was okay to leave Hannah. She told her she would call later, and not to worry about the festival, that they would handle it.

Maggie ran-walked down to the bakery to tell her Aunt Alice, who was Hannah's mother, what had happened, but her aunt's only response was, "Well, why in the world was Hannah running a snow blower? Weren't there any men around who could do that?"

Maggie was not surprised at her reaction, which was typical.

"We're too busy for me to go down there right now," Alice told Maggie. "Hannah will just have to cope without me."

Maggie told her that Sam was with her daughter, and Alice said, "What is she thinking, dragging Sam out in this weather? He shouldn't be driving in this."

Although there wasn't a cloud in the sky, the roads were clear, and Sam was completely capable of driving in any weather, Alice always treated him like an invalid, even though it drove Hannah crazy.

Maggie's mother was more concerned about the festival.

"They won't cancel it you don't think?" Bonnie fretted. "I'll lose a pot of money if they do."

Maggie hadn't considered that aspect. She thought of the store full of employees she was paying and selfishly allowed herself to worry a bit too.

Ed Harrison heard about the body from Mandy, who came over from the bakery to tell him. He grabbed his camera and rushed down to the festival grounds, where Scott's small team was taping off the area and keeping people back, but Scott refused to let him photograph the body.

"Sarah's on her way," Scott said, "and we don't know who it is yet."

"C'mon," Ed said, "just a photo of the general area."

"I'm not trying to be a jerk," Scott said, "but if a picture of that body ends up in the paper on Sunday I will be seriously pissed off."

"I swear I'll just get the area, and you doing your job."

"Okay, just a few, but hurry. Sarah should be here soon, and I don't want her to start off mad at me."

Ed kept his word and avoided the actual murder victim as he took photos. He did, however, get a good look, and a thought occurred to him.

"Is it Margie, do you think?" he asked Scott.

Scott frowned at his best friend and shook his head.

"No comment."

"Off the record."

"Yeah," he said as he nodded. "I think it probably is."

Ed whistled low.

"I know she was a pill, but who'd want to kill her?" Ed asked.

Scott shook his head, knowing he really shouldn't discuss his suspicions with anyone but Sarah.

"She was an awful gossip," Ed said. "But if people got killed over that, half the town would be dead."

Scott couldn't go into the suspected blackmail aspect of Margie's recent behavior, so he just shook his head again.

"Will you keep me informed?" Ed asked.

"As much as I can," Scott said, "but you'll probably find out more about it than I will."

"I'll let you know."

Sarah Albright and her team arrived within an hour and quickly took over. To his chagrin, Scott's role was reduced to mustering town forces to do Sarah's bidding. With Sarah's approval, Scott directed the city snowplow driver to create a path at the end of the alley behind the fire station down the steep hill into the field near where the body was, keeping an eye out for additional bodies, should there be any, however unlikely.

The mayor conferred with Sarah and with her approval decided not to cancel the festival. The volunteer firefighters put up snowdrift fencing all around the area and covered it with tarps to shield the crime scene from view. It was far enough from the main thoroughfare that it wasn't obvious to anyone passing, but word spread fast, and Skip and Frank had their hands full keeping curious people away from the area.

A concerned Mayor Stuart Machalvie was walking around assuring vendors and townspeople that no one was canceling the festival and imploring them not to scare the tourists away by talking about it as anything other than an unfortunate accident.

"Yes, a great tragedy, but purely an accident, I'm sure," Scott heard him telling someone. "Some poor drunk fella probably picked the wrong place to pass out, and must've frozen to death."

Scott had seen the amount of blood around the "poor fella," and didn't think that had been a side effect of passing out drunk. He was convinced it was Margie Estep's body, but couldn't imagine how she came to be there.

Maggie was working the first shift in the bakery caravan by herself, and although business started out slowly, by four o'clock, she was running low on brownies and had to call for backup merchandise. Patrick was selling cups of draft beer and hot mulled cider from the Rose and Thorn caravan next door, so he couldn't leave to fetch anything, and there was no one available to send. Hannah was supposed to have been assisting her, but Maggie didn't expect her after what she'd been through that morning.

It surprised her then to see Hannah show up with several boxes of baked goodies, escorted by her husband Sam in his wheelchair.

"What are you doing here?" Maggie asked. "You should be at home."

Hannah said, "I have to have something to do, or I'll go nuts."

Sam seemed determinedly cheerful, which was not at all like him. He hated crowds and Maggie knew this was not his idea of a fun day, at all. Maggie asked Sam if he wanted to work in the caravan.

"If you can get me up there," he said

With Patrick's help, they got Sam up into the caravan and onto a chair, where he handled the cash box while Hannah sold the baked goods.

Maggie left them to it and walked around the festival a bit, stretching her back, which was stiff from working in cramped quarters most of the day. The police had done a good job of hiding the crime scene. The two city fire trucks were parked in such a way that they blocked the area, and you could not see what was going on. Maggie glimpsed the back of Scott's jacket through the gap between the trucks and decided to buy him and the team some hot coffee. She stopped at the nearest caravan and bought a dozen large coffees, which they placed in two cardboard carriers for her. Skip and Frank were grateful for the gesture, and took the carriers from Maggie, promising they would make sure Scott and the sheriff's team got cups as well.

Maggie saw her sister-in-law Ava supervising the mitten fishing game, where little children "fished" with a piece of sticky hook-and-loop tape at the end of a string attached to a stick, trying to "catch" two mittens that matched to win a prize. It wasn't a hard game, the little kids loved it, and Ava made sure everyone won something.

Ava was glad to see her, saying, "Could you run things for a minute? I have got to go to the bathroom."

Maggie took over, and Ava was back in five minutes, thanking her for the break.

"I just cannot make myself use the porta-potties," she told Maggie, "so I ran up to the bar."

Ava asked her if she could sit with the kids that night, and Maggie said she could.

"I promised to help the guild ladies cook the bacon and sausages for the pancake breakfast in the morning, and we'll be up at the community center until at least midnight."

"I'll be glad to do it," said Maggie. "I'll take them to the bonfire if they want to go."

Maggie decided her mother and aunt could probably use a break at the bakery, so she headed back toward town. She met Caroline and Drew walking down Marigold Avenue toward the festival. Upon seeing Caroline dressed warmly in the clothing Maggie had lent her, Maggie felt a sudden immature urge to avoid her, but instead gave the pair a tight smile and said hello.

Caroline immediately ran up and hugged her, gushing, "I've been looking everywhere for you!"

It was all Maggie could do not to push her away, but she stood still and made no effort to hug Caroline back. When Caroline let go and looked at her in concern, Maggie stared her straight in the eye.

"I've been working for two days in a bakery that has my last name written on the outside of it; that shouldn't be too hard to find, should it?"

Caroline just rattled on as if she hadn't heard her, very much for Drew's benefit, Maggie could tell.

"I was telling Drew how wonderful you and Hannah were, driving all the way up to Pittsburgh to get me so early in the morning, and then lending me these clothes," she said. "It's just so great to have such good friends!"

Drew had a goofy smile on his face, obviously entranced with Caroline.

"Did you find everything you needed at the store?" Maggie asked her pointedly.

"Oh yes!" Caroline enthused, "and Jeanette gave me the bill, which I will take care of just as soon as I get some U.S. currency."

"The bank's open until 6:00 p.m. on Fridays," Maggie told her, pointing in the direction of the bank. "You still have time to get there before they close."

"Oh no," Caroline said. "I don't want to think about that kind of stuff until next week. Right now I just want to rediscover Rose Hill, play in the snow, and have all my old friends around me."

"And some new ones too, I guess," Maggie said, watching Caroline snuggle up to Drew and nuzzle his neck. Drew looked drunk on her attention. Maggie had seen that look on Caroline's boyfriends' faces before. She had also seen their devastated, tear-stained faces when Caroline discarded them just as suddenly as she picked them up.

'He's a big boy,' Maggie thought. 'He'll have to look out for himself.'

"Hannah's down at the bakery caravan, Patrick's next door, and Ava is running the little kids' games," she told Caroline, "if you still want to help."

"Sure," Caroline said, without much enthusiasm. "We'll stop by and see them."

Maggie knew Caroline was not going to be any help to them this weekend. She just hoped that by offering her work every time she saw her, she would make sure Caroline avoided her.

"I'll call you later!" Caroline said as they parted.

"I won't hold my breath," Maggie said as she walked away.

Back at the bakery, Bonnie and Alice looked worn out, and Mandy looked thrilled to see Maggie.

"Mandy and I can handle this," Maggie told the older women.

After they left, Mandy and her son Tommy both breathed a sigh of relief.

"You know I love all y'all," Mandy said, in her Chattanooga drawl, "but those old women were gettin' sorta cranky."

Maggie put on a Fitzpatrick Bakery apron and washed her hands.

"They've been here since 4:00 a.m.," Maggie said. "I'm surprised they didn't have you both in tears by now."

Mandy showed Maggie where they were in preparation for the next day's sales. She, Tommy, and Maggie worked flat out until 6:00 p.m. when Ava called to remind Maggie she was sitting with the kids that evening.

"I'm just now leaving," Ava told her, "and they'll be fine until you can get here. My place is full up with guests, but I've got help."

Mandy needed to get down to the Rose and Thorn caravan to work her evening shift. After a quick phone call from Maggie, and a generous bribe, two bookstore staff members agreed to cover the last couple hours at the bakery caravan, until it closed at 8:00, so Hannah and Sam could leave. Maggie called Hannah to let her know, and then she and Mandy filled a big box with bakery goods for the evening shift to take to the caravan.

After her staff members picked up the order, Maggie invited Tommy to go with her to Ava's, but he said Ed was taking him to the bonfire. Maggie gave him several ham and cheese turnovers for the two of them to eat for dinner. Tommy was a sweet, shy, gawky twelve-year-old, with a two-tone adolescent voice, a great work ethic, and a quiet way of fading into the background. Maggie was just waiting for him to turn 16 so she could coerce him into coming to work at the bookstore.

Situated just a block from Rose Hill Avenue on Pine Mountain Road, Ava's elegant Victorian home was in a prime location, and was busy all year long with both tourists and parents visiting their offspring at nearby Eldridge College. Every Victorian architectural element you could imagine was evident on the home's exterior, from the gingerbread trim and wrap-around porches to a cylindrical turret and the stained glass transom window over the front door. The Fitzpatricks had worked hard to restore the house to give Ava a way to make a living after her husband abandoned her. The Fitzpatricks were very much a "hand up" rather than a "hand out" kind of support group, and to her credit, Ava had done very well for herself under her own steam.

When Maggie entered the front room, she found two teenage girls surfing the Internet on Ava's computer with their homework laid out in front of them on the check-in desk. They greeted Maggie and told her the kids were in the family room. Maggie walked back through the arched hallway past the stairs that led to the second floor, through the large kitchen to the small family room. This tiny room was only a small nook in which the family could have some privacy to watch television or play, but it and the kitchen were the heart of their home.

Twelve-year-old Charlotte was curled up in a big armchair reading "The Secret Garden," probably for the third or fourth time. It was one of Maggie's favorites, too, and much like Charlotte, Maggie didn't like to be interrupted when she was deep into a book. Charlotte looked up and hardly seemed to register Maggie's presence before she dove back in.

Six-year-old Timmy was laying on his stomach, playing with some dark green plastic army men while watching "James and the Giant Peach," his favorite movie. Maggie had seen it with him so many times that she could recite most of the dialogue herself. They were glad to see her, but neither budged from their spots. If it had been Patrick arriving, they would have squealed and clamored for his attention, but Maggie didn't mind. She loved her niece and nephew, but she hadn't spent nearly as much time with them as Patrick had. He was like a father to them.

Timmy was entranced by his movie, so Maggie lay down on the couch and closed her eyes, just for a second. She woke up when Timmy crawled up next to her and snuggled down in the crook of her arm, his head on her shoulder. She scooted over to make more room for him, pulled a hand-crocheted afghan off the back of the couch, and draped it over them.

"You smell like Mamaw's work," he said in his raspy little boy voice.

Maggie kissed the top of his head, which was covered in bright red curls, just like hers.

"You smell like play dough," she said, and sure enough, there was some in his hair.

It was almost nine o'clock, and Charlotte was still reading, so Maggie relaxed again, cozy and warm with the little boy in her arms. She was too worn out to think about taking the kids to see the bonfire, and they didn't mention it.

At 9:00 p.m. Mandy left the Rose and Thorn caravan and ran down to where the enormous bonfire was burning. She had nagged at Patrick for an hour to let her go until finally, he'd relented. Delia and Ian were both working in the bar, and most people were at the bonfire, so the caravan wasn't that busy. She had promised to come back within an hour when Patrick anticipated the evening trade would start in earnest.

Mandy searched through the crowd until she found Ed and Tommy. They were near the front, and Tommy was standing in front of Ed, facing the fire, with Ed's hands on his shoulders. Mandy stopped a moment to watch them. To anyone who happened to see them but didn't know them, they looked just like father and son. Mandy wanted that so badly it made her heart ache.

She knew Ed was too old for her, too smart for her, too sensible for her. He wasn't exactly her dream date either, by any means, with his bald head and fuddy-duddy clothes, but he was good and kind and steady, and she was crazy about him. She was grateful that no one else had seen the prize he was beneath his ordinary appearance and snapped him up before she could.

She had confided her ambitions to Delia.

"People will be telling him he's too old for you," Delia said. "Ed's a man with principles, who cares deeply about what other people think of him."

"But I don't care how old he is."

"Folks might think he's taking advantage of you."

"But I'm the one chasin' him," Mandy complained. "I've never had to chase a guy. They're all the time chasin' me."

"Are you sure this is what you want?"

"It is, Delia. I never felt this way before. Seein' him makes my heart beat fast and gives me butterflies in my stomach. I can't sleep at night. I can't eat nothin'. It's drivin' me crazy."

"Sounds like love to me."

"It is, but no one believes me. Please, please help me."

"Alright, honey. I'll help you. If you're sure he's the one for you."

"I am. He is."

"I think the key is for you to be determined and sensible, and not give up. If he sees that you're serious about this and that it's not just a silly crush, he may eventually wear down."

"What if he's just not attracted to me?"

"Child," Delia said, "with what you have to work with, if he isn't interested, he doesn't have a pulse."

Mandy was determined to convince him using all the assets she had. She pushed through the crowd to the front and when she reached them, wrapped her arm around Ed's waist and poked Tommy in the side.

"Hey," Ed said, surprised, but to Mandy's relief he didn't shrug her off or pull away. He put one arm around her, keeping one hand on Tommy's shoulder.

'We make a family,' Mandy thought to herself, 'just like in my dream.'

Tommy looked around and smiled at his mom, knowing what she was up to.

The crowd's attention was now drawn to Mayor Stuart Machalvie, who was standing on a raised platform with his wife Peg and the rest of the town council. Peg had on a huge black fur coat with a matching hat and muff and teetered on her spiked heels. Oversized rings sparkled on each hand, and she was smiling as much as she could with her pale, shiny face shot full of nerve paralyzers and wrinkle fillers. Hannah liked to claim that Peg was a vampire, and slept in a coffin full of dirt in the basement of the Machalvie Funeral Home. With her blood-red lipstick and nails, she certainly looked the part.

"Welcome to the Rose Hill Winter Festival," the mayor said into the microphone, which gave some ear-piercing feedback.

The crowd cheered and applauded.

Ed whistled loudly to make Tommy laugh. He then excused himself to take pictures. Mandy took his place behind Tommy, who was almost as tall as she was. She set her chin on his shoulder and hugged him from behind.

"It is my great pleasure to introduce this year's Snow Queen, who recently returned home to Rose Hill after living for many years in New York City," the mayor said. "She is descended from one of the founding families of this town; they owned Eldridge Lumber, the Eldridge Coal Company, and also built Eldridge College. We are proud to have her back in Rose Hill and honored that she has consented to reign over this festival as its queen. I can't think of anyone more like royalty, or more deserving of a crown. Ladies and gentleman, I present this year's Rose Hill Winter Festival Queen, Miss Gwyneth Eldridge!"

The Pine County Consolidated High School band played "Isn't She Lovely" while the mayor helped Gwyneth up onto the stage. He placed a white satin sash with "Snow Festival Queen" written on it over her right shoulder and under her left arm while his wife Peg affixed a tiara to her sleek blonde head. Ed got close enough to get a good photograph, and saw that Gwyneth's hands were shaking as she approached the microphone. Her voice shook a little as she began to speak.

"When the mayor first approached me about doing this," she said, in her nasal British accent. "I at first declined the honor, thinking it should go to someone born and raised in Rose Hill. I was born in the English countryside, you see, and raised abroad. I only visited Rose Hill between school terms. But Stuart insisted, reminding me that the Eldridge family's roots run deep in the soil beneath this town. One is reminded that one owes it to the legacy of one's family to support the town events as one's mother and grandmother did before one. So here I am, living proof that there will always be Eldridges in Rose Hill."

She paused, and the mayor began clapping so that everyone would know she had finished. The crowd joined in, albeit without much enthusiasm.

"Please enjoy the festival," Gwyneth said and gave a royal wave.

Ed took photos of Gwyneth, the mayor, and the town council, in many configurations, and then returned to where he left Mandy and Tommy.

"I have to go back to work," she said. "Will you be over at the bar later?"

"I've got all the photographs I need, and this is too much of a crowd for me," Ed said. "How about Tommy and I go pick up Hank, then we'll order pizza and watch some TV together until you get home."

Mandy smiled widely and then kissed Ed on the cheek, much to Tommy's embarrassment.

"Thank you," she said. "I'll see you at home later."

She ran off before Ed could say anything else, and Tommy was grinning at him when he turned back around.

"Stop that," Ed said. "We're just friends, your mom and me."

Tommy tried hard to hide his smile, but it went too deep inside.

Maggie woke up at midnight when Ava came home escorted by Patrick. Charlotte was still reading, and Patrick rolled his eyes at her.

"She's just like Maggie was at that age," he said to Ava. "She'd stay up all night if you let her, reading some egghead book."

Patrick carried Timmy up the back stairs to the family's quarters, which was completely separated from the guest rooms for privacy and safety. Charlotte yawned, stretched, and reluctantly went off to bed.

"You look tired," Ava told Maggie.

"I was just about to say the same thing to you," Maggie said.

"You're welcome to stay," Ava said.

"No," Maggie said. "I like my own bed too much."

Patrick left to go back to work at the bar, and Maggie went the opposite direction toward home.

All of the businesses downtown save the Rose and Thorn were closed by midnight. The crowd at the festival grounds had dispersed, and the town was quiet and peaceful. There was smoke rising from the chimneys of dark houses, and bright stars twinkling in the dark sky. Snow crunched under her boots as Maggie crossed Pine Mountain road and continued down the alley on the other side, which led to her bookstore's back door. As she passed the dumpster behind the bank, Duke ran out from beneath it and followed her home. She let him in the backdoor but left in him the vestibule while she disarmed the security system, entered the bookstore, and looked at the sales figures for the day.

"Wow," she said out loud when she read the figure.

They had had a great day. She was so tired it was all she could do to reset the alarm, climb up the steps, and let Duke and herself into her apartment.

There was a message from Scott on her voice mail.

"Hey, just wanted to let you know it was Margie, looks like she was stabbed and bled to death. We haven't found the murder weapon yet. Sarah's all over this, so you know she'll be snapping her fingers, and I'll be jumping for the next few days. I'll talk to you tomorrow. Get some sleep."

Maggie had just enough energy left to wash her face and brush her teeth before falling into bed, and her last conscious awareness was of Duke jumping up on the foot of her bed, loudly purring as he settled there to sleep. Although mildly allergic to cats, Maggie didn't have the strength to shoo him off the bed.

Maggie went to sleep thinking about Margie's body in the snow bank down by the river. That night she dreamed that Margie was standing at the top of the town, on Morning Glory Avenue, rolling pink snowballs down Pine Mountain Road, and by the time they reached the river they were as big as houses.

Patrick walked Mandy home after the bar closed at 2:00 a.m., and attempted his clumsy version of a heart-to-heart chat.

"I know you have your sites set on old Ed, there," he said awkwardly.

"I do, and you can't talk me out of it," she said.

"He's way too old for you, you know."

"Everybody's all the time sayin' that, but he's only eight years older'n me. He's younger than you."

"But he's very mature and smart."

"And I'm just some stupid kid, is that it?"

"No, you know I don't think that. Listen to me. You're like me. We don't take everything as seriously as Ed does. We don't get so wound up about everything all the time. Ed cares about stuff like politics, causes, and justice. He thinks everything should be fair to everybody all the time. We know life isn't like that."

"I think it's great he cares about that stuff. Somebody has to, or things wouldn't never get any better."

"But do you wanna listen to all that bitchin' and moanin' about it all the time?"

"I don't mind it. I might learn somethin'."

"His wife was a smart newspaper writer like him."

"And that didn't last, did it?"

"You may have a point there."

"Are you going to help me or not?"

"I think it's a big mistake."

"Well?"

"I'll help you, I guess."

"I appreciate it. Now, what should I do?"

"He's a man, isn't he? Get him drunk and have sex with him."

"You're such a gentleman, Patrick."

"You asked me. I'm just telling you what I know works."

Ed was asleep on Mandy's couch when she crept into the trailer. His reading glasses had fallen down his nose, and his book was on the floor. Mandy picked both up and put them on a side table. Down at the end of the hall, she saw that Tommy was sound asleep in his small room, with the black lab Hank draped over the foot of his bed, so she shut his door. She went back to the living room and sat down on the coffee table, regarding Ed, sprawled out and snoring.

She imagined what it would be like to come home to him like this every night, and it gave her a warm feeling inside. She wanted him here, waiting for her, watching over Tommy. She wanted someone to carry in her groceries, to make sure the electric bill got paid, and to repair the toilet when it leaked. She wanted someone to tell she'd be home early, or wouldn't be home until late. She wanted someone who would care where she was, what she was doing, and whether she was warm enough, had eaten enough, and was happy. She wanted someone for Tommy, too, a father he could look up to and count on.

Ed stirred, woke up, and smiled at her.

"What are you doing, just sitting there?" he asked her as he sat up.

"I didn't want to wake you up. You look too comfy," she said.

Ed rubbed his face, looked at her fondly, and yawned.

"How was your evening?" he asked her.

"It was fine," she said, so happy to have someone ask her that simple question.

"That's good," he said. "Your son and I played some scrabble and watched TV way too late, and he didn't get to bed 'til midnight."

"That's okay. Thanks for lookin' after him."

"I was glad to do it. With all these strangers in town this weekend, it might be a good idea if I do the same tomorrow night."

"Thank you," she said. "That'd make me feel much better."

"Well," he said, getting to his feet, "I better mosey on home."

"You're welcome to stay," she said quietly.

"Mandy," he said, but before he could continue, she pushed him back down into a sitting position on the couch, climbed on top of him, and kissed him.

Ed's baser instincts were wide-awake now and quickly taking charge. He struggled for control.

"Wait a minute," Ed said.

"I don't wanna hear it, Ed," Mandy said, as she unbuckled his belt. "I know you want me. I can feel you want me."

"But Tommy's just down the hall," Ed protested.

"He's a sound sleeper," Mandy said as she popped open the button on his pants.

"I think we should talk about this first," Ed said weakly, his resistance evaporating.

"We can talk about it after," Mandy said, as she tugged down his zipper. "I'll get me a dictionary so I can cipher all those big words you like to use."

Ed laughed and gave in. He was undone, both literally and figuratively.

Hannah lay awake in bed while her husband worked in his office. Tears ran down both sides of her face onto the pillow beneath her head. She was still emotionally raw from the events of the day and kept reliving the moments when she discovered the body over and over, like a film in her head she couldn't stop. Although she knew Sam was exhausted, physically from maneuvering his wheelchair through the snow and mentally from having to interact with people all day at the festival, she still resented being alone in their bed. He had gone seriously, intensely silent on the ride home, and then seemed to be angry with her the rest of the evening. When Hannah tried to talk to him about it he brushed her off, when she persisted they fought, and as soon as they got home, he retreated to his office. Hannah needed him to hold her and be with her and let her talk about what happened. Instead, he had withdrawn as if he was punishing her.

Hannah thought about the calendar issue, as she was calling it, and wondered if it would make things better or worse for them. Sam could have several good months in a row, but then something would always happen, sometimes just a small thing, and he would completely de-rail. Hannah was always worrying about it but tried not to shield Sam from anything, or withhold her feelings or opinions, on the advice of his counselor. Sam's counselor told Hannah she had to live her own life and be herself and let Sam deal with his feelings. That was easier said than done.

Hannah went to the office door and spoke through it.

"Samuel," she said. "Will you please come out and talk to me?"

There was no response, even though the clicking sound of the keyboard stopped, and she knew he heard her.

"Please, Sam," she said. "I need you."

The clicking resumed, and she knew he was not going to acknowledge or respond. This angered her so that everything she wanted to say next was mean and hurtful, and likely to solve nothing. Hannah went back to the bedroom and locked the door behind her.

"You can sleep on the couch," she said to the locked door.

Hannah eventually went to sleep and watched the body-finding film, over and over, in her dreams.

Morning Glory Circle by Pamela Grandstaff

Chapter Six - Saturday

When Maggie arrived at her parents' house early Saturday morning, she found her father and grandfather enjoying a breakfast casserole her Aunt Delia had prepared for them. Delia hugged her niece as she entered the kitchen.

"I thought you could use a break," Delia said. "I have a little time before I have to be at Ava's. The bar and the caravan can't open until noon, so I'm going to help Ava until then."

Maggie collapsed into a kitchen chair and gratefully accepted the mug of hot tea her aunt handed to her.

"I woke up, saw the time, and just ran," Maggie said. "These event weekends are so exhausting."

The volume of the fishing show Fitz and Grandpa Tim were watching was turned up so loud it was an assault on their ears. Delia shut the door to the front room and took a seat across from Maggie.

"How was the bonfire last night?" Maggie asked her. "I thought about taking Ava's kids, but I fell asleep on their couch."

"I stayed up at the bar," Delia said, "but Mandy said the highlight was the crowning of the Snow Queen."

"Did Stuart get Gwyneth to do it?"

"He did."

"Complete with sash and crown?"

"It was said she had a little trouble keeping the tiara on her head."

"Did she do the queen wave?"

"Like Elizabeth herself."

"I'm so sorry I missed that. Did she make a speech?"

"Mandy said it was mostly bragging about her family."

"I guess we have to get used to her," Maggie sighed. "It seems like she's here to stay."

"You would think her brother having been murdered here would put her off Rose Hill."

"I guess you heard about Margie," Maggie said.

"Oh yes," Delia responded. "There'll be little else talked about in this town for days."

"Did Ian tell you what Scott found out about Margie?" Maggie asked.

"I've known about Margie Estep interfering with the mail for over two decades," Delia said. "If she hadn't been Eric's daughter she'd have been fired from the post office a long time ago. It was kind of Scott to protect Enid by not arresting her daughter; I just hope that doesn't get him in hot water now Margie's dead."

"I hadn't considered that," Maggie said. "Wouldn't Sarah just love to hold that bit of information over his head?"

"That woman has her sites set on your man, darlin'," Delia said. "You'd be wise not to underestimate her."

"I'm not worried," Maggie insisted. "He hates her."

"Hate is just the flipside of the coin of love," Delia said. "Or is that the coin of lust? I can never remember. I read that in a romance novel once."

Delia picked at some breakfast rolls that were on the table, nibbling on small pieces between sips of tea. Maggie felt uncomfortable discussing her feelings for Scott and decided to change the subject.

"At least Enid is safe now," Maggie said, referring to Margie's mother.

"I don't think Margie would have hurt her mother," Delia said.

"I hope that's true."

"I went to see Enid earlier this week, and she seemed happy at Mountain View," Delia said. "She said 'I feel like a lottery winner.'"

"Maybe not so much now her daughter's been murdered," Maggie said.

Maggie knew Scott would have been the one to share the sad news with Margie's mother. She just hadn't had a moment alone with him to hear how it went.

Maggie started picking at the other side of the plate of breakfast rolls, and when she tasted them found they were sweet and moist, with buttery cinnamon and pecan filling. Maggie's father yelled that he wanted more tea. Maggie got up and filled the kettle, then put it back on the gas ring to heat.

"I'd like to put that one in Mountain View some days," Maggie said to her aunt while nodding toward the front room, but Delia wagged a finger at her niece.

"Then you'd just be running the road to Pendleton every day instead of walking two blocks."

Patrick came downstairs and into the kitchen in his pajamas, and Delia waited on him hand and foot. She heated some of the casserole, made him some tea, and cut some rolls for him, while Maggie watched with disapproval.

"You're a lovely woman," Patrick told his aunt, "and there's some could learn from watching you how to take care of a working man."

"I work too!" Maggie said. "We all work in this family. It seems like that's all we ever do."

"Speaking of work, I'm sure you're needed at the bakery," her brother told her. "Mandy will probably be late this morning."

"Why's that?"

"Well, old Ed was at her trailer last night when she got home..."

"He wouldn't," Maggie said.

"Oh, he would, don't you kid yourself about that," Patrick said. "And for some reason, Mandy's determined to have him."

"But what do they have in common?" Maggie demanded. "What will they talk about? He's really smart, and she's a sweet girl, but she's not the brightest bulb."

130

"I don't think it's intellectual stimulation she's providing," Patrick said.

"There's nothing wrong with it," Delia said in Mandy's defense. "They are two consenting adults."

"Completely wrong for each other," Maggie pronounced. "It will never last."

"They may surprise you," Delia said. "There's more to a happy marriage than having all the same opinions."

"I seriously doubt there will be a marriage," Maggie said.

"Ed and Mandy sittin' in a tree," Patrick sang to his sister. The word he started to spell out next caused his aunt to smack him on the head, hard.

"Ow!" he said.

"I should wash your mouth out with soap," Delia threatened.

Maggie groaned as she stood up, and her aunt kissed her cheek before she left.

"Don't run yourself down," Delia told her. "Let other people help."

As Maggie passed through the front room, her father stopped her.

"We're out of rye bread. Tell your mother to bring some home. And tell her I said not to be as late tonight as she was last night."

Maggie felt a hot flash of anger pass through her at the thought that her mother was working around the clock because their financial welfare depended upon it, and her father wasn't fit enough to help out. She said nothing, though, because any angry words she said now would only make her feel guilty later. She reminded herself that her dad was in constant pain, and that made him self-centered. She kissed her father's cheek and said goodbye to Grandpa Tim, who blew her a kiss as she left the house.

Margie went to the bank to get change for the caravan cash box, then to the bookstore to pick up some hot drinks for the bakery crew. There were customers lined up out the door of the bakery when she arrived, and her mother said, "About time."

Maggie swallowed her retort, sat down the tray of hot drinks, and started loading up boxes of baked goods to take to the festival caravan. Mandy bumped Maggie's hip and stuck her tongue out at her, and they each giggled, provoking Bonnie even further.

"Dear Lord, why am I the only one awake and willing to work this morning?" Bonnie asked the ceiling.

"And what did you get up to last night, little missy?" Maggie murmured to Mandy.

Mandy blushed a deep pink, grinned like a possum, and waggled her eyebrows.

"I don't kiss and tell," she said quietly.

"I guess you don't mind leaving your cousin Hannah high and dry at the busiest time of the morning," Bonnie said. "She's called twice looking for change and stock."

Mandy said, "I'll send Tommy to help," and summoned her son from the kitchen, where he was helping Alice.

"That will leave us shorthanded," Bonnie complained.

Maggie was saved from further criticism by the appearance of her Aunt Delia.

"You're an angel," Maggie told Delia, giving her the change. She gave Tommy the big box and tucked Hannah's latte in amongst the wrapped treats.

"I can only stay down there long enough to deliver this lot," Delia said. "I have to cover the desk at the bed and breakfast this morning, and then help Ian in the bar after noon."

"Tell Hannah I'll be there as soon as I can," Maggie said. "Tommy can stay and help her."

The long line had dwindled a bit by 10:30, so Maggie put on her coat over her apron, ran-walked down the alley and then down Peony Street to the festival. She had missed the 10:00 parade down Rose Hill Avenue and most people had already made their way down to the festival site. When she got in the back of the caravan, Sam was friendly enough, but Hannah was grouchy and short with her. Maggie just got to work, and let it slide.

"I'm going up to the community center for some breakfast if there's anything left," Hannah said tersely. "I don't know when I'll be back."

"Alright," Maggie said. "Take your time. Tommy and I have this covered."

Hannah and Maggie helped Sam out of the caravan into his wheelchair, and then Maggie climbed back up inside and closed the door behind her.

"Hannah seems mad," Tommy observed.

"Hannah's had a bad shock," Maggie said.

"Finding that dead lady, you mean."

"That's made her short-tempered," Maggie said. "So we have to be patient with her."

"Like not talk back to her, even though you wanted to."

"Exactly," Maggie said. "As you mature you have to learn to be patient and not to let other people's bad moods or bad manners provoke you."

Gwyneth Eldridge approached the caravan just then and seemed to recoil at the display of yummy-looking baked goods as if they had snakes on display instead of cinnamon rolls and croissants. She had on a luxurious looking black cashmere coat and high-heeled leather boots, with her Snow Queen sash draped loosely around her fashionably gaunt frame. Her tiara was perfectly centered in her professionally streaked blonde bob, but her tastefully made up facial features seemed oddly frozen. It took Maggie a few moments to figure out that Gwyneth had had some "facial work" done recently, and she did indeed look ten years younger.

"Do you have anything low carb?" Gwyneth asked Tommy.

Maggie felt all her good intentions being sucked out of her as if by a skinny, tiara-topped vacuum cleaner, and before she could remind herself how mature she'd become, she snapped, "I'm sorry, Gwyneth, but did the word 'bakery' on the outside of this caravan not suggest anything to you?"

Gwyneth stormed off in a huff while Tommy laughed behind his hand.

"I obviously still have some work to do," Maggie conceded, "in the patience and maturity departments."

Maggie saw Scott in the distance, walking with the petite Sarah, and took a few deep breaths as she reminded herself that it was all about work. Just because she hadn't been with him since Hannah found Margie's body didn't mean he'd suddenly taken up with the woman she and Hannah liked to call "Tiny Trollop, the crime-fighting kitten," or "Tiny Crimefighter" for short.

As she turned back to help a customer, she saw Scott watching her over Sarah's head, and he smiled and winked at Maggie. She smiled in return and made the "call me" sign, to which he nodded, but then nodded toward Sarah and shrugged. Only Tommy's presence nearby kept Maggie's middle finger firmly clenched in a fist at her side, and not raised in salute at the back of Tiny Crimefighter.

A little later Sarah and Scott took a break in the station office, both to warm up and to compare the notes gathered from interviewing people all over town. Sarah had insisted Scott go with her, and enjoyed treating him like a subordinate in front of the citizens of Rose Hill. Scott was not surprised at how little progress they made, considering how condescending and demeaning Sarah's questioning technique was. The townspeople's facial expressions spoke volumes to Scott, but their statements to Sarah were deliberately obtuse.

"So why would somebody want to kill the nice little old lady who ran the post office?" Sarah asked him. "She had no husband, no kids, and no illicit love affairs that we know of, and lived her life solely for her invalid mother. Nobody had an unkind word to say about her."

"Margie was known to spread vicious gossip," Scott said. "She was the one who concocted the threat card that arrived in Theo's mail on the day he was murdered."

"I don't remember seeing that in your report," Sarah said, turning her dark hawk eyes upon him.

"There didn't seem to be any point with Theo dead, and his killer identified. It was just a malicious prank to her, and I remember you weren't too impressed with the evidence at the time."

"That's beside the point, Scott. That prank could be related to why she ended up in the deep freeze with a hole in her heart."

"I will be glad to write it up now if you want."

"You have to quit thinking of these people as your friends and neighbors, and start thinking of them all as potential suspects," Sarah said. "I've talked to you about this before."

"As I said, I will be glad to write it up now if you want."

"We've talked to at least fifty people, and not one of them mentioned the deceased was a gossip, a troublemaker, or anything other than an exemplary citizen who will be dearly missed."

"That's because it was you doing the asking," Scott said. "They won't speak ill of anyone to an outsider."

"Not even if it helps us catch a murderer who may be living among them?"

"This is a small town," Scott said. "There are strict societal rules that must be followed in small communities. Unless you grew up here, you couldn't possibly understand."

"So you should do all the asking, and I should just stand beside you and look pretty, is that it?"

"They probably won't speak frankly with you even present, I'm afraid."

"You know, this is a freakish backwater of a burg. I don't know how you stand it."

"I grew up here," Scott said. "People know me, know my character, and they trust me."

Scott didn't say that these exemplary qualities also sometimes made him the last person they'd call instead of the first.

"Alright, then," Sarah said. "You and your team do the local interviews, and when you come up with something that points the way to the killer, you let me know."

"You're leaving?"

"There's no point in wasting any more of the time and resources of the sheriff's office, is there?" she said. "We'll oversee the post-mortem, and I'll let you know what the results are, but I don't see any point in banging my head against a wall if no one will tell me anything useful. See if you can come up with anything and let me know."

"You'll be the first to know," Scott said. He couldn't believe he'd got rid of her so easily.

"I'll check in on you and see what progress you're making," Sarah said. "You can look on this as an opportunity if you're smart about it. You solve this case, and it will look very good on your application for a position with the county."

"I have no desire to work for the sheriff," Scott said. "I'm happy right where I am."

Sarah shook her head.

"You're skills are wasted in this town, just like they're wasted on Maggie Fitzpatrick. How's that going, by the way?"

"Maggie and I see each other."

"Naked?"

"Just for once, could you pretend that appropriate professional boundaries exist in our working relationship?"

"What are you, Amish?" Sarah said. "Real grown-up people not only talk about sex, Scott, they sometimes even do it for no good reason except it feels so gosh darn swell. When was the last time someone rode you so long and hard you passed out afterward from pure pleasure? I'm betting it's been a long, long time."

Sarah leaned over his desk as she spoke, way too close for his comfort, and Scott sat back in his chair.

"I scare you to death, don't I?" she said. "I'm exactly the kind of girl your mama warned you about."

"I'm just not interested, Sarah," Scott said. "I'm sorry if that hurts your feelings, but I love Maggie, and I'm not going to do anything to screw that up."

"You might think that," Sarah said, "but I think it's just a matter of time before you get tired of being rejected and give in to what you want, what I know you need. In fact, if you close the door right now, I can prove it. I'll have you flat on your back begging for mercy in two minutes. It would be so hot with us, Scott. I can feel it, can't you?"

"I'll let you know if I find out anything useful," Scott said, then stood up and pointed through the open door.

"I'll be in touch," she called as she sailed out, smirking.

Scott sat back down, propped his elbows on the desk and held his head in his hands. The front door chimed, and when he looked up his friend, Ed was walking toward him, looking concerned.

"Your head alright?" Ed asked.

"Yeah," Scott said. "It's just Sarah."

"That woman scares me a little bit."

"She should," Scott said. "Listen, I need a sounding board, and I don't want to be overheard. Care to take a walk with me?"

"You got it. I need to share some information with you anyway."

The two men left the station, crossed the street, and headed up Peony Street toward Morning Glory Avenue.

Scott told Ed about his morning spent interviewing people, and the less lurid details of the conversation with Sarah that followed.

"You can imagine how reluctant I am to share with Sarah the specifics of the deal I made with Margie," Scott said. "When I did all that, it was with the best interests of her mother at heart; I had no way of knowing I'd be investigating her murder a few weeks later."

"I wondered about that," Ed said. "You know, not much goes on in this town that everyone doesn't find out about. Are you afraid if you don't tell Sarah someone else will?"

"That's just the thing. We went around doing these interviews, and no one breathed a word about it. I'm touched by their loyalty, but it worries me how willing they are to be complicit in a cover-up."

"No one was sorry to see Margie lose her job, and after they found out what she was doing to her mother, she could not have found a sympathetic ear in this town. Everyone appreciates what you did for Enid, and I can't imagine anyone would want you to get in trouble for doing it."

"I did what I thought was right, but it was not exactly legal or through official channels. After Margie's body was found, I should have told Sarah right away what happened, but by doing that I would have given her all the ammunition she needs to get me fired. She would love to have that kind of power over me. If the people of this town protect me by not telling what happened, that's great for me, but what if a killer gets away with murder as a result?"

"She just gave you carte blanche to investigate Margie's murder," Ed said. "So do that. Find out who killed her, arrest that person, and let the chips fall where they may. Then you will have done the right thing regardless of the outcome for you, personally."

"You're right. I just need to figure out who did it and if I have to tell the truth about the deal I made with Margie I will. I may lose my job, you know."

"I know," Ed said. "But that's not the end of the world. We'd figure something out."

"You need another paper carrier?"

"I'd fire Tommy tomorrow."

"Thanks," Scott said. "You said you had some information?"

"Tony Delvecchio said his mother got a letter in the mail that upset her quite a bit. He thinks it was from Margie."

"I better go talk to her."

"He wants you to talk to him first if you would."

"I can do that. Is he at work?"

"No, he's helping out in the PJ's caravan down at the festival."

"I need to go down there, anyway," Scott said. "I'll see if I can talk to him."

"Listen," Ed said. "I know something about Tony that I've been keeping in confidence. I don't want to break that confidence if I don't have to, but it may relate to this letter."

"Is it something illegal he's done?"

"No, it's personal."

"Then keep it to yourself for now. I'm beginning to regret relaxing my policy about listening to gossip. I already know way more than I want to about most of the people in this town."

They parted ways at the top of the hill. Scott started back down toward the festival at the bottom of the hill, and Ed went to the library to look for a book about parenting adolescents.

Maggie was taking a short break during a lull when she saw her brother Sean walking through the crowd toward the caravan. She jumped out the back of the caravan and flung herself straight into his arms.

"Whoa!" he said, but picked her up and spun her around.

"What are you doing here?" she asked after he sat her back down.

"Well, you said you needed my help," he said, "so here I am."

Once inside the cramped quarters, Sean met Tommy, took off his coat and tied an apron over his black pants and charcoal-colored sweater. With his thick dark hair, bright blue eyes, and tall, elegant figure, Maggie thought he looked more like a male model than a corporate attorney.

"I've missed you at every turn this morning," he said. "Everywhere I've been, you'd just been and left."

"Where?" Maggie said. "Did you see Mom and Dad?"

"Yes," he said, making himself at home, seated on a high stool. "I went to the house, and you'd just left, then I went to the bakery, and you'd just left, so I came down here."

"What did Dad and Grandpa do when you showed up?" she asked.

"Well, Grandpa Tim cried, but it may be because I brought him a box of Cuban cigars, not knowing he's been forbidden to smoke. Fitz took the bottle of Irish whiskey I brought him, said 'don't just stand there like an eejit, fetch us some glasses,' and started pouring out shots, so it felt as if no time at all had passed."

"And Mom?"

"Oh, she cried, Aunt Alice cried, and Mandy wondered who the hell I was until I introduced myself. Is she the one who's sweet on Ed?"

"Yes," Maggie said, gesturing subtly with her head at Tommy, "and Tommy is her son."

"Ah, I see," Sean nodded. "It's fun to meet all these people you've been e-mailing me about."

Just then the caravan rocked back and forth, knocking Sean off his stool and some of the baked goods from the display. Patrick flung open the back door and stood with his hands on his hips, regarding his brother and sister.

"In case you've forgotten, counselor," he said to Sean. "The men in this family work in the bar and the gas station, and the womenfolk work in the bakery."

Maggie protested, but Sean took off his apron and followed Patrick to the Rose and Thorn caravan next door. Maggie and Tommy replaced all the plastic wrapped baked goods in their neat rows, and then leaned out so they could see what the two brothers were doing. Sean was tying on a pub apron while Patrick showed him how to run the cash register. Considering all that had happened in their family in the past, and all that had come to light recently, that had been as good a greeting between the two brothers as Maggie could have hoped for.

"He looks like Patrick, but skinnier," Tommy said.

"Don't let Patrick hear you say that."

"Why didn't he ever visit before?"

"He was busy with his job," Maggie said. "But I think he'll be back more now."

"Do you think Brian will ever come back?"

"I don't know," Maggie said, although she devoutly hoped her oldest brother would stay away.

That was one family reunion for which she didn't have high hopes.

Hannah returned to the caravan with a fresh load of baked goods and gossip. She had already forgotten she was mad at Maggie, having evened the score by staying away for two hours instead of one. She sent Tommy back to the bakery and shrugged off her coat.

"The latest scuttlebutt," she said, "is that Margie was stabbed in her hard little heart, rolled down yon hill behind ye olde tire store, and landed where I found her. She was covered with a four-foot drift, so it must have happened

Monday night or early Tuesday morning before we got the big storm."

Both women turned their attention to some customers and then, as soon as they walked away, Maggie said, "Go on."

"They found a cloth in the burn barrel behind the tire store that had been soaked in some chemical. When Frank smelled it, he almost passed out. They think someone knocked her out with that and then stabbed her. They haven't found a weapon."

"Sounds like chloroform. That's an old murder mystery classic, but I bet it's not easy to come by."

"It will be a few days before they have the toxicology report."

"So it was someone with access to medical supplies or a scientific lab of some sort."

Maggie mentally went through all the people she knew who were nurses or doctors. She didn't know any scientists or lab technicians.

"Hey Nancy Drew, I can see your mind computing," Hannah said, "but do you want to hear the rest?"

"Of course," Maggie said.

"Ruthie was with Margie's mother when Scott told her the sad news, and Enid's reaction was interesting. She was upset of course, but she was also irritated with Margie for being killed. She said something like, 'I told her if she didn't keep her nose out of everyone's business it would get cut off someday.'"

"Really?"

"Oh yes. Scott couldn't get any more out of her, but Ruthie thinks Enid might know more."

"I hope Ruthie keeps talking to her about it," Maggie said.

"She said she would let us know if Enid said anything else," Hannah said.

"We should go see her after all this is over," Maggie said, gesturing to the festival.

Hannah's husband Sam rolled up just then.

"I see you two putting your heads together, and I know trouble will be sure to follow."

Maggie thought he looked tired.

"How's the mitten fishing?" she asked him.

"I think I've fished my limit," he said, and then turned to his wife. "Can we go now?"

Hannah looked at Maggie, who nodded.

"Go, leave me here, I don't care," Maggie said. "It's only a few more hours."

Sean hailed Sam just then, and Sam rolled over to the pub caravan to talk to him.

"I could just run him home and be right back," Hannah offered.

"No ma'am," Maggie said. "It's a bakery policy that employees who find dead bodies get extra time off without pay."

"Gee, thanks."

"Are you doing okay?" Maggie asked her.

"Yeah, I think Sam's more shook up than me," Hannah said. "I feel kinda jumpy, but Sam's a mess."

"Why is he so upset?"

"He feels like he can't protect me," Hannah said, "and it makes him feel helpless."

"Uh oh," Maggie said. "That's not good."

"I just hope he snaps out of it. I don't think I have the energy to deal with another deep funk right now."

"Anything I can do?"

"No, but thanks. He'll stick to me like a decal for a few days but growl every time I talk to him, and then some government agency will get hacked by space aliens, and he'll have to go back to work."

"Did you talk to Sean?"

"Not yet. And look at your hunky brothers over there, drawing the woman to them like flies to honey. We need one in this caravan; hot men are good for business."

"I'm immune to it. I grew up sharing a bathroom with them, and all I remember is the farting and fighting."

"You're not telling me anything I don't already know," said Hannah, who had four older brothers of her own.

"Do you think we can get in Margie's house and look around?" Maggie asked as Hannah put on her coat.

"We just need a key," Hannah said, "and I know where we can get one."

Scott passed the Fitzpatrick Bakery caravan but saw Maggie was busy with customers, so he stopped to converse with Sean and Patrick instead.

"Good to see you," he said to Sean.

Sean leaned out over the front counter and shook Scott's hand.

"I thought I better start doing my filial duty," Sean said. "People were starting to think Patrick's the only son in this family."

"The only working son, that's for sure," Patrick said. "Wearing a fancy suit and having meetings all day isn't what I'd call honest labor."

"Ask Patrick if he's heard any good lawyer jokes lately," Sean said to Scott.

"I've got a million of 'em," Patrick said.

"And I've heard about half of them already today," Sean said.

Scott left them to their customers and walked on down to the PJ's caravan, where Tony and his nephew were selling slices of pizza and calzones. Tony motioned to Scott to come around to the back of the caravan, and Scott met him at the back door. Tony jumped down, and they walked back a few feet, where they could talk privately.

"I heard about Margie," Tony said, wiping his hands on his apron, which was spattered with pizza sauce.

"Mmm hmm," Scott said, and then was quiet.

"My mom got a letter in the mail; I think she got it Wednesday, but she just told me about it today. I think Margie may have sent it to her. She was pretty upset about it."

"What did it say?"

"Pretty much what Margie was referring to the day she threatened me. Asked if my mother knew what I was doing with a certain person late at night."

"Was there a request for money to keep it quiet?"

"No," Tony said. "It sounds to me like Margie just wanted to make sure my mom knew this information, to hurt her."

"I'm so sorry to hear about this. I'm going to need to talk to your mother."

"I figured you would. I told her she has to tell you about it. She doesn't want to but she will."

"Should I go to the house?"

"She's up at the community center right now," Tony said. "Just do it outside, away from her friends, if you don't mind."

"Don't worry," Scott said. "I will."

"Thanks," Tony said. "Oh, by the way, that sheriff's investigator came to talk to us, but we didn't say anything about the deal you made with Margie."

"I appreciate your good intentions," Scott said, "but I'm not asking anyone to lie for me. It may all have to come out."

"We don't see it as lying for you," Tony said. "You always do what's right by the people in this town, and we want to do what's right by you."

"Thanks," Scott said. "I appreciate the loyalty."

Up at the community center, Antonia Delvecchio did not look glad to see Scott but made a show of welcoming him into the kitchen, where a group of women were cooking and baking.

"Please have some coffee," she implored him. "Have some macaroons. I made them myself."

Scott couldn't resist the offer and was immediately plied with food from every direction. Afraid to offend anyone, Scott took a few bites of everything put in front of him. Several of the women took the opportunity to mention their unmarried daughters and extol their virtues.

"Sherry made the lemon squares, Scott," Mrs. Meyers said. "You wouldn't believe how hard that girl works at the college, but she still makes time to sew and cook. She's an old-fashioned girl. I just wish she could meet the right boy."

"Men these days seem to go for flash over substance," Mrs. Haddad said as she placed a plate of baklava before him. "My Julia is a beauty inside and out, but she doesn't paint herself up and display all that God gave her just to hang out in bars, like some I could mention. She's in town for the festival, Scott. You should stop by and see her. I know she'd love to see you."

Scott recognized that he was one of the very few unattached men under the age of fifty in Rose Hill, so he was used to these pitches. He felt sorry for their daughters, though, who he knew would be mortified to hear their mothers say such things. They were nice women, all of them, but everyone knew his heart was spoken for.

As soon as he finished all the desserts he could manage, Antonia said loudly, "Scott, would you mind to take a look at the thermostat outside the cloakroom? I think it's broken. I'll show you."

Antonia Delvecchio held herself in an almost imperious manner, but she also had a powerfully sensuous quality that was impossible to ignore. She led Scott across the common room out into a cold hallway where everyone hung their coats, and Scott was disconcerted to notice the sway in her walk was incredibly sexy. As she turned to face him, he noted her beautiful bone structure and Mediterranean complexion also seemed to have defied the aging process. Scott reflected that she must have been an amazingly attractive woman when she was younger, yet it had been the short, homely Sal who had won her heart.

After checking to be sure no one was in either restroom nearby, Antonia spoke in a low voice.

"Anthony told me I should tell you about the letter. Such lies! That witch, that Margie person; I knew she was a troublemaker. She was no good."

"Where is the letter?"

"I burned it," she said. "And I hope she burns in hell as well, may God forgive me."

With her emotions riled Antonia became a little more Italian, kind of like when Maggie's father drank he became a lot more Irish.

"What did the letter say?" Scott asked her.

"It was all lies about my Anthony. He was seen with someone late at night, so they must be lovers; that my heart must be broken to have a son such as this. I love all my sons, Scott, but Anthony, he is the closest to my heart, capiche? Of course, you do. You're close to your mother as well. My Anthony and I have such a close relationship, I would know if something like this was true, and it's not. He's the only one who has not married, this is true. But he is so special, and there has just not been the right woman for him. That's all it is. Anything else is just lies and evil thoughts from this person, this jealous Margie. I know she's dead and I must not speak ill of the dead, but anyone who would do such a thing, well...she doesn't deserve to live among decent people."

Scott thought he got the gist of the letter but wanted to be sure.

"She inferred that Tony is gay."

"She used an awful word, a word I would not repeat to you, to anyone."

"Did she ask for money?"

"No, she didn't. It was meant to hurt me, to ruin my relationship with my beautiful son, but it was not blackmail."

"When did you get the letter?"

"Tuesday. Salvatore picks up the mail, but it was addressed to me. I didn't tell him about this. It would kill him even to think it might be true. It's not true! Anthony has had many girlfriends. He recently broke up with a young woman who lives in Pittsburgh; he used to see her on the weekends. I never met the girl but she was lovely, he said so. She came from a nice family. Unfortunately, they were not Catholic, and she would not convert. Anthony knows how I feel about these things. He would never marry someone outside our faith."

"Did you try to contact Margie?"

"I didn't know it was from this woman. It was written on a typewriter with no signature. After I told Anthony about it, he told me about her visit to his office, and her threats. That's when we knew who it must be. Then she is dead, so there is no one to confront."

She shrugged as if to say, "and that was that."

"So there was no contact from her before or after you received the letter?"

"No, none. If she had come to me for money, I would have slapped her face. I would have spat on her. Such disrespect, and to my husband, a town council member and a respected businessman in this town for so many years. God forgive me, may she rest in peace, but if she had lived, well, I might have killed her myself."

"Mrs. Delvecchio," Scott said. "I'm investigating her murder. Please try to be more careful what you say."

"I'm an emotional woman, Scott. Pay no attention to what I say. When I'm upset, I say things I shouldn't. It's the Sicilian blood; it runs hot when my family is threatened. Please forgive me."

"And you didn't tell Tony about this until today."

"Yes, we are so close, you know, that I can't hide anything from him. Nor he from me."

"I appreciate you talking to me. I wish you had kept the letter."

"You won't tell anyone about it. What it said, I mean."

"I can't see any reason to."

"Lies!" she hissed as she pulled the sweater draped over her shoulders closer around her. "Wicked lies."

Scott thanked her and left the community center.

The bar caravan stayed open until 10:00 p.m., but Maggie closed the bakery caravan at 8:00 p.m. and Tommy helped her carry the money and leftovers back to the bakery. She passed Caroline on her way out. It was the first time Maggie had seen her without Drew attached to her hip.

"Hey!" Caroline called out cheerfully, "I've been trying to reach you all day!"

Maggie just kept walking, leaving Caroline staring after her.

"Verbally assaulting one Eldridge sister per day is my new limit," Maggie told Tommy.

The bakery had closed at 6:00 p.m., and it was dark inside when Maggie unlocked and opened the front door. She had just set the cash box down on the front counter when she heard something in the kitchen, and the hair stood up on the back of her neck. A metal pan or bowl hit the floor back there, and Maggie sent Tommy running out the front door, saying loudly, "Go to the diner and ask Pauline to call Scott."

Tommy met Ed coming out of the diner.

"What's happened?" he asked, seeing Tommy's face.

"Someone is hiding in the bakery," he said breathlessly. "Maggie's still in there."

Ed hurried back with him while dialing Scott on his cell phone. Maggie had turned all the lights on and was standing just inside the front door, holding a long wooden rolling pin like a baseball bat. They all waited there until Scott arrived, thankfully without Sarah.

Scott's first concern was Maggie, and as soon as he saw she was okay, he led the way to the kitchen. Scott slowly swung open the door and flipped on the light, but whoever it was had gone. The back door was standing wide open, letting big gusts of frigid air and swirling snow into the room.

The noise Maggie had heard was a pan of brownies, left out to cool with a dishtowel over them, flipped over onto the floor. Maggie got a broom and dustpan to clean up while Scott looked around in the alley.

"Looks like whoever it was is long gone," Scott said, noting the large, wet boot prints left on the kitchen tile. He examined the door, but it didn't seem to have been forced.

"The backdoor locks automatically every time you close it," Maggie told him, "so I know Mom didn't leave it unlocked. I came in the front, which was also locked."

"Who has keys?" Scott asked her.

"Everyone in the family," Maggie said.

Scott suggested they change the locks. Ed called Sonny Delvecchio, who owned the hardware store, and he said he'd be down in a few minutes.

The adrenaline rush quickly wore off, and Maggie felt herself go rubbery-legged and suddenly unable to deal with one more thing. Tears filled her eyes, so she turned and began wiping down the counter to hide them. Scott thanked Ed and nodded toward the door.

"I think I'll walk Tommy home," Ed said. "But if you need anything, Maggie, you just call me."

Maggie thanked him but didn't turn around.

As soon as he heard the front door shut, Scott came up behind Maggie, put his arms around her, and said, "Are you okay?"

Maggie wriggled out of his arms, saying, "If you are nice to me right now, I swear I will blubber like an idiot."

"I don't mind," he said, and she threw a towel at him.

"I mean it," she said. "Sonny will be here any minute, and I can't fall apart right now. I have too much to do. Tell me what's going on with you."

Scott hopped up to sit on the stainless steel worktable and rubbed his eyes, looking just as exhausted as Maggie felt. Maggie gave him a plate full of ham and cheese turnovers to eat, and he realized just how starved he was. She put on a pot of coffee, and he gratefully accepted that as well.

"You probably know more than I do," Scott said, and Maggie nodded, agreeing.

"How's Tiny Crimefighter?" she asked.

"Same as always," Scott said. "She's pissed at having to lower herself to investigate our rinky-dink crime, doesn't understand why she can't insult the truth out of everyone and thinks I'm just barely bright enough to handle it on my own."

"But she'd still like to sleep with you," Maggie said.

Scott laughed, though he blushed as well. There was a knock on the front door, and they found Sean outside.

"Ed told us what happened," he said. "I'm here to help."

Scott left Sean with Maggie to wait for Sonny and went back to the festival.

"I'd forgotten how handsome he is," Sean teased her after Scott left. "A man in uniform, too."

Maggie swatted him, saying, "Hands off, buddy, he's mine."

And with that exchange, Sean Fitzpatrick finally communicated to his sister Maggie that he was, in fact, gay, and Maggie, who had already figured it out, reassured him that it was fine with her.

Sonny arrived and was surprised to see Sean, who was in his youngest brother Paul's class in school.

"These are old locks," he said after he examined them.

"Probably the originals," Sean said.

Maggie called her mother to tell her what had happened but insisted she didn't need to come back over to the bakery. Maggie locked up the deposit in the safe and did some prep work for the next day. Sean talked to Sonny while he worked. Once Sonny finished, he gave Maggie two keys for each door and said he would bring more copies the next morning. When Maggie asked him how much she owed him, he shook his head.

"This one's on me," he said. "Professional courtesy."

Maggie quickly loaded him up with all the baked goods she could fit in the largest box.

Sonny shook hands with Sean, picked up the hefty box, and left.

The bakery phone rang, and Sean answered it. He listened intently for half a minute and then said, "will do," and hung up.

"Patrick asked if you would check on Ava," Sean told Maggie. "He's worried about her."

"How come?"

"She left the festival in a hurry this afternoon, and he hasn't been able to get her on the phone."

"Alright," Maggie said with a sigh. "Just what I need, one more thing to do."

"Tell you what. I'll take the keys to Mom, help Patrick until closing, and then meet you at Ava's. You got a couch I can sleep on tonight?"

"I do."

"I'll see you in a little bit."

"Sean," Maggie said, as her brother turned to leave, "I'm so glad you're here."

"Me too," he said and smiled as he went.

Maggie hurried over to the B&B and found her sister-in-law standing in the kitchen looking out the back door. When she turned around, Maggie thought Ava looked ill.

"What's wrong?" Maggie asked.

Ava got up and closed the door to the family room, where the kids were watching a television show, and also closed the door to the public area, where the two teenage girls were working, so they wouldn't be overheard. Maggie put the kettle on for tea, and when she handed a mug to Ava, she could see her hands were shaking.

"Mrs. Turner stopped by the mitten fishing game this afternoon, to bring Timmy to me, and to tell me she saw a strange man approach him at the festival."

"Oh, Ava, no. What happened?"

"Mrs. Turner said she saw a man walk up to Timmy and try to take his hand, and that Timmy yelled 'no' just like I taught him to. When Mrs. Turner called out, the man took off, and Timmy ran to her. He was very upset."

"Where was he when this happened?"

"He was supposed to be with Charlotte, but he wandered off, apparently. Mrs. Turner said he was over close to the mobile home park."

Maggie felt nauseated and now understood why Ava looked so ill.

"Is he okay?"

"Yes, he's okay. I haven't told you the worst part yet. He said he'd seen this man before."

"Where?"

"At the school, watching him on the playground. He says the man is a pirate."

"A pirate?" Maggie said with a dubious look.

"I asked him what the man looked like and he said, 'a pirate.' He was asking Scott the other day if he had ever arrested any pirates, and I didn't think anything of it. Oh my God, Maggie. He could have..."

She started crying then, and Maggie hurried around the island to hug her.

"I don't want them to see me like this," Ava gasped between sobs.

Maggie could feel herself coming close to tears as well. There was too much happening all at once, and they were all so tired.

"Run upstairs, get it all out, wash your face, and I will wait here. Go!" she commanded.

Ava did as she was told, and Maggie immediately called Scott.

Much later, after the kids had gone to bed, Patrick, Sean, Scott, Maggie, and Ava sat around the kitchen island, discussing the events of the afternoon.

"Timmy said the man had a beard, mustache, earrings, and long curly hair," Ava said. "I didn't want to push him too hard, but I did ask him to draw a picture of the man, and as he did, he described him to me. He said the man had long red hair like Aunt Maggie's."

Ava showed them the picture, drawn with crayons. It did indeed look like a six-year-old boy's version of a pirate with wild red curly hair.

"I talked to Mrs. Turner, and she confirmed the red beard but said he was wearing a toboggan so she couldn't see his hair," Scott said. "I called the principle, and he's going to alert the teachers. I'll have Skip and Frank take turns keeping watch at the school next week."

"It's Brian," Patrick said, and there was an audible intake of breath from everyone.

"If Brian's been living on Bimini for the last six years," Scott said, "he could easily have grown long hair like Maggie's and may very well look just like a pirate."

"But why would he sneak around?" Sean asked.

"He's trying to kidnap Timmy," Ava suggested. "To get the money Theo left me."

"He should be easy to spot," Patrick said quietly.

Patrick was much calmer about this than Maggie thought he would be. His quiet demeanor scared Maggie more than if he was yelling and breaking furniture.

"It may have been Brian who broke into the bakery," Maggie suggested. "He could still have a key to it."

"And to the station and the bar," Patrick said.

"And to this place," Ava said.

154

Scott dialed Sonny, who luckily had not yet gone to bed. Patrick left to meet him at the Rose and Thorn, and Scott agreed to stay with Ava until they returned to change her locks.

Sean walked home with Maggie.

"Why wouldn't he just show up and say, 'I'm back?'" Sean asked her. "Sure, everyone was pissed he left, but he didn't commit any crime."

Maggie told Sean about the blackmail photos of Brian and Phyllis Davis that she had discovered in the late Theo Eldridge's safe. She also told him about the huge loan Brian had taken from Theo, using life insurance on his wife and children as collateral, and how he cleaned out their savings account after he left.

"You think he sold his disappearance to Theo?"

"Yes, I do."

"So he's not likely to get a hero's welcome," he said, "and certainly not open arms from Ava."

"I think it's safe to say that marriage is over."

"Still," Sean said, "if it is Brian sneaking around, he must have done something more than cheat on Ava. Adultery may be despicable, but it's not illegal. The worst we could accuse him of is abandonment. We could sue him for back child support, but he wouldn't go to jail unless he refused to pay. No, there must be something bigger he's running from."

"Ava thinks he wants to kidnap the kids."

"Or kill her to get the money Theo left her," Sean suggested.

"I hadn't even thought of that!" Maggie said. "That's pretty morbid."

"I work with greedy relatives all the time," he said. "Even perfectly sane people can go a little crazy when a lot of money is involved."

"I guess we don't know what he's capable of," Maggie said.

"Has Ava written a new will since she got Theo's bequest?" Sean asked.

"I never thought to ask her," Maggie said. "I don't know."

"Do you think she would mind if I talked to her about it?" Sean asked.

"Ava doesn't offend easily," Maggie said. "If it would protect her kids she'd be anxious to do it."

Maggie didn't have to worry about Brian breaking into her bookstore because it was armed from the floor to the ceiling with security devices, plus smoke and carbon monoxide detectors. Since her house burned down, Maggie didn't believe in taking any chances.

"Are you sorry now you came back?" Maggie asked him, as she let him into her apartment above the bookstore.

Sean collapsed on her couch with his coat still on.

"No," he said. "Looks like I'm just in time for a Fitzpatrick family reunion."

Maggie fell back into her favorite cushy armchair and put her feet up on the ottoman.

"I hope he hasn't already broken into the bar or the service station," she said. "There's been a lot of money coming in this weekend."

"Should we warn Mom and Dad?" Sean asked.

"No point," Maggie said. "If Brian shows up at home he'll be welcome."

"The prodigal son returns," Sean said.

"It's a two for one special this weekend," Maggie said.

Maggie closed her eyes and could feel herself falling asleep. She was so tired that she felt dizzy.

"I told Patrick I'm gay and he seems okay about it," Sean said.

"Good, I'm glad," Maggie said, with her eyes still closed. "How'd that subject come up?"

"He asked me why I never come home, and I told him it's because I'm gay."

"What did he say?"

"He said, 'I figure you guys are born that way and can't help it,' and then changed the subject."

"Our Patrick, he has such a way with words."

"It's a pretty insulting thing to say because it implies being gay is a congenital disability, but I think he meant well. It could have been worse, I guess."

"I know he seems like a stupid jock," Maggie said, "but he's pretty smart and has a good heart."

"He's improved with age. I think I'll tackle Mom and Dad separately."

"It will be fine."

"Probably not, but thanks for saying that."

They were quiet for a few minutes, and Maggie thought that maybe Sean had fallen asleep.

"Is there anyone special back in Pittsburgh?" she asked.

"There used to be," Sean said, "but not for awhile now."

Maggie thought about all the single men in Rose Hill. There weren't that many, and she had no idea if any of them were gay.

"Sonny Delvecchio's wife just left him," Maggie said. "I know he's not handsome, but he's nice."

"You have him, then," Sean said, as he threw a pillow at her. "I prefer his brother Tony."

Ed Harrison kissed Mandy long and hard before leaving her mobile home in the wee hours of the morning. His dog Hank stood nearby, peeing on a shrub.

"You could stay," she said. "Tommy doesn't care."

"I care," Ed said. "I don't want people gossiping about you."

"I don't care about that," Mandy said, but let him go, closing the door behind him.

Ed noticed there was a light on in Phyllis Davis's old trailer. The last he heard, she was living in a rented room out behind the Roadhouse bar near the highway and was renting the trailer to someone. He thought he saw a movement behind the curtains and thought about the break-in at the bakery.

Mandy answered the door instantly at his knock.

"You changed your mind," she said.

"I've been doing that a lot lately," Ed said, and he and Hank went back inside.

Hannah lay awake, alone in bed, while Sam tapped away on the computer keyboard in his office. He had been quiet and taciturn again on the way home. When they got home, they argued, and he asked her if she was sorry she'd married a cripple.

"I don't think of you as a cripple," she told him, "but you're acting like an emotional one right now."

He barricaded himself in his office after their fight, and she knew he would probably sleep on the couch again. This was an old drama they played out, over and over. Sam was down and blaming himself for everything, and Hannah was fed up with comforting him over a bad thing that had happened to her.

"You don't understand how helpless it makes me feel," he'd said, "when I can't get to you and protect you."

"I don't need you to protect me," Hannah had responded, "but I do need you to quit making this all about you, and how it affects you."

"You don't know what the world is really like, Hannah. It's a dangerous, awful place, and you have to be on your guard all the time. The end can come out of nowhere in a split second. You aren't careful enough."

"I know the war was awful, and you feel like the world is out to get us, but I don't. I can't live my life as if it's a battlefield. It's not healthy."

"I have to. I can't help it. I'm sorry I can't be what you want."

158

"I wish you could just this once get your head out of your behind and stop whining about what you can't do, and be there for me in the ways that you can be."

"You shouldn't stay married to me if I can't be the man you need."

"Oh, I think you can, Samuel. I think you're just used to this one man pity party you're always throwing, and you don't know how to live life without it."

"I'm sorry I'm such a disappointment to you."

"Me too, buddy, me too."

Hannah felt lonely, tired, and sorry for herself. She hugged her pillow and cried until she fell asleep. She didn't dream about finding Margie's body. Instead, she dreamed about a baby that was so tiny she could hold it in one hand.

Caroline Eldridge offered the joint she was smoking to Drew, who shook his head.

"It's organically grown," she said. "I have an excellent source in South America."

"I think the contact high will be quite enough, thank you," he said. "It makes me paranoid and jumpy when I'm high, and then sluggish and stupid when it wears off. I have never understood the appeal."

"It makes me happy and horny," Caroline said.

"Then, by all means, have some more. Don't let me stop you."

They were lying tangled up in the blankets on his bed, where they had spent much of the weekend.

"I feel like I've known you all my life," she told him, then licked two fingertips and pinched the lit end of the hand-rolled cigarette. "I think we may be soul mates or twin souls and have shared many lives before. Maybe it was in Rome; I keep getting a visual of us wearing togas and walking among marble columns. I think maybe we were brothers. Or maybe it was in Atlantis. I had a past life regression once where I saw myself there doing something with healing crystals."

"Let's just focus on this life right now," Drew said. "I don't think you should move out to the lodge. Stay here with me until summer comes."

"But the monks are coming. I have to get the place ready for them."

"Celibate monks, right?"

"Don't be silly, of course they are. I hope you don't have any bourgeois hang-ups about sex. It has to be organic and free flowing between us for it to work."

"I'm not possessive. I won't smother you or tie you down. As long as we can be together whenever we feel like it, that's fine with me. I was getting lonely up here."

"You can come up to the lodge anytime."

"I'm going to have to get a better car if I'm going to be running up Pine Mountain all the time."

"You can have one of Theo's cars. He left me several."

"That's very generous, rich lady, but I'd prefer to pay my own way."

"Why don't we turn the barn into a veterinary clinic and you can move out there with me? There are already kennels there."

"It's a long way to ask Rose Hill people to drive."

"But you'll get the rich ski resort people from Glencora. They've probably all got spoiled pets. You could charge more and get paid what your work is worth."

"But don't the people in Rose Hill deserve proper care for their animals as well?"

"Sure they do," she said. "But that doesn't mean you shouldn't attract wealth to yourself. The more money you have, the more people you can help. If you were making lots of money, you could hire someone to work in the Rose Hill office. When I get Theo's money, I can invest in your practice, and you can pay me back over time, or not. Material things don't matter to me."

"We'll see. You aren't even sure you're staying in the country, remember?"

"I can't imagine leaving this bed right now," she said. "Besides, there's a lot of good I can do right here, with the monks staying at the lodge, and you setting up a practice in the barn. Maybe I could start a yoga studio in one of the buildings Gwyneth owns."

"There are lots of options when there's enough money involved."

"Stick with me," Caroline said. "I'm all about attracting wealth and putting it to good use. The universe rewards that kind of thing."

"I'd like to reward you by exploring your South American region," Drew suggested.

"You're in luck," Caroline said. "There's a boat leaving right now."

By the time Sonny left the bed and breakfast after changing Ava's locks, it was very late. Ava was sipping tea at the kitchen island. Scott joined her but declined anything to drink.

"I have too much caffeine in me as it is," he said.

"I can't sleep," Ava said. "I feel like as soon as I let down my guard something bad will happen."

"I can understand that. You ought to call Maggie; she'd be glad to come over and stay."

"No," said Ava. "She's even more exhausted than me. She needs her sleep."

"I would be glad to sleep on your couch if that would help. I'm so tired that I could sleep on a bed of nails right now."

"That's so kind of you, Scott. You really wouldn't mind?"

"No," Scott said. "Just throw a blanket over me, and I'll be out like a light."

Ava got him a pillow and a blanket while Scott unlaced his boots and took off his belt. It felt a little intimate getting semi-undressed in front of Ava, but she waited until he was down to his boxers and t-shirt, and as soon as he lay down she tucked the blanket in around him on the couch. She kissed his forehead and thanked him again.

"Don't worry now," Scott said. "I'll shoot anything that moves."

"If some of my guests wander into the kitchen looking for a midnight snack," Ava laughed, "it may be the last thing they ever do."

Ava locked up, turned off the lights, and went up to bed.

Scott, who was so sure he would fall right to sleep, now felt keyed up and wide awake. He went over all the Margie stories people had told him over the last couple days and realized he had a town full of suspects, many of whom probably had stories about Margie they would never share. If she had been going around town threatening to blackmail people, and sending poison pen letters, there would be more than one person who would have been glad to eliminate the threat she posed. In the wee hours of the morning, Scott finally fell asleep and dreamed about kissing a woman. It started out to be Maggie but ended up to be Ava.

Chapter Seven – Sunday

Tommy woke up before his alarm went off at 4:00 a.m., after hearing what sounded like a baby crying next door. When he went down the hallway to get his breakfast, he found Ed eating cereal out of his favorite bowl, and Hank eating dry cereal out of a tin pie plate on the floor. For a moment, he thought he might be dreaming.

"If this bothers you," Ed said, "I won't do it again."

"No, it doesn't," Tommy said. "Just leave me enough milk for mine."

Tommy had a hard time hiding his grin as he fixed his breakfast.

"Did you hear a baby crying earlier?" Ed asked him.

"Yeah, I think Phyllis is renting her trailer to an old lady with a baby," Tommy said. "I saw them yesterday morning with a cart of groceries. She's shy, though, and didn't wave back when I waved."

Ed felt better knowing it was a grandmotherly type living so near rather than some of the rough characters Phyllis knew.

At 4:30 a.m. Ed, Tommy, and the dog Hank walked to work together, and it felt completely normal to do so. If it bothered Tommy that Ed was staying all night with his mother, he certainly didn't show it. Ed felt so out of his element, so confused, but so happy all at the same time, he didn't know what the right thing to do or say was anymore. He could never have imagined he'd need to know what to do or say in a situation like this because it was so unlike him to be in a situation like this. All he knew was that right now he felt good, and he didn't want to ruin it by over-thinking.

"Are you going to the pancake breakfast later?" Ed asked Tommy, who shrugged.

"Yesterday was the Women's Guild, but today it's the Volunteer Firefighters," Ed told him. "They aren't as stingy

163

with the bacon. I'm going up later so you can go with me if you want."

Tommy just nodded, failing to suppress another huge smile.

When Scott woke up his friend, Patrick was standing next to the couch in Ava's family room, staring down at him in an unfriendly manner.

"Good morning," Patrick said.

"Hey," Scott stammered as he sat up. "What time is it?"

"It's 6:00," Patrick said. "Why are you here?"

"He's my new bodyguard," Ava said from the kitchen.

She was fully dressed for the day and looked radiant, even with the little hint of shadows beneath her big dark eyes.

"It's part of a new service we offer," Scott said, putting his feet on the floor and rubbing his face. "Personal security detail."

"Uh huh," Patrick said.

Ava smiled at them both and started the coffee.

"I'm on my way to the Volunteer Firefighters' breakfast," Patrick said. "Just thought I'd check in."

Ava continued to smile and putter around the kitchen, and Patrick continued to loom over Scott and look back and forth between the two. Finally, Ava shook her head and laughed at Patrick.

"Patrick, stop it. He was here when Sonny left last night, and I told him I was too scared to sleep. I coerced him into sleeping on that lumpy couch so I would feel safe."

"But Sonny changed your locks," Patrick protested.

"I know," Ava said.

"You could have called me," Patrick said.

"No, I couldn't," Ava said, pointedly.

"I think I'll give you two some privacy," Scott said, scooping up his clothes and heading for the half bath in the hallway.

"Not necessary," Ava said.

"Thank you, Scott," Patrick said.

When Scott came out of the bathroom, fully dressed, Patrick was gone.

"Is he waiting outside with dueling pistols, wearing a cape?" he asked.

"Don't worry," Ava said. "He's fine."

Scott gratefully accepted the coffee she offered and then ate two of the muffins she baked for her guests. Ava kissed him on the cheek before he went out the door.

"Thank you, Scott. I know that was awkward, but it was such a blessing to me. I slept better than I've slept in several nights."

"No problem," Scott said. "I'll just be sure to tell Maggie about it before she hears it second hand."

Ava laughed and shook her head.

"The hot-blooded, jealous Fitzpatricks."

"God bless 'em," Scott said, and went on his way.

Fitz Fitzpatrick surprised everyone by coming to the Volunteer Firefighters' breakfast at the community center. He sat in a wheelchair propped up with pillows, sweating profusely despite the cold. He wanted everyone to shake hands with his son Sean, and to brag about his job at a bank in the "big city."

Maggie watched her brother Patrick out of the corner of her eye, wondering if this big show of paternal pride would hurt his feelings. He seemed to take it in stride, though, flipping pancakes on a huge griddle and flirting with all the women within a five-yard radius.

Ava was there with Timmy and Charlotte, keeping both children within reach.

'Who could blame her?' thought Maggie.

Hannah was waiting tables, and Sam was keeping an eye on her from a wheelchair parked next to Maggie's father. Maggie was filling cups at the drinks table, watching everyone. Bonnie Fitzpatrick was in her element, serving baked goods she made herself, receiving many compliments, with her handsome and successful son Sean home for a visit. Maggie watched her go from table to table, beaming with pride.

"Where's the fatted calf, I wonder," Hannah said as she returned to refill her tray.

"Sean and I were just joking about that last night," Maggie said.

"I hear you may have another brother in town," Hannah said.

"Is that what the scanner grannies are saying?"

"No," Hannah said. "Patrick told Sonny, Sonny told his mother, and his mother told my mother."

"Looks like no one's told Bonnie yet."

"That's too near the fiery furnace for most people," Hannah said.

"Well, if he's in town, he can't stay hidden long."

"And what will happen if Patrick finds him first?" Hannah asked.

"There won't be much left of him for Bonnie to welcome home," Maggie said.

"Do you want the latest Margie gossip?' Hannah asked.

"Of course."

"The unofficial word is that the cloth found in the burn barrel was soaked in chloroform. Just like you thought, miss smarty pants, chloroform is no longer used as an anesthetic, hasn't been for years. It's a controlled substance that would not be that easy to get hold of."

"How'd you find this out?"

"Skip talked to someone he knows in the coroner's office."

"Scott would skin him alive if he knew Skip talked to you about the case."

"So don't tell him."

"What's their theory?"

"The murderer thought he was destroying the evidence. The thing is chloroform doesn't burn except at high temperatures; Skip found that out when he looked it up on the Internet. That's why the part of the cloth soaked in it didn't burn; it wasn't hot enough. The dry part caught fire, and the murderer left it in the burn barrel, thinking the whole thing would burn, but didn't wait to see it finished."

"Anything else?"

"That's all I've got. It's still early."

"We have to get in that house."

"That's covered."

"How?"

"Ruthie got a key from Enid to get clothes to bury Margie in. I told her we would take care of it."

"You're good."

"The police have been all over their place already, so they probably have all the evidence."

"Still..."

"We might be able to find something they missed."

"When are we going?"

"The coroner is releasing the body tomorrow, so we have to go tonight."

"The festival lasts from 12:00 to 6:00, and then we have to clean up and break everything down. So we're looking at what, 8:00?"

"The goose flies at 8:00," Hannah said.

Gwyneth came in with the mayor and circled the room, offering two limp bony fingers as a handshake. When she got to where Maggie stood at the drinks table, she pretended not to see her and greeted the woman next to her instead.

"Do you have any freshly squeezed organic juice?" she asked. "Or cappuccino?"

The woman looked at Maggie, but Maggie just bit her lip.

"I'm afraid not," the woman said nervously, and Mayor Stuart Machalvie apologized profusely to Queen Gwyneth for the inferiority of the offerings.

Maggie rolled her eyes but said nothing. She was trying to be good.

Caroline and Drew arrived, and Caroline greeted Maggie with a little more reserve this time.

"Hey," she said. "How are you?"

"Just fine," Maggie said, pointedly not asking Caroline how she was.

"Wow, this has been a crazy week, hasn't it?" Caroline said. "We haven't even had a chance to catch up."

Maggie just looked at Caroline steadily and said nothing, until the silence became uncomfortable for everyone.

"Well, I'll let you get back to work," Caroline said, and she and Drew went to sit down at a table.

Maggie felt her face flush, but she was determined not to feel guilty for being rude.

'What do I care?' Maggie asked herself.

Someone arrived to relieve Maggie at her post, so she took a break. Connie Fenton, the manager of the Eldridge Inn, was coming out of the restroom as Maggie was going in. She looked very pale and drawn. Connie had a brisk manner and was not one to show emotion, but she was suffering, Maggie could tell.

"Connie," Maggie said. "I was so sorry to hear about your cat."

"Thank you, Maggie," Connie said, her eyes brimming with tears. "Mrs. Wiggins was an old cat, and I loved her, but I hated to see her suffer."

"Hannah said she had kidney failure."

"She'd had problems for quite a long time. I was able to keep her alive by administering subcutaneous fluids through an IV until Dr. Rosen got there."

"You could do that?"

"I used to be a nurse, dear," Connie said. "But anyone could do it with a little training."

"She must have loved you to hang in there so long."

"Yes, that comforts me," Connie said. "But in the end, it was the best thing for everyone that she be put down."

Maggie didn't know what else to say, so she said, "see you later," and went into the bathroom, where she splashed her face and dried it with paper towels.

As she was drying her hands, she noticed a purse on the windowsill. She thought Connie must have left it there, but decided to check the wallet for ID to make sure. She unzipped the purse and fished out the wallet, and sure enough, Connie's driver's license was in it. As she was zipping it back up something else in the purse caught her eye. She quickly locked herself in a cubicle and took out the plain white envelope with Connie's address typewritten on the outside. She unfolded the single sheet of paper that was inside and read it quickly. When she was done, she carefully put it back in the envelope and tucked it back into the purse.

Maggie found Connie and gave her the handbag. Connie seemed flustered and embarrassed to have left it in the bathroom and thanked Maggie for finding it. Maggie scouted the room for Hannah, caught her eye, and indicated with a head motion that she should meet her in the kitchen.

"What, what?" Hannah wanted to know.

"Connie Fenton has a threatening letter from Margie in her handbag."

"How do you know?"

"She left her purse in the bathroom. I was checking for ID, and I saw it."

"What did it say?"

"It said, 'I know what happened on March 9, 1984. I will be in touch.' That was all."

"What do you think that's about?"

"I don't know, but obviously it's not something Connie wants anyone to know about."

"You have to tell Scott."

"I can't. He'll arrest me for breaking and entering her pocketbook."

"Well, he needs to follow up on it. What if Connie killed Margie?"

"I know she's a crazy germaphobe, but would she kill someone?"

"We're going to have to look into this."

When they came back out into the common room, they saw Eldridge College President Newton Moseby arrive and immediately begin working the room, shaking hands with everyone just like a politician.

"There's Newton," Hannah said. "Watch when he gets to Connie."

Sure enough, when he got to where Connie was seated, he pretended not to see her, although he shook hands with the person seated on either side of her. Connie's face flushed, she gathered her things and left in a huff. Newton seemed nonplussed by her behavior, and just kept on pressing the flesh and moving on down each row.

"See, they hate each other," Hannah said. "They were having a huge argument when Drew and I got to the Inn the other day."

"Or they share a molten passion that threatens to drown them both in a tidal wave of desire," Maggie said.

"That's just gross," Hannah said.

Bonnie interrupted them and said, "We need to get going, or we'll miss the second service."

Maggie walked down to Sacred Heart with her mother, who was fussing about the new keys.

"I went over this morning and checked, but nothing was taken," she said. "Sonny dropped off more keys and gave me a lecture about not handing them out to just anyone. I told him, 'if I can't trust my family who can I trust?'"

Maggie thought it wisest to keep her mouth shut.

Ed and Tommy had multiple helpings of pancakes, bacon, and sausage. Several people asked where Mandy was, and Tommy kept telling them, "She's working at the bakery today."

Many of these people winked at Ed, but he pretended not to notice.

Patrick took a break and plunked down next to Ed, telling Tommy, "Why don't you run down to the bakery and see if there's anything you can do to help your mom out."

Tommy obediently jumped up and went. Ed found himself resenting Patrick bossing Tommy around but restrained himself. Tommy was not his son, and Patrick had enjoyed a closer relationship with the boy for a longer time.

"So how's it going?" Patrick asked Ed.

Ed could feel himself blush and hated himself for it.

"Fine," he said. "Just fine."

"That's what I hear," Patrick said. "Let's be sure it stays that way."

"What do you mean?" Ed asked him.

"Well let's just say that Mandy and Tommy are part of our family, and I would hate to see them get hurt."

"Are you threatening me?"

"Astute observation. I can see why you work in the news biz."

"Patrick," Ed said. "I would never do anything to hurt Mandy or Tommy. You know that."

"Good. Then there will be no need for me to break both of your legs if you do."

"You aren't serious."

"As a heart attack," Patrick said and stood to leave.

"C'mon, Patrick," Ed said. "You're kidding, right?"

"Glad we could have this talk," Patrick said, and slapped Ed pretty hard on the back before he walked away.

Sean sat down in the seat his brother had just vacated.

"Is Patrick putting the strong arm on you?" he asked.

"Yes," Ed said. "I can't believe he's serious."

"He's pretty fond of Mandy. Maggie says if it weren't for Ava, Patrick and Mandy would probably be married by now."

"Well, that explains a lot. Thanks for telling me."

"I've only been back a couple of days," Sean said. "But I gotta tell ya, it's like a soap opera around here."

"Don't I know it," Ed said. "It's good to see you, though."

"Thanks," Sean said. "Listen, we think Brian might be sniffing around town, behind the scenes."

"That's just what Ava and the kids don't need right now," Ed said.

"If you see him, will you let me know? Before Patrick, I mean."

"Sure thing."

Scott looked over the lists he had been making in connection with Margie's murder investigation. After canvassing the town without Sarah in tow, he and Deputies Frank and Skip had found many people who were willing to share their negative experiences with Margie. Scott figured for every one person willing to tell a tale there were two more that had worse to tell but chose not to. Just like the investigation into Theo Eldridge's death, Scott now faced a town full of suspects, many of whom may have hated Margie enough to want her dead.

From interviews made about her last known movements on Monday night Scott knew she had an altercation with Sue Fischer outside their house on Lotus Avenue, and then Maggie saw her mailing some letters at the post office. Margie then insulted Maggie, and as she walked away, Maggie overheard Margie getting into it with Matt Delvecchio at the IGA. After that, no one had anything to report except her mother Enid, who said she heard Margie come in late that night but couldn't remember what time, and didn't hear her leave again.

Scott walked down to the IGA and found Matt Delvecchio stacking large bags of dog food on a pallet by the front windows. When asked about what Margie said to him, Matt shook his head.

"Margie was a lonely, bitter person," Matt said. "I never took anything she said seriously. On Monday night she hinted my wife was having an affair with my brother Sonny because she goes to the hardware store a lot. Sonny's wife just left him, and my wife is working there to help out, so Margie was right about the visits but didn't have all her facts straight. Not having the facts never stopped ole Margie from spreading a rumor."

"Any idea who might have hated her enough to kill her?"

"I've been hearing some awful stuff about her now that's she's dead, and if half of what they say is true, there could be dozens of people. It's all just gossip, though. You know how people are."

"What have you been hearing?"

"You understand this is just what's going around?"

"I understand."

"Well, my wife heard that Margie was blackmailing some people over what she found in their mail, and things she saw going on when she walked around town at night."

"Any names attached to these stories?"

"I wouldn't like to say. It's just gossip."

"Would your wife tell me?"

"Probably."

Scott thanked Matt and headed up Pine Mountain Road to Lilac Avenue, where Matt and his wife Diedre lived in a brick foursquare with a porch covered in what looked like twenty years' worth of lawnmower and bicycle parts. Diedre answered the door in her bathrobe, smoking a cigarette. She invited Scott in and led him to the kitchen in the back of the house through a dark hallway lined on each side by towering stacks of newspapers, magazines, catalogs, and books. Scott had never been in their house before, but quickly recognized the signs of a hoarder living there. In the kitchen, there was a narrow path to each appliance, plus room for two people to sit at an old chrome dinette table. Every other inch of available space was piled with flattened food packaging, egg cartons, and milk jugs, all in neat, orderly piles tied with twine and stacked as high as Scott was tall. It gave the kitchen an almost labyrinth quality.

"Excuse the mess," Diedre said, and Scott almost laughed out loud.

Diedre was a fortyish woman of medium height with a gaunt frame and frizzy dark hair. She had a habit of crossing one arm across her body to grasp the elbow of the other arm, which held a cigarette in its hand. This cigarette was never farther than six inches away from her face, with an ash so long it was mesmerizing to watch how it didn't fall off. As soon as she finished one, she lit another. The smoky smell permeated the house and Scott knew he couldn't stay long. He declined coffee and got right to it, asking her about the rumors.

"That Margie was a piece of work," Diedre said, and then inhaled deeply on her cigarette before blowing the smoke out in an upwards direction by extending her bottom lip. "She's got my mother-in-law tied up in a knot over some letter she sent claiming Tony's a big pansy. Listen, everybody in the family knows about Tony, but we don't care. He's a good guy, and he keeps that part of his life out of town, where it belongs. His mother just doesn't want to know, ya know?"

"Did Margie ask your mother-in-law for money to keep it quiet?"

"No, she just wanted to punish Tony for not writing her an insurance policy on the old lady. She had to make good on some of her threats, or no one would take her seriously, ya see what I mean?"

"Do you know of anyone she has blackmailed?"

Diedre looked at Scott speculatively and finally knocked an inch long ash off her cigarette onto a saucer on the table. Scott could feel a tiny headache start, right behind the sinuses between his eyebrows. The cigarette smoke was starting to make him feel sick at his stomach.

"I'm not going to do all your work for you, but I will give you some names to get you started," Diedre said. "You go talk to Trick Rodefeffer and Mandy Wilson. Ask those two what Margie had on them."

Trick's name didn't surprise Scott, but Mandy's did.

Scott walked up to Morning Glory Avenue, where Trick and his wife Sandy lived in a faux Tudor mini-mansion. Trick was still in bed when Scott rang the bell, and eventually answered the door in his pajama bottoms and a sweatshirt. He also invited Scott back to the kitchen, but unlike Diedre's and Matt's house, the Rodefeffer house was spotless, and the kitchen was a showplace of marble and stainless steel. Trick filled a coffee filter and started the coffee maker, but only put one mug on the table, in front of Scott.

Trick was the same age as Scott but looked ten years older. He had big bags under his pale blue eyes, and his thinning blonde hair was cut in a style made popular many years ago when Trick wore a puka shell necklace and drove a black Trans Am with a gold eagle painted on the hood. He got himself a beer out of the massive refrigerator, removed the cap with a practiced thumb flick, and plopped down on a stool across the wide kitchen island from Scott.

"What can I do ya for?" he asked.

"I guess you heard about Margie."

"Oh yeah, awful thing, just awful. Horrible, horrible thing. I hated the bitch, but still, stabbed in the heart and thrown over the hill like a sack of garbage. That's brutal."

"I understand you're handling the sale of her mother's house."

"I am, I am indeed. Mountain View owns it, so technically I am representing their interests."

"Did you have any trouble with Margie over the sale?"

"Trouble was Margie Estep's middle name, Scott, as you well know. That sour little minx had her nose in everyone's business, and mine was no exception."

"What did she do?"

"She intercepted a very private letter sent to me by a dear, close personal friend whom my wife does not know. She threatened to show it to Sandy. Very cold, very calculating, almost evil, some might say."

"What did she want?"

"My percentage of the sale of her mother's house."

"What did you do?"

"I love my wife, Scott, and five percent of that shack is not that many pesos, but money's money, am I right? I knew if I gave in once she'd be back for more. Pesky business, blackmail. It's a deep pit; a dark, deep pit. I told her I'd tell Sandy myself, save her the trouble. That made her so mad that I thought she was going to have a stroke."

"Did she show Sandy the letter?"

"I don't think so."

"Did you tell Sandy?"

"My wife's a terrific gal, Scott. She hears things, she sees things, and when she comes to me, I explain to her how appearances can be deceiving, facts can be twisted, and completely innocent conduct can be misconstrued by jealous busybodies. She may be mad for awhile, but she always comes around. It may take a piece of jewelry or a nice vacation to smooth her ruffled feathers, but we have a good life, and she likes being Mrs. Rodefeffer. I didn't want to upset her by sharing what Margie had done, and as far as I know, Margie never carried out her evil plot. All's well that ends well."

"Except for Margie."

"Nothing to do with me or mine, I can assure you. I couldn't kill anybody. I'm a natural born coward, and everybody knows it. I can't hunt or fish; hell, I can't even boil a live lobster; makes me sick to my stomach just thinking about it. Besides, the missus and I just got back from a trip to the Keys; we left last Friday and just returned yesterday evening. I think that puts me out of the Margie-specific time frame, doesn't it?"

"Has Sandy opened the mail that accumulated while you were gone?"

"Not that I know of, why?"

Enlightenment paled Trick's face under his Florida tan, and he jumped up and ran to the front hallway, where a basket of mail sat on a side table. Scott followed at a slower pace, and when he caught up to Trick, the man was frantically rifling through a pile of envelopes and periodicals. When he came to a plain white envelope with his wife's name and their address is typewritten on the front with no return address, he looked at Scott with wide eyes.

"You may have just saved my life, compadre."

Scott held his hand out and Trick reluctantly parted with the letter.

Mandy was working at the bakery, and Scott led her out into the alley behind it for their talk.

"What's up?" Mandy asked, her big green eyes wide.

"Did Margie Estep try to blackmail you?"

Mandy's face flushed and her eyes opened even wider.

"Oh, Scott," she said. "You don't think I done kilt that rotten egg."

"No, I don't," Scott said. "I'm just following up on everyone she tried to get money out of, and your name came up."

Mandy's eyes teared up, and Scott felt awful.

"Oh my Lord," Mandy said as the tears started falling. "You think I coulda done somethin' like that."

"No, Mandy," he said, and put an arm around her. "Don't cry, please. Whatever it is, I'll help you figure it out. I don't think you killed her, I promise."

"I didn't kill 'er," Mandy cried. "I hated 'er guts, but I wouldn't never kill nobody."

"I know that," Scott said, and gave her his handkerchief so she could wipe her eyes. "Just tell me what she threatened you with, and what you did about it. How much did she want?"

"I ain't got no money," Mandy said. "She knowed that."

"So what did she want?"

"She wanted me to be her friend."

"She what?"

"She wanted me to pretend to be her friend so people would think somebody liked her."

Scott almost laughed but stifled it.

"Poor you," he said instead. "I think I'd rather pay any amount."

"I know! I told her I didn't think anyone'd be fooled, but that's what she wanted. I kept puttin' her off, and I never did go to lunch with her like she wanted. She wanted me to have lunch with her three times a week in the diner, and I was 'sposed to laugh and act like I was havin' a good time. She was gonna pay for the lunch; I just had to show up and be nice to her."

"What did she threaten to do if you didn't go along with this?"

Mandy's voice lowered to a whisper, and she looked frightened.

178

"She would tell somethin' on me that I don't want told."

"Who was she going to tell?"

"It wouldn't matter who, it would get around and then I'd be ruined in this town."

"Whatever it is, and you don't have to tell me, I don't imagine it would matter to the people who care about you."

"I'm not gonna tell ya. I'm hoping she took it to her grave."

Scott thought of the letters Maggie saw Margie mail. Two were accounted for so far, and although Mrs. Delvecchio told Diedre about hers, how did Diedre also know about Trick's and Mandy's?

"I just have one more question for you. Was Diedre Delvecchio close to Margie somehow? Do you think Margie would confide in Diedre about what she was doing to people?"

"Diedre hated Margie 'bout as much as me. Diedre's sister took over Margie's job at the post office, and I guess she left a huge mess for Sadie to clean up."

"You know, I completely forgot Sadie is Diedre's sister. They aren't much alike."

"I know; Sadie's a sweetie. You can't imagine she could be sisters with that sourpuss Diedre. Matt Delvecchio is the nicest man in the world, and that Diedre gives him hell from the time he gets up 'til he goes to bed at night. She's got some weird mental problem where she don't throw nothin' away; have you heard about that?"

"I saw it with my own eyes," Scott said.

Sadie Marcum had just returned from church when Scott knocked on her door. She lived in a modest bungalow on Iris Avenue next door to Maggie's Aunt Delia and Uncle Ian. She led Scott back to her clean kitchen and poured him a cup of coffee. The newspaper was spread out on the kitchen table, and Scott could smell something delicious cooking in the oven.

"George is down to the festival grounds," Sadie said. "He's a Whistle Pig Lodge member, so he's working in that caravan. He'll be home for some lunch any minute. Are you looking for him?"

"I'm investigating Margie Estep's death," Scott said and watched as Sadie's face became purposefully expressionless.

"Mmm hmm," she said and crossed her arms in front of her chest.

"Your sister said you might know something about some letters Margie mailed on Monday," he said.

"My sister is mistaken," Sadie said. "I can't talk about the mail, Scott, you know that. I'd lose my job."

"This may help us catch Margie's murderer, Sadie. I need to know how many letters Margie mailed and who they were addressed to."

"I need this job," Sadie said. "George is laid off right now, and his unemployment only lasts three more months. This job was a like a gift to us from God."

"Tell him what he needs to know," George said from the hallway. Neither Sadie nor Scott had heard him come in. "You can't let someone get away with killing people, Sadie. We've got kids to think about."

George came in and shook Scott's hand before he sat down at the table.

"Spill it, Sadie Anne," he told his wife. "No job's worth a murder on your conscience."

Sadie was torn, Scott could tell. After a short silence, she sighed deeply and uncrossed her arms. As soon as she did so, her husband tenderly smiled at her, as further encouragement.

"There was a bunch of letters, just like you said," Sadie said. "We have to watch things like that because of terrorist attacks. I wrote down who they were addressed to, on account of the no return address thing. One was addressed to Antonia, and Diedre was at her house when she read it. She said Tony figured Margie must have sent it because he refused to write her an insurance policy on her mother."

"Where is that list?"

Sadie left the room for a moment and returned with a folded up piece of paper. Scott scanned the list and saw Antonia Delvecchio's and Sandy Rodefeffer's names were on it, but Mandy Wilson's name was not.

"Where would your sister get the idea that one of these letters had something to do with Mandy?"

Sadie looked very uncomfortable and her face flushed.

"Tell it all, hon," George said. "Clear your conscience."

"I held one of them up to the light," she said. "I saw Mandy's name written inside."

"Which one?"

"The one to Ed Harrison."

Sadie was near tears, and Scott was torn between reassuring her and scaring the hell out of her. George saved him the trouble.

"You've learned your lesson, now, haven't you?" George said. "That's how it started with Margie, probably, just a peek inside the mail out of curiosity, and before she knew it, she was blackmailing people and airing their dirty laundry."

"I would never do that!" Sadie cried.

"I think you'll be more careful in the future," Scott said.

"You can count on it," George said.

"Alright," Sadie said, dabbing her eyes with a dish towel. "You two can quit being so hard on me now."

George scooted his chair over so he could hug his wife, and Scott got up to leave.

"Is there anything else you know related to Margie that might help me find out who murdered her?" Scott asked them.

"No," Sandy said. "I've told you everything."

"If you remember anything else about those letters, please let me know," Scott said. "I won't get you in trouble for helping me."

"I will, Scott, I promise," Sadie said.

"We've all heard the gossip about Margie's mail tampering and taking money from Enid," George said. "Everybody knows the only reason Margie wasn't in jail was because you knew the shame of it would kill her poor mother. You did the right thing."

"If she'd gone to jail, at least she'd be alive," Scott said.

Scott left their house wondering, 'where in the hell is Ed and why didn't he mention his letter?'

Scott found Ed in the newspaper office working on his website. When Scott told him about the letters, Ed seemed perplexed.

"I haven't received anything in the mail from Margie," he said. "I pick up the mail every morning, and there was no mysterious letter any day this week."

"You've opened everything, then?"

Ed reached over and picked up a stack of envelopes and papers from his inbox, and carefully went through each one.

"Nothing."

"Mandy didn't tell me what it was Margie had on her," Scott said. "Has she confided anything in you?"

"She told me her husband got killed for agreeing to testify against a drug dealer, and how she drove Tommy up here looking for an aunt in Pennsylvania who it turned out died. Tommy was just a baby then, and she didn't have any other family. Her car broke down on the highway north of here, and Curtis towed it to Rose Hill. He felt sorry for her, and the Fitzpatricks pretty much adopted her; gave her a job and a place to live. Nothing she could be blackmailed over."

"These letters are all pretty vicious," Scott said. "I wonder what happened to yours."

"I didn't get it," Ed said. "You believe me, don't you?"

"Of course I do," Scott said. "If you find it, though, give me a call. I don't have to know what's in it; I would just like to tie up any loose ends."

"Who do you think killed her?"

"I think it was someone she was blackmailing. So far the letters just seem like hateful acts to upset people she wanted to punish. I think the killer was someone who could afford to pay, and the drop-off site was somewhere in the alley behind the tire store. Margie was expecting a big payoff, enough to fly to Hawaii and start a new life. I think Margie showed up to get the loot, the blackmail victim killed her, and then rolled her over the hill. I just wish I knew where she was keeping her stash of blackmail. We've been all over her house with a fine tooth comb, and there's nothing there."

"Could she have kept it stashed at the post office somewhere? In the ceiling or something?"

"I hadn't thought of that. The only problem with that theory is they had the locks changed after she quit, so she wouldn't have been able to get back in to retrieve any of it."

"Maybe the threat was enough. Maybe she didn't have to have anything to back it up as long as she knew there was something to the rumor."

"It's worth a shot. I'll get the key from Sadie and go have a look."

But there was nothing hidden above the tiles in the drop ceiling at the post office but spiders and dust.

By noon, Hannah and Maggie were ensconced in the bakery caravan, huddled around the heater. The snow was flying, and the wind was sharp.

"I hope the next six hours go by fast," Hannah said miserably.

By two o'clock, the field was packed with tourists and locals. They were playing games, competing in contests, and most importantly, spending money at the many caravans. Hannah and Maggie took turns watching the dog sled race out the back door. Instead of the dog pulling the sled, each contestant pulled a sled with a dog sitting on it, and the winner was the one who crossed the finish line first with a dog still sitting on the sled. Contestants were not allowed to secure the dogs to their sleds in any way, so many loose dogs were running around, chased by sled pullers.

"I think I recognize some of Theo's dogs," Maggie said to Hannah.

"I got them all placed in homes except the two beagle brothers."

"I'll tell you a secret, but you can't tell her I told you," Maggie said. "My mother has a real soft spot for beagles."

"You don't say."

"Bonnie says there is nothing cuter than a beagle pup."

"Thank you very much," Hannah said.

"How are we going to find out what Connie was doing in 1984?" Maggie asked.

"We need to ask some people who knew her then," Hannah said.

"Maybe we'll find something in Margie's house," Maggie said. "She had to keep her blackmail stuff somewhere."

It being Sunday, the Rose and Thorn caravan was closed out of respect for the local churches. Patrick and Sean were busy ferrying everything back to the Rose and Thorn in Patrick's truck. They delivered baked goods and change to Maggie and Hannah most of the afternoon while keeping an eye out for red-headed pirates.

Scott showed up at closing time and helped them break down the bakery caravan contents and drive everything back to the bakery. While Patrick drove his truck, Scott walked with Maggie.

"I stayed all night at Ava's last night, on the couch," he told her, as soon as they were alone. "I hope you don't mind."

"I already heard about it. That was nice of you."

"I've been running all over town today, and I didn't have a chance to call you."

"It's okay," Maggie said. "I'm not worried about you and Ava."

"That's good."

"Thanks for coming to help us clean up."

"No problem. Listen, I need to talk to you later," he said.

"What about?"

"Margie was blackmailing some people."

"So I hear."

"I have some things I need to check out first, but I have an interesting list to show you, and I want to run some scenarios by you."

"Sure," she said, and then remembered she and Hannah were going to snoop at the Estep's house. "I have lots to do this evening, but I should be at home by ten, why don't you come by?"

Scott grinned and waggled his eyebrows.

"Can I stay 'til breakfast?"

"Only if you want to share the couch with Sean," she said.

"He does have a good job," Scott said, "and a nice car."

Maggie bumped him with the box she was carrying.

"Don't switch teams on me now. I'm just getting used to the idea of you in my bed."

"Careful, now. If you keep talking like that, I'll take it as encouragement," he said.

"Then I'll stop," she said, but she was smiling.

Scott spent the afternoon following up on the twelve names on Sadie's list. Eight of the letters had been accounted for. The recipients he was able to speak to were appalled to realize Scott knew about the letters but quickly understood there was nothing to be gained by denying any knowledge of them. Ed's letter was still unaccounted for, so that left three letters.

After he parted with Maggie, Scott drove up Pine Mountain Road toward the state park and then out Rabbit's Fork Road to the home of Lieutenant Colonel Harlan "Mean" Mann, who worked for District One of the State Division of Natural Resources Law Enforcement Section. The locals just called him "the game warden," but not within his hearing. Scott was all for the protection of wildlife and the conservation of natural resources, but Mean seemed to take a special delight in torturing the lawbreakers he caught before he arrested them. Scott was dreading the prospect of finding out Mean had received a letter telling him Cal Fischer had been hunting out of season.

Scott found Mean cutting firewood out behind the modest A-Frame log home he lived in.

"What in the hell brings you out to this neck of the woods?" Mean asked Scott by way of greeting. "I figured you'd have your hands full over there in Thornytown. I heard that witch in the post office got herself killed."

"Hey Mean," Scott said. "You get any anonymous letters this past week?"

Mean narrowed his eyes and leaned on the handle of his ax, the blade of which was embedded in a thick log.

"I did," he said. "How'd you know about that?"

"Seems Margie sent some hate mail before she died," Scott said. "What did yours say?"

"Couldn't tell you," Mean said. "Somebody sends me a letter with a typewritten address and no return address, and it gets tossed directly on the fire. No telling what kind of terrorist nonsense might be inside."

"You get a lot of death threats, Mean?"

"I get my share," he said. "I've had my mailbox shot through more'n once, and someone set fire to my porch just before Christmas."

"Did the sheriff look into it?"

"The sheriff would be hard pressed to find someone who didn't want me dead," Mean said. "I take my job seriously even though most of the people in these parts don't think the laws apply to them. The sheriff sent that little gal out here to ask around, but nobody's gonna tell her nothin'. She's a pretty little gal that one is. I wouldn't mind to take her out back and..."

"Anyway," Scott interrupted, "that's all I was interested in knowing. Thanks for your help."

"You tell that Malcolm Behr I said he could kiss my ass," Mean said as Scott walked away. "He thinks I don't know he shot a deer out his bathroom window last month, but I got people tell me things. I ever catch him red-handed he'll go to jail."

"I don't know anything about that," Scott said and waved as he left.

Scott's next stop was the Roadhouse, where Phyllis Davis was living out back in one of a string of small, shabby rooms they rented out. She was so drunk that she could barely stand, but was sober enough to tell Scott she hadn't picked up her mail in Rose Hill in almost a month.

"Did I win the lottery or somethin?" she asked him.

"No, I just think you might have received someone else's mail by mistake," he said.

"You wanna stay and party with me?" she asked him.

Her eyes were straining to focus, and Scott imagined she was seeing more than one of him in the doorway. The room smelled like cigarette smoke and rotten food. Scott could see an unmade bed and a blaring TV in the background behind her.

"No, thanks anyway," Scott said.

Sadie was aggravated to see Scott and refused to open Phyllis's post office box without a search warrant.

"I can't do it," she said. "It's against the law."

"I'll be back tomorrow with a search warrant," he told her. "Just don't let Phyllis have her mail until I get there."

"I can't do that either, and you know it," Sadie said. "Is this some kind of test?"

"No," Scott said. "I'm sorry I asked. I'll see you tomorrow."

Scott parked in front of the Eldridge Inn and walked up to the entrance. It was a grand looking Edwardian mansion built to complement the style of the college president's former home, now Gwyneth's, which was next door. Scott rang the bell, and innkeeper Connie Fenton answered. Her face was drawn and pale, and when she saw Scott, she immediately said, "Why are you here?" in a very unwelcoming tone.

"I need to ask you about a letter you may have received last week," Scott said.

Connie's face flushed and she stepped outside, pulling the entry door shut behind her.

"How do you know about that?" she asked.

"Margie sent letters to several people, and your name was on a list. Can I see your letter?"

"I've misplaced it," she said. "I've looked everywhere for it, but I can't find it."

"What did it say?"

"Gossip," Connie said, "filthy gossip that no one would believe. I certainly wasn't worried by it."

"Would you care to share that gossip with me?"

"Certainly not," Connie said. "I don't traffic in filth, and I wouldn't lower myself to repeat it."

"Margie has been murdered," Scott said. "Your letter may give me a lead on her killer."

"Well, I didn't do it," Connie said. "When did it happen?"

"Monday night."

"Well, then," Connie said. "It couldn't have been me. I took Lily home from the Winter Festival committee meeting, and my car got stuck in her driveway. Curtis couldn't tow it out until the next morning, so I stayed all night out there. Ask her, she'll tell you."

"Thanks, Connie. I'm sorry to have to bother you."

Connie slammed the inn door as she went back inside, and Scott walked back to the squad car with a weird feeling about their conversation. After thinking about it for a few minutes, it occurred to him that Connie's reaction was odd. Instead of protesting that she couldn't possibly kill anyone, she seemed more eager to establish an alibi for the time of the murder. With a sigh over a day that seemed like it would never end, Scott headed out to Lily Crawford's farm to check Connie's alibi.

At 8:15 p.m. Hannah and Maggie were in Margie Estep's attic bedroom, having gone over every inch of the house without finding anything.

"This is discouraging," Hannah said.

"If she was blackmailing someone," Maggie said, "she had to hide the goods somewhere."

They pulled out every piece of furniture, but there were no doors into the crawlspace under the eaves of the attic.

"That seems odd," Hannah said.

"What?"

"We have an attic room at our house, and so do your parents, don't they?"

"Yeah, so?"

"We keep all kinds of junk under the eaves, and there is a little door to get in there," Hannah said. "It's the same at the Rose and Thorn. We keep the extra paper goods up there."

"So there should be an access door here somewhere," Maggie said.

"But there isn't."

"Maybe they just didn't put one in."

"Maybe Margie hid it."

They went from one corner of the low wall to the next, all around the small room, examining the paneling that covered the wall, picking at the seams. Every panel appeared to be securely nailed to a two-by-four stud behind it until they got to the panel behind the chest of drawers. There were no nail heads in the paneling. Hannah helped Maggie pull the dresser further out, and Maggie found the seam where one piece of paneling met the next piece exactly. To the naked eye and touch, it looked and felt almost seamless. When Maggie hooked a fingernail behind it and pulled, however, she discovered the whole panel was held in place with hook-and-loop tape attached to both the panel and the two-by-four studs behind it. When Maggie gave it a firm tug, the whole piece came away from the wall with a scratchy ripping sound, and there was a dark space behind it.

Maggie felt the hairs rise on her arms.

"This is creeping me out," Hannah said.

Maggie and Hannah pushed the chest of drawers completely out of away so the ceiling light would shine into the room.

"I see stuff in there," Hannah said.

Maggie brought a lamp over from Margie's bedside table and plugged it into the nearest outlet so they could see inside the crawlspace.

"Bingo," Hannah said.

With the light from the lamp she was holding, Maggie could see another lamp sitting just inside the crawlspace. She crawled in and turned it on, illuminating the area.

Hannah crawled in behind her, and they both sat cross-legged in the small space.

"Jiminy Christmas," Hannah said.

The crawlspace was filled almost completely with stacks and stacks of envelopes, periodicals, and packages.

"This is twenty years' worth of stolen mail," Maggie said.

"There doesn't seem to be any organization," Hannah said, looking at a few envelopes nearby. "The dates and names are all different, and they're just stuffed in here any old way."

"We're not going to be able to get through all this tonight."

Just then Maggie heard someone coming up the pull-down stairs to the attic and looked frantically at Hannah, but her cousin was paralyzed with fear. There was nothing they could do, and no way to hide. The footsteps crossed the room, and both women held their breath, eyes wide. Maggie's heart was pounding so hard she was sure whoever it was could hear it.

"I guess if I wait long enough in any murder investigation, you girls will do all the hard work for me," Scott said as he stooped down at the entrance to the crawlspace.

"Oh, thank God," Hannah said.

"Sarah's not with you, is she?" Maggie asked him.

"No, lucky for you, it's just me," Scott said.

He looked all around the crawlspace and whistled low.

"I should be embarrassed I didn't find this first," he said. "But then Sarah doesn't have to know I didn't."

"You're not mad?" Maggie asked him.

"What's the point?" Scott said. "I'll just have to remind myself in the future to keep a closer eye on you two every time someone's murdered. You're better than a pair of bloodhounds."

Hannah crawled out past Scott, not trusting this sanguine attitude to last.

"I think I hear my mother calling," she said and was quickly gone.

Maggie was still not convinced Scott wouldn't haul her to jail just to make some point. He was looking all around at the stacks and stacks of envelopes, padded mailers, and boxes of every size.

"I'll have to get Skip and Frank down here to take all this to the station," he said. "It's going to take days to go through it all."

"Will you return it to the intended recipients?"

"It's all potential evidence right now," he said. "I'm not going to think any farther ahead than that."

Scott backed out of the crawlspace, stood up, and offered Maggie a hand up as she crawled out. He pulled her to her feet, wrapped his arms around her, and kissed her soundly for a long while.

When Maggie finally wriggled loose, she felt dizzy and disoriented.

"What's wrong, Maggie," he asked her, grinning.

"We shouldn't do this here," she said a little hoarsely, heading for the ladder steps.

Scott just laughed.

"Chicken," he called after her, and then followed her down.

Ed and Tommy were playing Scrabble while Mandy put three frozen TV dinners in the oven and then set the table. Ed was beating Tommy, but the young boy was quickly getting the hang of the game.

"Hey," Mandy said. "Mr. Barrett met our new neighbor today."

"An old lady and a baby," Tommy said.

"No," Mandy said. "It's a man. Mr. Barrett said he helped him shovel out all the walkways this morning after he got home from workin' the night shift at the power plant. Mr. Barrett said he was real friendly."

"Mr. Barrett works at the power plant, or the new neighbor works there?" Ed asked.

"Mr. Barrett does. I don't know where the new guy works. He didn't say."

"He's staying in Phyllis's trailer?"

"Yeah, he said he's renting it."

"What color hair does he have?"

"What?" Mandy asked him. "Why?"

"Did he have long red curly hair and a beard? An earring?"

"I don't know; he didn't say. What're you talkin' 'bout?"

Ed told Tommy and Mandy about the man that tried to take Timmy.

"I couldn't stand that Brian," Mandy said. "He was always flirtin' with me in a way that made me feel like I needed a shower afterward."

"He might have come back to try and get that money Theo left Ava."

"Well, that's just awful," Mandy said. "What's Scott doin' about it?"

"Looking for him, of course," Ed said. "But he's got a lot on his plate just now."

"Bonnie never mentioned it."

"I don't think she knows."

"Well, somebody better tell her before she hears it through the grapevine, or there'll be hell to pay."

When Maggie got to her parents' house, she walked right into the middle of her mother giving Patrick a verbal spanking for not telling her about the "pirate" who approached Timmy.

"I had to hear it from a customer, Patrick, a customer! Do you know how stupid that made me look? My own grandson."

"I'm sorry, Ma," Patrick said.

"And you!" Bonnie said, pointing to Maggie, who stood frozen in the doorway. "You had all day to tell me about it, so what's your excuse?"

"I thought it was probably Brian, and I didn't want to tell you."

Her mother's mouth was open, ready to reject whatever excuse Maggie offered, but she hadn't expected that one.

"What?" she said in a whisper.

Patrick groaned.

Maggie's father had tuned out early in the argument, but now he was back in.

"What's this about Brian?"

"Timmy said the man had long red curly hair, and whoever broke in the bakery must have had a key, so I thought it might be Brian."

Maggie waited for one or both of her parents to bless her out, but it didn't happen. Bonnie sank down into a chair by the door to the kitchen and Fitz turned as far as he could in his recliner to look at Patrick.

"Son," he said, "do you think it could be Brian doing these things?"

"Curtis and Ian are keeping it quiet, but someone got in both the bar and the gas station last night and took some money," Patrick said. "Whoever it was used a key at both places."

"It's not true," said Bonnie, looking from Patrick to Maggie. "Why wouldn't he come home if he needed money? Why wouldn't he come to us in the daylight and ask us for help? He's our son, not some common criminal. He may have done wrong by Ava and the children, but I'm his mother. Why wouldn't he come to me if he needed something? No, it was someone else."

"Who else has keys to every Fitzpatrick family business?" Patrick asked the room.

"One of Curtis's boys then," Fitz protested. "Why does it have to be one of mine?"

"Red curly hair," Maggie said. "The man who approached Timmy had red curly hair."

"Those two things may not even be connected," Bonnie protested.

Everyone started talking at once, and no one was listening to anyone.

Maggie noticed Grandpa Tim was trying to say something, but everyone was talking over him.

Maggie went over and bent down next to him.

"What is it, Grandpa?"

Grandpa Tim's voice was little more than a hoarse whisper, ravaged as it was by emphysema and throat cancer. He could barely speak, but Maggie understood what he was saying.

"Shut up everybody," she said. "Grandpa Tim says Brian was here."

Everyone immediately stopped talking and listened carefully as Grandpa Tim struggled to get the words out.

"He was here," he said, in a hoarse whisper. "In the night."

Bonnie jumped up and began pacing and praying, "Oh my Heavenly Father, oh my Holy Mother, oh my Lord in Heaven..."

Fitz grumbled that the old man was probably dreaming.

Patrick and Maggie exchanged looks. Patrick put his arm around his mother and coaxed her into the kitchen. Maggie kissed Grandpa Tim and held his hands in hers.

"Did he have long curly hair?" she asked.

195

He nodded.

"Did he ask you for money?"

He nodded.

"Did he take anything else?"

Grandpa Tim gestured toward the kitchen, and Maggie felt sick at her stomach. She thanked him again and slipped into the kitchen, around Bonnie and Patrick, who were sitting at the kitchen table. Bonnie was crying into a tea towel, and a scowling Patrick had his arm around her. He watched Maggie remove the cookie jar from the top of the Hoosier cabinet as quietly as she could. She looked in, and just as she feared, it was empty. Patrick saw the look on her face and understood, nodded.

Maggie pointed to their mother and mouthed, "Should I tell her?"

Patrick shook his head and mouthed, "No way."

Maggie let herself out the back door and ran up to the next block, to her Aunt Delia's and Uncle Ian's house on Iris Avenue. Delia was folding laundry in the kitchen when Maggie knocked on the back door. She made some tea while Maggie told her what happened.

"How much money was in there?" Delia asked.

"I'm not sure. She's been saving for that trip for years."

"Your mother's been saving for a trip since Ian took me to Philadelphia to see Tony Bennett five years ago," Delia said. "Sometimes she says it's to see Tom Jones in Las Vegas, and sometimes she says it's for a trip to the Holy Lands. It was the money she earned making wedding cakes, and she only makes, what, four or five of those per year? She charges a hundred dollars for them."

"So she may have had twenty-five-hundred dollars in there."

"Do you think I should go over?"

"I don't know," Maggie said. "It would either be the perfect thing to do or the worst thing, and either way it will be my fault if anyone else knows about it."

"Well, whatever I can do to help, you know I'm glad to."

"Here I am carrying on about a couple thousand, and he probably cleaned you guys out of much more."

"We put a deposit in the bank last night on account of it was so much money. All he got was the base fund in the till."

"And at the station?"

"I don't know. Curtis isn't saying."

"Will you check on Mom later? You could just happen to drop by..."

"Sure, sweetie."

"I've thought of something else," Maggie said, "but I'm afraid to say it to anyone but you."

"What's that?"

"What if Brian killed Margie?"

"But why would he?"

"Maybe Margie knew something about him we don't know. Maybe she saw him first and threatened to tell someone."

"What I don't understand is why he's hiding if he's here."

Maggie didn't feel like airing the rest of her family's dirty laundry where Brian was concerned.

"I think he may be in trouble for something else he did somewhere else and is hiding here," was all she said.

"Your brother Brian was always too clever for his own good. If he had used that brain for good purposes, he could have done as well as Sean."

"I bet Sean is sorry I convinced him to come back this weekend."

Delia hugged Maggie and kissed her forehead.

"You're a good girl, Mary Margaret," she said. "I know your mother doesn't often say it, but she thinks it."

Maggie felt tears fill her eyes and she blinked them away.

"I've got to get back to Sean," she said. "He'll be wondering where I am."

"When is he going back?"

"Early tomorrow morning."

"It was a blessing he came back this weekend," Delia said. "That will help Bonnie and Fitz deal with the other."

A Greyhound bus pulled in the parking lot outside the Dairy Chef, and when the doors wheezed open, a group of men dressed in orange robes and sandals got off. Caroline ran up to meet them and bowed to each one in turn. She directed them to the church van, which was waiting with the engine running in the parking lot, and the monks filed on in an orderly fashion. A harried-looking woman followed them off the bus and started ferrying their luggage from where the bus driver was unloading it over to the van.

"You must be Rachel," Caroline said. "It's such an honor to meet you."

Drew and Caroline rushed to help her carry all the suitcases, duffel bags, and boxes tied with twine.

"Well, it's hi and goodbye, I'm afraid," the woman said when they were done, with an odd smile on her face. "You'll have to cope from here."

"What do you mean?" Caroline said. "I thought you and your husband were going to come with them and see to everything. You said on the phone..."

"My plans have changed," Rachel said, handing Caroline the last two bags. "My husband has been very accommodating of my devotion to the order, but he has a good job in California and isn't leaving it to live in this, well, to live here."

"But doesn't he understand what an honor it is to enable these monks to do their work?"

"My husband is a very good man, and he loves me very much," Rachel said. "But he's not about to leave a good job with health benefits and a 401K to wait hand and foot on a bunch of monks in the middle of nowhere, for no money. He paid for their travel to get here, but now we're done."

"But who will look after them?" Caroline asked.

"I guess you will," Rachel said as she jogged back toward the bus.

"Wait!" Caroline yelled, running after her. "I don't know how to look after them. What do I do?"

Rachel stopped at the door to the bus, pulled a folded piece of paper out of her purse and handed it to Caroline.

"I almost forgot to give this to you," she said. "This is their schedule and a list of some things that might be helpful to you. They're vegans, and they don't prepare food, serve food, or clean up after food is served. They don't buy things or handle money. They don't drive or operate machinery of any kind. They don't do laundry, make beds or clean bathrooms. It's considered an insult to show them the bottom of your feet, so don't cross your legs in front of them. They get up at four in the morning and go to bed at nine at night, and it's mostly meditation, chanting, and Dhamma instruction in between. They don't talk unless it's in class or absolutely necessary and you shouldn't touch them. The altar stuff is in the big blue bag, but Bhante Sujiva will set that up. If you have any other questions, call me. My number's on there."

"Wait! What if I pay you and your husband? I'm rich; I can do that."

"The truth is, I'm worn out," Rachel said. "I'm going to go home, sleep for a week, and then my husband and I are going on a real vacation, one in a hotel with room service. Good luck."

Having said all that she got back on the bus, the doors closed, and the bus pulled away from the Dairy Chef parking lot. Caroline walked back to the church van, where Drew was stowing baggage anywhere there was room. All the monks were sitting quietly, looking at Caroline expectantly. Caroline bowed, and they all bowed back.

"We're going out to Pine Lodge, which is your new home," she said, not knowing how many of the monks spoke English. "You'll have to forgive me if I do or say something that is incorrect. I expected Rachel to be here to help me learn all this, but I guess she's going home."

Drew looked at her in a kind of panic.

"What are you going to do?" he whispered.

Caroline raised her head high, determined to show him she was in full control of the situation and knew exactly what she was doing.

"We'll get you settled in tonight, and tomorrow I will make everything perfect for you, so your meditation work will not be interrupted."

Elbie, the church van driver, who had volunteered his services to take the monks up the mountain, looked at Caroline as if she was crazy. Caroline sat down in the seat behind him, next to Drew, and took a deep breath.

"Let's go," she said.

"I'll turn the heat up for ya," Elbie called back to the monks, and then in a quieter aside to Caroline, said, "The first thing you better do is get 'em all some thermal underwear and wool socks. The wind up on Pine Mountain will shoot right up them dresses."

Hannah stood in the darkened kitchen of the farmhouse she shared with Sam, looking out the window at the snow falling, and let the tears roll down her face. Sam was in his office, ostensibly working, but more likely avoiding her. Her crying upset him and made him cross, so she had to hide to get it done.

Jax and Wally were lying on the floor at her feet, providing what dogs give so selflessly: patience, loyalty, and love. When she and Sam fought, the dogs stuck to her like glue and barked and growled if he raised his voice. When Sam was in a dark place, like the pit he seemed to be falling back into right now, they would not make eye contact with him, and made it obvious they were guarding Hannah. It validated her belief that her husband was, in fact, a different person when he was depressed, and the dogs recognized this, but it saddened her that the comfort of dogs was denied to him because of it.

Hannah realized that what she was feeling, beyond shock at finding Margie's body, or anger that Sam could not be as emotionally strong as she wanted him to be, was fear. Fear that she might not be able to stay with Sam, even though she loved him. She would never admit it to anyone, but she was a little afraid of her brilliant, handsome, charming husband. Afraid of the person he became when he was in that dark place, and afraid each time he went there that he would not be able to find his way back, and be her best friend again.

She felt so lonely and vulnerable right now; she wanted to put Jax and Wally in the truck and drive away. She considered it, thinking it might lift this huge weight that seemed to be pressing down on her, making her want to do something, anything, to relieve the pressure. There were the prisoners out in the kennel to think of, though. She couldn't abandon them. The beagle brothers still needed a home, and when Sam was down, he couldn't be counted on to take care of anyone or anything, not even himself.

"If I were a better Catholic," she told the dogs, "I would go see Father Stephen."

She thought she knew what the priest would advise her to do about Sam. It would be some version of what the dogs provided to her: patience, loyalty, and love. All those things she promised in the church at the wedding, including, "in sickness and in health."

"Even when it sucks to be married," she told the dogs. "That's what they should make you say."

Hannah splashed water on her tear-stained face and dried it with a dishtowel.

"I need help," she said quietly. "I don't think I can do this on my own."

A thought popped into her head, one that she would have made fun of if anyone had dared suggest she try it. It was something their Aunt Delia often said, and when she did Hannah would always roll her eyes at Maggie. Hannah was desperate, though, at her wits' end, to the point where letting go and letting something bigger than herself sort it all out for her sounded like the perfect plan. At least then maybe she could get some sleep.

"All right, big guy," she said to the ceiling, "do your stuff."

The dogs looked up at the ceiling, and then at Hannah.

"C'mon boys," she said to the dogs, who jumped up immediately, and waited to hear the next command. "Let's go to bed."

Ava Fitzpatrick was also spending time at the window watching the snow come down. She kept hearing things in the house, and although she knew it was just her guests moving around, getting up and going to the bathroom, making the floorboards creak, she was afraid to close her eyes and go to sleep, for fear that Brian would sneak in somehow and kidnap their children.

Sonny had changed the locks, and Scott's team was patrolling the town, making sure to circle the bed and breakfast often. What she wanted, what would make her feel safe, was to have Patrick or Scott in the house. She couldn't have Patrick and didn't feel right imposing on Scott again, so instead, she woke up both of her children and told them they could sleep with her. Drowsily, they made their way to her bedroom and got in her bed. After she locked the door and wedged a chair under the knob, they all snuggled down together. The children went back to sleep quickly. Ava did not close her eyes until much later.

Scott helped his deputies with the removal of all the purloined mail from the attic space in Enid Estep's house to the break room at the station. He, Frank, and Skip put everything in file boxes, and those boxes, stacked six high in multiple rows filled the small room, so it felt more like Diedre and Matt Delvecchio's kitchen. By the time they finished it was past midnight, so he sent the deputies home and then locked the station door behind them. There was a doorbell on the outside if anyone needed anything. He made some coffee and sat down at the break room table with the first box. It was going to be a long night.

Lily Crawford was wakened in the middle of the night by her basset hound Betty Lou howling, and what sounded like a catfight outside. She jumped out of bed, pulled on her robe, and stuffed her feet into slippers before hurrying downstairs. At the foot of the stairs, she paused to listen. Betty Lou seemed to be down at the barn, and the cats, wherever they were, were yowling and carrying on nearby. Lily went to Simon's study, unlocked the gun safe, pulled out a double-barreled shotgun, and loaded it.

She found a flashlight, draped Betty Lou's leash around her neck, and left the house with the shotgun broken down over the crook of her arm. The snow was flying so thick she couldn't see very far ahead, and she kept walking off the stone path she couldn't see beneath her feet. When Lily reached the barn, she found Betty Lou howling at the heavy barn door, which someone had unlatched and left open just a few inches. The yowling catfight seemed to be taking place in the barn, and she could hear Penny the pony snorting and moving around in agitation.

Lily pointed the flashlight into the barn through the narrow opening and saw Penny was out of her stall, which she also kept latched. Her flashlight reflected off many pairs of cat eyes, and then a pair of human ones. The hair stood up on the back of Lily's neck, and she backed up. Betty Lou was howling and pawing at the door, but it was too heavy for her to move. Lily snapped the shotgun into one solid piece and cocked it, which made a sound no human being could mistake for anything else.

"You listen to me," Lily called out, although her voice shook. "Whoever you are, you have five minutes to get the hell out of my barn and down the road before the police get here. I have a loaded shotgun in my hands, and I'm a pretty fair shot, so don't tempt me."

She had a sudden thought, and added, "Brian, if that's you, you better get out of town, son, before Mrs. Wells finds you."

Lily used one hand to hook Betty Lou's leash to her collar and pulled the protesting dog back to the porch of the farmhouse. Once inside her kitchen, Lily released the dog but confined her to that room. She took the shotgun back to the study and looked out the window, toward the barn. The snow had lightened up a bit, and a spotlight on a pole by the driveway shone on the figure who left the barn, closed the door behind him, and walked quickly down the drive away from the farm.

Lily considered calling the police but was conflicted. If it was Brian, and they arrested him, he could tell the police things that would hurt her, and she could lose everything. She couldn't call Mrs. Wells; that would be just as bad as shooting him herself. Instead, she made her way back down to the barn, shotgun in hand, to check that Penny was okay. Betty Lou howled from inside the kitchen, furious at being left behind.

One of the milk house heaters had fallen over, so it had automatically shut off. Lily righted it, reset it, and turned it back on. Someone had gone through the cabinets as well, leaving all the doors open and a mess on the floor. Lily lay the shotgun down on the workbench and went to work cleaning up the mess. Penny shuffled over and nuzzled her pocket, looking for a carrot or apple. Lily rubbed the pony's velvety muzzle and apologized for the intrusion. She gave Penny a cup of pony chow, drizzled some thick molasses over it, and the shaggy pony happily munched away. She put some cat food out on the workbench for the barn cats, and while the others stayed hidden, Betty Lou's little kitten came out and greedily began to eat, purring deep in its throat as it did so. The small kitten had something snagged on its claw, and Lily recognized some long red curly hairs.

"Snicklefritz," Lily said to the kitten, "I have revised my opinion of you. You are better than a security system."

Lily imagined Brian had some deep scratches to show for his poor judgment in trying to bed down in her warm barn.

'Or maybe he was looking for something,' she thought.

She shone the flashlight at the trapdoor at the top of the ladder that led to the loft, but it was still fastened with a padlock on a strong metal clasp. That was a relief, at least. She hated to think what Brian would have done with what was up there.

Lily knew she could no longer ignore the events that were taking place in Rose Hill, or pretend they had nothing to do with her. She would have to make some difficult decisions, and soon. The lives of the people she cared most about were at risk, and old secrets were being revealed. It was just a matter of time before a trail of blood led right back to her door.

Chapter Eight - Monday

When Scott first surveyed the mountain of stolen mail cluttering the break room, he wondered how even to begin to examine it all. He felt sure the key to Margie's disappearance was in there somewhere. He put aside the magazines and boxes of mail-order merchandise and decided to concentrate only on looking in envelopes that Margie had already opened. He put on some latex gloves, took a long sip of hot coffee, and began.

At 3:30 in the morning, a third of the way through his examination of Margie Estep's stash of stolen mail, Scott found what would have been a very powerful motive for blackmail and murder. They were the kind of photos that would send a person to jail for a very long time; the same kind of photos Margie had used to ruin Willy Neff's life a few years previously.

The envelope they were in was newer and plain, with no writing or postmark of any kind on the outside. Scott wondered if the original envelope, with the original recipient's name and address, had been used to threaten the perpetrator, with the photos kept in reserve as a kind of insurance. There was no proof that any of this had happened, of course, but it was the kind of thing Scott was looking for. He carefully sealed the envelope of photographs in a plastic bag, put them in the station safe, and kept going.

At 4:30 he made another pot of coffee, and took a headache pill. Throughout the night Scott read many letters and learned many things about the citizens of Rose Hill that he immediately wished he hadn't. His list of potential suspects just got longer, and the growing stack of evidence shattered any illusions he may have had about what a quiet, peaceful town Rose Hill was. He finally had to designate a whole box for potential suspects, and everything that was potential blackmail fodder went into it.

At 5:30 in the morning Scott found a letter addressed to Maggie Fitzpatrick from her ex-boyfriend Gabe, postmarked a few months after he'd left her, almost seven years previously. This was a letter she had obviously never received. He sat holding it for a few minutes, deliberating whether to read it or not. He imagined handing it to Maggie, not knowing if its contents would blow apart all hope he had of a relationship with her. He stared at it until his vision blurred, and he felt additional twinges in his head. Finally, he tucked it into the interior pocket of his jacket and went back to sorting. He was determined to look at every piece of mail now, not only in case there was more blackmail evidence, but also in case there were any more letters addressed to Maggie.

At 7:45 a.m. Scott looked at the last open envelope in the last box, his head throbbing from both lack of sleep and thinking too hard. He took the file box full of the most incendiary information and locked it in his office. When Skip came into work at 8:00 Scott assigned him the daunting task of sorting and inventorying everything else.

"By the last name of the recipient, I think," Scott told him. "Then anything we need will be easier to find later."

He put on the jacket with Maggie's letter in the pocket and went home. A hot shower helped his head a little, as did the pill he swallowed before setting the alarm clock and falling into bed. Gabe's letter, still tucked inside his jacket, seemed to glow through the fabric, shine through the wall, and burn into his brain, until he wasn't sure if he could sleep with it in the house.

He considered burning it, and wondered if he could live with that decision, just as he'd learned to live with the agonizing decision he made almost seven years ago, the night Gabe left Maggie behind in Rose Hill. It would be so easy to do, would take less than a minute, and then it would no longer be a threat. The only problem was that the thought of destroying the letter felt so wrong it nauseated him.

Scott had come to realize that emotionally, Maggie was stuck in the same place she was seven years ago. Over the intervening years, Maggie may have grown to love Scott a little more and to grieve over Gabe a little less, but he knew she wouldn't be free to begin anything with him until she finally let go of Gabe.

Meanwhile, the truth had been waiting, ticking like a time bomb in the crawl space of Margie Estep's attic bedroom. Only after Maggie knew what happened and then made up her own mind, could Scott know for certain that she would choose him over Gabe. The only problem was she might not forgive him for his part in the events of that night. An envelope-shaped headache followed him into his dreams, where he met his old friend Gabriel, who had a lot to say.

Sean didn't wake his sister before he left her place at 6:00 a.m., but she heard him go. Maggie turned over and covered her head with her pillow, willing herself to sleep a little longer and put off starting the day, but it was too late. Her mind was already running through the list of things she had to do, and a list of things she wanted to think about.

If her brother Brian was in Rose Hill, where was he staying? Who would hide him? Maggie knew Scott had his hands full with Margie's murder investigation so she would have to find Brian herself. If he was stealing from the family and wanted to kidnap the kids, he must be on the run from someone or something. One good thing was, with all the festival tourists gone he would have a harder time hiding, especially with that long red hair and beard.

She also wanted to find out what Connie had done in 1984 that Margie had found out about. If Connie used to be a nurse, it might have had to do with something that happened to someone under her care. She would have to find out where Connie worked, and if anything bad had happened on her watch.

Maggie got up, took a shower, and then sat at the kitchen table, detangling her long red curls while waiting for the kettle to boil. At 7:00 she called downstairs to the bookstore and talked to Benjamin, who was working in the café. He checked the schedule and let her know that all the day's shifts were covered, so she didn't have to come in. Maggie thought her staff would probably be relieved about that. She tended to nitpick and nag when she worked the sales floor even though the staff was perfectly capable of running things without her there to supervise them.

Hannah called at 7:30.

"I'm relieved to find you at home and not in jail," she said.

"He wasn't mad," Maggie said. "I think we're wearing him down."

"We are assets to his law enforcement team," Hannah said. "He should thank us."

"I wouldn't push it," Maggie said.

"What are we doing today?" Hannah asked.

"I was just sitting here making a list. I thought we might visit Enid."

"Good idea. I think she knows more than she's said."

"We have to take Margie's burial clothes to Peg at the funeral home."

"You would dare to wake the undead in the light of day?" Hannah said. "I'll bring my wooden stake."

"Then I thought we might go door to door collecting money for the Humane Society or investigating a lost dog report that you haven't received."

"But what will we be doing?"

"Looking for Brian," Maggie said, "and asking people when they saw Margie last."

"You think the two are connected?"

"We know Brian's been skulking around town at night, and we know Margie was doing a lot of walking around in the dark herself."

"And if Margie saw him, he would know she would tell the whole town."

"So if he's on the run for some reason, and wanted to shut her up..."

"I'll be there in twenty minutes."

Ed Harrison sat in the newspaper office and fiddled around with the website he was building. His grandfather had started the newspaper, and then Ed's father had run it until he died. The Sentinel's subscribers were an aging population, and it was not attracting any younger replacements. As papers all over the country were gobbled up or going under, replaced by tabloids and websites, Ed had begun to feel more and more like a dinosaur pretending the air wasn't turning cooler. He could no longer ignore the events that seemed to be leading to the demise of the business he was raised to believe was essential to daily life, like food and water. He didn't know what he would do if the paper went under.

Ed's mind wandered. He couldn't figure out how he had mislaid the letter from Margie, or who could have picked it up. There were people in and out of the paper office all day every day, and many people had access to his mail; he didn't see any reason to lock it up. Mandy visited the most, probably, but if she didn't know about the letter, she wouldn't be looking for it. He hadn't asked her about it, either. It was none of his business, and their relationship was so new he didn't think he had a right to demand to know all her secrets. He had decided not to worry about what the information was, but he was still concerned as to where it ended up.

He also kept thinking about the man renting Phyllis's trailer, and Tommy seeing an old lady with a baby living there. Abruptly, he decided to go down there and see if he could get someone to answer the door. When he got to the trailer the walk was shoveled clear, so there were no shoe prints visible, and no one answered the door. He decided to check in at the station and let Scott know about the new residents. When Skip informed him Scott was at home, sleeping off a 24-hour shift, Ed decided not to wake him and went to the diner for some breakfast.

Ed took his usual seat at the end of the counter at Davis's Diner near the coffee service station so he could help himself to refills. He could remember watching his father do the same thing for many years and ruminated that he was not only sitting on the same stool but was probably drinking out of the same mug his father once used. He ate the same specials, talked to the same people, and wrote about the same town events that his father had. His father, he reflected, probably never had an affair with a much younger woman who had an adolescent son. After Ed's mother ran off when Ed was still in grade school, Ed's father hadn't wanted anything to do with women, romance, or what he called "foolishness."

The owner's daughter Pauline nodded a greeting to Ed as she waited on a nearby customer, and then gave the order to her husband Phil through the high window to the kitchen. Ed sipped coffee until she brought his usual order.

"How you doin', Ed?" she asked him.

"Just fine, Pauline. Yourself?"

"I'm down but not out, as they say."

"Having trouble finding a new waitress?"

"We aren't even looking. Mom's selling the place."

"Well, I'll be darned. What will you do?"

"We're moving to Florida. Phil's got a brother down there who owns a fishing boat, and we're going in with him. Mom's not getting any younger, and the winters up here are hard on her."

"I don't know what we'll do without you," Ed said.

"Maybe you'd like to buy the diner," Pauline teased him. "You and Mandy could run it."

"No, no, no," Ed protested. "That sounds like too much hard work for me."

"I guess you heard about that Margie."

"Yeah, it's all very strange. She ever give you any trouble?"

"We got a post office box in Pendleton ten years ago on account of her. She once tangled with my mother over something my daughter did, and I guess Gladys tore a strip off her hide. She never bothered us again."

"Gladys is tough as nails, isn't she?"

"Her mother was a single mother back when that was a disgrace to a family," Pauline said. "They both raised me to hold my head up high and not be afraid to spit in anyone's eye. That came in handy with a daughter like Phyllis. And my grandson, may God forgive him."

Her eyes filled with tears and Ed gripped her hand, gave it a squeeze.

"Well, I'm sorry to see you go. You'll be sorely missed."

"If you know anybody who would be interested, let us know."

Pauline went around the counter to wait on some customers. Ed got himself a refill of coffee. He was trying to think of anyone he knew that might be interested in the diner. When Pauline came by he stopped her.

"The Delvecchios may be interested," he said.

"I already talked to Tony," Pauline said. "So they know about it."

"Who is renting Phyllis's trailer?" Ed asked her.

Pauline shrugged.

"Beats me. We don't see much of our daughter since she moved out to the Roadhouse. I hear she's not doing well."

"I'm sorry to hear that."

"I thought when I had a baby girl that she would grow up to be my best friend. Instead, she fought me tooth and nail from the minute she saw daylight. It was like she resented us for having the nerve to bring her to life. She's my daughter, and I love her, but Phil and I are ready to have some kind of life without all her drama and misery."

Ed couldn't think of any appropriate response, so he just shook his head, and said, "I am so sorry."

Pauline had tears in her eyes again as she patted Ed's arm.

"Be glad you don't have any kids," she said. "They just break your heart."

Ava Fitzpatrick finished making out her grocery list, gathered up her purse and coat, and headed to the grocery store. Charlotte and Timmy were in school, under the protection of their teachers and principal, with Frank sitting in a squad car just outside the entrance. Her last B&B guests had checked out, and she was looking forward to a few days with no new guests. Her fridge was bare, so she was going to pick up some basic provisions, plus some special treats for the kids.

Ava slowly pushed her cart through the aisles, picking out anything she fancied. Since she'd received notice of Theo's generous bequest, she had been allowing herself to spend a little more freely than she would have before. It may take a year for the will to go through probate, Sean had told her, but after that, she would have generous quarterly payments to count on, and she was looking forward to it. It felt to Ava that she had been frugal and gone without her entire life, and she was ready to enjoy herself a little more.

Out of the corner of her eye, she was startled by a flash of red hair. She turned quickly and saw that it was only the curly red hair of a baby being carried by an older woman who Ava assumed was its grandmother. Ava was struck by how much the child looked like Timmy at that age, and pushed her cart over to the produce section as if magnetized, to where the woman stood picking through the bananas.

The baby, who could not yet be a year old, had a snotty nose and red eyes and didn't look as if it felt well. The child was fussing a little, and the old woman shushed it. As she got closer, Ava was shocked by the resemblance of this child to her son Timmy. In a dazed, odd moment, Ava felt as if this baby was Timmy, and that this woman had kidnapped him. A sudden panic seized her, her heart was pounding in her chest, and she felt compelled to speak.

"What a beautiful baby," Ava said and smiled as she approached.

The old woman was startled. She quickly turned the baby's face away and covered it with the grimy blanket she had wrapped around it. She said something that sounded as if it was in another language and waved Ava off.

"Are you visiting someone in Rose Hill?" Ava persisted.

The older woman abandoned her grocery basket and hurried to the front of the store. Ava left her cart with her purse in it and ran after the woman. As she neared the checkout counter, just as the woman pushed out the front door, Ava tripped over the edge of a display and fell face first onto the floor, spraining her wrist as she attempted to break her fall. IGA owner Matt Delvecchio vaulted over a stack of soda cases to be the first one to assist her. As soon as Ava got to her feet, she ran outside, but the woman with the baby was gone.

Holding her wrist, with Matt right behind her, Ava ran to the street corner and looked in every direction.

"She couldn't just disappear," Ava said.

"Who are you talking about?" Matt asked her.

"That old woman with the baby."

"I'm sorry," he said. "I didn't see anyone."

Ava went back inside the store, where Matt gave her a bag of frozen peas to hold on her wrist and retrieved her cart and purse.

"Can I just put these on your account and deliver them?" he offered.

Ava, still feeling dazed, thanked him as he hung her handbag over her shoulder.

"You should get that wrist looked at," he said as she left.

Ava stood outside, taking deep breaths of cold air, holding the bag of peas on her painful wrist, and wondered if she was finally cracking up. She hadn't had much sleep the night before, so maybe she was hallucinating. As soon as the street was clear of traffic, she crossed over to the bookstore, looking for Maggie, but Benjamin said she'd gone out with Hannah. Ava left a message for her and then left the bookstore.

Ava's wrist ached and was beginning to swell. She was embarrassed about her behavior in the grocery store and hoped no one who saw it would add that to the gossip about her already circulating around town. She considered calling Patrick but decided not to. It wasn't fair to keep dragging him into her messy life, and she was determined to keep her distance.

"You look lost, Ava," Delia Fitzpatrick said, encountering the young woman as she walked out of the bank.

"I think I may have lost my mind," Ava said.

"You want to talk about it?"

"Do you have a minute?"

"For you, my dear, I always have time."

Back in the kitchen at the Rose Hill Bed and Breakfast, Delia expertly wrapped Ava's wrist in an elastic bandage.

"I think it's just sprained and not broken," Delia said, "but sometimes sprains hurt just as badly. You should keep an ice pack on it, alternating thirty minutes on and thirty off, and keep it elevated. Take something for the pain if it gets bad."

"I forgot you used to be a nurse," Ava said.

"You never forget basic first aid," Delia said. "It came in handy when all the kids were younger. Someone was always falling off a bike or slamming a finger in a car door."

Ava told her about the old woman and the baby in the store.

"Now that I'm thinking back, it seems more like something I imagined," Ava said. "But at the time it seemed to me that the woman had kidnapped Timmy, who was somehow this baby."

"You've been under way too much strain," Delia said. "Maggie filled me in on what's been going on. It's no wonder you're on edge."

Ava blinked back some tears, and Delia busied herself making them some tea.

"There's something I haven't told anyone," Ava said. "I've kept it a secret for so long it feels like a cancer inside me."

"You know I can keep a confidence," Delia said. "I won't judge you."

"I know," Ava said. "You've never let me down."

"It probably isn't as bad as you've made it in your mind," Delia said. "Maybe it won't seem so large a burden after you share it with someone."

"No, it's bad," Ava said. "It's about Theo."

Delia hugged Ava and looked at her with deep sympathy.

"I thought it might be."

Someone was pounding on Scott's front door, but he thought it was part of the dream he was having. In his dream, Gabe was pounding on the door of the house he used to share with Maggie, up Possum Holler. The house was on fire, and although Scott knew that Maggie had got out safely, Gabe thought she was still inside. Scott watched Gabe break down the door and rush inside the burning building, but did nothing to stop him. The house began to collapse, and Scott knew Gabe would be killed, but he just stood by and watched. Scott woke up in a cold sweat, and then realized the pounding was taking place in his waking life. It was his deputy Frank at the front door.

"Eldridge College President Newton Moseby committed suicide in his room at the inn," he said. "He left a letter confessing to Margie's murder."

Scott hurriedly dressed and went with Frank in the cruiser to the Eldridge Inn. The paramedics were still there, along with an ambulance and the fire station rescue vehicle. Connie, the innkeeper, was standing on the front porch, sobbing hysterically, clinging to Lily Crawford. Connie tried to talk to Scott, but she was crying so hard she was incoherent. Scott thought she might be having a nervous breakdown.

"Take her to the kitchen," Scott told Lily, "and call Doc Machalvie. She may need a shot of something to calm down."

Scott made his way through the phalanx of rescue workers to the top of the interior stairs, where Malcolm Behr, the fire chief, stood in the hallway outside one of the rooms. Malcolm was a tall, powerfully built, very hairy man, whom most people just referred to as "Bear."

He shook a baggy with an empty pill bottle in it at Scott.

"Overdose," he said. "Looks like he did it last night."

Scott dreaded looking at the scene but knew he had to. He took a deep breath and went into the room with Malcolm close behind. The president of Eldridge College lay on the bed, with a sheet drawn up over his body and face. One arm was uncovered, extending out beyond the bed, the other lay close at his side.

Malcolm pointed to a laptop computer open on the desk. He tapped the touchpad with the end of his pen, and the screen lit up, revealing what read like a confessional suicide note.

Scott read out loud, "I can't stand the guilt, so I am ending my life. Tell my wife and daughter I love them very much and I am sorry for what I have done."

"That's a suicide note, plain enough," Scott said.

"If this was one of those murder mysteries," Malcolm said, "we'd suspect someone typed that after they killed him."

"We still might. He doesn't say what it is he feels guilty about, though."

"Here," Malcolm said. "Look at this."

Malcolm pointed to a stack of photos in Newton's open briefcase, sitting on the nearby dressing table. The photos were very much like the ones locked up in Scott's safe at the station. There was a piece of paper under them, on which was typed, "$100K in a grocery bag in the barrel behind the tire store at midnight Monday or your crimes will be revealed."

"That barrel is right up the hill from where Margie's body was found. It's at the base of the stairs in the alley just beyond the old tire store," Malcolm said. "That's where your guys found the cloth they think has chloroform on it."

"But is he saying he's sorry for killing Margie or just for having those photos?"

"Both, I'd wager."

"It's not completely clear to me that he is saying he killed Margie," Scott said.

"Well, she blackmailed him, and now she's dead, and he's saying he's sorry, and he's dead."

"I'm just not sure yet," Scott said. "I need to think this through."

"It's an awfully tidy-looking crime scene," Malcolm said. "If it was murder surely there'd be signs of a struggle."

"You sure you didn't want to be a policeman instead of a fireman, Malcolm?"

"I read too many murder mysteries, I know," Malcolm said. "It makes me suspicious of everything and everyone. Drives my wife crazy."

"Anyone call his wife yet?"

"I leave that privilege to you," Malcolm said. "I'm going to take my boys and go."

"Thanks," Scott said.

Scott went downstairs and found Doc Machalvie in the sunroom behind the kitchen, talking to Connie in a calm, soothing tone while he gave her an injection. Scott waited until Connie was resting comfortably on a chaise with Lily nearby and then gestured to Doc that he'd like a word.

He showed Doc the pill bottle in the plastic baggy.

"Do you know anything about these?" he asked.

Doc put on his reading glasses and read the label.

"Anti-anxiety medication," he said. "I don't recognize the doctor's name."

"How many would he need to overdose?"

"With alcohol, two or three, I'd guess. Without alcohol, I'd say probably twice that many. It would depend on what tolerance he had developed. May I see him?"

Scott led the doctor up the stairs to the room, where Doc put on some latex gloves and pulled back the sheet. Scott instinctively turned his head away, and then forced himself to turn back and look.

"Hmmm," Doc said.

"What's that mean?" Scott asked.

"I know this is hard for you to do, son, but look closely at this."

The doctor lifted up the corpse's eyelid to show Scott a red web of broken blood vessels in the eye underneath.

"Is that unusual?" Scott asked him.

"It's unusual in a narcotic overdose," Doc said, "unless there was violent vomiting, which there's no evidence of here. But it's very normal for someone who's been smothered to death."

Scott felt a chill run up his spine.

"You're sure about that," Scott said.

"The coroner will be able to verify it," Doc said, "but it looks very much like someone may have fed him an overdose and then helped him along. Of course, that's just my opinion."

"Jesus," Scott said.

"I am not at liberty to say where and when, but I've seen something like this before."

"I understand," Scott said. "You can't divulge medical information."

"Nothing was proved, you see," Doc said, looking at Scott meaningfully.

"I get it," Scott said.

"I wonder if you do," Doc said, but Scott was no longer listening.

He was debating whether to call Sarah or not, but Sarah saved him the trouble by showing up.

"You want me in on this?" she asked from the doorway.

Scott asked Doc Machalvie to tell Sarah what he had told him. Sarah listened intently and watched as Doc repeated his demonstration with the eyelids, and then looked at Scott.

"I think he's right," she said, "and that means this is now a county case. Do you agree?

Scott felt demoted but resigned.

"By all means," he said. "The most important thing is we find out who did this."

"Where's the innkeeper?" she asked.

"I just sedated her," Doc said.

"Are there any other suspects or witnesses you've put safely to sleep somewhere?" Sarah asked Scott.

Scott felt his face grow hot with embarrassment.

"She was hysterical and making herself ill."

"Maybe because she killed him," Sarah said.

"Well, at least she can't get away now," Doc Machalvie told her. "You can handcuff her to the wicker settee and put armed guards all around her."

Sarah didn't see the humor in the situation. She took out her cell phone, called the county dispatcher, and asked to have her team assembled.

Doc Machalvie excused himself, and Scott helped him up off the floor from where he knelt.

"Good luck," he whispered to Scott as he left. "You know where to find me if you need me."

Scott sat with Lily Crawford on the back steps of the inn, out of Sarah's hearing.

"Could Connie and Newton have been having an affair?" Scott asked her.

"I guess it's possible," Lily said. "Connie is very high strung, and her cat just passed away, so she was already very fragile, emotionally. Newton didn't seem the type, but I guess you never know."

"Hannah said she overheard Connie and him arguing last week."

"Connie and I are friends, but she's very guarded. She doesn't share personal things with me."

"What did she do before she ran the inn?"

"She was a nurse. She took care of Mrs. Eldridge for several years before her death."

"Theo's mother?"

"Yes. After Mrs. Eldridge died, her husband put Connie in charge of the inn as a kind of retirement arrangement. She's guaranteed the job for her lifetime."

"Someone told me Gwyneth treated Connie like a maid while she lived at the inn. I can't remember who that was."

"I wouldn't be surprised. Gwyneth has an oversized sense of entitlement, and would have been used to seeing Connie as a servant in her parents' house."

"And it was Gwyneth who kicked the president and his wife out of their house when Theo died, and she inherited it."

"I believe his wife is in Florida with their daughter."

"That reminds me, I need to contact her."

"I don't envy you that part of your job."

Scott stood up and helped Lily to her feet.

"You always turn up when people need you," Scott said.

"I could say the same for you," she said.

"Yeah, but that's my job."

"I somehow think you'd turn up just the same," Lily said and squeezed his hand before letting go.

After Scott made the call to the deceased's widow, he went back outside to take some deep breaths of cold air. He didn't have to do that sort of thing much, and it never got easier. He said a silent prayer for Newton, his wife Delores, and their daughter. When he went back inside, he looked around the spacious and elegantly appointed front room and foyer, and then walked through the dining room and sitting room of the grand mansion. There was a wall of bookcases on each side of the fireplace in the sitting room, and the shelves were packed with romance novels and murder mysteries. He thought of Malcolm Behr and what he'd said about the suicide being staged to cover up for murder.

Sarah found him there.

"Find out anything from the widow?" she asked.

"She was very upset," Scott said. "She'll be here tomorrow."

"The doctor said Connie would be unconscious until morning, so I'm leaving someone with her."

"What can I do to help?"

"The other guests who are staying here will need to be interviewed, but my team will take care of that. You could go to the college and snoop around his office. Do you know his secretary?"

"I do. Her name's Darlene, and she goes to my church."

"We need to get in there before Darlene cleans up any evidence, and she's more likely to let you in."

"I'm glad to be of service."

"That's good to hear. I was planning to go to Margie's funeral tomorrow. Do you want to go with me? We could get a beer afterward."

"I'm on night shift tomorrow night," Scott said. "I'll be at the funeral, but I need to get back to work after."

"Suit yourself," she said. "Oh, and by the way, congratulations on finding all that loot in Margie's attic. Can't think how we missed that."

"There are some pictures in the station safe a lot like those in Newton's room."

"Even better," she said. "I'll have to watch out, or pretty soon you'll be gunning for my job."

"Don't worry," Scott said. "I'm happy where I am, doing all those jobs that are beneath you."

"I'd love to have you working beneath me," she said, moving into his personal space so that her breast rubbed his arm.

Scott jumped away, and she laughed at him.

"You're getting awfully jumpy," she said. "It's not good to stay so frustrated. Why don't you let me take care of that for you?"

Scott's face flushed and he had to make a concerted effort to control his temper.

"See you at the funeral," he said, and walked away, conscious of her checking out his backside as he did so.

Maggie and Hannah went to the Mountain View Retirement Home in Pendleton to see Enid. She was sleeping, but they got to talk with their friend Ruthie.

"She's upset about Margie's death," Ruthie said. "As much as you imagine she would be. But she's also confused, maybe because so much has happened in such a short time. She keeps asking everyone when Eric is coming."

"Her dead husband."

"She thinks he's coming to take her to the funeral."

"That's so sad."

"I've been spending a lot of time with her because she knows me and she's calmer with a familiar face around. Last night she said something very telling. She said, 'Mary Margaret did some very bad things.' I asked her what kind of things. She said, 'I told her someday all her bad chickens would come home to roost.'"

"What do you think she meant by that?"

"She wouldn't say any more."

"We don't want to wake her," Hannah said, but she was asking if they could.

"She needs her sleep if she's going to be fit to go to a funeral tomorrow," Ruthie said. "I'm worried about her blood pressure."

"Who's been to visit her?" Maggie asked.

"Let's take a look at the book," Ruthie said. "Everyone has to sign in and put down who they're visiting."

Out in the lobby, Ruthie spun the registration book around and looked back over the previous seven days.

"You and Hannah, Lily and Connie, both of your mothers and your Aunt Delia, Father Stephen and Sister Mary Margrethe, and of course, Scott."

"I wonder if she told any of them anything interesting."

"Well, you'll never get anything out of Father Stephen, but maybe the others got something."

Maggie and Hannah took Margie's nicest outfit (which wasn't saying much) to the funeral home, and when they rang the bell at the back door, Peg opened it almost immediately.

Peg had on a bright red pantsuit accessorized by black jet jewelry that matched her severely arched eyebrows, spidery lashes, and bell-shaped hairdo. Her makeup was dark and dramatic as always, but her lips looked newly plumped up and sore around the edges.

She stood in the doorway amidst a choking cloud of perfume, and asked, "How can I help you?" in a most unwelcoming tone.

"Nosferatu," Hannah said under her breath from where she stood behind Maggie.

"Pardon me?" Peg said impatiently, although her puffy lips gave the "p" an extra pop.

"We brought Margie Estep's burial clothes," Maggie said.

Peg brusquely thanked them as she jerked the hanger out of Maggie's hand and slammed the door in their faces.

"What in the hell happened to our friendly neighborhood creature of the night?" Hannah asked Maggie. "It looks like she kissed the business end of a bee."

"Some sort of lip implants?" Maggie said.

"The better to kiss Gwyneth's bony butt with, I guess."

Mayor Machalvie was intent on wooing Gwyneth Eldridge now that she controlled the majority of the Eldridge family's wealth, and Peg had been spending a lot of time making sure that any wooing that was done was strictly businesslike and unromantic. To that end, she had assigned herself the role of Gwyneth's new best friend and kept looking for ways to get close to her.

Maggie and Hannah stopped in at the bakery next, to ask their mothers about anything Enid might have said that was interesting and found out about the college president killing himself.

"I heard he confessed to killing Margie in his suicide note," Hannah's mother Alice said. "There were some awful photos and a blackmail note directing him to leave money in the burn barrel, right up the hill from where Margie was, well, where Hannah found her."

"Well, that takes care of that," Maggie said to Hannah. She was sorry to hear about the suicide but was also relieved her brother Brian wasn't involved.

Bonnie was still mad at her daughter for not telling her about Timmy's "pirate," and for accusing Brian of stealing money, so she was pretending her daughter wasn't in the room. Maggie went back to the kitchen, where Delia and Mandy were baking.

"I guess you heard about Newton Moseby," Maggie said, and both women nodded.

Delia hugged her and whispered in her ear, "Your mother hasn't mentioned the cookie jar money yet."

Maggie just shook her head, and then looked more closely at Mandy.

"You look different," she said. "What have you done?"

Mandy giggled, and Delia laughed out loud.

"She's in love," Delia said, and Mandy flung a handful of flour at her, even though she was still smiling.

"Well whatever it is, it suits you," Maggie said.

Ed Harrison abandoned his website work once again and drove out to the Roadhouse to talk to Phyllis Davis. He found her seated at the bar having coffee and smoking a cigarette. She looked thinner and older than the last time he saw her, just a few weeks previously. It looked like the deaths of Theo and her son had taken a toll on her.

"Will you look at what the cat dragged in?" she asked the bartender, a heavily tattooed biker named Ray whom Ed knew from the summer softball league.

The Roadhouse had a softball team that was just as rowdy and prone to get into fistfights as you would expect a team sponsored by a biker bar to be. They also, however, procured more toys for the annual Holiday Season toy drive than any other sponsor and hosted a summer Harley riding event called the "Tats for Ta Ta's Fun Run" that raised money for breast cancer research. Ed nodded at Ray, the man returned the gesture and poured Ed some coffee as he took a seat next to Phyllis.

"What brings you all the way out to sin city?" Phyllis asked him, striking what she no doubt thought was a seductive pose. The smeared makeup left over from the previous night, the deep lines on her face, and her rat's nest of dark hair with its thick stripe of gray roots made the pose more pitiful than sexy.

"I had to come out this way, and I thought I'd drop by to see how you're doing."

"That's a load of crap, and we both know it. Cut to the chase, Eddie boy. What do you want?"

"Who's renting your trailer?"

"Ha!" Phyllis said. "Wouldn't you like to know?"

"Is it Brian Fitzpatrick?" he asked her, and she couldn't cover up her initial reaction, which was surprise.

Ed also noted Ray's reaction, which was a brief, pointed look.

"Nah, some old granny and a kid," Phyllis said. "I thought Brian Fitzpatrick was dead."

"Well, then his red-headed ghost is roaming the streets of Rose Hill," Ed said.

"Wouldn't surprise me," Phyllis said. "He and Theo are probably having a blast, haunting all those holier than thou church cats. You can't have any fun in Rose Hill anymore, Ray. It's against the law."

"Well, take care of yourself," Ed said, and covertly gave Ray a $20 bill for the coffee, and told him to keep the change.

Ed waited outside for a few minutes, and Ray eventually followed him out, as he hoped he would.

"You think Brian's back?" Ray asked him.

"I have reasons to believe so, yes," Ed said.

"Well, if he is, he hasn't been out here, and if he's smart, he'll stay hid."

"Why's that?"

"When someone takes off with half a million of someone else's money, he would be wise to stay gone."

"Whose money was it?"

"I'm not going to say, 'cause I like you, and I don't wanna hear you were found floating down the Little Bear with your throat cut."

"I thought maybe it had something to do with Theo Eldridge."

Ray snorted.

"Theo Eldridge was small beans," he said. "The fat cat Brian ripped off eats guys like Theo for breakfast."

"If you see Brian, or hear anything, will you let me know?"

"There's a price on his head," Ray said, "and I don't have a retirement account. I tell you what, I'll call you second."

Scott found Maggie at work and told her what was happening with Newton.

"Doc seems to think someone may have helped him along," Scott said. "That makes me think it might have been Connie."

Maggie told Scott about finding the letter in Connie's purse, and Scott wrote down the date in his notebook.

"I know I shouldn't have looked at it, but I couldn't resist," Maggie said. "It had to be one of the letters Margie sent."

"Connie refused to show it to me or tell me what it said. You're sure about the date?"

"Yeah, I'm sure."

"I swear I have more leads than I can follow up on. I need a dozen deputies. Thanks for telling me about the letter."

"I'm just relieved you aren't throwing me in jail for snooping in Connie's purse."

"Here's a crazy idea. Do you think Newton and Connie could have been having an affair?"

"You think Connie killed him because he wouldn't leave his wife?"

"I don't know. She was hysterical when I got to the inn, but she's kind of kooky anyway, and she did find his body."

"But why else would she have drugged him and smothered him?"

"That's what I want to know. I'm going over to his office next, to see what I can find out there."

After Scott left Maggie found that she couldn't concentrate on paperwork. She had a store full of staff, so she went over to work in the bakery kitchen with Delia so Mandy could have some time off.

"You know," Maggie told her aunt while they worked side by side in the hot kitchen. "Hannah and Drew walked in on an argument between Newton and Connie last week. You think he could have been having an affair with her?"

"I have no idea."

"You wouldn't tell me if you did know," Maggie said. "You are one secret-keeping high-security vault when it comes to your friends, you are."

"I'm no friend of Connie Fenton's," Delia said, and Maggie was surprised by the sharpness of her aunt's tone.

"Tell that story," Maggie demanded. "Tell it right now."

"No, I won't," Delia said. "Because nothing was ever proved, and even if I don't like the woman, I won't have vicious gossip about her on my conscience."

Maggie was like a bird dog on a turkey's trail now, but no amount of badgering would pull the story out of her aunt.

"Did this take place in March of 1984?" Maggie prodded.

"Not another word," Delia said and turned a stern look on Maggie. "I mean it."

"Who else knows this story?"

"You are persistent; I'll give you that," Delia said. "But no. Change the subject."

Maggie knew there was more than one way to crack a nut. She tackled her Aunt Alice, who, although she was Hannah's mother, was not too bright and never knew when to keep her mouth shut.

The first opportunity she got, she cornered Alice behind the register.

"Did Delia and Connie have some kind of falling out?" she asked her.

"No," Alice shook her head, "not that I know of."

"Did they ever work together, back when they were both nurses?"

"Delia worked at the old folk's home in Fleurmania for awhile after Liam died, to help pay the medical bills. Connie worked there too."

When Ian and Delia's son Liam died of leukemia at nine years of age, it had devastated the whole Fitzpatrick family. In addition to the weight of their grief, his parents were also stuck with a mountain of medical bills. Small business owners in Rose Hill couldn't often afford the luxury of good health insurance. Liam had died just before Christmas in 1983.

When Maggie left the bakery that afternoon, she went back to the bookstore to get her VW bug, intending to drive out to Fleurmania. Instead, she got caught up in some work-related responsibilities, and the opportunity passed.

When Scott passed under the stone archway that separated the grounds of Eldridge College from Rose Hill, he felt as if he had entered another world. A generous endowment from the Eldridge family paid for the manicured grounds and meticulous upkeep of the century-old red brick buildings, built in the Gothic architectural style. The college was an expensive private school, known to accept wealthy progeny both kept out of or kicked out of other expensive schools.

Scott stopped to have a word with the security guard on duty, a local man he knew well. The school employed lots of Rose Hill citizens, and with good benefits and decent wages being the norm, there was very little job turnover.

Everyone already knew about the president's death. His secretary Darlene, with red eyes and nose, started crying again as soon as Scott entered the office.

"I just can't believe it," she said, pulling a fresh tissue out of the box on her desk.

"It's awful, I know," Scott said. "Did you have any idea he was upset about anything?"

"Nothing that bad," she said. "I mean other than Gwyneth kicking them out of their home, and having to live at the inn with Connie, and all her nuttiness."

"What was Connie doing?"

"You know, Scott, Newton's wife Delores is the sweetest woman I've ever known, and she never has a bad thing to say about anyone. But she had to go to her daughter's house in Florida because Connie was driving her so crazy."

"In what way?"

"Connie's a germ freak; everyone knows that. Delores said she followed them around sterilizing everything they touched. That would be enough to make me nuts, but she was also nosy. Delores said she caught Connie snooping in Newton's room, and they fought it. Also, I guess Connie has some old cat she lets roam around everywhere, and Delores has a phobia about cats."

"Wait a minute. Delores and Newton had separate rooms?"

"Oops, I shouldn't have let that slip. When you work for someone as long as I've worked for Newton, you get to know personal things. Newton had a bad snoring problem, so they slept in separate bedrooms. She was always after him to get tested, you know, for that sleep apnea, but he refused."

"Did Newton ever say anything about Connie?"

"Said she was mad as a March hare, and he didn't know how long he would be able to stand to live at the inn. There are no big houses available in Rose Hill, you see, and it wouldn't look right for the college president to live just anywhere. They were considering buying something in Glencora, and commuting from there."

"Did Margie Estep ever come to see Newton here?"

"Margie? No, why would she?"

"I just wondered. What was on his schedule last Monday night?"

"You're certainly piquing my curiosity now, Scott. Let me look. Last Monday was the board meeting, so we were here until 7:00 p.m. and the board dinner that followed lasted until 10:00 or so. I went home after the meeting, but I know he stayed the whole time at the dinner. Lucille, who works in food service, said he had a long talk with one of the board members after everyone else left. It kept her staff from cleaning up and going home, and they were kind of mad about it. You know those executives, they never think about the lives of the service personnel who wait on them hand and foot."

"Which board member was it?"

"Lucille didn't say, but I could ask her."

"Would you? It's probably not important, but I have to follow up with anyone he talked to last week."

Darlene made the call and then gave Scott the name and phone number of the board member.

"Anything else going on that would have been upsetting to him?" Scott asked her.

"Not really," she said. "Newton's a really easy going guy. I mean was."

Tears began to flow again, and Scott apologized for having to ask her so many questions.

"I just can't imagine why he would kill himself," Darlene said. "He wasn't depressed about anything that I could tell."

"If you think of anything else you'll let me know?" Scott said.

"Of course," she said.

"Okay if I look through his desk?" he asked. "I can get a search warrant if you want."

"No, you go ahead," Darlene said. "If I ask someone higher up, they'll probably require it, so let's just not ask anyone."

Scott looked through the president's office but didn't find anything out of the ordinary. He copied down the man's schedule for the past week, but nothing appeared suspicious about it. He used the president's phone to call the board member, who had already heard about his death.

"The board has scheduled an emergency conference call this evening so that we can appoint an interim administrator," she informed him.

Scott guessed the board's bureaucratic concerns must outweigh their emotional ones. The man's body was barely cold, and the woman seemed heartlessly business-like. She also didn't remember anything odd about their conversation, which she said concerned an amendment they were considering making to the bylaws to increase the number of board members. Scott knew there was nothing a bunch of rich, powerful people liked more than multiplying the number of people in a room who liked to hear themselves talk, so he wasn't surprised the board was expanding.

When Scott asked what her relationship was with the president, the woman laughed.

"Newton?" she said. "Sorry to laugh. God rest his soul, I know, but he may well have been the dullest man I ever met."

Scott thanked her for her time and hung up. Darlene was on the phone as he walked through the outer office, so he waved and went on.

Scott didn't know Newton very well. He knew Delores better, as she was a pharmacist at Machalvie's drug store and on several town committees. She was a soft-spoken, kind woman who seemed to have a lot of common sense, and she was always friendly to Scott when they met. The scandal of her husband killing someone and then committing suicide would be devastating enough to any wife. If there was some hanky panky going on with Connie as well, plus the blackmail, and maybe a murder dressed up to look like suicide, Scott wondered how Delores would handle it. Scott wished he could question Connie, who Sarah would no doubt tackle as soon as she woke up. Instead, he went back to his office and wrote up his notes on what he'd just done for Sarah to review.

Later in the day, a call came saying the search warrant for Phyllis's post office box was ready to be picked up at the county courthouse, and Scott rushed it down to the post office. Sadie solemnly handed over Phyllis's mail, and Scott took it back to the station. He couldn't believe what he read in Margie's letter to Phyllis. He made a photocopy of the letter and then drove up to Morning Glory Circle, where he parked in front of Mamie Rodefeffer's house. Her maid let Scott in and directed him to Mamie's sitting room, where the old woman was reading a paperback book through a page-sized magnifier.

"What is it?" she demanded. "What do you want?"

"I have something very private to discuss with you," Scott said. "Can we be excused?"

He glanced at the maid, who looked very interested.

"Get out," Mamie told the woman, "and shut the door behind you. I'm going to open it every five seconds just to see if you're listening."

The maid looked insulted but did as she was told.

"They spy on me and make fun of me," Mamie said. "They don't know I can hear everything they say. I may be legally blind and old as the hills but I'm not senile, and I have excellent hearing. Sit down, sit down. What's so important?"

Scott explained to her about the letters Margie had sent and showed her what was mailed to Phyllis Davis. Mamie placed it under her page magnifier and held both up to her nose as she read.

"Hmph," she said as she read. "Ha!"

When she finished she used her cane to stand up, walk to the fireplace, and before Scott could stop her, she threw the letter on the fire. He wasn't too upset, as the one he'd shown Mamie was the photocopy of the real letter, which was in the station safe.

"Is it true?" he asked her.

"That dreary little mouse turned out to be a dirty rat, didn't she?" Mamie said. "Hah!"

"She's also a dead rat."

"Do you think I killed her?" Mamie asked him as she resettled herself in her armchair. She peered at him through magnifying lenses that made her eyes look twice their size.

"Did you?"

"No, of course not," Mamie said. "But think how exciting it would be to stand up in court and confess to a murder. 'I did it!' I could say. My father would roll over in his grave, of course, but my mother might have approved. Homicidal tendencies flow in our bloodline, apparently."

"Tell me about it," Scott said. "How did you find out?"

"My father told me on his deathbed. What an old fool he was. He practically gave the glass factory to Theo Eldridge so the truth wouldn't come out, but then he was worried Theo would try to blackmail me with the same information. My mother could not have children, and our family needed heirs. Her maid was a young, willing idiot and my father was very generous. She gave him my younger brother and me. My father set her up in business afterward. She had another child out of wedlock after she left our employment, a daughter who was not my father's, and when the maid died her daughter took over her business."

"Davis's Diner."

"Yes, Gladys Davis is my half-sister; Pauline is my niece, and so on."

"Phyllis is your great niece and Billy was your great, great nephew."

"And Billy murdered Theo, the man who blackmailed my father. That vicious circle is complete, I should say."

"Billy killed Theo thinking he would inherit his money when he was your heir."

"And would not have hesitated to do me in as well, I'd wager. That family is what I would call poor relations, in every sense."

"So what will you do?"

"Nothing. What should I do? Can you imagine my nephews' faces if they found out about it? Richard probably wouldn't care, but Knox, with his political aspirations and very high opinion of himself? How would that smutty rumor play out in political circles, do you think? His grandmother was a maid who ran a diner; his father was born on the wrong side of the blanket, his second cousin is a prostitute and his third cousin a murderer."

"Theo may have already blackmailed Knox with that information."

"Blackmail's results are so often at odds with the intended outcome, don't you think? I can't imagine why anyone practices it anymore."

"I can't think of any legal reason why I should publicly reveal this information," Scott said. "But don't you think you have a moral imperative to help the Davis family?"

"You don't look like the blackmailing type," Mamie said, and then wagged her finger at him. "Remember how it always ends."

"I'm not threatening you," Scott said. "Gladys and Pauline are good people, and they're struggling financially right now. They don't have to know who it was that helped them."

"What makes you think I have any money?" Mamie said. "Is it this house? Looks can be deceiving, Chief Gordon."

"It was just a suggestion," Scott said. "I appreciate your candor, and I promise your secret is safe with me. No strings attached."

"Hmph," she said. "Hah!"

Scott made his way out of Mamie's impressive home and noticed as he went that everything was perfectly dusted and polished. It smelled like lemon furniture polish and old money. He wondered how much she had left.

Ava Fitzpatrick made sure her children had a quiet, low-key evening with no stress or over-stimulation. She was as nervous as a long-tailed cat in a room full of rockers, which was something her father used to say. She was determined not to let her stress affect her children, so she got them focused on a book and a video while she prepared for the next day.

Several of Connie's customers had checked out of the Eldridge Inn and into the Rose Hill Bed and Breakfast after the death of fellow guest Newton Moseby, so Ava had plenty of chores to keep her busy. Her housekeeper had washed sheets and towels all day, and the last load was tumbling in the dryer.

Ava was concentrating on the breakfast portion of her business by mixing up a huge batch of muffin batter to refrigerate overnight in an airtight container. In the morning, she could just scoop it into muffin pans and bake it, and it made the morning routine much easier. Everything was harder to do with only one working wrist, but Ava was managing.

The phone rang, and Ava answered, "Rose Hill Bed and Breakfast, Ava speaking."

"Hey gorgeous," her husband Brian said.

Ava felt light-headed and gripped the counter with her free hand, then winced at the pain in her sprained wrist.

"What are you doing?" she stammered. "Where are you?"

"Can't a devoted husband call his darling wife just to see how she's doing? The place looks nice, honey. And the kids! That Charlotte is going to be a knockout, just like her mama."

Ava stretched the phone cord as far as it would reach, hurriedly shut herself in the laundry room and turned off the dryer so she could hear.

"How dare you!" she said, trying to keep her voice down. "Why can't you leave us alone?"

"I would like nothing better, sweetheart. All I need is some money to make that happen."

"Of course, I see. How much?"

"I heard your old boyfriend left you a pile of cash."

"I can't touch that. It's in a trust."

"You can borrow against a trust, my precious, for the full amount. Ask any banker."

"You would take that from us, the only security we have?"

"All you have to do is bat those eyes and shake that sweet ass, honey, and you can have anything you need from any man with a heartbeat. If you want me gone, you have to pay."

"Was that your baby I saw in the grocery store today?" she asked, "With an old woman who doesn't speak English?"

Brian was silent, and Ava could hear a dog bark in the background of wherever he was.

"I have to go, sweetie," he said, "but I'll be in touch. Go to the bank tomorrow and get that loan paperwork rolling. As soon as I get that money, you'll never have to see me again."

He hung up before she could say anything else.

Ava stared at the phone.

"Mommy," asked Timmy, from outside the door, "what are you doing in there?"

Ava took a deep breath and turned the dryer on before she opened the door.

"Nothing, sweetie," she said, embracing her little boy, "nothing at all."

Hannah stayed late at her father's gas station, finding things to do and people to gab with until Curtis eyed her and said, "What's up little bird?'

Hannah felt tears fill her eyes, and she blinked hard to stop them.

"Tell your old papa what the matter is," he said and hugged her tight in his arms.

Hannah shook her head, and her eyes filled again.

"It's Sam," she said.

"I figured that," Curtis said, letting her go. "He got them blue meanies, again?"

"He's headed in that direction," she said. "I just don't know if I can go through it again."

"Has he called his counselor?"

"I asked him to, but he told me to mind my own business."

"That doesn't sound good."

"He's staying locked up in his office. When he does come out, we fight, and he's getting darker and darker inside. I can see it happening."

"You wanna stay at our place for a bit? Maybe give him some breathing room?"

"No, but thanks. I've got to be a grown-up girl and work it out myself."

"That's my girl. Just don't you let him drag you down in there with him, ya hear?"

"Don't worry," Hannah said. "I won't."

But in her heart, she could see she was a little further down the path with Sam than she wanted to admit.

Ed was trying to look casual as he watched the trailer next door through Mandy's front window.

"I had to get on Tommy for peepin', but I never took you for a pervert," Mandy said.

"I'm sorry," Ed said. "I'm just naturally curious, which comes in handy when you write news stories for a living."

"Well, go on over there and knock."

"I did that earlier, and no one came to the door."

"Maybe they weren't home then. You want me to do it?"

"No, no, I'm just being silly."

"Well, come on over here and be silly with me on the couch."

"Mom," Tommy said sternly.

"Oh, get over yourself," Mandy said.

Tommy rolled his eyes and went back to his homework, which lay spread out on the coffee table, but he was smiling. Ed's dog Hank was lying on the floor with his head on Tommy's lap, looking very content.

"You write anything about that guy what offed hisself?" Mandy asked.

"Newton Moseby was his name. Yes, I wrote that up today, and sent it to the city paper for tomorrow's edition."

"You put it on your website?"

"No, I haven't launched that yet."

"Sounds like a boat or a rocket ship."

"Did Newton ever come in the bakery or the bar?"

"Not that I ever knew. I couldn't even tell you what he looked like."

"What about Connie?'

"Ed," Mandy laughed. "Are you interviewing me?"

"I guess I am."

"Well, then I have a hot news flash for ya. Miss Miranda Wilson says, 'My boyfriend needs to leave his work at the office, and concentrate on his woman when he comes home.'"

"I get it."

"Oh yeah, I think you can count on that."

"Mom!" Tommy complained.

"Put your headphones on then! I'm sparkin' with my fella."

"I saw them today," Tommy said.

"Saw who?" Mandy asked.

"The old lady and the little baby."

"When?" Ed asked him.

"Today when I got home from school I saw her pulling a wire cart with some groceries in it. I asked her if I could help but she shouted at me in Spanish, so I left them alone."

"It was nice of you to offer," Mandy said.

"Please be careful with strangers, though," Ed warned.

"You think the worst of everyone," Mandy accused.

"Your last neighbor killed a man," Ed reminded her.

"You got a point there," Mandy said. "We better move."

"That isn't a bad idea," Ed said.

"You makin' me an offer?" Mandy asked.

"No, I just meant maybe you should move to a safer neighborhood."

"But we ain't good enough for your house, that it?"

"I didn't mean that at all. It's just awful soon for us to be making that kind of commitment, don't you think?"

"You plannin' on dumpin' me?"

"Of course not," Ed said, and then gestured at Tommy. "Maybe we should talk about this privately."

"No way," Mandy said. "Me and Tommy are a team, and we been thinking you're on our team too. We need to know if this is just, just…"

"Tryouts," Tommy supplied.

"Yeah," Mandy said. "What he said."

"We just started seeing each other," Ed said. "Don't you want to see if it works out between us first?"

"What's to work out?" Mandy said. "I love you, and you love me, don't ya?"

"Mandy, I am not ready to have you move in with me."

"But you and Hank crashin' here every night, and us all eatin' every meal together, that ain't moved in? Just 'cause your baseball card collection ain't stayin' here with ya?"

"I'm sorry, I don't know what to say. This is all very sudden for me, and I wasn't, I don't, I mean, I wouldn't want…"

"No, I get the message," Mandy said, and it was the first time Ed had ever seen her get seriously angry.

She stood up, went to the door, and took his coat off the hook on the wall.

"Mandy, don't…"

She opened up the front door and threw his coat out into the snow. His snow boots followed.

"Out," she said. "If we're just wastin' our time with you, let's not waste one more minute."

"Please don't do this," Ed said.

Tommy huddled where he sat, cross-legged at the coffee table, trying to pretend he wasn't there. Hank got up and followed Ed to the door.

"Go!" Mandy insisted, and Ed had no choice but to go out the door in his stocking feet.

"It was nice while it lasted," she said, as he went out the door. "You can quote me on that in your damn newspaper."

Ed and Hank had barely cleared the door when she slammed it behind him.

Ed stood out in the cold, with freezing wet feet and wondered what in the hell just happened.

Chapter Nine – Tuesday

When innkeeper Connie Fenton woke up and saw the sheriff's deputy waiting for her, she immediately began crying hysterically, gasping for air, and complaining of chest pains. The deputy drove her to the emergency room at the hospital in Pendleton, where a doctor was running some tests.

County investigator Sarah Albright was furious about this turn of events and was taking it out on Scott. He had come off another night shift at 8:00 a.m. and should have gone home to sleep, but instead was sitting in his office listening to a litany of Sarah's complaints about his police work. She was ticking them off on her fingers as she went.

"You didn't immediately inform the county dispatch when you suspected the inn was the scene of a homicide, and if I hadn't stopped by the station, I wouldn't have known about it until you got around to calling me if you had bothered to call me at all.

"You let a prime suspect be sedated, and you let another civilian linger at the scene without supervision. That Crawford woman could have helped Connie dispose of the evidence. She may have been in on it from the start.

"You should have taken Connie's statement while the body was still on the premises. She's had all this time to get her story straight, and now we have to wait again while she pretends to have a heart attack.

"You let a dozen people walk through that crime scene and put their hands all over everything, and let a doctor who was not assigned to the case touch the victim.

"You didn't get a search warrant for the president's office before you went through it, and now the college will probably sue.

"I don't know why you call yourself a police officer. You're more of a criminal activity enabler."

"That's enough," Scott said quietly.

"And Tweedledee and Tweedledum out there," she continued, gesturing to the outer office, where Skip and Frank were pretending not to listen, "are worse than worthless. You might as well have hired two monkeys as those two retards."

"That's enough," Scott said a little louder.

"What did you say?" she said, finally hearing Scott.

"I said, that's enough," he said calmly. "I've had enough of you insulting this town and everyone in it. I've had enough of you demeaning my staff with your unprofessional behavior. I want you to take your condescending attitude, your FBI training, your Washington, DC violent crimes unit experience, and your rude, hostile comments, and leave this station right now."

"What is wrong with you?" she asked. "Are you insane?"

"I am formally requesting that you leave this station, and if you need anything further from my team or me, you can submit your request in writing. I will then consider whether we have enough resources available to help you. I think you'll find that from now on we will probably be too busy to help."

"You can't just kick me out of here."

"On the contrary, I can, and I am. I called a buddy of mine at the county courthouse and had him look up the official guidelines. If a city does not have resources adequate to assist in a county investigation, the county cannot insist that the city comply more than is reasonable."

"You stupid hillbilly, I will get you fired."

"And I will make a formal complaint against you for sexual harassment."

She blanched.

"You wouldn't."

"I'll start with a call to your boss," he said, "and work my way up from there. I'm willing to bet it won't be the first complaint they've received about you. I also have a friend who owns a newspaper. It comes out this Sunday, and I think you'll be interested to read all about my sexual harassment lawsuit in there. I wonder if that will have any effect on your ambitious career plans."

Sarah stormed out of the station. They could hear her slam her car door and gun the engine.

"You want me to arrest her for speeding?" Skip asked eagerly, as they stood at the window and watched her peel out, make an illegal u-turn, and drive away, tires squealing.

"No," Scott said. "She might shoot you, and I need you up at the grade school on pirate watch."

"Can I get you anything?" Frank asked him after Skip left to go up to the grade school. "Some coffee, a doughnut or something? That was incredible. I mean, really, really awesome."

"No, Frank, but thank you," Scott said. "I'm going home to get some sleep. Don't call me unless something important's on fire or someone else gets murdered, and Sarah Albright does not count in either case."

Tommy was sitting in class, and the teacher was demonstrating how to solve an equation on the blackboard, but Tommy wasn't listening. He was worried about the baby. When Tommy went home for breakfast at 6:00 a.m., after helping Ed deliver the big city daily paper, he saw the old woman leave the trailer next to theirs without the baby. She had a small suitcase with her and seemed to be in a hurry. Tommy knew a bus came through town around that time each morning and stopped in the parking lot in front of the Dairy Chef to drop off and pick up passengers. He wondered if she was hurrying to catch it. He stood in the driveway of the mobile home park and wondered if he should follow her. He didn't hear the baby crying, and the suitcase wasn't big enough to put a baby in. So where was the baby?

Tommy waited until she got several yards ahead of him before he started following her. When he got to the corner of Peony Street and Rose Hill Avenue he waited, hiding behind the corner of the Rose and Thorn bar. The old woman crossed the street, walked half a block, and then stood outside the Dairy Chef, under the porch overhang, with a shawl pulled closely around her head and shoulders. She wasn't dressed warmly enough for the brisk winter weather, and Tommy thought she was probably feeling the cold. When the bus drew up and parked the driver stowed her suitcase in the baggage compartment, and the old lady got on the bus. When it pulled away, she was still on board.

Tommy didn't know what to do. He considered going to the newspaper office and alerting Ed but hesitated. Ed and his mother were fighting, and he had done his best to stay out of their way and prove what a great kid he was. He had been involved in a murder case by following someone a few weeks previously, and all kinds of trouble had followed involving Ed. He didn't want Ed to get the idea that he was always sticking his nose in where it didn't belong and stirring up trouble. Ed might decide not to make up with his mom if he did.

Tommy went back to the mobile home park and listened at the door of the trailer where the old woman had been staying. He couldn't hear anything. He knocked quietly, and then a little louder, thinking he would have to make up some reason for intruding if someone answered. No one answered. He tried the doorknob, but the door was locked.

'She must have left that baby with someone,' he thought, as he walked over to the trailer where he lived with his mother.

While he ate his breakfast, Tommy listened for the baby to cry, as it often did in the morning, but today there was no crying.

'That baby is probably back with its mother,' he told himself as he left for school. 'The old lady was just babysitting it.'

Now in Algebra class, he couldn't quit thinking about that baby. His hand went up before he was even conscious of what he was going to do.

"Yes, Tommy," said Mrs. Cavender.

"I feel sick," he said, and she gave him a pass to go to the nurse's office.

Tommy walked quickly past the nurse's office and out the side door of the school. He saw the patrol car sitting out front, and skirted around the hedges that lined the street so Skip wouldn't see him. Tommy crouched low and ran across Peony Street, and then down Magnolia Avenue until he made it to the alley behind Sunflower Street. There he stood up straight and ran as fast as he could, slipping and sliding in the ruts of snow and ice. He was heading for the newspaper office to get Ed.

Behind the Rose Hill Bed and Breakfast, Ava Fitzpatrick was putting trash out in the alley, using only her right hand to protect her swollen left wrist.

"Tommy," she called out when she saw him running. "Why aren't you in school? What's wrong?"

Tommy stopped and tried to catch his breath before he spoke, but he felt panicked to get going again, so he attempted to tell her.

"A baby," he gasped out. "A baby's been left by the old lady in the trailer next to ours."

He bent over to try to ease the cramp that had developed in his side, the side where his broken ribs had just about healed.

Ava's eyes grew huge in her head, and she dropped the trash where she stood.

"C'mon," she said, grabbing him by the arm. "I'll drive."

Ava didn't even wait for him to buckle his seatbelt before she backed the minivan out of the driveway and tore down the slippery alley as fast as she could. Tommy got his safety belt fastened and then stared at Ava in awed admiration. This was like something on television.

248

"Hold on," she told him, as she made a sharp right at the juncture of the two alleys, and then a sharp left onto Peony Street. She could see no one was coming, so she zipped across Rose Hill Avenue without even stopping at the stop sign. Another sharp right just down the hill brought them into the mobile home park, and she slid to a stop in front of Tommy's trailer.

Tommy jumped out and ran to the trailer next door with Ava right behind. They could hear the baby crying loudly. Ava pounded on the door, and no one answered. Ava tried the knob, and it was still locked.

"Help me," she said and started battering the door with her shoulder.

Tommy and she both slammed into it together, and the flimsy door flew open with a bang against the wall inside. They fell in, and Ava gasped as she tried to catch herself once again, re-injuring her already sprained wrist. She thought she heard it snap this time, and the pain was excruciating.

Tommy helped her up, and they rushed down the hallway to where the screaming originated. The baby lay in the middle of a messy bed, with a red face and eyes streaming with tears. It coughed and gasped for breath. She scooped the child up and held it close to her chest, making soothing noises. The baby wailed in response.

"Look for diapers," she told Tommy.

Tommy looked around the bedroom, which was an awful mess, but there were no clean diapers or baby stuff. He checked the bathroom, the other small bedroom, the kitchen, and the living room. He found lots of dirty dishes and smelly, used diapers, but no clean ones.

Ava followed him out to the main room with the baby and wrinkled up her nose at the smell.

"Let's just get out of here," she said.

Tommy helped her to wrap the baby in a semi-clean towel she found draped over a chair, and they left the trailer.

"Can you drive?" she asked him.

Tommy, who was only twelve, was shocked to be asked.

"Sometimes my mom lets me start the car," he said, "but I've never driven it."

"I don't have a baby seat," she said. "You get in the backseat, put on your seatbelt, and hold the baby. I'll go slow."

Tommy did as he was told. The baby was still crying, but not as hysterically as before. It smelled awful and had thick green snot flowing out of its nose. It coughed and wheezed, and that sounded bad even to Tommy, who didn't know anything about babies.

"You'll be okay," Tommy told the baby. "We'll take good care of you."

Ava drove slowly up to Rose Hill Avenue, waited for a break in traffic, then turned right, and parked in front of the pharmacy. She jumped out, ran around, slid open the side door of the van and awkwardly took the baby from Tommy, wincing at the pain in her wrist.

"Open that side door," she told Tommy, pointing at a door between the pharmacy and the hardware store that led to a set of stairs up to the second floor, where Doc Machalvie had an office.

His receptionist, Mildred, was in the outer office. She took one look at wild-eyed Ava holding the coughing baby and sent them straight in.

Ava turned back to Tommy as she went in, and said, "Go downstairs to the pharmacy and tell Meg to give you everything a six-month-old baby would need. They can put it on my account."

Mildred motioned to Tommy and said, "You stay put, sweetie, and I'll go. I know what to get."

Tommy knew he was in twenty kinds of trouble, but he also knew he'd done the right thing. He sat down on one of the wooden chairs in the waiting room and waited for a grownup to tell him what to do next.

Inside his office, Doc Machalvie took the wailing, coughing baby from Ava and gave her an ice pack for her wrist.

"Whose baby is this, Ava?" he asked her.

"Tommy found it abandoned in the trailer park," Ava said. Her heart was pounding, and she was out of breath.

"You sit over there and calm down," he told Ava. "If you and I are calm, the child will know it's safe here."

The baby was a boy. Doc examined him thoroughly, took his temperature, and listened to his lungs and heart. He also used a bulb syringe to suck the snot out of the little guy's nose, which made the baby howl in indignation. Through it all, Doc spoke softly in a warm, comforting voice, and eventually, the hysterical crying wound down into the grumpy, complaining crying of a baby who's just had enough, needs something to drink and a quiet place to go to sleep.

Ava's wrist was throbbing, so she could only watch as Doc gave the baby a warm bath in his office sink. She admired his gentle handling and soothing manner with the frightened infant. The baby's skin was raw and chapped from diaper rash, so Doc put some ointment and powder on it and diapered him with an incontinence pad he cut down to size.

"I haven't done any of this in a long time," he told Ava.

"Neither have I," Ava said.

Doc swaddled the baby tightly in a clean towel and cradled him against his chest with one arm while he wrote out some prescriptions.

"I'm going to give you a couple of prescriptions, Ava, but I know you've been through upper respiratory bugs with your children, so you know what to do. A steamy bathroom or a vaporizer, and a mentholated rub will help loosen up the congestion. He's not dehydrated or malnourished, so I don't think he needs to be hospitalized. Keep him fed and

251

warm, but not overheated. Call me if he gets worse. I'll stop in to check on him on my way home."

"Thank God," Ava said. "I can take him home with me."

"He looks like a Fitzpatrick," Doc said, giving Ava a pointed look.

"I think he probably is," Ava said.

The doctor looked long and hard at Ava but did not ask any of the questions she thought he probably had.

"You'll need to file a report with the police, and they'll want to talk to me," Doc said. "You think long and hard about what you want to say, and I'll back you up."

"Thank you, Doc."

"Once Mildred gets back, she can hold him while I look at your wrist."

Mandy ran into the newspaper office in a panic. She was still in her bakery apron, hairnet, and plastic gloves.

"The school called," she told Ed, out of breath. "Tommy's missin'."

Ed jumped up, got his keys and jacket, told Hank to stay, and Mandy followed him to his truck, tears streaming down her cheeks.

"We'll check at home first," he said. "I'll call Scott on the way."

Just as he started the ignition, Bonnie Fitzpatrick came running out of the bakery waving her arms and yelling, "Wait, wait!"

Ed rolled down his window.

"Ava just called; he's with her."

"What in the world?" Ed said.

"She said for you to go on over to her place, and they'll be there shortly. He's fine."

Ed drove Mandy over to Ava's bed and breakfast and pulled in the back driveway just as Ava pulled in. Ava got out of her van wearing a sling and a cast on her arm and slid open the door to the backseat. Tommy was sitting back there holding the baby, who was now sound asleep.

Ava put her fingers up to her lips as Mandy and Ed started to ask questions.

"Don't be mad at Tommy," she whispered. "He saved this baby's life."

Ed carefully took the sleeping baby from Tommy, carried it to the back porch, and waited until Ava opened the door, which she had left unlocked earlier.

Tommy got out of the van. Mandy hugged him hard, and then pulled his hair.

"Ow," he said. "I'm sorry."

"I don't care how brave you been," Mandy said. "You shoulda called me."

She kissed his cheek and hugged him again, then wiped her eyes and pinched him hard on the arm.

"Ow, I said I'm sorry," Tommy said.

"I love you," Mandy said, "but you gotta quit scaring the life outta me like this. I'm gonna get wrinkles and high blood pressure."

"I'm sorry," he said. "It all happened so fast. That old lady left on a bus this morning, and she didn't have the baby. She left him all alone in the trailer, and he's real sick. Doc Machalvie said it was good we got there when we did."

Mandy looked long and hard at Tommy, and tears filled her eyes.

"You done the right thing," she said. "Lord knows I woulda done the same."

"I love you, Mom," Tommy said, and hugged his mother.

"Alright, come on inside," she said. "I wanna know everything that happened, and don't you dare leave anything out."

Tommy and Mandy got the bags full of baby supplies out of the back seat, closed the van door, and went in the house.

Later that afternoon the late college president's wife and daughter arrived at the bed and breakfast, checked in, and went straight up to their rooms. Delia was covering the front desk for Ava, who was supervising Mandy feeding the baby boy in the kitchen.

"It's been a long time since I done this," Mandy said.

"You're doing just fine," Ava said. She was frustrated about being unable to hold the baby due to her cast and sling. "It all comes right back to you, doesn't it?"

Mandy didn't answer her. Instead, she kissed the top of the baby's head, and tears filled her eyes.

"Tommy's okay, isn't he, Mandy?" Ava said. "I'm so sorry we didn't call you right away."

"It's not that," Mandy said. "I just wonder how anybody could abandon a precious little one like that. What kinda person does that?"

"My ex-husband, I think," Ava said. "He has a history of this sort of thing."

"You think this here baby is Brian's?" Mandy asked incredulously.

"He looks so much like Timmy he almost has to be," Ava said.

"I think all babies look pretty much alike," Mandy said.

"But a mother never forgets what her own baby looks like. You're a mother, Mandy; you know what I mean."

But Mandy didn't answer; she just kissed the baby again and then wiped her eyes.

Ed had volunteered to take Tommy back to school, prepared to plead his case to the principal. Bonnie Fitzpatrick called soon after, to say she was coming over, unable to stand not knowing what was going on.

"He's a hungry little fella," Mandy was saying as Bonnie came in the back door. Bonnie bent around Mandy's shoulder, took a good look at the child, and then looked at Ava.

"Oh my Lord Jesus," she said.

"I know," Ava said.

Bonnie immediately took the baby and the bottle from Mandy and sat down in a kitchen chair.

"You go on back to the bakery now," she told Mandy. "I left Alice by herself."

Mandy took the command in stride, as she always did.

"Yes ma'am," she said and waved goodbye. "By Ava, thanks for lookin' out after my son."

"Please don't be too hard on Tommy," Ava said. "It's my fault we didn't call you sooner."

"He shouldn't a left school like that, without callin' me, but I'm not gonna whup him," Mandy said. "It turned out alright."

After Mandy left, Bonnie kept looking at the baby, then looking at Ava and shaking her head.

"The spitting image," she said.

"I know," Ava said, smiling.

Delia came into the kitchen and put an arm around Ava.

"Looks like you've got a new grandbaby," she told Bonnie.

Bonnie smiled tenderly, and a couple of tears fell from her eyes onto the baby's blanket. Then just as quickly, her face grew stormy, and she looked accusingly at Ava and Delia.

"And where I'd like to know, is his father, my son?"

Ava shrugged and reached over to touch the baby's cheek.

"I don't care," she said. "I know he's your son and my husband, but a man who would abandon a baby like that, again, has lost the right to claim him."

"He might not have known the baby was alone," Bonnie protested. "And no one has told me yet what happened. Why am I always the last one to know anything?"

Ava got her caught up but left out the part about Brian calling to demand money, so of course Bonnie defended her son.

"You don't know his side of it," Bonnie said. "He may be able to explain everything."

Ava just sighed, and Delia squeezed her arm in support.

"I hate to be a party pooper," Delia said to Ava. "But you probably better call Sean and find out what legal things you need to do now."

Bonnie sat the baby up to burp it and wiped his runny nose.

"You go on and do that, Ava," she said, as she gently thumped the baby's back. "I'll take care of my grandson."

After Scott slept a few hours and took a quick shower, he decided to go to the bed and breakfast to give his condolences to the late college president's wife. Now that he had officially separated himself from the case, he couldn't turn around and investigate it, but because he had been the one to call her with the bad news, he felt he owed her a visit.

He was surprised to find Delia at the front desk in the parlor, and Bonnie walking the floor with a redheaded baby in her arms. Ava came down the hall from the kitchen with her arm in a cast and sling and got Scott caught up on the day's events.

"I guess no one thinks to call the police when these things happen," Scott said when she was done.

"I'm sorry," Ava said. "It all happened so fast. I didn't think; I just went."

"This will have to get reported, though," Scott said. "I can't just let you have the baby."

"I just got off the phone with Sean," Ava said. "He said I should call you right away. He said I would need to report the baby abandoned, and that you would probably need statements from Doc Machalvie, Tommy, and me. I'm supposed to request that you make me the temporary guardian."

"It may not be as easy as that," Scott said. "You'll need a judge to sign the order."

"Judge Feinman lives right up the hill," Bonnie said. "He'll sign it."

"A relative would be the logical choice of guardian," Scott said. "But what do I tell Judge Feinman is the relationship between you and the baby?"

"We think he's Brian's son," Ava said. "So I would be his stepmother, I guess."

"I'm related to him by blood, though," Bonnie said. "I'm his grandmother."

Ava looked at Bonnie, and the two women locked gazes.

"A blood test will have to be done," Scott said, "to prove he's related to Bonnie. I'm willing to recommend either of you for temporary guardianship, as long as I have Children's Protective Services' blessing and Judge Feinman's approval. Who's it going to be?"

"Do you promise to hear him out when he shows up?" Bonnie asked her daughter-in-law.

Ava did not break eye contact with Bonnie, but she paused for a long moment before she spoke. Everyone in the room could see her internal struggle, and no one made a sound.

"He's my husband, Bonnie," Ava said finally, sweetly. "Of course I'll listen to whatever he has to say."

Bonnie looked at Scott and nodded in Ava's direction.

"Ava can have him. You tell us what to do, and we'll do it."

When Tommy got out of school, his mother was waiting, and she walked him to the station so Scott could take his statement. The Children's Protective Services social worker was a Sacred Heart Sunday school teacher who knew everyone involved, and she rushed the paperwork through by calling in some favors. Scott took the agency forms, Tommy's, Ava's, and Doc Machalvie's statements, and the guardianship request to Judge Feinman for his signature.

When Scott got to Maury Feinman's house, the judge was expecting him. He was also eating a hot, freshly baked cinnamon roll, straight out of a big bakery box recently delivered from Fitzpatrick's Bakery. His secretary Frannie, who was a notary as well as the second lucky recipient of a large bakery delivery, was also in attendance.

"Lucky kid," Maury said, signing the paperwork. "I wish I'd been rescued by that family."

Maggie found Hannah sitting in the back row of the viewing room at Machalvie's Funeral Home, watching everyone arrive for Margie's funeral.

"Where were you?" Hannah asked. "I've been calling around town trying to find you."

"It's a long story," Maggie said. "But it ends with Ava holding a baby Brian abandoned in the trailer park."

"You are freaking kidding me."

"No," she said. "The kid looks just like Timmy did when he was a baby."

"Get out."

"I know, right?"

"Rose Hill is a crazy place to live these days."

"My family is what's making it crazy, I'm afraid."

"At least Brian didn't murder Margie," Hannah said, gesturing to the coffin up front.

"But where is he?"

Hannah shrugged.

"There are not very many people here yet," Hannah said, looking around. "Do you think no one will show up?"

"Oh, they'll be here," Maggie said. "Nobody in Rose Hill misses a funeral."

"Or a funeral reception," Hannah said. "But I think I'm going to pass on that. If you find the body, you don't have to spoon out the potato salad. At least I think that's the rule."

"Did you look at her?" Maggie asked Hannah, nodding toward the coffin.

"I skipped that too. I think I'm doing okay, and then suddenly I'm not."

"But more importantly, how is Sam doing?" Maggie asked sweetly.

"I know, what a big selfish baby, right?"

"I'm sorry, that was mean."

"No, you're right. It happened to me, and he's made it all about him, per usual."

"Are you doing okay, really?"

"Yeah, I'm fine."

"Except when you're not."

"Yep, that just about sums it up."

"Newton's wife and daughter arrived today. They're staying at the bed and breakfast."

"Poor them. I wonder how old Connie is doing."

"Aunt Delia said something cryptic about Connie," Maggie said. "I guess they worked together at Pine Crest Manor in March 1984, and Delia is not a fan."

"Oh, really? Pine Crest Manor in Fleurmania, where the deer and the Fleurmaniacs roam? When are you going, then?"

"First thing tomorrow morning. Want to join me?"

"I can't. I promised Drew I would assist him with some house calls and surgeries."

"Ew."

"No, it's not. It's really very interesting and scientific."

"Digging around in dog and cat guts? Please."

"It's my kind of thing, not yours, so shut up."

Everyone seemed to wait until the last minute to arrive, but right before the service started, the room filled up with people. Ruthie and Lily brought Enid in a wheelchair, and it was sad to watch her look at her daughter in the coffin, and then weep throughout the service. Maggie's mother and Hannah's mother both sat up front with Enid. Scott came in late and inched around to sit in the seat next to Maggie. Sarah came in after he did, and stood by the door.

'If looks could kill,' Maggie thought, as Sarah glared at her.

Afterward, Maggie sat in Scott's SUV with him and waited for the parking lot to clear.

"So, Newton killed Margie and then killed himself?" Maggie asked him.

"I'm still working on that," Scott said. "I still have some suspicions Connie's involved somehow."

Maggie considered telling him what she was planning to do in regards to investigating Connie on her own but decided not to. He'd just tell her to stay out of it, and then they'd fight.

"You want to talk about it?" she offered.

"No, I need to think it through some more first," he said. "I saw your new little nephew, by the way, and he looks just like Timmy."

"Thank you for facilitating that."

"Your mother greased all the wheels; I just made sure the legal processes got followed. Every person who needed to be involved in making things happen turned out to have some close connection to your family, the church, or both. Your mother is like some Celtic mob boss."

"She's using her powers for good, though."

"God help us if she ever turns evil."

"Now Ava has the baby, and that's the important thing," Maggie said. "Say what you like about her, she's a terrific mother. He couldn't be in better hands."

"I thought for a minute there your mother and Ava might arm wrestle for him."

"I heard Bonnie blackmailed her into taking Brian back if he turns up."

"Not when I was there," Scott said. "All I heard was that she had to give him a fair hearing."

"You just don't speak Bonnie's language. Ava is not related to that baby by blood. If Brian turns up, he holds all the cards where the baby's concerned. If the birth mother or Brian can't be found, Ava doesn't have any real rights to that baby except through Bonnie. That makes Bonnie the boss of Ava in this particular situation."

"Your mother would force Ava to take Brian back using the baby as leverage?"

"Have you met my mother? Remember the Celtic mob boss?"

"That's amazing. All that went right over my head."

"Of course it did; you're a man. Speaking of mothers, where's yours?"

"She's visiting my sister in Winchester for a couple weeks."

"Ah, I wondered why she wasn't in church."

"Would you like to join me for a pizza and some beer tonight? Say around 8:00."

"I really wish this town would get some Mexican or Chinese food, but yes, I'd be delighted."

"I want to tell you about how I kicked Sarah Albright out of my station this morning."

"You did not!"

"Oh, I did. I may live to regret it, too."

"I wish I could have been there. Did it feel as good as you hoped it would?"

"You would have been so proud. It wasn't as dramatic as you throwing Gwyneth out of the bookstore, but I like to think it had a charm all its own."

"I tell you what," Maggie said. "I'll come for dinner, and I'll bring my toothbrush."

"Don't be cruel."

"I'm not kidding. I think heroic behavior like yours should be rewarded."

261

Scott leaned over and kissed her, and the driver in the car behind them honked his horn.

"Ignore it," Scott murmured and kissed her again.

Hannah went from the funeral to the homes of some of her scanner grannies. She wanted to make sure they were doing okay and to gather any new gossip she could get. The truth was, she was in no hurry to go home, where Sam was fast brooding himself into a major depression. When Hannah finally got home later that evening, there was a suitcase sitting by the door. Sam had his wheelchair pulled up to the kitchen table, where he was writing something.

"What are you doing?" Hannah asked him. "Where are you going?"

"I was just writing you a note."

"You're leaving me?"

"There was a breach of security at a government contractor's company in Boston, and I have to go."

"Since when? Don't you pay people to do the technical part?"

"They want me. It's my company's name on the line, and I have to go."

"Just like that."

"It happens, Hannah. It's the nature of my business."

"Samuel Harold Campbell, you are lying to me."

"I'm not. Why would I lie?"

"Because things just got tough here in Marriage Land. Because I found a dead body and you made it all about you, and you know you were wrong, and feel guilty. Because you don't know how to be anything but the selfish schmuck that you are, so you run off instead of staying here and working it out with me. Then you'll come back pretending nothing happened. It's what you always do, you big jerk."

"That's really nice, honey, I'll miss you too."

"You can go to hell," Hannah said. "Chicken shit bastard."

"Thanks, I will have a safe trip. I'll call you when I get there."

"Don't bother," Hannah said. "I won't answer the phone."

Hannah went to their bedroom and slammed the door behind her. She waited until she heard the van crunching up the driveway before she came back out. Both the dogs were sitting by the bedroom door, looking concerned.

"He's left us again," Hannah told Jax and Wally and began to cry. "That son of a bitch has left us again."

Jax and Wally both licked her hands and whined.

Maggie walked into the station at 8:00, and found a candlelit table set for two in the break room.

"Isn't this against some sort of policy?" she called out, "or health code?"

Scott came out of his office flourishing a paper towel over his arm as he offered her a plastic bottle of root beer.

"I trust the vintage will be to Madam's liking," he said.

"Mmm, my favorite."

"I also asked them to leave off the onions and garlic, as a courtesy."

"Fine Italian cuisine from 'Casa P and J' I see."

"Only the best for you, my dear."

"You know," Maggie said, "this wasn't exactly how I pictured this romantic evening in my mind. The setting, for one thing, doesn't really put me in the mood."

"What do you mean? We've had a couple of really hot moments in this station," Scott said. "What about the time I almost arrested you and threatened to lock myself up with you in the cell all night?"

"I will never forget that, it's true."

"Did you bring your toothbrush?"

"It's in my purse, but if you think I'm staying here..."

"Not to worry, I have plans for that later."

After the pizza dinner, Scott turned up the radio for some romantic dancing. The trouble was neither of them could dance. They twirled and bobbed around the break room, giggling, until Scott's romantic dip ended up with both of them laughing in a heap on the floor.

"We can have romance anywhere," Scott said, "as long as you and I are together."

"Listen to you, getting all squishy," Maggie said. "It's almost sickening."

"I would love to get all squishy with you," he said and kissed her in a way that proved it.

"I seem to remember that couch in your office being sturdy," Maggie said when they finally came up for air.

"If it isn't, the desk is," Scott replied.

Scott jumped up and helped Maggie up, and embraced her with a long, lingering kiss.

Maggie's cell phone rang.

"Ignore it," Scott said forcefully. "That is a command from the Chief of Police."

"There's too much going on for me to ignore it," Maggie said. "You know that."

Maggie opened her phone and said, "Hello, this better be good."

Scott watched her, praying it was nothing, and that they could get back to what they were doing.

"I'll be right there," Maggie said and closed her phone.

"Nooooooo," he whined.

"Sam's left Hannah," she told him.

"No way."

"That's what I think too," Maggie said. "But she's beside herself and insists that he has. I have to go out there."

"Then take the Explorer," he said. "Unless you want me to come too."

"No, it better be just me, I think," Maggie said. "I will take you up on the offer of your vehicle, though."

"I'm running a tab for you, but eventually you will have to make all this up to me."

"It's a deal," she said. "This is probably how it will always be, though; someone calls or pounds on the door, and then you or I go running."

"As long as you know that when you call, I will always come running," he said, hugging her tightly, and breathing in the scent of her hair.

"I am so glad of that," she said.

"I love you," he said. "You do know that."

"I love you too," she said quietly, so quietly he thought he might have imagined he heard it, and then she left.

Caroline flopped down next to Drew on the bed in the master suite at the lodge, and he put down the book he was reading.

"I don't understand this book at all," he said. "Something about the heart diamond sutra and how everything is an illusion."

"When you're ready the information will be clear to you," Caroline said. "My legs feel like limp spaghetti."

"They don't do anything for themselves, I've noticed," he said. "If they drop something, by accident, say, they just keep on walking."

"They're holy men," Caroline said. "They raise the consciousness of the whole planet just by using their energies for that purpose. They can't be bothered by lower plane, corporal issues like cleaning and cooking and picking up things."

"Look at you, though, you just came back from South America for a rest, and you're exhausted. You can't keep this up, and I have to go back to Rose Hill in the morning. I have my own work to do."

"Please, can't you just stay here another day? I'll have the routine down by tomorrow night."

"I can't stay, I have appointments. And look here, it's too much for even two people to do. You need someone to buy groceries, someone to cook, someone to clean up after each meal, someone to pick up after them and do the laundry."

"But who?"

"Aren't there other people who volunteer like you do who could come and help you?"

"No one who's currently speaking to me," she said.

"Well, I don't know what to tell you," he said. "It seems unreasonable for this group to just descend upon you and expect to have all their needs tended to with no compensation."

"You don't understand," she said. "It's a privilege to enable them to spend all their time meditating."

"So you'll get huge karmic points in the next life or something?"

"I don't do it for a reward; I do it because I am meant to do it. They came to me for a reason, and although I don't know what that is yet, eventually it will become clear. I keep waiting for the universe to guide me, to show me what to do, or to bring help, but my guides are silent."

"Your guides?"

"It's all this sex we've been having. I've lowered my vibration to the point that I am all down in my body, in my second chakra, and my crown chakra is blocking out the messages from my higher self."

"You're what is what?"

"You wouldn't understand," she said. "You're fixed earth and I'm mutable air."

"I think you're so tired you're babbling. Why don't you get some sleep?"

"That's just like a five," she said, as her eyes closed. "You observe and judge, but you don't want to feel anything."

"Just rest now," he said. "You aren't making any sense."

"Maybe Mercury is retrograde," he thought she said, but he could hardly hear her.

Drew turned off the lights and covered her with a blanket.

"Sweet dreams, Caroline," he said.

"Namaste," she said, and within minutes she was snoring.

Hannah was not crying when Maggie arrived at the farm, but she was still very upset.

"Tell me what happened," Maggie insisted, coaxing her to sit down at the kitchen table. "Can I fix you something to eat or drink?"

"I'm not hungry," Hannah said, miserably.

Maggie knew it was bad if Hannah couldn't eat her way through it.

Hannah told her what had been going on, and gave her a blow-by-blow account of all the fights, leading up to Sam's strangely calm exit this evening.

"Isn't it possible it was work related?"

"I guess," Hannah sniffed. "Although the timing is way too convenient."

"Maybe taking a break isn't such a bad idea. You two weren't resolving anything together, so maybe some time apart would be a good thing."

"I'm glad he's gone, in a way," Hannah said. "It just makes me so mad that he doesn't have the will to stay here and fight this out with me."

"He's probably had enough fighting for one lifetime," Maggie said.

"He's never going to get better," Hannah said. "He worked hard with his counselor for a long time, and got to the point where he seems recovered, but he is never going to be like I want him to be. I just have to quit wanting too much."

"Didn't you know all this when you married him?"

"That's not fair, Maggie. I was in love with him. Love's blind."

"And balding," Maggie said.

"And gets migraines," Hannah said, smiling.

"And can't dance," Maggie said.

"I just want, when something bad happens to me, to know I can call him, and he'll be there for me," Hannah said. "He doesn't have to be able to run to me on two legs, and physically protect me. I just want him to be strong for me, emotionally, and let it be about me, and what I'm feeling."

"And you told him that."

"Twenty times at least. He can't get past blaming himself and then pushing me away."

"I'm so sorry."

"I'm sorry too. I'm sorry for myself and sorry for him. Hell, I'm sorry for everyone tonight."

"Are you sure you couldn't eat something?"

"Maybe a little something," Hannah said. "I think there's some cake left in that tin over there."

Maggie fixed Hannah a generous slice of cake and a glass of ice cold milk.

"What were you doing when I called?" Hannah asked her.

"Nothing important," Maggie said.

Ava had introduced Charlotte and Timmy to the new baby when they got home from school, and they were both entranced. She told them that he was lost, and they were going to keep him until they figured out what happened to his parents.

"He looks just like you, Timmy," Charlotte said.

"What's his name, Mommy?" Timmy asked.

"I don't know," Ava said. "What shall we call him until we know?"

"Tickle Bug," Timmy laughed.

"No," Charlotte said. "He should have a proper name."

"I was thinking maybe we could call him Fitz," Ava said, "after your Papaw Fitz."

"Papaw will like that," Charlotte said. "Can we take Fitz to see Papaw?"

"He has a little cold right now, so he needs to rest where it's quiet. We'll take him this weekend to see Papaw Fitz."

"There will be a big Fitz and a little Fitz," Timmy said.

Ava had enlisted Gail Goodwin, one of the women who worked as a housekeeper at the bed and breakfast, to go up in the attic and bring down the Moses basket she had used for both Charlotte and Timmy when they were babies. Gail lined it with soft blankets, swaddled the baby, laid him in it, and then sat the basket on the couch where Ava could watch over him. Delia was taking care of the guests and was on hand to change his diapers when needed or to give him a bottle. When Ava finally sent Delia home, saying she'd be fine until morning, it was midnight, and her children were tucked up in bed.

When the phone rang, she was ready.

"Hey sweetheart, did you go to the bank today?"

"No, Brian," Ava said. "I was busy rescuing the baby you abandoned in the trailer park."

"What are you talking about?"

"I'm talking about this beautiful little red-headed boy that some old woman was looking after, who left on a bus this morning without your son."

"How about that," Brian said. "It sounds to me like he found a soft place to fall, though. Takes after his old man, I guess."

"I shouldn't be surprised you don't care," Ava said.

"He's alright, isn't he? You were a lousy wife, Ava, and I can tell you're still a relentless nag, but everyone knows you're a great mother. Stop bitching at me and let's get back to the money issue. I really need to get out of Dodge pretty soon."

"I have a new demand."

"You've got that backward," Brian said. "I make the demands here."

"No, I've been considering my position, and I think I won't give you any money. I think you should come home. I'll have the police waiting for you when you get here."

"You bitch."

"And relentless nag, don't forget."

"What's this demand?"

"First of all, where's the baby's mother?"

"Forty leagues under the sea," he said, "probably fish food by now."

"I don't want to know anything more about it. I want you to sign papers giving me full custody of this baby. As soon as they're signed and notarized, I'll give you the money."

"How do I know you won't double cross me?"

"I could have set you up and had you arrested when you came to pick up the money here. You must trust me somewhat."

"I know you want me gone so you can shack up with my brother."

"Oh, I do. But I want this baby taken care of first."

"Sure, I can do that. Tell you what, I'll even call my little brother Sean and have him make the arrangements. But if I see one cop hanging around, darlin', I'm gone. That baby will go into foster care, and there won't be a thing you can do about it."

When Ava hung up the phone, she was shaking all over. She called Sean, who agreed to do as she asked, but suggested she get the police involved, at least covertly.

"He's so smart," Ava said. "He'll know."

"How are you going to get the money?"

"Brian said I could borrow against the trust Theo left me."

"Not this one," Sean said. "Theo set it up like Fort Knox."

"What will I do?" Ava asked. "I can't protect this child from him without those papers."

"I'll give him the money, and you can pay me back as your trust funds are released."

"Sean, it's too much."

"I'll tell him we could only borrow ten percent of its value. That will be enough to make him disappear again, but won't clean you out."

"Do you think he'll settle for that?"

"He'll have to."

"He said the mother is dead," Ava said.

"He'll have to have a death certificate to prove it," Sean said. "Does he have one?"

"You'll have to ask him."

"What happened to her?"

"I don't know, and I don't want to know."

"Okay," Sean sighed. "I assume he'll call me sometime soon."

"Thank you so much," Ava said. "It seems like the Fitzpatricks are always coming to my rescue."

"You're one of us, Ava, don't forget that. We're your family."

When Ava hung up the phone, she was startled to see a well-dressed, gray-haired woman at the back door. She looked familiar to Ava, who couldn't remember where she'd seen her before.

Ava let her in, saying, "Were you looking for a room?"

"No, dear," the woman said. "I'm looking for your husband."

"He's not here," Ava said, startled. "My husband has been missing for a long time."

"I know you've been communicating with him, Ava," she said. "Why don't you invite me in? You're in no immediate danger. I just need to talk to you."

"What's your name?" Ava asked as she let the woman in the kitchen.

Ava peeked in at the sleeping baby to make sure he was okay. The woman followed her glance, walked over to the basket on the couch in the family room, and looked down admiringly.

"I'm Mrs. Wells, dear," she said quietly. "Isn't that a lovely baby? Look at all those beautiful red curls."

The woman's words were sweet, but something about her was making Ava very uneasy. She instinctively wanted her away from the baby and quickly inserted herself between them.

"I'm sorry to seem inhospitable, Mrs. Wells, but it's very late, and I have had the most stressful day."

"I know all about your day," the older woman said, giving her a kindly, warm pat on the arm. "Let's have some tea and get acquainted. I won't keep you long, and it will be very worth your while, I promise."

Ava felt like she was walking through a dream. She made tea, and the two women sat at her kitchen table, looking just like two new friends getting to know one another at a tea party. That appearance could not have been further from reality.

Ed found the letter from Margie over the visor in his truck, where he had stuck the mail he picked up on Tuesday and then forgot about it. He took the letter in his house and sat at the kitchen table with it for awhile. He thought about Mandy and all she'd been through in her life. He wondered what she could have done that would be bad enough for Margie to be able to use the information to blackmail her into being her friend.

It was just after two in the morning when Ed picked up the letter and took it to the sink, where he used a match to set it on fire. He let it burn in the sink until it was nothing but black ash. Then he took Hank to Mandy's trailer and knocked on the door, holding a stack of newspapers and roll of packing tape. As soon as she opened the door, Mandy jumped from the doorway into his arms. He had to drop the newspapers and tape in the snow in order to catch her.

"I was just surprised is all," he said, in between her kisses. "I love our team, and I do want a long-term contract."

"Shut up and kiss me," she said. "I been missin' you somethin' awful."

"I brought tape and newspaper to help you pack," he said. "But it's all wet now."

"I don't care about any damn tape," she said and squealed as he picked her up and carried her back in the trailer, slung over his shoulder.

Hank followed them in, climbed up on the couch, turned around twice, and lay down to sleep.

Scott lay awake and thought about the letter still tucked into the inside pocket of his jacket. He meant to talk to Maggie about it, but everything was going so well between them he couldn't bring himself to take a chance on ruining everything.

'What if I'd never found it?' he thought to himself. 'What if I burn it? No one knows about that letter but me. No one has to know.'

He got up and went to the front room, intending to take the letter and destroy it. He wanted to do it, had convinced himself he had a right to protect Maggie from the contents. Anything written inside could only hurt her, after all. When he took the letter out of his jacket pocket, he once again experienced the overwhelming feeling that he was about to do wrong. There was no mistaking the feeling, or the cold sweat that accompanied it. He put the letter back in his jacket and went to the window, which was frosted with ice. He rubbed a spot big enough so he could look out at the snow-covered lawn and a night sky full of stars.

'I want her so badly,' he thought. 'But if I go about it the wrong way I will never forgive myself.'

He knew he had to give her the letter. Once she read it, she could decide for herself if what he did was wrong or not. It had been seven years, but it might as well have been yesterday as far as Maggie was concerned. She may be willing to hold Scott in her arms, but he wasn't convinced he occupied the first place position in her heart.

Chapter Ten – Wednesday

Maggie hadn't been to Fleurmania in several years. The little town was tucked away in the foothills of Pine Mountain, just like Rose Hill, but on the other side of Bear Lake. It was half the size of Rose Hill and was well off the beaten track as far as tourists were concerned. There was a large Mennonite Church there, but no folksy tourist attractions. As a consequence, the town was peaceful but poor.

At Pine Crest Manor, Maggie found the administrator was a Mrs. Kathleen Dougan, someone who went to school with her father and mother.

"Your dad was the most handsome boy you ever did see," she said. "He had that black curly hair and bright blue eyes. We all had mad crushes on him, but he only had eyes for your mother."

Maggie knew that wasn't entirely true, according to her mother, but she let this nice lady have that fantasy. She played 'remember when' and 'do you know' with her for a little while, and then got to the reason for her visit.

"You remember my Aunt Delia?" Maggie asked her.

"Of course I do, how is she?"

"She's doing well. Ian's retired now, but they still have the bar, the Rose and Thorn."

"It was such a shame about their little boy. He was the sweetest thing."

"Yes, he was. Did Connie Fenton work here at the same time Delia did?"

Mrs. Dougan's demeanor immediately changed.

"Unfortunately, yes," she said.

"Why, what happened?" Maggie asked.

"Nothing I'm allowed to talk about," she said, "if I want to keep my job."

"I certainly don't want to jeopardize your job," Maggie said, clearly wishing she could.

She could tell Mrs. Dougan was dying to say just what she thought of Connie Fenton, so Maggie told her about the president of Eldridge College dying in the Eldridge Inn, where Connie was in charge, and Mrs. Dougan's eyes got bigger as she listened. After Maggie finished telling her all she knew, the administrator got up and left the room for a minute, before coming back with a thick file.

"I have to run out to my car and look for my cell phone," she told Maggie in a loud voice, as she thumped the file down right in front of her on the desk. "It might take me awhile. You help yourself to anything you need while I'm gone. I'll lock the door, so no one disturbs you."

With that final remark she left the office, and Maggie wasted no time in opening the file to read through the contents. By the time Mrs. Dougan came back twenty minutes later, Maggie had learned all she needed to know. She thanked the woman profusely.

"I'm sorry I couldn't tell you what you needed to know," Mrs. Dougan said loudly, as they walked through her secretary's office.

"That's okay," Maggie said. "I understand."

Maggie walked out of Pine Crest Manor and down the steep stairs set into the hillside to where she left her car on Main Street. There weren't many businesses open in Fleurmania, just a gas station and a general store. Maggie went into the latter to see if they had any root beers.

Morris Hatcher came out as she walked in.

"Hatch!" she said just as he said, "Maggie!"

"What in the devil's name are you doing in this godforsaken town?" he asked her.

"I came to see someone at Pine Crest," she said.

"You haven't changed a bit," he said. "How's your family?"

"They're all just fine," she lied. "How about your bunch?"

"It would take me all morning to get you caught up, and I have to get back to work."

He pointed to the gas station down the block.

"Is Marvin Bledsoe still running that place?" Maggie asked.

"He is, and about to drive me crazy. He hasn't changed much either; he's just fatter and meaner."

"How about if you put the VW up on the rack and talk to me while you change the oil? He can't fuss about that."

"Sure, bring that old buggy on down here. I'd like to see what kind of rubber bands and paper clips you got holding her together these days."

"I'm going to buy myself a root beer, and I'll be right down."

Morris Hatcher had been Hannah's boyfriend in high school. Then his good-for-nothing father drank himself to death, and his mother died of cancer, leaving Hatch at age sixteen with four younger siblings to look after. He dropped out of school, went to work for Marvin as a car mechanic, and broke up with Hannah, who was devastated.

Maggie bought her soda and then drove her vintage VW Beetle down to Marvin's gas station. Marvin Bledsoe was a gigantic man who'd already had one leg amputated because of diabetes, but still, he sat in the gas station all day long drinking whiskey in RC Cola and accepting money for gas and car repairs. He started out nice in the morning, but by afternoon he was a different person altogether.

It was still early, and Marvin was in good form. He was sitting behind the counter in his wheelchair, chewing the fat with a couple old coots.

"Hey Red," he said when Maggie walked in. "How's that ole man a yers?"

"Fitz is fine," Maggie said. "How are you doing, Marvin?"

"Oh, I can't complain," he said with a wheezy laugh. "Nobody'd listen even if I did."

"I'd like Hatch to take a look at my VW if that's alright with you. My oil light just came on, and I'm afraid to drive it all the way back to Rose Hill."

"Sure, sure," he said. "Go on in."

Maggie walked through the connecting door to the service area, which seemed very familiar to her, having an uncle with a service station very much like it in Rose Hill. She threw Hatch the keys, and he brought the VW in and raised it up. He found Maggie a milk crate to sit on and placed it near the gas stove. He draped a newspaper over it.

"That should keep your britches clean," he said, and she thanked him.

Hatch's hands were stained black from his work. He wore a pair of faded blue coveralls with the name "Dwayne" embroidered on the chest; they were several sizes too big and hung on his thin frame. Hatch had never been what you would call a handsome man, with a lanky, bony frame, a long neck with a pronounced Adam's apple, and a big hooked nose. He had large dark eyes and a friendly smile, though. His features were further improved by the black goatee he wore to cover up his receding chin. In high school, he'd had long, silky, straight black hair, which many a girl envied, but now he wore it nearly shaved. When he smiled, a chipped front tooth was still apparent. He always looked tired as a teenager, with dark circles under his eyes. They were still there.

"How's Patty?" Maggie asked first.

Hatch's sister, Patty had been in Maggie's class, a very shy girl who quit school the year after Hatch did to help look after the younger kids.

"Well, that's a kind of sad story right there," he said, as he drained the old oil out of the pan. "She took up with a fella from over to Familysburg, and he got her hooked on that meth. I don't know if she's alive or dead, to tell you the truth. I haven't heard from her in over a year. I got her child living with me, though. He's about seven, and he's a good 'un. Smart, you wouldn't believe how smart that boy is. Gets all A's on his report card. Better'n I ever did, that's for sure."

"I'm sorry to hear that about Patty," Maggie said, thinking Hatch would never be free from raising someone else's kids.

"She may kick it yet. I guess there's some that do."

"What about Boyd?"

"He's done good. He went in the army, got himself a promotion this past year. He's running the procurement department down at a base in Texas. He doesn't come home much, got a family of his own now, two little girls and a real nice wife."

"And Lessie?"

"She went to beauty school and works at a place in Morgantown. She's married to a steady, nice guy who's a meter reader for the gas company. They don't have any kids yet. Her job keeps her busy, so she doesn't get home much either."

"And Trudy?"

"Trudy graduated from high school 'bout five years ago, and she's working at the Megamart in Friendsville, sharing a place with another girl she works with. She's got her a real nice Christian boyfriend, and I expect she'll marry him and have a bunch of little Sunday-schoolers before long."

"So it's just you and Patty's boy?"

"Joshua. Yep, it's just me and Joshie now. I never did get married; I just didn't have room for anybody else, ya know what I mean?"

Maggie thought of how Hannah had suffered when he broke her heart in high school. Hannah, who didn't seem to be able to have kids of her own; she would have married him in a heartbeat and been a good mother to all those kids. Things might have turned out differently for everyone if she had.

"How's our Hannah?" Hatch asked her as if reading her mind. "You two still joined at the hip?"

"Pretty much," Maggie said. "If I don't see her every day I talk to her four or five times."

"How's she getting along?"

"She's good," Maggie said.

"I heard she married Sam Campbell. She happy?"

"She's doing fine," Maggie said. "She's still the animal control officer for the county; she and Sam took over the family farm. She keeps pretty busy."

"She got any kids?"

"No, not yet."

"I see her dad every once in awhile when he tows somebody through here. You tell her I said hi."

Hatch and Maggie played the "remember when" and "do you ever see" game until the oil change was done, and then Maggie paid Marvin while Hatch backed her car out of the service bay.

"You tell your Uncle Curtis I want to sell him this place," Marvin said to Maggie.

"Why would you want to do that, Marvin?"

"I'm gettin' old, girl, and I want to move to Florida."

"It's way too hot in Florida," Maggie told him. "You've got that mountain blood in your veins, and it's too thick for the beach."

"You tell him I'll make him a good deal," Marvin ordered, in between sips of RC and the whiskey Maggie could smell from where she stood. "I mean it."

Maggie waved to him as she went out, and took her keys from Hatch.

"Your buggy's in good shape for a senior citizen," he said. "I adjusted the timing belt and cleaned your spark plugs while I was in there, but Marvin don't have to know 'bout that."

"I really appreciate it," Maggie said. "It was good to see you again."

"You ever hear from Gabe?" he asked her.

Maggie still felt a sharp pain in her heart at the mention of his name.

"No," she said. "I don't know where he went or what he's doing."

"Well, I don't want to spread gossip, but I heard he was in prison down in Florida."

Maggie's heart thumped hard in her chest and the pain increased.

"That's not true," she said. "He couldn't be. For what?"

"Possession with intent to sell," he said. "A huge shipment of drugs is what I heard."

"That can't be true," Maggie said. "Gabe didn't do drugs, let alone sell them."

"I'm just tellin' ya what I heard. He and Patty's man had the same supplier."

"That's just vicious gossip," Maggie said. "I don't believe a word of it."

"I won't argue with ya, woman," Hatch said. "I know ya too well, and I'd never win."

Maggie just kept shaking her head.

"Patty's man is thinking of someone else."

"Alright," Hatch said. "Sorry I said anything. You mad?"

"No, I'm not mad."

Hatch looked at her with those big soulful dark eyes, reflecting a life of sorrow and hard work.

"You take care," he said to her. "I'd give ya a hug, but I'm too dirty."

"That's alright," she said. "Hug received, just the same."

Maggie cried a little on the way back to Rose Hill; for Hatch and his orphans, for Hannah and her troubled husband, and in a burst of self-pity, for herself and Gabe.

Several people nodded to Scott as he entered the Rose and Thorn, and one or two people took the opportunity to leave, but he was used to that. Patrick was serving drinks, and his Uncle Ian was holding down one end of the bar, entertaining the tourists. On top of the other end of the bar, oddly enough, what looked remarkably like a small beagle was sprawled out asleep, its head resting on a folded bar towel.

Patrick lowered the volume on the Alison Krauss CD he was playing, and said, as Scott sat down at the bar, "Sorry about giving you so much grief about clearing out the bar the other night. I know you were just doing your job, and we did have way too many people in here."

"Don't worry about it," Scott replied and nodded at the dog. "Who's your friend?"

"That's Banjo," Patrick said, as he resumed polishing glasses. "I'm dog sitting him for Hannah. Caroline asked her to find homes for all Theo's dogs, and Hannah's kennel is full up. She found a home for his brother, but this one is still available."

"Just dog sitting, huh?" Scott said with a smirk.

"It's just for a few days until she gets something else sorted out," Patrick insisted, but Scott knew better. "Lazy Ass Laddie doesn't like him, so my mother had him tied up behind the bakery, bossing him around something awful. I brought him down here so he could relax where it's warm."

"Aren't you worried about the health department?" Scott asked.

"You mean Floyd?" Patrick said, and gestured with his head toward a booth along the side, where county health inspector Floyd Ransbottom raised a frosty mug to them at the mention of his name. "Banjo here's been buying him beers since we opened, and I gotta tell ya, Floyd doesn't seem too concerned."

Scott shook his head and went down to the end of the bar to see if he could buy Ian a beer, but Ian waved him off.

"I can't drink 'til after dinner. I'm driving the bus mornings and afternoons again," he said.

"That's a long drive now," Scott said, "and to a big school."

"Have you seen that consolidated school?" Ian asked him. "It's a massive thing. I don't know how the kiddies find their way around it without a map. Full of computers and you can't imagine what all. It's all technology these days. Everyone's on the wild world enter web."

"Do you use the e-mail, Ian?" Scott asked him, knowing his former mentor hated not only computers but any machine he couldn't take apart and repair himself.

"No, son, let me tell you what I like to do. When I have a message for a fella, I like to use this thing I got called a telephone. It has a cord attached to the wall what connects it to every other house in the nation. Or I haul my fat arse over to where the person I want to communicate with hangs his hat, and give him my message personally. All these spoiled brats with their texturing and wee boxes and what have you, they may be richer than we were, but they are a damn sight poorer in some ways, I can tell you; they're not a smidgin' brighter either, and that's the shame of it."

"No discipline problems on your bus, I imagine," Scott said, knowing full well he was only winding the older man up.

"You got that right," Ian said. "Every semester during the first week of school I put one of 'em off the bus on the side of the highway and leave 'em there. It makes an impression they won't soon forget."

"You don't really," Scott said, a little concerned.

"No, I do, I really do," Ian insisted. "I tell Delia the day I'm doing it, and she follows along behind and picks the child up. No harm, no foul. But it makes my point."

Everyone in the bar laughed except Scott, who closed his eyes and wished he hadn't asked.

Gwyneth arrived at the lodge and was horrified to find Caroline hanging dripping wet sheets on a clothesline draped across the great room.

"What are you doing?" she gasped, watching the water drip on the expensive oriental rugs and hardwood floors.

Caroline looked at her sister in exasperation as she climbed down the ladder she was using.

"I'm conserving electricity by not using the dryer," she said.

"You have all those monks out here, why don't they do some of the work?"

"It's a long story," Caroline said, wiping her brow, "and I know you wouldn't understand, so I'm not going to try to explain it to you."

"Oh, are they the beekeeping kind? I really hope they're not the dog training ones; we just got rid of all those horrid beasts."

"No, they are not beekeepers, or dog trainers, they are meditators, and I don't have any help," Caroline said. "I'm doing this all by myself."

"Why didn't you call me?"

"I hardly think of you when manual labor is involved."

Gwyneth smiled at her sister and took out her cell phone.

"I thought you said your cell phone didn't work in Rose Hill," Caroline said.

"I switched to the local provider. Turns out I now own the land on which their tower sits. My service and service for all my staff is now free and unlimited. They'd like to put up another tower between here and the ski resort, darling, and I told them I'd talk to you about it."

"You never cease to amaze me."

"Donald," she said in dulcet tones to the person who answered her call. "Stop whatever it is you're doing and bring Louise and Martina up to the lodge. My sister is having an emergency, and we need you here. Call me on the cell when you get here, and I'll give you further instructions."

"That's really not necessary," Caroline said weakly, as Gwyneth ended the call and gave Caroline a critical up and down look.

"Nonsense. Put on your coat, I'm taking you to the spa in Glencora. It's not the Red Door, but it will have to do."

"Gwyneth, I can't go. I have the lunch dishes to do, and then I have to shop for more food. They only eat breakfast and lunch, and they don't eat that much, but there's so many of them."

"My staff will see to that. Caroline, I despair of you, I really do. You need to hire people to do the menial tasks for you so you can focus on the important things you are meant to do."

"What I'm meant to do?"

"Yes, are you hearing impaired? You're obviously near the point of a nervous breakdown and need your sister to guide you."

"To guide me? Oh my Goddess," Caroline said, covering her mouth with her hands.

"Stop blithering," Gwyneth said. "Darling, tell me something. Would it kill you to run a brush through your hair? And I hate to say this, but you smell like a goat, and not the good, sweater-making kind. Is basic bodily hygiene against some spiritual principle you uphold, dear? Honestly. Your pores! You look like you haven't had a facial in over a year."

Caroline started laughing and laughed so hard she snorted.

"You're making an odd noise, Caroline," Gwyneth said. "Please stop. It's so unattractive."

"The angels did hear me," Caroline said, raising her hands up toward the ceiling, "but you're the last person I thought they'd send."

"That's magical thinking, Caroline," Gwyneth said. "There is no such thing as fairy godmothers or angels; there are only neuroses, disorders, social systems, and resources."

Caroline came forward and wrapped Gwyneth in a big bear hug before her sister could stop her. Caroline was much taller, and she lifted Gwyneth off the ground, despite her sister's protests.

"I honor the divinity within you, Gwyneth," Caroline told her.

"That's nice, dear," Gwyneth said. "But you're crushing the cashmere that's upon me. Put me down now, please."

Caroline put her sister back down and ran to get the ski jacket Maggie had lent her.

"My goodness," Gwyneth said, as she attempted to straighten and smooth out her expensive coat. "Such a display."

Gwyneth looked around the lodge speculatively with her inner interior decorator eye.

"She's going to ruin this place if I don't take her in hand, I just know it," she said.

Just then, Gwyneth noticed a small man dressed in an orange robe staring at her from the hallway to the kitchen. He made prayer hands in front of his body and bowed low, smiling.

"Oh, hello," Gwyneth said, making a little wave.

The man backed away from her, down the hallway, bowing the whole way.

'That's not so bad,' Gwyneth thought. She quite liked the degree of deference shown to her in the bowing and backing, and the orange robe provided a real pop of color in the room.

Caroline came back with her coat on and said, "I'm ready."

"You know," Gwyneth said, as they went out to the waiting car, and her driver rushed to open the door for them. "I wouldn't mind having a couple of those monks at my place."

"I don't know if you can split them up like that," Caroline said.

"Well, at least ask them," Gwyneth snapped, "before you tell me 'no.'"

Mandy left the bakery with a plate of hot ham and cheese croissants on a plate and popped in next door to the newspaper office. Ed was sitting at his computer, working on the website. He grinned when he saw her, and she gave him a quick kiss on the cheek before she sat the plate down on the worktable in the middle of the room.

"Still working on it, I see," she said, looking over his shoulder, her arms sliding down around him in an intimate way.

"Yeah, but it just seems too easy."

"Why does a thing have to be complicated," Mandy said, sliding around to sit on his lap, facing him, "in order to be good?"

Ed lost himself in a long kiss, and the smell of her hair and skin, and only just remembered they were sitting in the window of the news office when someone honked their car horn outside and whistled.

"Whoa," Ed said. "You better sit over there, out of my reach."

Mandy jumped up and gave him another quick peck on the cheek before she sat down on a stool next to the worktable. Ed's black lab got up off his cushion by the stove, wandered over, and stuck his nose under her arm, asking for some attention. Mandy rubbed his head and ears as he leaned against her in blissful ecstasy.

"You have the same effect on Hank as you do on me," Ed said, and Mandy gave him a wicked smile.

"What are we gonna do Friday?" she asked. "I got the night off, remember?"

"Well, we could go out to eat, stay in to eat, play cards or scrabble. I could rent a movie if you'd like."

"I want to go out on a real date," Mandy said. "Just you and me."

"What about Tommy?"

"He can stay with Delia or Bonnie. Bonnie's got a new dog he can play with."

"Alright then," Ed said. "We'll go wherever you want to go and do whatever you want to do."

"You're a great boyfriend," she said. "I'm gonna put on a dress and high heels for you."

"I can't wait."

Mandy sailed out of the newspaper office, waving and blowing kisses back at him. Ed caught the reflection of his own goofy grin in the window and rolled his eyes at himself. Hank was looking out the door after Mandy with his tongue hanging out, panting.

"I know exactly how you feel, son," Ed said, and then shook his head. "I hope we know what we're doing."

Ava was sitting on the couch in her tiny family room, watching the baby boy sleeping in the basket. She was both happy and melancholy, as the baby fulfilled some inner longing she didn't know she'd had, but at the same time reminded her of the pain she went through when Timmy was a baby, and she'd felt so alone and afraid.

Timmy had only been three months old when Brian disappeared. He'd said he was driving over to Pendleton to get some parts for a car they were working on at the station, and a week later he cashed a check in Miami that cleaned out their savings account. Some church people took up a collection to pay for a private investigator, but he didn't find any trace of Brian.

Ava and Brian had been married fourteen years when he disappeared. Brian was charming and outgoing in public, but short-tempered and demanding at home. No matter how hard Ava tried, she couldn't seem to do anything right in his eyes. If she got 99.99 percent if it right, that .01 percent she got wrong was what he cared about most. She did everything she could to be a good wife, but he cheated on her blatantly and repeatedly, drank too much, and wore her down with his insults and allegations. He was possessive and jealous, hated it when men looked at her and accused her of trying to elicit the attention. He blamed her for having to give up his college baseball scholarship to marry her, and for burying him alive in Rose Hill. He complained bitterly about her to his mother and drove a wedge between the two women that had yet to be removed.

After he left Ava was frightened and bewildered, but she was also secretly relieved. Sometimes, although she knew it was a grievous sin, she wished he was dead so she could be free of worrying about him coming back and terrorizing her and the children with his bad moods and clever, cutting tongue. Dependent upon his family and the church, with two small children and no income, Ava learned to play the part of the grateful, obedient daughter-in-law in order to please her rescuers. She'd leaned on Patrick too much, and knew that she was playing a dangerous game by allowing him to take Brian's place, but she needed someone, and he was willing. They were lucky they kept their affair hidden as long as they did.

Patrick came in through the back door into the kitchen and then stood in the doorway to the tiny family room.

"He looks just like Timmy, doesn't he?" she asked him.

"He does," Patrick said, and sat down on the edge of the easy chair across from the couch, so close their knees touched.

"He's feeling better too," she said. "He's less congested today."

"I'm worried you'll get too attached to him, and then someone will take him away," Patrick said.

"Over my dead body," Ava said, in a fierce but quiet voice.

"It may just be a coincidence," Patrick said. "The coloring, I mean."

"He has the same swirl of hair on the crown as Timmy and Brian. And look," she said, as she unfurled one tiny little hand and showed Patrick how his index finger was longer than the middle finger. "You have that. Brian and Timmy both have that."

"We got that from Dad," Patrick conceded. "Maggie has it, too."

"I don't need a blood test to know," she said. "He's Brian's."

"He has a mother somewhere who's probably frantic about him missing."

"I think she must be dead," Ava said. "I can't tell you why I think it, but I do. He feels like an orphan."

"So you think Brian's dead too?"

"Am I awful to wish he was dead?"

"He's my brother, Ava, I can't wish that. But at the same time, I'd like to ring his neck."

"I was so young when I fell in love with Brian. I didn't know who he really was. When I did know, it was too late."

"Nobody blames you for what he did to you and the kids."

"You don't know the whole story, either."

"I don't need to know," Patrick said.

"But I want you to know. I want you to know what happened that summer before Brian and I got married. It's been eating me up inside all these years, keeping it a secret."

"I don't want to know. That's all in the past. Let's leave it there."

"But it's not, Patrick. The past is back, and it's trying to kidnap my son. It's abandoning helpless babies, and it's stealing from the family businesses. It's just a matter of time before it gets to me. The past is circling this house, and it will find a way in."

"I can stop him. I won't let him hurt you."

"It's way too late for that. And it's more than just Brian now, way more."

"We can handle anything if we're together."

"It's a weakness, this thing between us, not a strength. We have to stop it."

"I can't stop. I won't."

"We have to; before we lose everyone we love, and everyone who loves us."

"I don't care what anyone else thinks."

"Except we need them; the family, the church, our friends, the whole town. We need them to love us in order to be safe. We have to do what's right in their eyes so they'll protect us."

"You're just scared and upset right now."

"It will destroy the family if we keep on."

"We can keep it a secret. We'll just be more careful."

"Listen to me. Bonnie knows. I don't know how, but she knows. She can take this baby away from me just like that, and there will be nothing I can do about it."

"So you're choosing him over me."

"I have to. He's helpless, and he needs me."

"I need you."

"It's wrong, and we both know it."

"Jesus, Ava, you're killing me. I can't live without you."

"You'll be fine. I'm going to save this baby, and we are going to do the right thing, for everyone."

"If Brian were dead, then we could be together."

"I didn't hear that. Don't say it again. Don't even think it. If he does turn up dead, we don't want anyone looking at you for it, because of me."

Patrick and Ava stared at one another for several seconds, and then Patrick got up and left, shutting the door hard as he went. The baby startled and opened his eyes, screwing up his face to cry, but Ava lifted him, albeit awkwardly due to her sling, and held him against her body, rocking him and cooing softly until he fell back asleep.

"Don't you worry,' she said, "I won't let your daddy take you away, even if I have to kill him myself."

Delia came back to the family room, looking concerned.

"Was that Patrick?' she asked.

"He just left," Ava said, smiling at the baby, who was making a nursing motion with his lips.

"There's someone here to see you," Delia said, and Ava noticed the older woman was wringing her hands.

"A well-dressed woman with gray hair?" Ava asked in a steely voice.

"No," Delia said, and then lowered her voice. "He says he's from the FBI. Agent James R. Brown."

"Send him in," Ava said with a sigh. "He might as well join the party."

Maggie found Scott sitting in his office at the station. She let herself in and closed the door behind her.

"You will never guess what I found out about Connie."

"She's the little girl in the blackmail photos," Scott said.

"She is?"

"Maybe. It's a new theory I'm working on. I really think she's involved in this somehow. Hannah saw her fight with Newton, and she had the best opportunity to kill him."

"I think she killed Newton too, just like she killed an old man at Pine Crest Manor over twenty years ago."

"What?"

"I found out she worked at Pine Crest back when Delia did. Delia really dislikes Connie, but won't say why, so I went out there and talked to the woman who runs the place. She wouldn't tell me what happened, but she arranged for me to see a certain file concerning a lawsuit filed against Pine Crest for accusing Connie of murder."

"I'm not sure you should be telling me this, but go on."

"An old man died, and Doc Machalvie had suspicions about the way it happened, on account of the blood vessels being burst in the eyes."

"He tried to tell me about this," Scott said, "but I wasn't really listening."

"Connie was the last one with the man, stayed with him in his room all night the night he died. She was paid extra by the man's son to stay with him, and when she was accused of killing him, the son paid for her lawyer."

"So the son paid her to kill the old man?"

"No one knows. It ended up Pine Crest had to pay Connie a big settlement for firing her. She walked away a free, rich woman, and no one is allowed to talk about it."

"She killed him just like she killed Newton."

"What are you going to do?"

"I can't do anything. I burned my bridges with Sarah, and now I'm off the case."

"Someone could tip her off, anonymously."

"It's all inadmissible though, isn't it?"

"I'm telling you there is a file this thick out at Pine Crest with statements, photos, and everything. Can't they subpoena that file if it's for a murder investigation?"

"I don't know, I'm thinking."

"Well, you better think faster. Connie could be packing her bags for Mexico."

"She's back at the inn now. They couldn't find any reason to hold her."

"Do you think she could have been having an affair with Newton, killed Margie to protect him, and then when he wouldn't leave his wife for her, she killed him too?"

"I thought of that, but Connie has an alibi for the night Margie was killed."

"What alibi?"

"Lily was with her every minute, from the business owners' association meeting and all night afterward. During the time we think Margie was killed."

"I forgot that was the same night. She was there; I was at that meeting too. We had our meeting and then worked on Winter Festival projects until 1:00 in the morning."

"After the meeting, Connie took Lily home, and her car got stuck in the driveway. She called Curtis to come pull her out, but he said she'd have to wait until morning, 'cause he had so many other calls, so she stayed all night with Lily."

"So she wasn't at the inn the night Margie was killed," Maggie said. "And Lily would know if she left the house."

"I asked her. She said Connie snored the house down all night and Lily barely slept."

"So Newton could have made the drop, killed Margie when she showed up, and come back to the inn late, and no one would have noticed."

"That's possible."

"What are you going to do?" Maggie asked.

"I'm going to go talk to Doc. What are you doing this afternoon?"

"I have to do some work at my store. I haven't paid bills or placed any orders in over a week."

"I'll be in touch," he said.

He jumped up, came around the desk, and kissed Maggie warmly.

"I have a rain check I want to cash in tonight," he said with a grin.

Maggie felt her face flush warm at the thought.

"How about you come to my place tonight," she said, "and we won't answer the door or the phone."

"Hannah okay?"

"I think so. You know they go through this at least once every year."

He shrugged his jacket on and leaned down to kiss her quickly one more time.

"I will see you later," he said and left.

As Maggie stood up to leave, she noticed an envelope lying on the floor, where it must have fallen out of Scott's jacket. She heard the front door of the station slam, so it was too late to stop him. She picked it up and turned it over. It had her name and address on it, written in a familiar hand.

"Oh my God," she said, and her hand flew to her mouth.

"You okay, Maggie?" Frank called out.

"Yeah," Maggie said, her voice trembling. "I just remembered someplace I gotta be."

She stuck the letter in her back pocket, ran out of the station, and got in her VW. Later on, she couldn't remember driving home. She walked up and down the long hall of her apartment for awhile, just trying to slow down her breathing so she could think. Her heart was beating so hard in her chest she felt lightheaded. She placed the letter on the kitchen table. She tried to organize her thoughts, which were racing and tumbling in her head.

Scott told her he went through every piece of Margie's stolen mail the night after she and Hannah found it, so he'd had this letter since Monday morning. That meant he had the letter the previous night, when they spent the evening together, and almost slept together.

Gabe had disappeared in early March; in two weeks it would be exactly seven years. The postmark, from Miami, Florida, was from June of that same year.

Maggie picked up the envelope, removed and unfolded one page of notebook paper covered front and back with Gabe's jerky, messy handwriting. She flattened it out on the kitchen table and started reading. When she finished her eyes were clouded by tears, but she didn't have the strength to get up and find a tissue. Of all the tears she'd shed over the last seven years, none were as bitter as the ones that fell now. She sat and cried, not bothering to wipe them away. Her heart, which had been patched up and glued back together just like an old china teapot, shattered once again into a million pieces.

Scott left Doc Machalvie's office frustrated because the doctor refused to tell him anything about the case at Pine Crest, other than to nod as Scott told him what Maggie found out.

"I can neither confirm or deny any of that," Doc said. "I can't afford another lawsuit."

Scott felt like he was in an impossible position. He needed Sarah to have this information, but he didn't want to get anyone in any trouble for sharing it. He called Hannah.

"You got it," Hannah said. "I planned to drop in on some of my scanner grannies today anyway. This afternoon I'm helping Drew out at the veterinary office, but I can drop in on a few more on my way home."

"I need to make sure it gets back to Sarah," he said, "and that you'll keep the source a secret."

"Don't worry. By the time this gets across town and back, there will be six people claiming they were there when it happened. This is super juicy gossip."

"It's not gossip, it's the truth."

"You can split hairs all you want, Scott, but you are starting the hottest rumor in this town since Ava inherited money from Theo."

"I feel dirty all the sudden."

"That's between you and Maggie."

Scott was not allowed to investigate the case, but he still felt obligated to drop by the bed and breakfast to give his condolences to Delores Moseby, the late college president's wife. He had been distracted from doing so on his previous attempt by Ava and the abandoned baby.

Delia was working the front desk again. She looked grim, and he assumed it was from all the stress of covering so many jobs for everyone.

"You must be feeling stretched thin about now," he said.

"I go where I'm needed," Delia said shortly, getting up to close the door that led down the hall to the kitchen, explaining, "The baby's sleeping."

Scott told her he knew about the trouble Connie got into at Pine Crest. Delia's face flushed, and she pursed her lips.

"I can't talk about that," she said.

"That's okay," Scott said. "You don't have to."

Mrs. Moseby came down after Delia called her room. She was pale and unsteady on her feet, and her daughter supported her. Delia left the front parlor to give them some privacy.

"I am so sorry for your loss," Scott said to them both when they were seated.

"Thank you," Delores said. "You were always very helpful to Newton when the students caused trouble in town."

"Has the county sheriff's office been in touch with you yet?"

"Yes, but I don't know why the county had to be involved. They say I can't have his body until Friday, and I still have arrangements to make."

"Have you been allowed back in your rooms at the inn?"

"No, and I have personal items there to collect. Can you do anything about that?"

"I'm sorry, Delores, it really is out of my hands."

"I have a mind to just go over there and get my things, no matter what they say."

"I wouldn't do that," Scott said. "It might delay things even longer."

Delores sent her daughter to the kitchen to get her a cup of tea. As soon as she left, Delores leaned forward toward Scott and lowered her voice.

"Will it be in the papers, about those photos?"

"It won't be in the Sentinel," Scott said. "Ed Harrison isn't one to sensationalize things. As far as the daily paper, it just depends on what information the county releases."

"Such a scandal," Delores said, shuddering at the thought. "I won't be able to walk with my head up in Rose Hill after this. I've decided to go back with my daughter to Florida, and we'll have a small memorial service there. I called Stuart and told him I wouldn't be back to work at the pharmacy. I just can't face anyone."

"Were you still at the inn the night of the board meeting?" Scott asked her.

"No, I left early in the evening to drive to Pittsburgh, because I had an early morning flight the next day, and there was a storm forecast."

"Did Newton seem agitated or upset about anything?"

"No, he was sorry he couldn't come with me, but he seemed fine to me."

"I heard you had a run-in with Margie at the pharmacy awhile back, and your tires got slashed."

Delores's face flushed, and she gave Scott an affronted look.

"Are you questioning me, Scott? I thought you said you weren't investigating the case?"

"No, you're right, I'm not. Just a habit, I guess."

"Well, I'm sure you'll agree I've had enough prying and personal questions already. That Albright woman was very rude to us, kept us waiting for almost an hour, and then had an ugly attitude. I have half a mind to call her supervisor and say so."

"I'm sorry to hear that."

Delores's daughter came back with her tea and Scott thanked Delores for her time. Before he left, he had a thought.

"Couldn't Connie bring your things over to you?"

"I wouldn't lower myself to ask her. I don't care if I ever see that crazy woman again as long as I live."

"Sorry," Scott said, and beat a hasty retreat.

Scott thought he might just drop in and see how Connie was doing, as a concerned neighbor, no matter how many blocks away he happened to live. When she answered the door, her face was even more haggard and gray than the last time he saw her. She invited him into the kitchen and offered him some tea.

"No thanks," Scott said, worried she might dose the tea with something that would put him to sleep, and then finish the job with one of her decorative needlepoint pillows. "I was just visiting with Mrs. Moseby over at Ava's."

"I had to check out all my guests and send half of them to Ava," Connie said. "I hope she's grateful."

"I'm sure she is," Scott said. "Delia's over there helping her out. I didn't know you and Delia were nurses together when you were younger."

Connie gave Scott a sharp look.

"What did she tell you about that?"

"Said that it was so long ago she couldn't remember anything about it."

"Her son had just died, so I expect it's painful for her to look back."

"I expect so. Where did you work together?"

"Pine Crest Manor in Fleurmania. I don't even know if it's still there."

"I believe so. That's a tiny little town, isn't it?"

"Mm-hmm," Connie said. "I guess so. I haven't been there in years."

"Connie, when you found Newton, did you see the pictures in his briefcase?"

"No," she shook her head. "I checked his pulse and called 911. Then I waited downstairs for the paramedics."

"But you didn't try to resuscitate him yourself?"

"There was no pulse, and his body was cold to the touch. There didn't seem to be any point."

299

"Did you check his pupils?" Scott asked.

Connie's face went pale.

"No, I didn't. Why are you asking me all these questions? Sarah said you weren't helping her with the case."

"Just a habit, I guess. It just bothers me to have people being murdered left and right on my patch. It hurts my self-esteem as a police officer."

"Newton wasn't murdered. He committed suicide."

"I'm not so sure about that."

"Someone was blackmailing Newton, and he killed himself rather than be exposed. That's what the suicide note said."

"Did you read it before or after you called the paramedics?"

"I don't remember."

"And the open briefcase with the pictures was sitting on the dressing table right next to the desk."

"I don't remember."

"Were you the little girl in those pictures, Connie?"

"I certainly was not! Why would you even think that? That's an awful thing to say."

"How would you know if the pictures were awful or not, or if they were of you or not if you didn't look at them?"

"Alright, I did look at them. I saw he was dead so I read the blackmail note, and I saw the pictures. He deserved to die, looking at pictures like that. Nobody should want to look at filth like that and do whatever filthy thing he was doing. I run a clean establishment, and everyone knows it. I won't have filthy people like him bringing shameful, awful, filthy things into my inn. That room will never come clean. Never."

She was wild-eyed, and her hands trembled as she spoke.

"He took the overdose, but he was still alive when you found him, then," Scott said.

"No, he was cold. I checked his pulse. I told you that. Don't you try to trick me."

"He was still breathing, so you helped him finish the job, didn't you Connie? He was on the edge, and you just helped him over. He was going to die anyway. He wanted to die."

"No, I didn't. I swear."

"You held a pillow over his face and pressed it down, held it there until the job was done. It was easy to do. He was almost dead anyway, wasn't he? Who could blame you? It was him that wanted to die."

"You're crazy," she said. "I don't have to listen to this."

"They're going to subpoena the files at Pine Crest, Connie, where you did the same thing to that old man. Everyone will know then what you did. They'll know you did it again."

"They didn't prove anything. They had to pay me thousands of dollars for saying such awful things. I'll sue them again if they tell. They're not allowed to tell."

"The judge will make them tell. You committed the same crime again, so all bets are off. Everyone involved will have to tell testify against you in court, or they will go to jail. You did it again, so they can tell and not get in any trouble. Everyone will know now exactly what you did."

"You can't prove it," she said quietly, her eyes red and glassy.

"But you had to do it, didn't you? He was already dying. He was ready to die. It was better that he be put down, wasn't it? Better for everyone."

"He brought that filth into my house," Connie said.

"Everyone will understand. You were just cleaning up the mess he made. You were just helping him clean up the awful, filthy mess he'd made in your house."

Connie was staring into space, her eyes completely glazed over.

"He was so ashamed he tried to kill himself," Scott said. "He didn't want to wake up, but he might not have taken enough."

"I couldn't tell," Connie said. "I couldn't wake him up. I shook him, and he didn't wake up. That's how I knew he meant to do it."

"You were just cleaning up his mess. You were just helping him do what needed to be done."

"He was almost dead, anyway," she said in a whisper.

"And you just helped him go," said Scott.

"Yes," Connie said.

"You helped him die."

"Yes," Connie said.

Scott had his cell phone in his hand under the table, where he had speed-dialed his voice mail, and recorded their conversation. He only hoped it had picked up her last words, her quiet confession. He closed it and stuck it in his pocket.

Hannah led the docile, emaciated dog she had just rescued into the waiting room at Drew's veterinary clinic, and tethered him to the heavy oak bench along the wall. The dog, a friendly but skinny hound dog in dire need of a bath and some food, lay down on the floor and looked pitiful. The dog had been scavenging near the dumpsters behind the Dairy Chef and was easy for Hannah to catch using hamburgers donated by the restaurant owner who had reported the stray.

Hannah sighed as the newest in a series of lazy, dim receptionists Drew had just hired ignored her presence and continued to blab on the phone in what was obviously a personal call. This one's name was Destiny, and although ostensibly an adult, she wore her hair in a toddler tail on the top of her head, and had on a pink sweatshirt featuring a couple big-eyed kittens and the words "Cuddly" printed in sparkly letters on the front.

Knowing it was useless to expect the woman to give actual customer service, Hannah went behind the desk and got out the forms she needed to set up the dog's new patient file. Destiny was filing her long sparkly nails while complaining to someone on the phone about her allergies, and intermittently snuffling back a prodigious amount of phlegm.

"It's all these animals," she whined into the mouthpiece. "If it weren't for all these animals this job would be perfect for me."

Destiny snapped her gum and scooted her chair over to make room for Hannah to get anything she needed off the desk. Hannah rolled her eyes so hard they felt sprained afterward.

Hannah filled out the new patient form and was just finishing when Drew came out of the back room. The dog was lying as flat on the floor as was possible with his head between his front legs, looking worried. He wagged wanly at Drew but kept his submissive posture as the vet approached.

"He's a big fella, but he's awfully skinny," Drew said. "Lucky you found him."

Just then there was a low rumbling in the dog's belly, a gulping sound in his throat, and Drew backed away just in time to avoid having his shoes puked on.

"Still using the hamburger technique, I see," he said to Hannah.

"Ewwwww!" complained Destiny. "Do I have to clean that up?"

Drew led the dog back to the small kennel room, and Hannah followed, noticing a familiar looking fawn-colored boxer in one of the recovery kennels.

"Is that Trixie?"

"Yep," Drew replied. "Minus one pound of cheese, a salami, a bag of chips, and a loaf of bread."

"Sounds like a party. What was it last time?"

"Three pounds of raw spare ribs."

"You should install a zipper in that dog, Drew. It would save you some time later."

"Trixie's owner is coming by later to pick her up. I'll be sure to suggest that."

"What are you gonna do with this new one?"

"It's a slow day. I'll examine him, and if he's in good enough shape, I'll worm him and get his shots all up to date."

"Suits me. I've got two stone-cold killers, three mangy mutts, and a hospice case out at my place, so I have no room."

Hannah helped Drew get the trembling, timid dog up on the examining table, then talked softly to calm him while Drew examined him and gave him the necessary injections. Hannah then helped get the dog into a cage far enough away from Trixie so she wouldn't catch any cooties he might have.

She was glad to have the work to do as a distraction, because her husband still hadn't called her, and she had no idea where he was, other than "Boston." His home office was locked up tighter than a bank vault, and he wasn't answering his cell phone, at least for her calls.

"Thank you so much," Drew said to Hannah. "I wish I could afford to hire you."

"Maybe someday I'll get a big grant for a real shelter, and I'll be able to hire you," Hannah said.

"You know," Drew said. "I probably shouldn't talk about this yet, but Caroline wants to convert the barn at the lodge into a veterinary practice, once she gets her inheritance. She said it seemed a shame to let that empty space go to waste."

"I found homes for all of Theo's dogs, you know. That's why it's empty."

"I know, and Caroline is really grateful."

"I did that all on my own time, using county resources."

"She gets that, she really does. I'm sure she'll make a big donation. She just doesn't have any of Theo's money yet."

"Doesn't she have a big trust fund already?"

"She does, but so much of that is pledged to different charitable organizations that she really doesn't have much left to live on."

"Wow, what a saint," Hannah said, but the sarcasm went right over Drew's head.

"She does give a lot of her time and resources. It's one of the things we both feel strongly about. She's single-handedly taking care of a group of Buddhist monks right now."

Hannah rolled her eyes in a way that he couldn't see.

"Well, I'm happy to help you out," Hannah said. "The euthanasia jobs are not my favorite, but I'm glad to be there for support."

"Speaking of which," Drew said. "Did I tell you the weird news about Connie's cat?"

"No, what?"

"She told me I could donate it to the vet school, so I sent it, and when they performed the autopsy, they found out what shut the kidneys down."

"What's that?"

"Chloroform."

"You're kidding me."

"No, it's true. If a cat ingests or inhales chloroform or any strong chemical for that matter, it can shut the kidneys right down, especially in an old, sick cat like Connie's. They want to know, hell, I want to know, how did that cat get exposed to chloroform? It hasn't been used as an anesthetic for years. I don't even know how someone could get some if they wanted to."

Hannah was already putting on her coat.

"I have to go," she said. "Sorry to rush, but I have to find Scott right away."

Hannah tried first at the station, then at Scott's house, calling people as she drove. Maggie didn't answer, and neither Skip nor Frank knew where Scott went. Hannah finally decided to just start driving the streets, looking for his SUV. She finally found it, parked in front of the Eldridge Inn.

Connie answered the door, her eyes red and swollen, looking awful.

"Hey Connie," Hannah said, trying to look past her. "Can I talk to Scott?"

"He's not here," Connie said and drew the door close in behind her.

"His Explorer's here," Hannah said, pointing at the SUV parked in front of the inn.

"Well, he isn't here," Connie insisted.

Connie's voice was shaky, and she wasn't looking Hannah in the eye. All the hairs stood up on the back of Hannah's neck.

"Okay," Hannah said. "If you don't mind, I'll just have a look around without him, then. When I saw his Explorer here, I thought maybe he got my message about the snakes."

"Snakes?" Connie said, eyes wide, clutching her shirt collar together.

"Yeah, Gwyneth was on her way over here to bring you a coffee cake, and she saw a huge snake in your driveway, so she ran home and called me. I don't want to panic you, but you really should be careful until I've caught them all. There are probably three or four dozen of them crawling all over the neighborhood."

"It's twenty degrees outside," Connie protested. "How can there be snakes out in the middle of the winter?"

"The city was working on a water main under Lilac Avenue," Hannah said, "and they broke up a hibernating nest of 'em. There could be twenty to forty snakes crawling around in the sewer lines under the Inn right now."

"Oh no!" Connie said. "Filthy snakes!"

"You just go on back inside," Hannah said, as she backed away, pretending to check under the porch as she did so. "I think I just saw one looking out at me. Damn, that's a big snake."

Connie went back inside and slammed the door. Hannah whipped out her cell phone and called the station.

"Connie Fenton's done something to Scott, and he's inside the Inn," she told Frank when he answered. "You and Skip get over here but don't use your sirens. Bring a shotgun. I told her we were looking for snakes."

Hannah went back to the county animal control truck, unlocked the glove box, got her taser out, and switched the safety off. She also grabbed a big burlap bag and surreptitiously stuffed a long braided-leather dog leash into her coat pocket. She knew Connie was watching her out the window, so she held the bag open and approached the porch as if she were going to bag a snake with it, taser in hand. She knelt down out of sight of the windows and put the dog leash in the bag, then twisted the top closed and stood up. She held the bag out away from her body at arm's length and shook it a little, so it looked like something was alive in there.

Connie came out the front door.

"Did you catch it?"

"I caught one of 'em," Hannah said, "but I can see where they've gone through a hole into your basement. You better let me come in and look."

"No," Connie said sharply. "You'll track mud on my clean floors. You go around back, and I'll open the cellar door for you."

Hannah did not want Connie to lock her out of the main house with Scott in there somewhere, obviously incapacitated. She thought fast.

"Oh Connie, watch out, snake!" Hannah screamed and flung the burlap bag with the dog leash in it right at the woman.

Connie screamed and ran back inside the house with Hannah right behind her. Hannah could hear the squeal of tires behind her as the police cruiser fishtailed up the street, crossed the lawn, and came to a stop at the front steps of the Inn.

Connie realized Hannah was following her and stopped, turned in the hallway, and blocked her way, screaming, "You can't come in here!"

Hannah knocked the woman aside using a football rushing technique she'd learned from her big brothers, and ran into the kitchen. Scott was sprawled out face down on the floor with a wound on the back of his head, bleeding onto the sparkling clean white tile floor.

Hannah heard a noise behind her and turned around just in time to see Connie coming after her with a small iron skillet raised over her head. Hannah fired the taser at her, and Connie then demonstrated the effects of the "high" voltage setting by dropping the pan, jerking violently, and falling to the floor, where she writhed in pain.

As Frank and Skip rushed down the hallway, Hannah stepped over Scott's still body and stooped down to check his neck for a pulse.

"He's alive!" she shouted and then burst into tears.

Chapter Eleven – Thursday

Patrick unloaded the last of the empty liquor bottle boxes from the back of his pickup truck into Mandy's trailer by standing in the truck bed and tossing them to Tommy, who stood in the trailer doorway. When they were finished, Patrick jumped down and came inside, where Mandy was wrapping her collection of mismatched drinking glasses in newspaper.

"You've got it made, woman," Patrick said. "I got all the boxes you could want, and old Ed has all the newspapers."

Mandy smiled so hard she almost twinkled. She was beaming with happiness, and Patrick wished he could feel happy for her. What he did feel was mad, but he wasn't sure why.

"This okay with you?" he asked Tommy.

"Yeah," Tommy shrugged, "if it makes Mom happy."

"If Mama ain't happy ain't nobody happy, am I right?" Patrick asked Tommy, pulling him into a bear hug. "You're not too big for this, right? I'm not creepin' you out or anything, am I?"

"No," Tommy laughed.

Patrick wrestled him to the floor and held him there in a headlock.

"And this is okay too, right? I'm not that heavy."

"Agh!"

"Patrick, get off a him. He needs to go to school, and you're 'sposed to be helping me."

"Alright, that's enough horseplay, kid," Patrick said, pulling Tommy off the floor and dangling him by the back of his pants. "Let's roll him in newspaper and stuff him in a box."

"You're worse than a kid," Mandy said, but she was smiling affectionately at him as she said it.

"You're gettin' me in trouble with your mom," Patrick said, setting Tommy upright on his feet. "You better go to school."

"Bye Mom," Tommy said. "See you later, Patrick."

After he'd gone, Patrick sat down on the couch.

"You sure you want to do this?" he asked her in a serious tone.

"Of course I'm sure. I told you, this is what I want."

"For Tommy, or for you?"

"For both of us. Look, I'm tired of doin' it all by myself all the time. I'm tired of bein' lonely and pitiful. I been waitin' for my real life to start and this is it."

"But is it Ed you want, or was he just handy?"

"Patrick! Ed's 'sposed to be a friend a yours."

"I know. I just can't shake the feeling that this is all a big mistake. I'm fond of you both, but I can't picture you together 'til death do us part."

"You almost sound jealous."

"Hardly. I could've had Ed anytime I wanted him."

Mandy threw a pillow at him.

"Very funny."

"Well, I'm single, and I'm handy, and never once did you offer to make me breakfast in bed."

"I would have, Patrick, but we both know you ain't really been available."

"I am now. She kicked me to the curb."

"That's just temporary. Ava's in the middle of a poop storm right now, and she's just tryin' to keep you clean. When all that clears, I bet you end up with exactly what you want."

"You think?"

"I know it."

"I hope so. What can I do to help?"

"Well, you could move in here, so I don't have to store all this crap in Ed's garage and sell this place."

"Done."

"Really?"

"Yeah, I need to get out of my mom's house," Patrick said. "I'll rent it from you."

"I'll do ya one better'n that. Just pay the utilities and fix stuff when it breaks, and we'll call it even."

"Deal."

They shook on it.

"Your mom's gonna throw a fit," Mandy said.

"Yes, she is," Patrick said, "and I'm gonna tell her it was all your idea."

Ava Fitzpatrick needed to use a phone not currently being monitored by the FBI or the unsavory Mrs. Wells, which she now assumed was the case at her home. She considered all her options before she put on her coat and picked up the baby, using her good arm and the cast-covered one she was supposed to be resting.

"I'm running down to the church," she told Delia, who was sitting at the front desk.

The strain of being everyone's confidante plus covering various shifts at all the family businesses was starting to show on Delia's face, so Ava had not shared her latest scheme with the kind woman.

"That'll do you good," Delia said. "You sure you don't want to leave him with me?"

"No," Ava said. "I want him right where I can see him at all times."

"I can understand that," Delia said, "after the week you've had."

Ava kissed Delia's cheek, and Delia felt the baby's forehead.

"He's much better today. His fever's gone."

"His congestion is just about cleared up too," Ava said. "He's looking like himself again."

He was a smiley baby and gave Delia a toothless grin over Ava's shoulder as they left.

Midge McCallister was the church secretary, and she loved babies. She was sorry to hear Ava was having phone troubles and was glad to hold the baby while Ava used the phone in the counting room, which was a storage room where the collections were counted. As Ava closed the door between the counting room and the outer office, Midge said she was taking the baby down to see the children at the pre-school in the basement.

Ava called Sean's cell phone, and he answered on the second ring.

"I think the FBI has bugged my home phone," she told him. "Yours probably is too."

"Do you want me to call you back from a payphone?" he asked her. "I'm walking down the street, and I can see one from here."

Ava gave him the number, and within a minute he called her back.

"Jesus, Ava, the FBI? What did Brian do?"

"Well, let's see, according to agent James R. Brown, who paid me a visit yesterday, my husband married some rich woman, she had this baby, and then she disappeared mysteriously on a scuba diving trip in the Bahamas, right after Brian took out a big life insurance policy on her."

"Oh, no," Sean groaned.

"No, wait, there's more. There's also the little matter of a bar he burned down in order to collect insurance money, and some people he swindled out of investment money for a new bar."

"Lovely," Sean said. "Anything else?"

"A nicely-dressed little old lady named Mrs. Wells came by the house yesterday, to tell me Brian owes her a half million dollars for a shipment of drugs he misplaced, and if I want to make sure my family stays safe I need to give any money I have to her, and not to Brian."

"Ava, this is really bad."

"I know," her voice quavered.

"Okay, take a deep breath, and let's think this through together."

"I'm so sorry I dragged you into this."

"Forget that; we're family."

"I was awake all night trying to figure out what to do. Do you think we can mortgage my house and pay this woman off that way? I can't have that threat hanging over my family's head."

"We should go to the police," Sean said. "Why didn't you tell the FBI agent about her?"

"She wasn't kidding around," Ava said. "She offered to knock fifty thousand off the debt if I let her know where to find Brian. Unless everyone we know and love wants to go into the witness protection program, I don't think telling the FBI is an option."

"Okay," Sean said. "I can arrange the mortgage, but it will take a few days."

"She's given me thirty days."

"Good. We can meet that deadline. Your home and business are easily worth that, so don't worry."

"There's more. The FBI knows Brian is coming to your office this morning."

"Will they be waiting for him?"

"They agreed to arrest him after he comes out of your building, and not before. That way I get custody of the baby and your bank doesn't have to be involved. This is in exchange for your and my cooperation with their investigation. If Brian calls and tries to change the time or place of the meeting, don't agree to it."

"He called me at home last night. He said 9:00 a.m. sharp in my office."

"Mrs. Wells probably knows that too. If he's lucky, the FBI will get to him before she does."

"Oh my," Sean said. "This is really happening, isn't it?"

"I'm afraid so. Is the paperwork ready for the custody change?"

"It's all set. A friend of mine from law school handles private adoptions, and he owed me a favor. Brian says he has the death certificate for his wife, and if he really does, that will make it legal and binding. My friend will be here, my assistant will be a witness, and she's a notary as well. You still have to sign, and everything will have to be filed, but it's as good as a done deal as long as Brian signs this morning."

"Is this going to jeopardize your job?"

"I don't think so. I hope not."

"I keep saying I'm sorry, but I really am."

"It's okay. I'm just not used to this sort of crime drama in real life. I'm a little nervous."

"God bless you, Sean," Ava said. "Please call me later. I should be home all day."

"Wish me luck," Sean said and hung up.

Ava found Midge in the basement, where the pre-school children were having fun making the baby laugh. She thanked Midge and took little Fitz from her, and he snuggled against her shoulder. As she climbed the steps to the ground floor, she met Father Stephen coming down, and she introduced the baby.

"He's my stepson," she said. "It's a long story."

Father Stephen was in his late sixties and was still a handsome man, tall and lean with striking blue eyes, a white beard and mustache, wire-rim spectacles, and a head full of thick gray and white hair. He had been the priest at Sacred Heart for thirty years and knew Ava well.

"I have some time now, Ava, if you need to talk," he offered in his deep, warm voice.

"Thank you, Father, sometime soon, I promise," she said, with a smile, "but just now I need to get this little one home."

Ava considered going into the sanctuary to say a prayer, asking for protection, guidance, and forgiveness for all the illegal activities she was engaging in, but decided she didn't have time.

"Please bless us," she said under her breath, as she passed between the statue of Mary and the large crucifix hanging in the nave. "I'm doing the best I can."

On the way back to the house Ava saw a large black luxury car gliding slowly down Pine Mountain Road toward town, and suddenly remembered where she'd seen Mrs. Wells before. When she took her children out to Lily Crawford's house the previous week, so they could slide down her snow-covered hill on an inner tube, she'd seen Mrs. Wells talking with Lily in the driveway before leaving in a big black car just like it.

'What in the world was Lily doing with Mrs. Wells?' Ava wondered as she quickened her pace in order to get home before the car could circle the block.

When Ava got back to the house, Maggie was sitting in the front room talking to Delia. Maggie's eyes were swollen and red. Ava handed the baby to Delia and rushed to her sister-in-law's side.

"Maggie, what's happened?"

Maggie handed her a letter, and Ava sat down to read it.

"Oh, no," she said when she saw who it was from.

Delia sniffed the bottom half of the baby, who was fussy.

"I think little Fitz needs his diaper changed," she said and went down the hall.

When Ava finished the letter, she looked at Maggie and burst into tears, so Maggie cried again too. Hannah walked in just then.

"What in the hell's going on?" she demanded. "Why is everybody crying?"

Maggie took the letter from Ava and handed it to Hannah.

"Oh, crap," Hannah said when she saw who it was from.

She sat down on the chair behind the front desk and read through it, as Maggie and Ava wiped their faces and blew their noses.

When she finished, Hannah handed the letter back to Maggie and then pointed at her.

"This is just Gabe's version of events," she said. "You remember that."

"But I believe the part about Brian," Ava said. "I think that's exactly what happened."

"I saw Hatch yesterday," Maggie said, "in Fleurmania."

"What's he got to do with this?" Hannah asked.

"He told me he heard Gabe was in prison in Florida for drug trafficking," Maggie said. "I didn't believe it."

"So you're turning your back on Scott for giving Gabe the option of leaving town instead of being arrested," Hannah said, "without even giving him the chance to explain."

"Scott was hiding the letter," Maggie said. "He must have found it in Margie's crawl space. He didn't give it to me when he could have. I only found it after it fell out of his coat pocket."

"I admit, that sounds bad," Hannah said.

"He could have destroyed it, and then you never would have known," Ava said.

"That's true," Hannah said. "He was probably just waiting for the right time to give it to you."

"But he's known all this time," Maggie said. "For seven years I have tortured myself, trying to figure out what happened, and why Gabe left, and all the time Scott knew. Don't you see? I can forgive him for giving Gabe the option he did, but not for keeping it a secret from me."

The phone rang. Ava answered it, and then took it around the corner into the hallway.

"What would you have done differently?" Hannah asked her. "I mean if you'd known."

"I don't know," Maggie said. "But Scott took away my opportunity to decide for myself. He decided what was best for me because it was what he wanted for me."

"Scott almost died yesterday," Hannah said. "I tried calling you all evening, but you weren't answering the phone."

Maggie didn't say anything for a few moments and just looked at Hannah.

"I heard you saved his life," Maggie said, finally. "Delia just told me about it."

"I told Connie there were snakes under her house and then I tased her. I was awesome. Like Wonder Woman, really."

"How is he?"

"Go see for yourself. I'm headed out there around noon, and you can come with me."

"No thanks."

"C'mon. It's not fair to just cut him off without listening to his side."

"Hannah, I don't care what's fair or right. I'm telling you, I don't want to see Scott Gordon right now. I'm glad he's not dead, but beyond that, I really don't give a damn. Suddenly Gabe is not the man I thought I knew, and it turns out Scott is not the man I thought he was, either. Right now, I'm done with both of them."

"Okay, okay," Hannah said. "But I'm still going."

Ava came back in, looking very relieved.

"I have some good news and some bad news," she said.

Maggie lay her forehead down on her crossed arms on the front desk and rolled her head back and forth, saying, "I can't take anymore."

Delia came back in with the baby and Ava took him in her arms.

"The good news is that I am now legally this little guy's mother," she said.

Hannah congratulated her and Delia hugged both Ava and the baby. Maggie kept her head down on her arms, although she said, "congratulations" to the desktop.

"What's the bad news?" Hannah asked.

"His real name is Ernest Hemingway Fitzpatrick."

Maggie raised her head to laugh out loud.

"That poor child," Delia said.

"So do we call him Ernie or Hemmie?" Hannah asked.

"I think we'll stick with Fitz," Ava said.

"So how did you get custody?" Maggie asked. "Wouldn't Brian have to sign something?"

"He did," Ava said. "In Sean's office this morning he produced a death certificate for the mother, a birth certificate for the baby, and transferred all parental rights to me. I just have to sign and then it's official; I've adopted him."

"Where's Brian now?"

"I don't know if you'll think that's bad news or good news, so I'll let you decide," Ava said, and then filled them in.

Sarah Albright showed her identification to the nurse on duty, who led her back to Scott's room. Scott was reclining against the raised upper half of his hospital bed, staring out the window. He heard Sarah enter the room and turned and looked at her, but his face did not change its passive expression. Sarah came around to the other side of the bed, put the flowers she'd brought on a side table, and sat down in the chair next to the window.

"How're you doing?" she asked.

"I'm fine," Scott said.

"Does it hurt?" she asked, pointing to his head.

He turned so she could see where they had shaved his head and stitched the wound, and then pointed to the IV he was hooked to.

"I've got pain meds," he said.

"No complications, then."

"Nope. It turns out my head is just as hard as my mother says it is. Still, they're keeping me another night for observation. I'll be out tomorrow."

"Do you want to talk about the case?"

"It's not my case to talk about," Scott said.

"I think you proved otherwise in a very dramatic way yesterday, don't you?"

"Why are you here, Sarah?"

"Well, first of all, to apologize. I was way out of line, a lot of the time, and I deserved to get thrown out of your station."

"Who are you and what've you done with Sarah Albright?"

"Ha, ha, very funny," she said. "I mean it. I was wrong, and you were right. I was an arrogant ass, and you didn't let me get away with it. I'm here to try to set things right between us."

"Why?"

"Because we make a good team. Because I'd like us, if we can't be friends, to at least be colleagues who respect each other. I'd like to try that."

"Did you get in trouble or something?"

"No, I'm not in any trouble, and neither are you, in case you were wondering."

"Right now I don't care about any of that."

"I was right about Connie," she said.

"She killed Newton," Scott said. "Her confession's on my voicemail."

"Don't worry, she's telling anybody who will listen. She's completely lost her marbles now, although she could just be laying the groundwork for an insanity plea."

"I'd testify to that."

"We found out who killed Margie, by the way."

"Newton? Connie?"

"Nope. Newton's darling spouse Delores."

"That sweet lady, really?"

"That sweet lady indeed, with premeditation and malice aforethought."

"How'd she do it?"

"Two days before Margie was murdered, Delores caught Connie snooping in Newton's room, in the act of opening his briefcase. They had words, and Delores kicked her out of the room. Delores then found the pictures and the blackmail threat and confronted her husband with them. He denied the photos were his but admitted he was planning to pay the blackmailer rather than be publicly accused of so damning a crime. They argued, and she told him if he gave in to the blackmailer the demands would never stop. Newton insisted he was going to make the drop as instructed, and Delores said if he did she would leave him."

"On Monday night Delores went to the pharmacy after it closed, used her key to get in, and stole some chloroform they still had on hand from way back. Back at the inn, she took a knife from Connie's kitchen, the small glass bottle of chloroform she'd stolen, and a cloth with which to apply it, and put them in her purse. Connie's cat came in her room while she was assembling her murder kit, and hissed and growled at her when she tried to kick it out. Delores was deathly afraid of cats and feared all the noise it was making would bring other guests out of their rooms to see what was going on, so she chloroformed it and took it back downstairs."

"She told everyone that she was driving to Pittsburgh, where she would stay over for an early flight. Instead, she parked her rental car up on the corner of Rose Hill Avenue and Peony Street so she could see if the blackmailer approached the drop-off site by the steps next to the tire store or through the alley behind the fire station. Whichever way the blackmailer went, then Delores would go the other."

"She saw Newton make the drop at midnight, but the blackmailer didn't show up right away. Delores waited six hours in the freezing cold before Margie made her move. In the early morning hours, when she saw Margie walk up Peony Street and turn down the alley, Delores ran up Rose Hill Avenue and down the steps next to the old tire store, and hid behind the tires in the alley. When Margie pulled the money out of the old burn barrel, Delores chloroformed her, stabbed her with the knife, and then rolled her down the hill. She took the money, set the chloroform cloth on fire, tossed it in the barrel, and threw the knife down a storm drain up on Rose Hill Avenue. Then she drove to Pittsburgh and got on the next plane to Florida."

"Did she confess all this?"

"Only after we confronted her with all the evidence. First, we found out there was chloroform at the pharmacy where she worked part-time, and that she had a key. She also showed up on their security surveillance video at the pharmacy on Monday night when she was supposed to be in Pittsburgh.

When I questioned Connie, she mentioned arguing with Delores a few times about her cat being in their rooms. Your buddy, the veterinarian, sent the cat to his alma mater, where they autopsied it and found chloroform in its system. Delores mailed the blackmail money to herself in Florida so she wouldn't risk it being discovered by airport security and then opened a new bank account with the funds on the day it arrived. My team put all the pieces together and then we had her."

"So did Newton write the suicide note and try to kill himself?"

"Connie wrote that message. When she couldn't wake him, she went through his briefcase, looking for his pills, and found them, along with the blackmail note and photos. She thought he was committing suicide because of the blackmail."

"Why in the world did he keep the photos?"

"Delores said it was in case the blackmailer made additional threats. If she came back for more, he planned to

322

press charges, even knowing the consequences to himself. He needed the photos and blackmail note for evidence."

"Margie had more photos, so she probably would have gone back for more."

"He was willing to pay this once, I think, but no more."

"Where is the wife now?"

"She's in the county lockup, interviewing lawyers while her daughter gets her bail together."

"When I talked to her, it did seem like the scandal bothered her more than losing her husband."

"She almost got away with it. If Connie hadn't killed him, Newton and Delores might both be vacationing in Florida right now."

"So he didn't try to commit suicide?"

"He took enough of the drug so that he was unconscious, but not enough to kill himself. Delores said he would often forget he had taken one pill and take another, and he was under so much stress that may have made him more forgetful. He had some wine at the board dinner, so that probably also contributed it. When Connie found him unconscious, saw the photos, the blackmail threat, and the vial of pills, she just assumed he had taken an overdose. She smothered him, wrote the suicide note, and then left the briefcase open so the connection would be clear."

"Where's Connie now?"

"She's in the psych ward with a state trooper outside her door. Your buddy Hannah tased the daylights out of her. She also saved your life."

"That's what Frank said."

"How did Connie get behind you?"

"The phone rang, and when she got up to answer it, she knocked her cup of hot tea over on the table. I jumped up when it spilled all over me. She handed me a tea towel to wipe off my pants, and I looked down for just a second."

Sarah shook her head but didn't make any smart remarks.

"For what it's worth," she said. "Connie says to tell you she's really very sorry."

"Oh, well, that's okay then."

"That's what I thought," Sarah said, and smiled.

Scott took a deep breath, and then rubbed his eyes as he exhaled.

"What time is it?" he asked her when he looked up.

"It's 8 a.m. Friday morning. I was the first in line, and frankly, I was expecting your mother and Maggie Fitzpatrick to be guarding you like a couple of junkyard dogs."

"My mother doesn't know about it, and I don't want her to know. She's in Virginia visiting my sister."

"And the love of your life?"

"Maggie hasn't been to see me yet. Do me a favor, will you? Hand me that jacket over there. I get dizzy when I try to stand up."

Sarah handed Scott his jacket, and he checked the interior pocket, which was empty.

"Maggie probably won't be in to see me," he said.

He closed his eyes, and Sarah assumed he was in pain from his head wound.

"You're kidding me, right?" she said. "I thought yours was the great romance of the twenty-first century."

"I guess not."

"You've had some crappy week, huh?"

"You could say that."

"The silver lining, not that you care, is that you helped me solve two crimes, which made me look very good to my boss, which come to think of it, is my silver lining more than yours; but thanks."

"Don't mention it."

"And we're good?" she asked.

Scott pointed at Sarah.

"No more potshots at Rose Hill or its crazy, murderous citizens. No more insults about my staff. And no more hitting on me."

"Scout's honor," she said and held up a few fingers in a salute.

"Then we're good."

Sarah left, and Scott closed his eyes. A little while later a nurse woke him to record his vital signs and check his IV, and then he went back to sleep. When he opened his eyes again, Hannah was in the room.

"What time is it?" he asked her.

"It's lunchtime," she said. "Are you going to eat this?"

Hannah pointed to a tray of food on a rolling cart next to Scott's bed.

"No, help yourself, please."

Hannah seated herself on the end of Scott's bed, pulled the rolling cart over, and started in on Scott's lunch.

"So I hear you saved my life," he said. "Thanks for that."

"It's a hilarious story," Hannah said. "I'll have to tell you about it sometime."

"But not now?"

"No, I think this is a story that will only improve with age, along with some embellishments I haven't had the time to think up yet."

"I heard there were imaginary snakes involved."

"I am, as you often remind me, a natural born liar."

"Tell me, Hannah, have you had enough excitement in your life lately?"

"Not nearly enough. I'm thinking of getting a cape and calling myself the Masked Mutt-Catcher. My superpowers are corpse detection and the electrocution of skillet-wielding innkeepers."

"How are you and Sam doing?"

"Not good. Not good at all. That's another hilarious story I'll have to tell you sometime."

"I'm very sorry to hear that. Any stories about Maggie you'd care to tell me?"

"That one, not funny at all."

"She read the letter, I guess."

"Oh yes," Hannah said. "But I think I'll let you two work that out. I've got my hands full with my new crime-fighting career. Ed took my picture for the paper. I offered to do a virtual reenactment, but he said that wasn't necessary. He interviewed me and everything."

"Where is Ed?"

"He'll be over later. He and Patrick are moving Mandy and Tommy into his house today while the sun's still shining. We're supposed to get yet another big snowstorm later."

"That's a sudden development; Mandy and Ed, I mean."

"It's not, not really. You've just been busy."

"Any sign of Brian?"

"He's been picked up by the FBI for questioning over the suspicious manner in which his Bahamas baby mama died, among other nefarious crimes."

"So the baby was his, but who was the old lady?"

"We don't know yet."

"You know, the low flat line on the Rose Hill crime statistics graph has made a sharp upturn over the past few weeks."

"I think this crap has been going on for a while," Hannah said. "It just hasn't seen the light of day until now."

"Thanks, that's a cheery thought for the new head of law enforcement."

"Speaking of which, has the tiny paw of the law been to see you?"

"If you mean Sarah, then yes, first thing this morning."

"For what it's worth, she was really kind to me after the whole breaking and entering and zapping the crap out of Connie incident."

"That's good to know."

"It doesn't mean I want to be her new best friend or anything, I just thought I'd let you know."

"What can I do about Maggie?"

"Not a thing," Hannah said. "Not a blessed thing. You need to leave her be for a while. And that's my learned, sage advice."

"I don't know if I can take that advice."

"I can't either. The longer Sam goes without calling, the more I pester him."

Hannah pushed the rolling cart aside and jumped up.

"Thanks for lunch. You look like hell," she said and kissed him on the cheek. "I gotta scoot."

"Thanks, Hannah, for everything."

"You don't have to thank me," she said, posing with her hands on her hips. "It's all in a day's work for this crafty crime-fighter."

Hannah saluted and left the room, and Scott closed his eyes again. A nurse woke him long enough to record his vital signs again, and then he slept for a while longer. When he woke next, Ed was in the room.

"Who am I, where am I, how did I get here?" Scott said in a fake, weak voice.

"Tracked mud into Connie's clean kitchen is what I heard," Ed said. "She doesn't put up with that kind of crap. Showed you some discipline."

Scott showed Ed his head wound.

"Ouch," Ed said. "You should tell people it was a bad haircutting accident."

"What time is it?"

"It's six o'clock. They just brought you some supper. Looks pretty awful to me, but if you're hungry…"

"No thanks, I'm living on ice chips and painkillers these days."

"I heard that's how Keith Richards lost his baby weight."

"You're very funny this evening. One might almost say chipper. Love is in the air, I guess."

"We'll see," Ed said, but he was smiling.

"I heard you got two new roommates today. That's a good indicator."

"Gossip sure travels fast, even in here."

"Everybody's talking about it," Scott said. "The nurses on this floor think you're too old for her, but the surgical interns think you should go for it. The pediatricians are just concerned about Tommy."

"I saw Maggie today."

"Wow, I did not see that one coming so soon," Scott said. "Give me a second."

"She's really upset," Ed said. "I offered to bring her so she could talk to you about it but she didn't want to come."

"Did she tell you why she's upset?"

"She said you hid a letter from her, a letter from Gabe."

"I did. I found it in Margie's stash."

"What did it say?" Ed asked.

"I have no idea," Scott said. "I didn't read it."

"But you didn't give it to her. She said she found it after you dropped it."

"I was going to give it to her."

"You had only the best intentions, I'm sure."

"I didn't burn it, which I considered doing."

"So you don't know what it said."

"No, do you?"

"No," Ed said. "She didn't tell me."

"Well, she hasn't been to see me even though I almost died yesterday, so it couldn't have been too flattering."

"You want to tell me what you think it said?"

"I don't know what Gabe said happened, but I can tell you my version, and then you can tell me what you would have done."

"Okay."

Ed closed the door, sat down in the chair by the window, and listened. After Scott finished his story, Ed didn't say anything for a few minutes. The silence deepened in the room as the sky darkened outside and snow began to fall. Silence seemed like the only appropriate response to a story filled with so much regret and loss.

"I would have done the same thing," Ed said finally.

"Thank you," Scott said, and then put his head in his hands and wept.

Ed sat with his friend until the nurses threw him out, and then went home to his new family.

ACKNOWLEDGMENTS

Thank you to my mom Betsy. Thank you to first readers Ella Curry, Joan Turner, and Terry Hutchison. Thank you to my friends at the Huntington Museum of Art, especially John, Judy, Chris, and Linda.

Thank you to Tamarack: The Best of West Virginia, for selling my paper books in your beautiful building.
And last, but not least, I want to thank the people who buy and read my books. Thank you so much.

If you liked this book please leave a review on Amazon.com (Thank you!)

IRIS AVENUE

Book 3

CHAPTER ONE - Sunday

Ray Caliban slid a hunting knife into the holster on his belt, where it would be hidden by the bottom of his leather jacket. He glanced down at his alibi, who was sleeping off the knockout drug he'd slipped her the night before. As he left the motel room behind the Roadhouse Lounge he looked around for other potential witnesses, but it was that time in the morning when even the hardcore partiers were unconscious, and there were no early risers at the Roadhouse Motel.

Ray was amped up on methamphetamine. His days all seemed to be twenty-four hours long on meth, and he hadn't slept for three. Ostensibly a bartender at the Roadhouse, Ray was actually an illegal drug distribution rep, and the bar was his district office. He made enough to support his own habits, keep up the Harley, and pay for some female company whenever he wanted it.

Ray left the parking lot and walked down the narrow lane that led to the railroad tracks by the Little Bear River, about a hundred yards behind the Roadhouse. He crossed the tracks and slid more than walked down the steep hillside to where an old fishing shack stood next to the river.

Ray scanned what was left of the snow for footprints or tire tracks but saw none. He drew out his knife before he checked to be sure the shack was empty. He returned it to the holster while he scanned the riverbank and hillside on each side of the water.

The only sounds he could hear were the rushing water and the wind in his ears. This part of the river featured shallow rapids over a rocky bed. The current was swift and deadly in the middle, but there were deep, dark, still places along the bank where trout were known to hide. It was a clear, beautiful morning in early March but the sharp wind made it feel like February.

As time passed, his ears began to sting from cold. He repeatedly tipped up on his toes before setting his heels back down and opened and closed the snap on the knife holster.

He lit a cigarette with shaking hands. The previous murders he'd committed were reactions to sudden turns of events, fueled by adrenaline and the need to survive. He didn't like having all this time to think about it beforehand.

A flash of bright color on the other side of the river caught his attention. A man emerged from the thick underbrush on the steep hillside there and slid down to the narrow riverbank, causing a small avalanche of dirt and rocks. Ray realized that when the man called the night before he hadn't specified on which side of the water he would appear, and had assumed when he said 'by the shack' he meant this side. Ray didn't know of any other shacks, he didn't have a boat, and it appeared this man didn't either.

The man across the river cupped his hands around his mouth and shouted something, but Ray couldn't hear for the rushing water. He focused his full attention on the man, who was now waving his arms, pointing, and shouting, Ray couldn't figure out what he was trying to communicate. It seemed to Ray as if he was indicating Ray should stay there and the man would somehow cross over.

What the man was actually pointing to was the person who was creeping out of a huge drainage pipe in the hillside behind Ray. This man had a knife and was stealthily approaching Ray's back.

The person creeping up behind Ray had also been waiting for the man across the river. This person had no compunction about killing Ray, who was simply an obstacle to be removed, a complication to be eliminated; the next move in a brutal game. Thus he didn't hesitate when he reached his victim; he seized and dispatched him before the man had time to react.

Within minutes the riverbank by the fishing shack was deserted, and the man across the river had fled. Ray tumbled and rolled through the freezing cold rapids until he reached a calm stretch of water, where he floated on his back, his body turning in lazy circles as he went downstream. His eyes were wide open, but he could no longer see the brilliant blue sky.

Iris Avenue is available on Amazon.com